UNTIL THAT DISTANT DAY

BOOKS BY
JILL STENGL

WITH HEARTSONG PRESENTS:

Eagle Pilot
Finally, Love
A Child of Promise
Time for a Miracle *
Grant Me Mercy
Myles from Anywhere * **
Faithful Traitor
Lonely in Longtree *

STORIES REPRINTED IN:

Wisconsin Brides *
The Farmer's Daughter Romance Collection **

BARBOUR NOVELLA COLLECTIONS:

"A Woman of Valor" in *The English Garden* *
"About Face" in *Christmas Duty*
"Fresh Highland Heir" in *Highland Legacy* *
"Colder Than Ice" in *A Christmas Sleigh Ride* and *Christmas on the Prairie* **
"Buried in the Past" from *Hidden Motives*
"Liberty, Fidelity, Eternity" from *Masquerade*
"The Spinster's Beau" from *Mackinac Island*
"A Right, Proper Christmas" from *English Carols and Scottish Bagpipes*

STORIES REPRINTED IN:

* *The British Brides Collection*
** *A Prairie Christmas Collection*

UNTIL THAT DISTANT DAY

JILL STENGL

ROOGLEWOOD PRESS

Raleigh, NC

Published by Rooglewood Press
www.RooglewoodPress.com

Printed in the United States of America

ISBN-13: 978-0-9894478-3-6

This is a work of fiction. Names, characters, incidents, and dialogues are products of the author's imagination and are not to be construed as real. Any resemblance to actual events or persons, living or dead, is entirely coincidental.

Cover art and book design by A.E. de Silva

To you, Anne Elisabeth. Who else?
Thank you for prodding me to get back into writing,
for telling it straight when my work stank,
for being so thrilled when I finally got it right,
and for producing this gorgeous creation!
I am so blessed to be your mother.

CHAPTER 1

I WAS BORN BELIEVING THAT the world was unfair and I was the person to set it right.

One of my earliest memories is of Papa setting me atop a nail keg in the forge; I could not have been older than two at the time.

"Colette, give Papa a kiss," he said, tapping his cheek.

"*Pourquoi?*" I would ask. "Why?"

"Come and sit on my knee."

"*Pourquoi?*"

My response to every order was the same, asked with genuine curiosity. I did not understand why his watching friends chuckled. Why should I press my lips to Papa's sweaty, prickly cheek? Why should I hop down from the keg, where he had just placed me, and run to sit on his knee, a most uncomfortable perch? I felt justified in requesting a reason for each abrupt order, yet he never bothered to give me one.

Maman, when thus questioned, provided an answer in the form of a sharp swat. This I could respect as definitive authority, although the reasoning behind it remained dubious.

My little brother Pascoe was born believing that the world was his to command. As soon as he acquired his first vocabulary word, *"Non,"* he and I joined ranks in defiance of established authority.

Many impediments cluttered the path of destiny in those early years: parents, thirteen other siblings, and educational difficulties. As we grew into adulthood, more serious matters intervened, even parting us for a time. But I will speak more of this later. For now let me assert that, no matter the obstacles thrown in our way, our sibling bond seemed indissoluble; the love between us continued unaffected by any outside relationships.

Pascoe and I were young adults when revolutionaries in Paris threw aside the tyranny of centuries and established a new government based on the Rights of Man. From the seclusion of our little village in Normandy we rejoiced over each battle fought and won; and when our local physician, a man who first mentored then employed Pascoe for several years, became deputy to the National Assembly from our district, a whole new world opened at our feet.

My story truly begins on a certain day in the spring of 1792, in the little domain I had made for myself in the kitchen at the bottom of Doctor Hilliard's Paris house. Perhaps it wasn't strictly my domain, for it did not belong to me. I was merely the doctor's housekeeper and could lay no real claim. Nevertheless, the basement kitchen and the garden connected with it were more mine than anything else had ever been; and I loved that small, dark room, especially during the hours when sunlight slanted through the bubbled-glass windows high in its back wall, making bright, swirling shapes on the whitewashed walls, or each evening when I arranged my latest culinary creation on a platter and left it in the warming oven for the doctor to discover whenever he arrived home. That kitchen was my home. Not the home I grew up in, but the home I craved.

On this particular day, however, it did not feel the safe haven I had always believed it to be. Loud voices fell from the next floor where the doctor and Pascoe were in conference, disturbing my calm. When I closed the doors to the stairways, the angry voices slipped in through the open kitchen windows. I couldn't close the windows without smothering of heat. Yet I needed to block out the sound, to make it stop.

So I slipped a filet of sole into a greased skillet, set it on a bed of hot coals on the hearth, and let it brown until golden on both sides. The hiss and sizzle did not quite cover the shouting, but it helped. Then I slid the fish onto a waiting plate lined with sautéed vegetables fresh from my kitchen garden, and I topped all with an herbed wine-and-butter sauce. A grind of fresh pepper finished off my creation.

But my hands were still trembling, and I felt as if something inside me might crumble to pieces.

Pascoe often shouted. Shouting was part of his fiery nature, a normal event. He shouted when he gave speeches at *section* meetings. He shouted about overcooked meals or inferior wines. He shouted when his lace jabot refused to fall into perfect folds.

But Doctor Hilliard never raised his voice in anger. Doctor Hilliard was never angry. He never displayed emotion. At most he might indicate approval by the glance of a benevolent eye or disapprobation by the merest lift of a brow.

Yet there could be no mistaking the two furious voices overhead. I well knew Pascoe's sharp tenor with its sarcastic edge; but never before had I heard the doctor's resonant voice crackle with passion.

I managed to slide the hot plate onto the warming shelf alongside a crusty loaf of bread and closed the door, using a doubled towel to protect my shaking hands. Behind me, the door to the back stairway flew open, and Pascoe burst in as I spun to face him.

"Gather your things; we are leaving." His eyes blazed in his pale face, and the jut of his jaw allowed for no questions. He clapped his tall hat on his head as he passed through the room.

I snatched up my bonnet, shoved my feet into my sabots, and grabbed my parasol. "What has happened?" I asked just above a whisper.

"I'll tell you once we are away from this house." His lips snapped tight. His chest heaved with emotion, and he grasped a portfolio so tightly that his fingers looked white.

We left the house through the back door, climbed the steps to ground level, and passed through my kitchen garden. "Watch out for my strawberries," I warned, but Pascoe walked as if blind. Concern for him hastened my steps. Since the doctor's house was last in the row, the side gate of my garden entered an alley between buildings.

The heat of the Paris streets and alleys suited my brother's mood, as did the crush of traffic on the main thoroughfare. Street vendors cried their wares; carriages, carts, sedan chairs, horses, donkeys, and even the occasional goat cart filled the pavements; and café tables cluttered the walkway.

Pascoe blew along in his own private storm, heedless of passersby. He was not a tall man; in fact, he was smaller than average. Yet people tended to move aside when they saw him coming. I followed in his wake, panting and anxious. Pascoe and stress made a precarious combination.

Caring for this beloved brother had long been my major purpose for existence, an ongoing quest to right any wrongs preventing him from achieving his own life goals. I considered us a team functioning in tandem, with Pascoe in the lead position.

I paid no heed to our direction or location; staying with Pascoe was my only concern, and at times I wondered if he intended to leave me behind. He walked as he did everything, with purpose and effortless grace. Head high, shoulders back, lungs pumping efficiently, he moved so quickly that I was obliged to trot much of the time in order to match his pace.

Only when we stepped onto Pont Royal did I realize where he had taken us. "Pascoe, may we stop on the bridge, *s'il te plaît?*"

He slanted me a glance and slowed his pace. At the center of the span he stopped, and I struggled to catch my breath, gasping, *"Merci."*

The air was cooler here after showers earlier in the day, and the river flowing beneath us reflected patchy blue sky, giving it the illusion of fresh clarity. I had often stood here in the past, admiring the view of grandeur unequaled in my experience. Directly across Pont Royal lay the Palais du Louvre and Palais des Tuileries in all their glory. Despite my disapproval of royalty and privilege, my heart responded to their magnificent trappings. By comparison, much of my life in Paris felt enclosed and dingy. Either I worked inside a dark house or I walked filthy streets surrounded by buildings that obscured all but a strip of sky overhead. Here, from the bridge, I could behold vistas to raise my thoughts to lofty heights.

But as I stood there beside Pascoe on that stormy spring day, I noticed none of this glory. Leaning over the parapet, I lowered my gaze to the water rushing inexorably beneath our feet. Not fountain water or rainwater mixed with sewage in the street gutters, but a genuine river flowing directly through the city. Running water swept all before it, cleansing and desolating.

A sharp breeze caught at my bonnet. Startled, I looked up to see dark clouds building on the horizon. Sunlight glinted off Pascoe's bright hair, yet behind him loomed a storm. He leaned back, propped his elbows on the parapet, and crossed one neatly shod foot over the other. Although he dressed as befit a leader among the *sans-culottes*, my brother managed to impart a stylish air to trousers, waistcoat, and cravat decorated in patriotic red, white, and blue, and his coat was cut to perfectly fit his athletic figure. His current pose suggested relaxation and ease, but I knew better.

I followed his narrowed gaze across the river, to a roofline barely visible above the trees of the Jardin des Tuileries. It was the National Assembly Hall where the Legislature met each day. Where Pascoe had worked with Doctor Hilliard for the past two years.

The lingering anger in my brother's eyes worried me. Every protective instinct rose to his defense.

"Tell me what happened, Pascoe."

A muscle twitched in his lean cheek. "Doctor Hilliard has aligned with the Girondins."

"Ah bon?" I could not feign surprise at this news.

"He and I have finally, irrevocably parted ways."

The defiant words struck me with sadness. Doctor Hilliard, while not exactly a family friend, had at least been the Girardeau family's physician for many years. Long ago he noticed Pascoe's potential and drive and took him under his wing, mentoring and advising him; and everyone knew that his recommendation had ensured Pascoe's acceptance at Oxford.

In recent months the doctor had attempted to rein in the more radical wing of the Assembly, urging restraint, patience, and cooperation. However, the constant interference, conspiracy, and outright treason of the Royalists had eroded Pascoe's patience until he aligned himself with the Jacobins, those refusing to tolerate further compromise and negotiation with enemies of the Republic.

"I can see how it would be difficult for you and him to work together," I began, "when your visions for the future of the Republic—"

"Tais-toi!"

I stiffened. *"Pardon?"*

The thoughts and emotions flowing over his face were easy to read. Realizing that rudeness had been a mistake, he composed his features into an expression of loving concern. That very look told me what was coming, and I braced myself for confrontation. When Pascoe spoke again, his tone was gentle and reasoning:

"Do not feign ignorance, *ma poulette*. You must know reconciliation is impossible, as is your continued position as the doctor's housekeeper. This break will compel us both to spread our wings and find our true places in the city, places connected with the future, not with the past. Paris offers endless opportunity to a free woman of your talent and intelligence."

A dozen different responses flitted across my mind, but he had heard them all before. For nearly a year now, Pascoe had urged me to leave my housekeeping position. First, in his cajoling, amusing way, he pointed out that a *sans-culottes* leader laboring as a domestic servant was a symbolic travesty.

My response? "Symbolism means little when compared to a regular income."

Switching to a protective note, he next warned me of the dangers of a single woman working alone in the household of an influential man.

"Doctor Hilliard takes care never to be alone in his house with me," I assured him.

This tactic failing, with biting sarcasm Pascoe had mocked my posturing as a chef.

I calmly replied, "Until you actually sample my culinary efforts, your criticism means nothing."

As a last resort, he attempted to shame me. "You labor in the garden, hands in the soil like a farm girl. You hate agriculture, dirt, and insects as much as I do, Colette. Admit it!"

"I despised gardening back home in Biron, but that was when I had no choice in the matter. Now I find pleasure in cultivating and arranging flowers and in raising produce fit to grace a gentleman's table."

Although no heated words had yet passed between us on the matter, it had nonetheless grown into an invisible battle waged between the charmingly irresistible lever and the obdurately immovable rock.

When I said nothing, he turned to face me, still leaning one elbow on the parapet. Concern and repressed irritation filled his eyes as they studied me. His wide, mobile mouth assumed various shapes as he considered his next words. I could only return his regard, longing for him to understand my heart.

"Colette, *ma chère,*" he said, "this matter goes far deeper than a contest of wills between you and me. Current political tensions in the Assembly, in the city, are volatile. You must trust in my greater understanding of politics and economics, and in my broader experience of the world and its foibles. Trust me when I say that for you to continue serving in Doctor Hilliard's household would be an error with ramifications you cannot begin to comprehend."

My tender feelings withered in a sudden gust of resentment. His greater understanding! Had I not listened, a captive audience, while he read every classic tome on government and civilization written since the dawn of time? Had I not learned Latin under his tutelage and many times debated the merits of democracy, oligarchy, monarchy, theocracy, and every other method of government known to mankind? Yet whenever it suited him to think so, I was a weak woman who must trust in his superior knowledge of the world.

I folded my arms. "Explain these ramifications to me, *mon ange,* and I shall try, with my inferior female mind, to comprehend."

He swore and swung around to face the parapet, gripping it with his bare hands. "Why must you be so stubborn?"

"And you are not?" I touched his shoulder but he shrugged me off. "Pascoe, *mon cher,* the steady income from Doctor Hilliard keeps me solvent from month to month. There is nothing even remotely political about my work, and it has no connection with you. Let us speak of this no more."

"It has every connection with me, and I shall continue to speak of it until you come to your senses!"

"You are free to speak, and I am equally free to ignore."

A raindrop splashed on my hand. Dark spots appeared on his shoulders. "The storm is coming; we'll be caught in a downpour," I said. "And we'll be late for tonight's meeting if we don't hurry home."

He hailed a passing calèche, and moments later we clattered across the bridge behind a pair of skinny bays. Once again the crowded streets of Paris buried fleeting moments of glory beneath the daily struggle for existence.

Not for a moment did I believe the subject would be dropped.

CHAPTER 2

DINNER THAT NIGHT WAS a tense and hurried affair. Pascoe's mood was still foul, and our two younger brothers who lived with us had apparently been arguing as well. As our plates were removed and the next courses served, Étienne met my gaze and asked, "You have a *section* meeting tonight?"

Before I could open my mouth, Claude addressed him. "I am attending the meeting. I shall attend every meeting and demonstration if I so choose. You cannot stop me."

Étienne said not a word, yet sparks flew when his gaze clashed with Claude's. I glanced from them to Pascoe, but he merely raised a sardonic brow and focused on his lamb chop.

I have not yet mentioned the fact that every last one of our parents' fifteen children possessed red hair, not to mention blue eyes of various hues. The hair set the Girardeau family apart in our community but did nothing to nurture a sense of individual importance. I, the eldest daughter and fifth child, had struggled to establish any sense of distinction while serving as a second mother, of sorts, to three younger sisters and six younger brothers. (I never counted Pascoe in this number for, although I was his elder by eleven months, he was my peer.)

Étienne, eldest of the "little" brothers, was quite possibly the largest Girardeau of all. At twenty-one he had already filled out with brawn and sinew, and he towered above Pascoe and me. As a child he had looked for fights and tended to gravitate toward gangs of older bullies. Countless times I lectured him while tending his split knuckles, bleeding nose, and swollen lips. I cannot flatter myself that my sisterly advice in any way affected his choices, yet somehow this pugnacious boy had matured into a young man so reserved that at times he seemed to me like an ox—all muscle and no passion.

Claude, by contrast, expressed his thoughts and feelings so freely that I sometimes despaired of his ever acquiring dignity or tact. At seventeen he was like a headstrong, leggy, handsome colt not yet broken to the bridle.

Both blacksmiths by trade, like most of the Girardeau men, Étienne and Claude worked in a forge not far from our shared house, putting in long hours making weapons on order from the government.

"Why would Étienne attempt to stop you from attending our meetings?" I inquired of Claude. There must be some reason for his contentious attitude.

"He says I shouldn't go because Papa and Maman would disapprove." Claude looked from me to Pascoe for support. Pascoe continued eating, pointedly ignoring us.

"Is this true, Étienne?" I asked, fixing my large brother with a quizzical eye.

"*Oui.*"

"Why do you believe Papa and Maman would disapprove?"

Étienne met my gaze. "The political situation here is precarious; it's no place for a boy. He should return to Biron and work for Blaise."

From Étienne this was an impressive speech. He must have thought long and hard on the situation before making such a direct pronouncement. But it was no use. Blaise, our older brother who took over the family forge when Papa and Maman emigrated to America, had enough on his hands managing his own family; he certainly did not want responsibility over high-strung Claude.

Claude growled like an angry dog. "I am no boy. Blaise does not want me. Papa and Maman sent me here."

Étienne's response was quick: "They did not anticipate this level of strife in the government, let alone in the streets."

He did not mention it, but I knew the political involvement at the forge must add to his concern. Arnaud Lamorges, my friend and Étienne's employer, was a leader among our *section's sans-culottes*, and the other smiths he employed took active parts. Claude was undoubtedly bombarded every day with encouragement to join our protests and demonstrations.

"I want to join the Guard," Claude stated.

"You are too young," Étienne returned.

"I won't go back to Biron!"

I could not handle yet another shouting match that day, but these brothers were past my control. I gave Pascoe's shoulder a nudge. "Pascoe, say something!"

He gave me a disapproving look. "Why should I get involved? We can hardly bind the boy, strap him into a carriage, and send him back to Normandy." He shifted his gaze to Étienne, his voice deceptively mild. "Or I suppose you *could,* my herculean brother, but there is the question of whether or not you *should.* In your effort to protect young Claude from possible physical harm by imaginary enemies, you might succeed in dismembering him."

At this tacit support from Pascoe, Claude perked up. "Or I might dismember him first, *hein?"* he said, sounding extremely boyish.

"*Ça suffit!*" I said. "Enough of such talk." I turned to Étienne. "These periods of political strife generally blow over in a matter of weeks, and I expect the current one will as well. The deputies in the Assembly bicker and fuss, but they always seem to make the right decisions eventually. If we can be patient another week or two while they put pressure on the King, I'm sure he will give in to the people's demands and everything will proceed smoothly. Besides, Claude is doing important service for our country by making weapons for our army."

Claude gave a triumphant whoop.

Étienne looked away. Had he actually expected me to second his opinion?

"I wish you would come with us to the meeting, Étienne," I said, feeling guilty, which was ridiculous, since no matter which way I looked at it, his suggestion was impractical.

I disliked the idea of Claude's joining the military, but the possibility of his actually enlisting seemed remote. Even if he did enlist, he wouldn't necessarily fight. I saw members of the Paris Guard loitering around town all the time, picturesque and useless in their uniforms.

Yet when I met Claude's bright gaze, a shiver of apprehension ran through me.

Since we were running late, Pascoe ordered a closed carriage for the two of us; Claude was riding ahead with friends. As soon as the carriage door closed and Pascoe sat in the facing seat, I sensed the imminent continuation of our earlier argument. Mercifully, our *section* headquarters was not far away.

His following suggestion took me entirely by surprise. "*Ma poulette,*" he began, speaking the familiar endearment in a businesslike tone. "You say you cannot find work providing a steadier income than your current position. I have pondered the matter for some time, and I submit you are mistaken." He leaned forward and took my gloved hands in his. "These little hands need never again be red and roughened by hard labor, and you could wear fine silks and jewels."

I braced myself, warily studying his cool, sardonic expression. "Oh?"

"Oui. Have you considered becoming a courtesan? You are attractive and amusing and intelligent."

Shock silenced me for a long moment. "What prompted this idea, pray tell?" I inquired coldly, removing my hands from his grasp. Unwilling to let him guess how his suggestion disturbed me, I followed up my question with a wry smile. I doubt he was fooled.

Pascoe's tone became persuasive. "I have observed that *la Florinda* is highly respected and moves in the best circles of society. She lives well and has no financial doubts."

In recent weeks I had frequently observed Pascoe in the company of *la Florinda.* Until this moment I had believed their association to be entirely political.

Hurt pride and concern for my brother twined into a knot in my gut, but I made myself laugh. "I suppose I should be flattered you imagine I could find success in that profession, Pascoe. Or should I be insulted? How does a woman react when her brother tells her she could be a successful prostitute?"

He frowned. "Not an ordinary prostitute. *La Florinda* selects her clientele with an eye to her own professional and social advantage. She is a generous creature who would offer guidance if you asked, I'm sure."

This conversation struck me as not only tragic but also rather ludicrous. "Why do you imagine I would even consider such a lifestyle?"

"I should think the answer obvious. The life of a courtesan is filled with pleasure and luxury." He made an expansive gesture with both hands and gave me a shrewd smile. "Like me, you rejoice in your freedom and enjoy pleasure when it comes."

"Do I? My experience with such pleasure has left only scars."

His tone softened. "Only because you expected the impossible. Take me for your example: I have never truly loved anyone but you, *ma sœur,* and I am satisfied. To love a woman would be foolish, for what is there to love? A beautiful face and form I can admire and enjoy for a time. But the person within is inevitably tiresome."

I laughed a little too brightly again, striving to conceal my mounting disgust. "So you regard only men as worthy of love?"

"You never heard such an opinion from me," he replied, amused yet feigning affront. "Men are disgusting creatures. I cannot understand why you women would want one. And yet I am pleased your sex is so blind, for I gain by it."

He certainly did and always had. No man had a right to be as attractive to women as Pascoe. They succumbed in swarms to the lure of his moody blue eyes, each one convinced she alone offered the love he craved. They expanded their minds and engaged him in political debate, each one positive he never smiled at another woman with that hint of awe and dawning respect. Endeavoring to captivate him, they quoted poetry, studied fencing, rode dangerous horses, defied convention, engaged in clever witticisms, and probed the depths of his soul with philosophical inquiries. Yet he quickly tired of them all.

Now he smiled at me. "*Ma chérie,* I ask only that you consider my suggestion. I desire your happiness as I desire my own."

"You," I said, my smile warming despite myself, "are beastly."

"And happy." He tipped his hat.

The carriage stopped before the hall entrance. Pascoe jumped out first, placed the step-stool, then offered me his hand. I let him help me down then waited under cover while he requested the driver to wait. It was raining again. Claude must have had a wet ride on horseback, but he always became sick to his stomach while riding in a closed carriage.

While waiting, I stroked the rippled stone mane of one of the plump lions guarding the mansion's door, alertly serious about their duty. Such a beautiful place it was! The gardens were divine, just now approaching their peak. Sadly, gardeners no longer tended the flowerbeds; but the roses, bulbs, and perennials displayed their beauty with complete disregard for political change, vibrant even beneath the steady gray downpour.

This mansion, in which our *section* held its meetings, was the erstwhile home of an aristocrat now dwelling in England. Its location near the Invalides made it easily accessible to most of our people, and children loved to run and play on the grounds. I encouraged them not to deface the handsome building, but some of the boys could not resist scribbling mottos and effigies on the walls.

I secretly dreaded entering the overcrowded hall, but I followed my brother into the heat and crush. A looming cloud of tobacco smoke nearly obscured the marble frescos framing the room.

Pascoe escorted me to an area with a clear view of the podium set up beneath the musicians' gallery. He would undoubtedly be the night's key speaker, for he not only had connections with leaders of other *sections*, his legal work in the Assembly also allowed him access to the latest developments in that governmental body.

After announcements, updates, and a few very dull speakers, Pascoe was called forward. He pushed through the crowds, stepped up on the platform, set his hat on the stand so that all present could easily view his pale face, raised his hands, and paused to survey the room as silence fell.

His first cry captured the crowd: "People of Paris, it is time to take action! Our deputies in the Legislative Assembly are divided in purpose and fail to take strong action against the King and his vetoes. Our armies lose battles because of traitorous officers, yet the government merely wrings its hands and waits. And who suffers? As always, we, the people of Paris! Our money buys less and less! Our women cannot find food for our children! Can we let this inefficiency, this criminal neglect, continue? Our brothers in the east *sections* have determined a plan of action, an open demonstration against the King and his Court, and we are all to take part!"

This announcement produced a frenzied cheer; Pascoe reigned supreme. I watched in awe as he held the crowd in the palm of his hand: crying out in anger at injustice and crimes against humanity then wooing commitment to the Cause with pathos and pride.

"Your brother has a silver tongue," a deep voice muttered beside me.

I glanced over and couldn't help returning a smile. "He does indeed. *Bonsoir,* Monsieur Fillion."

"*Bonsoir,* Madame DeMer. You are looking lovely, *comme d'habitude.*" Saint-Jude Fillion worked at the forge with my little brothers and had introduced Claude around to his own circle of acquaintances. I was not altogether sure this was beneficial, for Fillion's set struck me as a bit wild. He was good-looking in a tough and vigorous style, originally hailing from a village not far from Biron. I guessed his age at twenty-three or four, several years my junior.

He would have spoken again, but I hushed him. *"Chut!* Listen to your *patron.*" For Arnaud Lamorges, owner of the forge, had joined Pascoe on the dais and now questioned him regarding details of the demonstration.

From their discussion I gathered that 20 June, the third anniversary of the Tennis Court Oath, a landmark of our Revolution, would be the propitious day. The National Assembly planned a mild celebration involving the planting of a Tree of Liberty in the Jardin des Tuileries.

"But we plan a demonstration of our own," Pascoe proclaimed. "A powerful uprising, violent if need be. This will gain the King's full attention!"

"Violent?" I said, more loudly than I had intended. Several faces turned my way in irritation. "How violent?" I muttered at Monsieur Fillion.

His eyes twinkled as he laid one finger over his lips. I grimaced at him but subsided for the time. I was familiar with details of the Fall of the

Bastille, the Market Women's Siege on Versailles, and other clashes between the People and the Royalist government in recent years; yet during my two years in Paris I had personally experienced no violence. As far as I was concerned, that part of the Revolution was finished. We had an army for the purpose of fighting battles on distant battlegrounds. Cities such as Paris were intended for civilization, not war. I often reminded the women of our *section* that we must be a humanizing influence over the men who seemed to crave brutal conflict.

After final arrangements had been made and the meeting began to break up, I repeated my question. Saint-Jude Fillion shrugged. "As violent as need be, like he said. We are all to carry pikes, those of us who cannot carry firearms. But we'll have many members of the Guard along, *bien sûr.*" He gestured toward the uniforms dotting the crowd around us.

"But why the weapons? Are we at war with our own people?" I asked.

"Au contraire! There will be no violence unless the Royalists or their troops attempt to stop us from demonstrating. They have shot at us before, you know," he reminded me darkly.

"Oui, bien sûr," I said vaguely, suddenly awash in worry. "Claude is too young to carry a pike. He will want to carry one, but it must not be allowed."

He shrugged. "Tell Étienne to control the lad; he isn't my responsibility."

"He won't listen to Étienne, but I think he might listen to you."

Deep dimples flashed behind dark stubble when Saint-Jude Fillion smiled. "For your sake, I'll do what I can. But I warn you: Claude is bull-headed."

"That is certain; he is a Girardeau." I thanked the young smith with a grateful smile of my own. *"Merci,* Monsieur Fillion."

Soon afterward I excused myself and made my way toward the podium. I was not unaware of Saint-Jude's rather flattering interest, but more pressing matters occupied my thoughts. Besides, he was too young.

CHAPTER 3

A RNAUD LAMORGES BECKONED to me. All of the smiths who worked at his forge were powerful men and most of them were tall; but Monsieur Lamorges was larger than all, a great bear of a man, impossible to miss in a crowd. I ducked and wove my way through the throng to reach him.

"*Bonsoir,* Colette," he said. "You could not convince Étienne to join us, eh?"

"*Non,* he remains quite without interest in politics. Did Adrienne come tonight?"

Two deep lines formed between his brows. "She prefers to stay at home and rest, though she fears being alone at night. I worry about her, Colette. Will you come and visit her soon?"

"*Certainement.* Why do you worry?"

"I can't help it," he sighed. "I just do."

My history with Adrienne Lamorges extended back to her childhood. I remember her well as a plump, shy little girl who carried a rag doll with her everywhere she went, even to church. Her mother, Madame Picot, had been cook at Maison Cerisier, the country home of Doctor Hilliard. When the doctor moved to Paris in the early days of the National Assembly, Madame Picot had declined to leave Biron, but Adrienne leaped at the chance to live in Paris. She and I served together as first and second housemaids for four months before she quit her job and struck out to find her fortune in the city.

I had lost contact with her until this past winter, when she showed up at my—that is, the doctor's—kitchen door, bedraggled, pregnant, and all of eighteen years old. Exercising what Pascoe called my "severe mother-hen tendencies," I brought her in, fed her, warmed her up, and lent a sympathetic ear to her tale of woe. After leaving her position, she said, she had sung on the stage as part of a chorus, a childhood dream. Then the man of her dreams entered her life, loved her for a time, and sent her away.

"Was he an admirer from the theater?" I inquired.

She wiped her nose on her sleeve and firmly closed her mouth.

I didn't press her, for I might have behaved the same in her situation. I took her with me that day while marketing and visiting the poor, and she seemed comfortable enough with the *canaille* in our *section* despite the vermin, the sewage in the streets, and the terrible crowding of tiny rooms in derelict buildings. My last stop that morning was at the forge, to deliver bread and cheese to my brother Étienne.

As we entered the open-sided structure, heat struck our faces and produced instant sweat. I hurriedly laid the food on Étienne's bench without distracting him and turned to leave.

Only to find Adrienne in conversation with Arnaud Lamorges himself, the man who never stopped working for social reasons. They apparently knew each other, so I lingered near my brother's anvil and watched their interaction. Monsieur Lamorges's interest in Adrienne was obvious; he regarded her with an expression quite near beatification. Her opinion of him was less clear, although I thought her expression lightened as their conversation continued.

I am not by habit a matchmaker, yet I clearly heard the chime of wedding bells . . . or perhaps it was merely the clanging of hammers on steel. At any rate, my guess proved accurate: Adrienne married Arnaud Lamorges within the week and moved into the small house behind the forge.

He was aware of her expected baby and fully understood that she married him for protection and provision, not for love. Yet the man was so smitten that none of this mattered. I often wondered if Adrienne understood the rarity and value of such love. She seemed content enough in her new situation, although she worried constantly about giving birth.

Since I occasionally served as midwife to the poor women of our *section*, Adrienne had begged me to count her among my patients. I visited her frequently, mostly to listen while she voiced her fears . . . which had transmitted to her doting husband.

Arnaud occasionally spoke of paying me once the government paid him for the weapons delivered. I smiled and expected nothing. I had become fond of the man since his marriage to my friend.

"I expect she will be fine," I told him now. "Adrienne comes of sturdy country stock."

"I hope you are right. I'll be a good father to her baby, come what may."

"I know you will, Arnaud."

He glanced past me, and his expression aroused my curiosity. Turning, I beheld Pascoe in the company of *la Florinda*. Memory of my brother's suggestion rushed over me and turned my stomach slightly queasy.

I turned back to Arnaud. "Tell Adrienne to expect me soon," I said brightly.

He nodded and bowed in farewell.

I tried not to be too obvious in watching my brother and his companion, but curiosity overcame my pride. Florinda Mordant, known by her admirers as *"la Florinda,"* was a woman of indeterminate age—I guessed her at near thirty—and no extraordinary beauty. Yet men seemed to find her fascinating. There must be more to her than immediately met the eye.

Pascoe's interest in the woman would soon fade; it always did. But in the meanwhile, I would be second in his priorities.

To my surprise, Pascoe came home with me in the carriage. "I had expected you to spend the evening with your lady friend," I said with only a trace of cynicism.

"La Florinda? Eh. I had hoped to introduce you tonight, but she had a client."

I rolled my eyes but made certain Pascoe couldn't see. He would be quick to call me judgmental, and I knew I couldn't rightly defend myself if he did. But I liked to pretend my own superiority without risking Pascoe's incisive wit, ever ready to whittle away at my precarious pedestal.

"She reminds me of you in many ways," Pascoe continued. "Outspoken, intelligent, well-read, witty." He paused then added in a wry tone, "I suppose you would qualify instead as 'well-read-to.'"

"Très drôle," I said flatly. Pascoe only referred to my deficiencies when he wished to put me in my place, an effective ploy.

Rain pounded the carriage top; I felt sympathy for the driver and his horses. In the darkness of the carriage I heard Pascoe yawn. The sound reminded me of his pale, slightly strained appearance.

"Are you feeling well, *mon cher?"* I asked gently.

"Well enough." His voice was curt, warning me not to pry. But I was not by nature one to shy away.

"Have you suffered an attack recently?" I leaned forward and pressed a hand on his arm. "You have left the doctor's employ, but will you remain in his care?"

"What do you think?" His voice rose, and he shook my hand off, turning his shoulder to me, an effective barrier. "I can take care of myself, Colette. Don't try to fix me."

"Don't shout at me! You may refuse to speak of it, yet the question remains, and I shall worry."

"Suit yourself, but leave me alone."

In a brief flash of lamplight through the carriage window I saw his hand opening and closing as it lay on his knee.

My brothers and I rented Maison Beau Temps, a fully furnished house located just off one of the main boulevards. I had thought it extravagant for our needs, but Pascoe overruled my objections, a fact that continued to rankle since he was frequently away overnight and often neglected to pay his part of the rent and expenses.

My one consolation? The house, along with several others in *faubourg* Saint-Germain, was equipped with piping to bring water from the Seine into its kitchen, a marvel of modern engineering.

The servants Pascoe hired to care for our elegant abode demanded an exorbitant rate for second-rate service. But we were lucky to have them, for domestic servants were difficult to find in Paris during this turbulent time. This situation had led to my current housekeeping position.

When he first came to Paris, Doctor Hilliard had brought along several of his long-time servants from Biron, adding me as a second housemaid at Pascoe's suggestion. Adrienne Picot had not been the first or last to leave his employ. One by one they all deserted him for more exciting jobs, and each departure had increased my responsibilities and salary. By the time the last housemaid gave notice, I had already learned every skill necessary to run the small household. The doctor was largely self-sufficient and cared for his own personal needs, which simplified matters, and he rarely hosted visitors other than Pascoe; now even that professional tie was gone.

Why had I remained after my friends left? Perhaps originally I felt a sense of loyalty to the doctor who had tended my family members through various illnesses, mourned with us at gravesides, and now labored long hours as our district's representative. Possibly fear of the unknown or lack of initiative on my part had been involved. Now I remained because Doctor Hilliard trusted me to run his household efficiently, and I valued this confidence, as well as my generous salary.

My one complaint? The doctor's decidedly unpretentious house lacked water pipes. In dry weather I either toted water for household and garden needs from the nearest fountain or hired children to carry it for me.

The morning after the *section* meeting I walked the busy streets between Maison Beau Temps and the doctor's house, struggling to tamp down a rising fear. Pascoe could not force me to leave my position, but what if the doctor wished to cut all ties with the Girardeau family?

Stepping through the alley gate into the fresh green of my kitchen garden was almost a magical transition. I closed the gate and drew a deep breath. I needed to pull weeds and pick strawberries, but such tasks were my pleasure. Last night's rain had filled my water barrels and watered the entire garden, an extra blessing.

I found my kitchen clean, a tidy fire burning on the hearth, and fresh coffee brewed. The familiar sights and smells were a hopeful sign. I left my wooden sabots by the door, hung up my hat, tied on an apron, poured myself a cup of coffee, and sat down at the table, intending to plan the day's errands and tasks.

But my mind wandered.

As a child, I had found Doctor Sébastien Hilliard both terrifying and fascinating. A tall, thin man wearing a plain gray periwig with curls above his ears, his face sober, his dark clothing pristine, always on horseback, he had inspired a sort of heart-pounding dread whenever I glimpsed him about his rounds.

Rumor flew about Biron village that he was an atheist, and in our Catholic community this was tantamount to possessing two heads or the tusks of a wild boar. Pascoe and I used to hide in the lilac bushes under a window at the doctor's house, hoping to overhear something sensational; however, I recall hearing nothing more exciting than cracking twigs beneath our feet, my nervous breathing, and Pascoe's angry whispers to be quiet when a spider on my hand made me squeal. The two of us laid all manner of plans to vandalize the doctor's house, thereby no doubt intending to discourage his atheism; but we never followed through, for which lapse I am now most thankful.

Then one day Pascoe wrestled me over the side of a footbridge and into the brook, where I had the misfortune to land on a submerged rock. To my horror, Maman summoned the surgeon, and I lay waiting in mute fear for his arrival, dying a dozen hideous deaths in imagination. I smiled at the memory, for Doctor Hilliard had been anticlimactically gentle and efficient in wrapping my cracked ribs.

As an adult, I still found the doctor both terrifying and fascinating.

I heard steps descending the stairs leading to the dining room, and the connecting door swung open. I jerked back to the present, nearly spilling my coffee. "Oh! Doctor Hilliard, I assumed you had gone," I said, rising quickly.

This did not bode well; the doctor was never at the house when I arrived. He seemed at a loss for words. His lips compressed into a long line, and his eyes were very dark. Then he gathered himself and said in a suppressed tone, *"Excusez-moi de vous déranger*; I thought—I did not hear you arrive. But you are here."

After making this obvious observation he strode to the fireplace and appeared to study the chimney crane with its assortment of hooks and hangers. The top of his head brushed the ceiling beams. As always, his cravat was neatly tied, his jacket smoothly fitted to his shoulders, his wig brushed. And, just as surely, his long, slightly bowed legs clad in breeches and stockings made me think of a grasshopper.

I cannot account for my silence. At this point I would usually have asked boldly about the future of my employment. Perhaps the anomaly of a discomposed Doctor Hilliard stole my tongue.

"Madame DeMer," he began. "That is . . ." He faced me. "Madame, do you intend to leave my employ?"

My relief must have been evident. "I should like very much to stay if you wish it, monsieur. I hope my work is acceptable."

His lips relaxed into something near a smile. "Better than acceptable. 'Invaluable' is the word I would choose. And today . . . today, madame, I must . . . that is, I would make an unusual request of you."

He paced before the hearth, hands clasped behind his back. "After many years away at school, my daughter, Leonie, is coming to live with me here in Paris. She will arrive soon, later this week. I realize I have delayed too long in requesting this favor, but if you would be so kind as to prepare a boudoir suitable for a girl of seventeen, I would be extremely grateful and will recompense you for your trouble."

"I shall be pleased to do it, monsieur," I said honestly.

He approached, placed a stack of coins on the worktable, and backed away. "If this amount is insufficient, you will notify me, *s'il vous plaît*. Purchase anything you think she might enjoy. I trust you will not find Leonie's daily presence in the house inconvenient. I believe she might prove helpful to you, for her mother trained her in housekeeping skills. And I am certain your company will be a comfort to her. She was ever fond of the Girardeau family."

"I am pleased for you, monsieur," I said, "to soon have your daughter home."

He acknowledged the remark, bowed, and made a quick exit.

After refilling my cup from the pot, I pondered this imminent change in my situation. Purchasing pretty accoutrements for a young lady's boudoir would be a pleasant variation from my normal routine, although I would be hard-pressed to make all ready in time.

Spending every day in Leonie's company was a different matter altogether. I remembered her as a child who sat with her mother in church and played with my little brothers. She would have been only eight when I married and moved away from Biron. Before I returned to the village as a widow, Leonie's mother died and the child was sent away to school.

Whether or not this arrangement would work depended on what type of girl Leonie had grown to be. One thing I knew for certain: The doctor would pay me generously for any extra labor. And if the situation proved intolerable, I could please Pascoe by finding employment elsewhere. Doctor Hilliard would certainly give me a character reference. However, it would be difficult to find another position as ideal as this one. Few employers, male or female, would allow such freedom as I currently enjoyed.

My real question concerned the lines I had observed between the doctor's brows. What about the impending arrival of his daughter could so disturb the man's peace?

A vase of fresh flowers on the bedside table added the right final touch. Irises, stock, hollyhocks, delphinium, and foxglove from the informal garden beyond my kitchen garden filled Leonie's boudoir with color and fragrance. I had chosen patterns of cheerful summer colors for the curtains, bedding, and floor rugs, with silk tassels and plump pillows to soften the severe lines of the walnut furnishings and offer bright contrast to the paneled walls.

I could only hope she would be pleased.

The upstairs rooms were stiflingly warm, but there was little I could do about this. Leaving the windows ajar to at least keep the air moving, I took the back stairs down to the kitchen where dinner had simmered and sizzled unwatched while I arranged flowers. Tender slices of ham in a spicy sauce would melt into fluffy, nutty rice, served with lightly sautéed fresh vegetables from my garden. The doctor enjoyed my sourdough baguettes, so I baked every third day to be certain his supply was never exhausted. If a few loaves went stale, I made bread pudding or a seasoned stuffing for a roast fowl.

A woman knows when a man appreciates her cooking. The doctor communicated approval by devouring everything I left for him. I was satisfied.

Would his daughter be as easy to please?

I had been running up and down between the front door and my kitchen for nearly an hour, keeping the food moist and warm, checking the dining room to be certain the centerpiece flower arrangement hadn't wilted and no many-legged creature had crawled from it onto the tablecloth or dishes.

When a carriage pulled up to the door, I checked my reflection in the hall mirror and straightened my cap, then opened the door and curtsied to the young woman mounting the front steps. She entered and stopped short.

Ice-gray eyes surveyed me from head to toe. The doctor must be supervising the unloading of her trunk. I heard his voice outside and the thud of something heavy hitting the ground. I was left to make the best introductions I may. I could read nothing in the young lady's gaze, but I returned it with a pleasant smile that brought no responding warmth to her face.

"You are a Girardeau," she said.

"*Oui,* mademoiselle," I replied respectfully.

She was tall and slim. In her angular yet still childishly soft features I saw a strong resemblance to her father; she had his significant nose. And when she looked down that significant nose at me from her superior height, I suddenly felt small, stupid, and stumpy. An unusual sensation for me; it was not often another woman could put me from my ease.

I struggled to recall any time when I might have personally offended the child Leonie. Had I shouted at her? Snubbed her? I had no memory of such an event. Maintaining my welcoming smile with some difficulty, I said, "Dinner is nearly ready. Would you like to freshen in your boudoir first, mademoiselle?"

She had not quite mastered her father's expressionless stare. *"Oui, merci."* Her voice gave the impression of a taut wire ready to snap.

I was leading her upstairs as the doctor entered. "I'll send up your luggage immediately, Leonie," he said.

She might have motioned or smiled at him; I cannot say for certain, for she was behind me. But I believe she totally ignored him.

I showed her into the room, hoping for some indication of pleasure. There was none. She removed her gloves and bonnet, then contemplated her reflection in the mirror over her dressing table. I glimpsed her reflected eyes and wondered if I might be mistaking exhaustion for antagonism.

"Which sister are you?" she asked.

"Colette."

"I remember. You married Jean-Antoine DeMer, *non?*"

"I did, but he died a few years later," I said. "I am a widow."

"Oui, I know," she said in a matter-of-fact tone. "And your baby died. I was sad when I heard of it."

I did not believe her claim of sadness; it was simply the established response. Although I neither expected nor desired a gush of empathy, this complete lack of feeling was chilling in a girl so young.

I did not try to sustain my weakening smile. I let it fall away, replacing it with an expression of polite blankness equal to her own. "I hope you will be comfortable in this room," I said. "If you need anything, tell me, and I will acquire it for you. Dinner will be served in ten minutes."

My exit was too quick, but I had no desire to hear her continue to relate my history in that flat tone. Although she had been only a child when I married, she no doubt heard plenty about my wicked deeds, foolish choices, and tragic consequences—all of it humiliating, heartbreaking . . . and true.

Two carriers lugged a trunk along the corridor as I headed for the back steps. If mademoiselle expected me to unpack her trunks, she could think again.

CHAPTER 4

BACK IN MY KITCHEN I focused on regaining impartial perspective. The girl was very young, after all, and she must be fatigued after travelling so far. She could not truly be as heartless as she seemed. First impressions were seldom fair or accurate.

All of this was true, yet none of it salved my hurt feelings. I found myself slamming pots and rattling cutlery a little more than usual as I made my final preparations for the meal.

The doctor waited for a good twenty minutes, spending much of this time pacing from his library across the hall to the salon, perhaps stopping to pour himself a brandy or two, then on into the dining room, and back. I could easily hear his footsteps through the ceiling. Once he came downstairs to ask, "Will the dinner keep? Shall I run up and encourage Leonie to hurry?"

"It will keep," I said, a little too shortly. I regretted my abruptness the moment the words left my mouth. After all, was it fair to punish the doctor for the offenses of his daughter? I forced my face into a conciliatory smile. "Your daughter is undoubtedly tired from her journey, monsieur."

He nodded. After another perambulation, he reappeared in the doorway. "Your arrangements in my daughter's boudoir are exceptional, Madame DeMer; I looked in there last night. I lack words to express my gratitude." He spoke in a level tone, but had he been anyone other than Doctor Hilliard, I would have described the look in his eyes as anxious.

I spoke before I thought. "Would you like me to stay a bit longer this evening, monsieur?"

A startled glance, and he looked away. "If it is no trouble, madame. We would be grateful."

He was grateful; I heard it in his voice. His daughter's reaction remained to be seen.

"Do you wish to have the meal served in courses?" I asked. "What about the wine?"

"I'll serve the wine. If you will place the platters on the table, we can easily serve ourselves. Why set a precedent we do not intend to follow?" He seemed to relax slightly as he spoke. "I dislike pretension even with regard to dining."

Just as I carried up the soup tureen, Mademoiselle Leonie entered the dining room, head high, shoulders back as if braced for conflict. I saw her glance around the room then narrow her eyes, first at me, then at her father as he hurried to escort her to her seat. While he poured the wine, I brought up platters of food.

"Where are the other servants?" Leonie asked with an edge to her voice as I returned to the kitchen. "Where are Madame Picot and Madame LaSalle? Did they not come to Paris with you, Papa? Where is everyone?"

The dividing door closed behind me. I heard their voices rise and fall as I descended the stairs, but I dared not eavesdrop. Although it was not difficult to imagine the direction of her thoughts, I trusted the doctor to end her misgivings. I had nothing to hide.

Yet her voice held emotion beyond suspicions of immorality. Five years apart would account for a certain level of awkwardness between father and daughter, but not loathing. I could understand why the child Leonie might have lived in awe of her father. His precisely-ordered and reserved manner could be off-putting to a sensitive child; I had felt it myself. But my personal experience as Doctor Hilliard's servant and his reputation among his old servants gave me no reason to believe he might have been an abusive father or husband.

There was mystery here both puzzling and intriguing. Gossip had always circulated in our village; I had been its focus often enough to both dread its effect and doubt its accuracy. Yet tragedy had unquestionably struck the Hilliard family during the years I lived in Caen with my husband, and it had resulted in Madame Hilliard's death. Soon afterward, Leonie had been sent away to convent school and her father began his meteoric rise on the political scene, Pascoe ever at his side.

Pascoe. He might have useful insights. I decided to pick his brain at first opportunity, not for gossip, but for clarity—*if* he would even speak with me of anything connected with Doctor Hilliard.

I set coffee to brew and arranged cheeses on a silver-rimmed platter with tiny matching plates and cheese forks. After a reasonable time had elapsed, I returned to the dining room and encountered a smothering silence. Neither the doctor nor his daughter looked up at my entrance. The doctor contemplated the pattern of the tablecloth as though studying an absorbing political dissertation. Leonie merely studied her own hands folded tightly in her lap.

The situation was intolerable. I had to intervene.

"Might I interest you both in a caramelized custard?" I asked brightly.

They turned to me then. Their eyes regarded me as if I were an angel come to relieve their torment.

"Madame DeMer," Doctor Hilliard said, "would you be so kind as to serve it in the salon and join us there? I believe Leonie would enjoy hearing news of your family, as would I."

Having thrown myself into the breach, I had no choice but to agree. While they withdrew to the salon, I cleared the table, filled the coffee pot, and added custard cups, the cheese platter, and plates to a large serving tray.

That cloying silence had followed them into the salon. Determined to dispel it, I chattered as I carried the tray into their midst. I cannot recall what I said—some ridiculous platitudes, no doubt. It felt strange to serve them while intending to join their party, and stranger still to have the doctor pour the coffee. My coffee was weak, but no one complained.

Leonie occupied an elegant mauve-striped canapé, the only handsome piece among the room's furnishings. The red velvet cushions of Doctor Hilliard's ornately-carved and gilded chair had faded to pink, making an incongruous background for his simple elegance. On the wall above his chair hung a still-life painting of a green-marbled cheese, unnaturally red apples, and a dead pheasant wearing a traumatized expression. I perched on the edge of a large armchair with a green satin seat that sagged to trap the unwary sitter. Exotic-looking flowers burgeoned and birds with gaudy plumage rampaged over the hooked rug at our feet.

These furnishings had come with the house and in no way reflected the doctor's taste, which was some comfort. But I could not help wondering what Leonie thought of them.

I soon learned.

"That is a hideous painting," she stated. "The composition is dreadful, and the colors are badly blended. I could do far better."

"You studied oil painting?" I asked with genuine interest.

"I did, for all five years of my schooling. My teacher, Sister Olivia, often said I was the most promising student she had ever taught. Do you enjoy art, Madame DeMer?"

I decided to give the conversation a light touch. "My endeavors in the field of art have been purely mercenary, I fear. Pascoe long ago discovered my skill and exploited it for his benefit."

Leonie appeared both puzzled and annoyed. "In what way?"

"I have a skill for copying what I see, which he quickly put to the practical use of forgery. He extricated himself from several difficult situations by writing a letter and having me copy an official signature to its closing."

Leonie gaped at me. "But that is wicked!"

"I realize this now, but at the time we were a pair of incorrigible children desiring to retain our freedom. Never fear; I have not committed forgery in many a year."

She obviously found my attitude appalling but said no more.

The doctor had remained silent during this exchange. A quick glance informed me of his amusement, which was encouraging.

I had been asked for news of my family, so as soon as everyone was served with coffee and custard, I complied. "You may be interested to learn, Leonie, that my parents recently emigrated to America, taking several of my siblings with them."

"Your little brothers, I assume?" Leonie asked.

"My little brothers are no longer little. Henri is now fourteen, and Claude tells us he is grown quite tall."

Leonie looked up. "Henri is fourteen? I cannot imagine it. Then Louis must be fifteen and Elliot, sixteen—"

"We lost Louis to lung fever several years ago." My voice sounded gruff, which I had not intended, but the pain was still raw. "He was not yet twelve."

Our second-youngest brother had never been strong; from infancy he seemed to catch every illness harder than the other children did. Doctor Hilliard had successfully nursed Louis through one ailment after another, but the purulent lung fever took him within a few days.

Leonie's stricken look surprised me. "I am so sorry," she said. "He—"

Her voice broke and she tried again. "Louis was a gentle soul."

This time I believed her words of sorrow and briefly wondered if there might, after all, be a heart behind those cool eyes.

"His loss left a great hole in our family." My parents had lost several children in infancy, and we mourned every one. But Louis had lived long enough to firmly establish his place among us. "Even from heaven he is counted among the fifteen Girardeaux."

I glanced at the doctor and saw sadness in his eyes. I hoped he didn't think I blamed him for Louis's death. Leonie had faced toward me while we conversed, balancing her saucer and plate in her lap and essentially turning her back on her father. I took care to direct my conversation to both of them, but I could not remedy the slight.

I needed to speak of something cheerful before we all broke down in tears . . . or at least before I did. So I talked about the brothers now running the forge in Biron, the siblings who had emigrated, and others who had married and scattered about Normandy. "Étienne, Pascoe, and I share a house not far from here; and, as I said before, Claude recently joined us. He and Étienne work at a forge here in Saint-Germain, supplying weapons for the military."

Leonie went perfectly still, so briefly I thought I had imagined it, then quickly sipped her coffee, swallowed rather hard, and cleared her throat. "I should like to see your brothers." Her cup clattered in its saucer.

"I am certain a visit could be arranged," I said. "You and Claude are of an age; I expect you and he were playmates as children."

Her mouth softened. "I have many happy memories of your family. I missed them very much when . . . when I was sent away."

This hint of softness caused me to wonder if she might possibly be pretty when she smiled. *If* she ever smiled, which was doubtful.

"I miss them, too, although I find three brothers considerably easier to manage than eleven at once, especially since I can no longer drag the younger ones about by the ear."

A quiver that might have been amusement touched Leonie's face. "Once Étienne dropped a basket of clean laundry and ran off to play fox and geese with us. But you grabbed his ear. I don't think he took three steps before you caught him."

My laughter echoed in the stuffy room. "Did I really? I would need to climb a stepstool to take Étienne by the ear these days."

Again Leonie nearly smiled. She turned to set her empty cup on the tray, keeping her eyes downcast. The doctor watched her, and I could not guess at his thoughts.

"Would anyone like more coffee or cheese?" I inquired. When they both declined, I rose to collect plates and cups. *"Eh bien,* I must get back to work or the daylight will slip away from me."

To my great surprise, Leonie followed me to the kitchen. "Allow me to assist you, *s'il vous plaît.* I am used to working in the kitchens at school," she said bluntly.

What could I say? She followed my instruction, paring curls of hard soap into a basin, then pouring hot water from the kettle while I added cold water from the rain barrel. She washed and dried the china and silver while I scoured the cooking pans with ashes. My hands were cracked and calloused; I noticed hers were also red and rough, no strangers to hard work.

As we hung up our aprons, Leonie confronted me directly. "Madame DeMer, why are you my father's only servant? What happened to the others?"

"Did your father not tell you? They left to find other jobs. I keep in touch with a few of them."

"Why did you stay when they left?"

"Ma foi, I enjoy working here. I have my own garden, and I can cook whatever I like," I answered lightly.

Her eyes narrowed. "How well do you know my father?"

I gave her a direct look. "I know Doctor Hilliard as a kind, respectful, and generous employer. That is all."

She studied my face then nodded. "*Bonsoir,* Madame DeMer." With that, she used the back stairs, probably to avoid her father.

As I donned my bonnet and sabots, Doctor Hilliard appeared again in the other doorway. "I shall hire a sedan chair for you, madame. It is quite late, I fear."

"I was pleased to help welcome Mademoiselle Leonie into her new home," I said as sincerely as I could manage. He met my gaze, and my false smile faded into a rueful but genuine one. "She will find her way, I think."

He opened his mouth as if to speak but then gave his head a shake and turned away.

Maison Beau Temps was dark but for a candle lamp on the entry hall table. After hanging up my bonnet, I followed the smell of pipe smoke to the balcony off our salon and found Pascoe lounging on a padded wrought-iron chair. On such a sweltering evening, the small balcony offered at least the illusion of fresh air. Blooming perennials from the gardens below offered sweeter scents than the Parisian streets, for certain.

"You're late," he observed.

I brushed this off with a wave of my hand and sat in the second chair. It was too heavy to move, so I sat on its edge and faced him. "I'm glad you're here tonight, for I find I am full of questions. What can you tell me about the Hilliards?"

By starlight I could gain no inkling of his thoughts. "Which one in particular?" he finally asked, then returned his pipe to his lips and drew.

"Leonie arrived in Paris today."

He carefully blew a wraithlike smoke ring. "*Ça alors!*" He sounded bored. How could he be comfortable in that hard, lumpy chair? With his legs extended and crossed at the ankles, his elbow supported by his other hand, and his head slightly tipped back, he was the picture of elegant repose.

"You knew she was coming?" I was certain I had not mentioned it to him.

"I expected she would come. Now her grandfather has emigrated, the doctor would feel safe to bring her out of hiding."

"What about her grandfather? Was he not some nobleman? Tell me everything; I've forgotten anything I knew."

"Everything?" Pascoe sounded amused. The glowing tobacco in the pipe bowl turned his nose and eyes dimly red. *"Eh bien, alors."*

The following is the tale he told to me, though not in his exact words.

In the summer of 1774, Sébastien Hilliard, a medical student working with a famous surgeon in Berne, met a young woman on holiday in Switzerland with a relative. He was nineteen; she was twenty-four. Following a quick and secretive courtship, Marie Louise de Falaise agreed to elope with him. Only after their vows had been spoken did she reveal she was the eldest daughter of Pierre-Camille Hilarie Louis de Falaise, the Marquis de Champs-Auguste.

The marquis demanded the marriage be annulled. When Marie refused and revealed she was pregnant, he disowned her. Doctor Hilliard, after his training ended in 1776, turned down a lucrative offer from a hospital in Prussia and settled instead on a modest estate in Normandy near the obscure village of Biron with his wife and baby daughter. His medical practice brought little profit, but the estate farms provided a good income. Rumor in the village maintained that a wealthy patron had anonymously funded Doctor Hilliard's education and purchased Maison Cerisier, but no one could give details.

Madame Marie Hilliard, a devout Catholic, was active in the community until her second confinement. A boy was born but lived only a few days. Due to complications of delivery, Madame Hilliard's health declined.

Doctor Hilliard took her to Switzerland, Prussia, and England to be examined and treated by leading specialists of the day, but no one could help her.

Over the following years, Madame taught and raised their daughter while her husband began to pursue a lifelong interest in politics and government. His writings, and later his oratorical skills, gained both local and national recognition, and he traveled often to Paris.

One June afternoon in 1787, the doctor carried his invalid wife into the front garden, as he often did on fine summer days, and then returned to his office at the back of the house, where he and his assistant debated political issues. Leonie, age twelve, read aloud to her mother while Marie did needlework.

A great coach-and-six, complete with liveried servants, drove up to the gate, and Madame's father, the marquis, emerged. No one witnessed their encounter but, apparently, it turned bitter, for by the time the doctor and his assistant—Pascoe himself—heard the row and emerged from the house, Madame Hilliard lay prostrate on the ground and the wicked nobleman ran for his carriage. Doctor Hilliard fired a few pistol shots after the coach but did no damage. The evil marquis escaped, and Madame Hilliard died soon afterward without ever regaining consciousness.

During my youth I had paid scant attention to the trials of my neighbors. I never knew or cared to know the nature of Madame Hilliard's illness. My own troubles had occupied my thoughts to the exclusion of others. And I had married and moved away several years before her death.

As I lay sleepless in bed that night, pondering Pascoe's story, several details disturbed me. The arrival of a coach-and-six would have stirred interest throughout the community. Surely some maid or gardener had sneaked glances out a window or over a wall at the marquis arriving in so much state. And even if every servant had been miraculously lacking in curiosity, the events of that tragic day were witnessed by at least one living person: Leonie Hilliard. She was twelve years old at the time, old enough to know what she saw and heard. Why, then, were important details left so unclear?

CHAPTER 5

ARLY THE NEXT MORNING I descended the front stairs just as Étienne and Claude left for the forge. Pascoe lingered to talk to me. "You look anxious, *ma chère*. Did my story last night disturb you?" He brushed a stray hair from his sleeve and adjusted his neck cloth at the hall mirror.

"I have mislaid my little printed calendar," I said truthfully while searching through my reticule. I felt reluctant to talk further with him about the Hilliards.

"A calendar?" He glanced back at me over his shoulder. "What use have you for a calendar?"

It was an honest question, but my hackles rose. "I use it for my social business." To supplement my income, I organized social events for the wives of Assembly deputies of all political persuasions. "I'm doing quite well. Next week I'll be hosting two events."

His amusement softened into concern. "Of course you are," he said in a conciliatory tone which served only to irritate me further. "You know,

Colette, very few of our compatriots in the *section* can read. Compared to most of them, you are a highly educated woman."

"There is a difference between never having learned to read and not being *able* to learn." I opened the escritoire in the salon and paged through a stack of papers, mostly handwritten letters as useful as ciphers to me. *"Ah, voilà."* The calendar's numbered squares and swirling decorations were familiar. I tucked it safely away.

He smiled at me from the salon doorway. "The difference looms large to you but small to others. It shouldn't matter so much. Why does a woman need to read or write?"

"To correspond with my mother and sisters," I said, pausing to glare at him. "To be able to read notes or invitations or posters or warning signs. Not to mention letters from loved ones, instead of always depending on someone else to read them to me."

His only response was a shrug. "I am curious. How do you manage to create guest lists for your social events? And to address invitations?"

"The hostess does that part. I do the ordering and arranging. I can add up costs easily enough. So far, no one has guessed my secret." But it was difficult to hide at times. "I hate being stupid."

At this, Pascoe strode over to confront me directly. With one knuckle he tipped my chin up. All mockery fled his expression. "You are one of the brightest people I know. Don't take me seriously when I tease; it takes all the fun out it when you feel hurt." He kissed my forehead, gave me a wink, and walked out the front door.

On hot summer days I did my gardening in the morning hours, while the vegetable plot lay in shade. After donning sturdy gloves and an apron, I picked up a trowel and headed outside to battle for my vegetables.

A tiny piece of country dropped into the center of Paris was my garden, shaped like a child's drawing with meandering fences and randomly planted trees. The back wall of the house composed the only straight side of the polygon, connecting a fence of high wooden slats on the west to a shorter, gated fence on the east, dividing the garden from the alley. These two fences wandered about until they met the south fence, a gated wrought-iron structure dividing my garden from another alley. The west fence swerved around the trunks of four large trees—two beeches, one alder, and one linden—which shaded not only this garden but also the one adjoining it. Beneath and between those trees I cultivated a variety of shade-loving perennials and shrubs, and several fruit trees.

Fifteen feet from the house, another fence divided this small paradise of shade and color from the kitchen garden, where I grew enough fresh vegetables to feed several families. No one could accuse me of taking shortcuts when it came to the defense and development of my garden produce and, with the doctor's permission, I shared its abundance with needy widows and invalids in our *section*.

As I have mentioned before, I paid several of the *section* boys to carry water from the nearest public fountain to fill the two rain barrels behind my kitchen. This was a difficult chore in summer, for there was less rain to aid with the filling, and those water barrels served for household needs as well as the garden. But the boys were allowed to eat whatever fruit was ripe in the garden as they labored, so my list of eager workers was extensive.

This narrow slice of earth in *faubourg* Saint-Germain was a delight to me. I loved its certainty, its surprises, its generous rewards for hard work and faithful care. I loved cutting and arranging flowers to beautify the dark old house. I was never happier than when digging, mulching, and weeding in the vegetable plot or peeling, slicing, and sautéing in the kitchen.

Leonie joined me in the garden nearly an hour later. With her hair bound up beneath a work cap, she might have passed as a maid herself. "May I help you?"

"Do you enjoy gardening?" I asked doubtfully.

She shrugged and knelt on a strip of straw mulch. "We worked nearly every day in the kitchen garden at the convent. We grew some very fine melons and squashes."

I handed her a trowel, and she set to work. Her hands were quick and sure; the weeds rapidly piled up in the mulch cart. I was satisfied.

Taking the opportunity, I did my best to draw her out . . . or at least to draw out information. "Did you enjoy your school days?"

"Sometimes. We were like an enormous family of girls, so you can imagine the bickering and the competition."

"*Tout à fait!* The four girls in our family bickered enough for a dozen." I grinned, but she did not respond. "It sounds like a nightmare. However did the nuns manage so many girls?"

"They were good to us, although Sister Beatrice was often short-tempered, which a nun really shouldn't be. I received an excellent education, I am sure."

"A nun is as human as anyone else. I should think the sisters' position in a girls' school would guarantee sainthood more surely than martyrdom." Despairing of coaxing a smile from her, I made an observation. "You sound more resentful than grateful for your education."

"I'm sure I do." Her voice was clipped.

"What happened? Were you abused?"

"*C'est pas vrai!*" She sat back on her heels and stretched her lower back.

All these half-answers began to irk me. "If no one mistreated you, why do you sound as if you were hung on the rack or dunked as a witch?"

Her gaze flickered to my face, and I glimpsed hesitation amid the annoyance. "Much of what angered me then, and still angers me now, was being exiled so completely from my former life. I want nothing more now than to find my grandfather and persuade him to let me live with him."

"Your grandfather," I repeated. For a long moment I sat there and let my brain spin this thought around. Why in the world would she wish to live with the grandfather who disowned her mother and possibly caused the poor lady's death?

She gave me a sharp look and shook her head. "Do not speak of this further." The command rang with authority. I could easily believe her the granddaughter of a marquis. Discretion closed my lips for the time, but I had no intention of bending to her will.

We labored on in silence, listening to starlings chattering in my shade trees.

"Our shade is nearly gone," I remarked at last. "But thanks to you, we have finished the job."

She gazed at the neat rows of produce with satisfaction. "Now what shall we do?"

"I need to run to the market and visit a friend—actually, the friend is Adrienne Picot, or she was before she married. You must have known her."

"We grew up together. Take me with you, *s'il vous plaît*."

I wondered then if I should have been more discreet, if I should first have asked Adrienne if she wished to see Leonie Hilliard. "I am willing, but I don't know how Adrienne will feel," I said plainly.

Leonie was quiet a moment, her face as unreadable as ever. "If she does not wish to see me, I will not be offended." She sounded sincere, even slightly humble.

"Perhaps you might wait outside her house while I mention you are in Paris and see how she reacts," I said. "If she says she wants to see you, I'll tell her you're waiting outside. If not, I won't tell her."

Leonie agreed. So we walked to market, each carrying a full basket.

"Why do we carry food with us to market?" Leonie inquired. "There is no room to add purchases."

"You will see."

As we passed through the *section*, children greeted us, and I handed out pieces of fruit. One boy stopped on the brick-paved street in front of Leonie and stared up at her, goggle eyed. Since he was blocking her path, I figured introductions were in order. "Mademoiselle," I said, "may I present Martin Danican? Martin, this is Mademoiselle Hilliard, my new friend."

Leonie glanced at me then reached into her basket and withdrew a plum. "I am pleased to meet you, Martin."

His face lit up. "You are pretty," he announced, accepting the gift.

Without batting an eye, she curtsied. *"Merci."*

He gave a whoop and ran off to join his friends. Leonie gave me a questioning look.

"Martin often runs errands for me," I explained. "I believe you have a new admirer."

She seemed pleased but said nothing.

I decided on a brace of ducks for that night's dinner, and also added a slab of cured ham to my basket. Since Leonie expressed a taste for cheeses, we indulged in a small round of Camembert and wedges of several other favorites. A jug of cream, a package of sugar, and a pound of coffee filled our baskets. Satisfied, I started toward the forge. The baskets were now very heavy, but Leonie did not complain.

"I know Madame Picot was your family's cook," I said. "Did you and Adrienne play together often?"

"We played dolls together, and her mother taught us to cook." Leonie's voice became slightly animated. "We grew apart as we got older, yet I have often missed her."

"Now she is married and expecting a child," I said.

"I hope she will wish to see me," Leonie said sincerely.

I had my doubts. Adrienne had always been prone to sudden shifts of mood. Pregnancy only exacerbated this tendency, and I never could predict which way the winds of her humor would blow from day to day.

We could hear and smell the forge long before it came into sight. I led Leonie around back to the little house where Arnaud's bride dwelt. It was a noisy home at best, but the house's stone walls shut out at least some of the shouting, clanging, roaring, and hissing from the forge.

Leonie sat on a crate against the back wall of the forge, rigidly upright amid spider webs and rusted bits of metal. "I'll wait here."

I had to admire her determination.

Adrienne answered my hail with "Enter." I found her down on her knees, sweeping out the hearth. This one room served as bedroom, sitting room, and kitchen. A tiny loft and a lean-to for food storage comprised the rest of Adrienne's home. She looked up and awkwardly rose to greet me. "Colette!"

"Bonjour, petite mère," I said, happy to see her active. "How are you feeling?" I deposited both baskets on her worktable.

"I still have pain in my hip and back, but not as bad as sometimes." She ambled over to peek into a basket. "Did you bring strawberries?"

"Strawberries and cream. I'll fix them; you sit down and put your feet up." Once she was settled with her feet propped on a stool, I said, "Do you know that Doctor Hilliard's daughter, Leonie, is in Paris? She arrived yesterday."

Adrienne's face brightened. *"Ah bon?* I did not know! She was sent away to school many years ago, after madame died."

"She expressed interest in seeing you, Adrienne. She says you and she were close friends at one time."

"Mais oui! Did she really ask about me? After all these years." Adrienne's voice held a note of wonder. "I expected she would forget. I should like to see her, but . . ." She glanced around. "Do you think she would want to come here?"

"Actually I know she would want to come here, because she asked me to bring her along with me today. But she stayed outside in case you didn't wish to see her."

"Hein! Leonie is waiting outside?" Adrienne looked ready to leap to

her feet, so I left off cutting strawberries and motioned for her to stay in place.

"*Non,* you stay here. I'll bring her to you." And I beckoned to Leonie from the door. She hopped up eagerly and hastened to enter.

The following hour was filled with talk, and for once I listened without often interrupting. Both girls talked more than I had ever heard from either, reminiscing about old times. Leonie gave Adrienne a painted-silk fan she had made, and Adrienne fanned herself so vigorously while she talked that loose hair wafted around her flushed face.

I served them strawberries-and-cream and then removed ingredients from my basket and began to peel and chop. The slab of ham plus onions, garlic, barley, and an assortment of garden vegetables filled a cast-iron kettle, and I strained water from the rain barrel to make broth for a hearty soup. Heat exhausted Adrienne in her condition, so she had difficulty cooking in the stuffy house even with the doors open. Soup made a meal she and Arnaud could eat for days, hot or cold.

I also mixed bread dough, using starter brought from home. The fireplace had no bake oven, so I set the dough to rise in a Dutch oven.

And talk floated about me all the while. In my opinion, Adrienne was putting on a show of happiness for her old friend. She patted her swollen belly with pride, spoke of her husband's ownership of the forge and his weapons contract with the government as if his successes were her life's joy, and not-so-subtly pitied Leonie for having been cloistered in a convent for five years. Her smiles and laughter rang a bit hollow.

Leonie was more difficult to read. She spoke only positive words about Adrienne's situation, yet I doubted her sincerity. Was she aware that her presence intimidated Adrienne? Perhaps their friendship had always looked this way: Adrienne, the elder by a year, pushing to appear superior yet always giving in to Leonie's will. The two girls were hardly more than children yet, I thought, glancing over at their rounded hands and faces. Yet Adrienne would soon be a mother. I was near her age when my baby girl was born.

I was determined to prepare Adrienne for the responsibilities of motherhood. Helping to raise my army of younger siblings had adequately prepared me to be a mother, but nothing could have prepared me for my daughter's death.

The one positive result of my past mistakes was sincere sympathy with other bruised hearts. I often encouraged Adrienne to pick up and move on with life as I had done . . . or as I hoped she would believe I had done. I longed for her to find contentment in her new situation, to value Arnaud's devotion, to adore her baby despite its father's failings. I suppose I was trying to live vicariously through her, to force a success where I had failed. This was unfair to Adrienne, yet I could not seem to help myself.

At present, Adrienne seemed determined to inspire envy in her old friend. She was unlikely to succeed. Leonie, for all her current show of friendliness, lived and moved in a sphere well above this humble cottage. Well above the likes of Adrienne and me.

CHAPTER 6

"LEONIE AND I HAVE had a lovely chat," Adrienne said in a strained tone, "but I am rather tired now, Colette."

I recognized the plea for help and wiped my hands on my apron. "I'm sure you are. We'll leave you to get some rest. I moved the soup to the back of the fire so it will simmer, and you can place the Dutch oven over the coals."

"Would you do it, Colette?" she begged. "I know I will forget."

"It hasn't risen yet. Never mind; I'll tell Arnaud. You go rest now."

"Would you help me to bed?" she asked, and I knew she wanted to speak with me alone.

"Mais bien sûr, ma chère. Leonie, pack up our baskets, and I'll rejoin you in a moment." To her credit, Leonie set to work without a word.

The bed was in one corner of the room, hardly a private place. I helped Adrienne to climb in. She was still more than two months from delivery, but the poor girl suffered almost constant back pain, and her face often had a drawn appearance. "You can rest now, *chérie.* Perhaps after the excitement of Leonie's visit, the baby will be ready to sleep." I smoothed lank hair from Adrienne's forehead and squeezed her hand.

"Will you come back tomorrow?" she begged quietly, clinging to my skirt. "Alone?"

"I cannot return until Thursday; tomorrow is the big demonstration."

Adrienne looked resentful. "Always the Republic is most important," she muttered.

A heavy step sounded on the floor behind me. "Adrienne?" It was Arnaud.

"I'm all right," she assured him. "I just needed to lie down. Colette brought my old friend Leonie to visit." She raised her voice. "Leonie, this is my husband, Arnaud Lamorges. Arnaud, Mademoiselle Hilliard. My mother worked as cook in her parents' house in Biron." A tautness in her voice concerned me. "We played with the Girardeau boys."

Leonie curtsied as Arnaud regarded her with mild interest. *"Bonjour,* Mademoiselle Hilliard," he said.

"Bonjour, monsieur. I am pleased to meet the husband of my good friend."

"We are just leaving," I told him. "There is soup in the kettle and bread dough rising. Will you set it to bake once it rises?"

He thanked me and agreed to rescue my bread. "The men are taking a rest to eat. You might stop by the forge for a moment if you wish, since mademoiselle is an old friend."

This permission surprised me, for Arnaud was usually strict about no visits in his forge. I suspected he made the exception in an effort to please Adrienne, but if so he was mistaken, for she wore a sour expression when we left the house.

"Visitors," Arnaud announced in a stentorian voice as we rounded the corner. Some of the forge's wall sections could be propped up to allow free air flow, although any air flowing through the area was stiflingly hot.

The five smiths sat on benches in the open, still wearing their leather aprons, their faces and arms sweaty and sooty.

"I have brought an old friend to visit," I announced. "Mademoiselle Leonie Hilliard, daughter of Doctor Hilliard, newly arrived in Paris."

Étienne was first to rise, and Claude followed him quickly. The other three men stared at us then clambered to their feet. To my surprise, Leonie set down her basket and approached my brothers, giving her hand to each and not seeming to mind the soot.

Saint-Jude Fillion ambled over to greet me, beaming all over his blackened face. "You are a welcome sight in the middle of a work day. However did you convince Lamorges to let you in?"

"I didn't." I watched Claude work his charm on Leonie. If anyone could win a smile from her, I would put money on my baby brother.

Saint-Jude followed my gaze. "You said she is Doctor Hilliard's daughter?"

"*Oui,* just returned from school."

"She looks like him," he said.

"A little, I suppose." I really wanted to eavesdrop on Leonie's conversation, and Saint-Jude's questions prevented this. It was silly to stand here and be irritated. I should either go join the other group or talk to him.

"Does she ever smile?" He was working so hard to strike up conversation, I finally took pity on the poor boy.

"Not often. Are you looking forward to the demonstration tomorrow?"

His face lit up again. "I plan to be in the thick of things! Can you dance the ça ira?"

"Not very well. Can you?"

"I most certainly can. I'll teach you, and we'll show the world how it should be done."

Arnaud called the men back to work a moment later, and Leonie and

I slipped quietly away, carrying our baskets. "So what do you think of my little brothers?" I asked.

"They have certainly grown." She sounded friendlier than usual, which was encouraging.

"Especially Étienne," I remarked. "But Claude will fill out in the next few years. They were born to be smiths—all long arms and big shoulders."

She said nothing, so I kept talking. "They work long hours at the forge, but Claude still finds time to socialize." I gave her a sidelong glance and added, "Being Girardeaux, they might have had their pick of women in Biron. One young woman outright proposed marriage to Étienne before we came to Paris."

Leonie slowly turned her head and stared at me. "Who?"

I smirked. "I wouldn't want to mention names. Apparently, he and the other little brothers were building a wrought-iron fence around her father's property, and she daily hand-delivered baked goods for their enjoyment. Claude tells me he put on weight that summer despite the hard work. But Étienne was apparently unimpressed, for he is as yet unattached. She was probably not religious enough for him."

"Étienne is religious?"

"Very. Devotedly. Blindly."

After a step or two, Leonie asked, "Was Adrienne . . . I mean, at her house today, was anything wrong?"

I accepted the change in subject without question. "She is hot and miserable and feels unattractive. I believe she will regain her spirits once the baby comes."

Leonie nodded. I could not read the girl's face at all. It was frightfully frustrating.

"Her husband is good to her. He is a kind man," I said. "And his situation is secure, working for the government. He is very patriotic and has been active in the Revolution from the beginning. He was in the middle of the action on Bastille Day."

"How old is he?"

Her tone startled me. "I would guess around thirty-five? I'm not sure. Why?"

Leonie said nothing, so I dropped the topic. When we arrived at the house, she insisted on helping with the cooking. I assigned her to make a dessert, and she competently prepared a fruit compote, adding spices with a generous hand.

While scalding the ducks for plucking I commented: "Your father informed me that your mother trained you in housekeeping skills. Knowing she was a fine lady, I confess I doubted. But you truly do know how to cook."

An expression that might have been gratification briefly touched her features. "My mother insisted I have cooking lessons. I told you how Adrienne's mother taught the two of us girls together in the kitchen at Maison Cerisier."

"Why did your mother think you should learn to cook?"

"She thought a woman should be prepared to do every job in her household, for she might someday have a need to know basic skills."

Perhaps madame had been more egalitarian in her views than expected. Or . . . "I wonder if she and your father often went hungry when they first married," I mused. "She would not want her daughter to experience this. How embarrassing to feel ignorant and useless before one's new husband!"

"Ignorant?" Leonie glared. *"Au contraire!* My mother was skilled with a needle, could speak five languages, and played the harpsichord beautifully. She was far from ignorant."

"Yet none of those skills can fill the stomach." I don't know why I pursued the subject. Curiosity can be hazardous. "Did she take in sewing or tutor languages to supplement her husband's income?"

Angry though she was, Leonie kept talking. *"Non.* They were obliged to hire servants while they lived in Switzerland, which Papa could ill afford." Some of her sulk ebbed away. "You are right; Maman felt useless and humiliated."

"I admire her for deciding you should have a practical education," I said. "Did she teach you needlework and music?"

"She taught me needlework, and I learned to play the harpsichord and to sing very well. I can speak and read German and English," she said, "and I can read some Italian, though I cannot speak it."

Laying the scalded ducks on the table, I began to strip off feathers. I glanced over at Leonie's set expression. "Your mother did her utmost to prepare you for whatever future might come. Who could ask more, *hein?*"

Leonie did not look at me, but I saw her shoulders relax a little.

"You mentioned your desire to live with your grandfather who, I understand, is a nobleman in exile. Would you wish to marry a title? Or would you marry for love?"

"Neither," she met my gaze and answered firmly. "I would marry for respect and friendship. I would marry a responsible man who would be faithful to me and love his children."

A hard light glittered in her eyes then faded into sadness. Listlessly she stirred the simmering compote.

"I cannot say I ever considered such things when I was your age," I admitted. "I thought only of pleasure. But pleasure alone doesn't make a good marriage."

The pleasure with Jean-Antoine had lasted until I got sober. And pregnant. By the time I spoke my marriage vows, any "pleasure" was buried under so much sorrow that it might well never have existed at all.

I was just as happy when Leonie excused herself and went upstairs; I liked having my kitchen to myself. I hung the compote on a hook where it would keep warm, then built up the fire, set hasteners to reflect the heat and a pan to catch the drippings, and arranged the ducks on hooks beneath the bottle jack. Then I wound up the spring mechanism and let the ducks revolve over the fire to roast.

Just as I finished this task, I heard the front door knocker pound. Removing my apron as I ran up the steps, I cautiously looked out the front window in the salon and was startled to see Claude on the steps. He caught sight of me in the window and grinned. When I opened the door, the first words out of his mouth were "Is Leonie here?"

"You're clean!" I said. He must have rushed straight home from work, washed the soot from his hands and face, changed into a clean shirt, then run here at top speed. "What are you thinking, *garçon fou?* Leonie isn't your sister, and you two are no longer children. You cannot simply knock at her door and tell her to come out and play."

"Then let her walk with me. I'll take her to Jardin du Luxembourg."

"*Non,* you will not." I pushed a finger into his chest to keep him out of the house. But before I could say more, Leonie spoke from the landing.

"*Bonjour,* Claude."

"*Bonjour,*" he answered hastily. "Leonie, tell Colette you want to talk with me. She's trying to send me away."

Leonie looked to me. "We shall walk beneath the trees in the garden." She addressed Claude. "My father will soon be home, so we cannot talk long."

Claude moved to step around me, but I pushed him back to the step. "Not so hasty." Leonie's high-handed manner provoked me, I confess. "A better plan is for you both to join me in the kitchen. This way, I can chaperone and you can make yourselves useful while you talk."

They both looked irked, but I cared not a whit for that. I set them to work, and aside from Claude's tendency to drop things—I allowed nothing breakable in his hands—they were surprisingly efficient. He cracked a large pile of almonds for a sweet *galette* while she minced garlic and other spices for the pilaf.

I let Claude talk uninterrupted for a time. He laid out his plan to escort Leonie to the next day's demonstrations and waxed eloquent on the need for such a protest against the King's interferences. She asked who all would be coming, which I interpreted as an attempt to learn whether or not she and Claude would be chaperoned.

"Colette will be around," Claude said hastily. "She will likely be right up front with the leaders. And we will be surrounded by respectable people. Many other women. Mothers. Everyone of importance will be there. We Girardeaux are active in the *sans-culottes* movement, you know."

"These *sans-culottes* are pushing for faster change from monarchy to republic, are they not?" Leonie inquired. "And the Girondins, my father's party, disapprove."

From her tone I gathered that this disapproval rendered the protest more, not less, appealing.

I made a few decisions while they discussed plans. When the *galette* was baking and everything else had been prepared for the dinner, I stood before them, fists planted on my hips. "Claude, I fully appreciate your desire to introduce Leonie to our people and our goals. However, any plans you make are contingent on Doctor Hilliard's approval."

Both opened their mouths to object, but I interrupted. "If you desire my support in presenting your plan to the doctor, you will accept my stipulations. Tomorrow is likely to be somewhat chaotic; such extemporized demonstrations generally are. You two may not run around Paris together without attendance. I shall make every attempt to be a pleasant companion, but whether you welcome my presence or not, you will accept it."

Claude began to bluster as I fixed my gaze on Leonie and said, "You will ask your father's permission before attending the demonstration."

Leonie's already sullen expression turned stormy. *"Bah!* I don't care whether he approves or not."

I lifted one brow. "If he objects, I shall advise him to take you with him to the Assembly tomorrow rather than risk your flouting his authority and mine and running off to spend the day with my brother."

She narrowed her eyes. "Shall I tell him what I know of the alternate demonstration planned by the *sans-culottes*?"

I really would have liked to smack her. Instead, I smiled sweetly. "You may tell your father whatever you like as long as it is the truth. Do you both understand my conditions?"

The wind taken from their sails, they nodded, and Claude, glowering mutinously, took his leave shortly afterward; I suspect he feared facing Doctor Hilliard directly.

I instructed a morose Leonie how to carve the ducks and added last touches to the sauce. "And don't forget to shake up the oil and vinegar before you sprinkle the vegetables," I was reminding her when Doctor Hilliard stepped into the kitchen, still peeling off his gloves.

"*Bonsoir, mesdames.* Whatever you are preparing smells delectable, as usual." The room seemed smaller with him in it, though he was only slightly taller than Claude. I hurried forward to take his gloves and hat, but he refused my help. "*Mais non!* You are busy. I can hang up my own things; I usually do, you know." He seemed to be in a good mood.

Leonie spoke up immediately. "I have a request to make of you."

The doctor turned his attention to her. "What request is this, *ma fille?*"

I hurried to the oven and removed the *galette* while Leonie laid out her plan. By her manner I would have thought her a complete stranger to him.

"Madame DeMer?"

"*Oui?*" I gave him my full attention.

"You plan to attend the celebration tomorrow and are willing to chaperone my daughter and your brother for the day?" He tapped his hat brim against one open hand.

"I offered to do so, monsieur."

"Rumor has reached the Assembly of uprisings among the *sans-culottes.* If events were to turn . . ." he paused to seek the right word. "If events were to turn unpleasant, may I trust you to safeguard my daughter?"

I stood my tallest and lifted my chin. "With my life, monsieur."

He briefly searched my face. "I shall consider this request and give my answer in the morning."

Then Leonie and I were alone in the kitchen. Leonie glared at the place where Doctor Hilliard had stood, her lips pressed into a flat line.

"You should honor your father," I whispered sharply.

Rebellion burned in her eyes. "You don't understand," she returned.

"It doesn't matter if I understand. You do. The dinner is prepared; you may serve it."

I gathered my things and slipped out the back door. It was still light enough to walk home, so I did.

CHAPTER 7

PASCOE CAME HOME AFTER dinner that night. I half-heartedly teased him about being a stranger in his own home, but the words were too true to be amusing and fell flat. Although he was outwardly composed, I sensed his nervous tension. Our younger brothers were in no mood to endure his sarcastic gibes, so I coaxed him out to the balcony to sit with me awhile.

"Oh, *mon cher*, it's been too long since we had a good talk," I said, struggling to shift my iron chair closer to his. It might as well have been welded to the balcony floor.

Pascoe reached over and moved it for me with one hand. *"Merci,"* I said, but my tone made him chuckle. He did not look like he should be so much stronger than I. But he was. I hated this, and he knew it.

He settled back in his chair and drew on his pipe, blowing smoke rings of varying sizes. "I've missed you too, *chérie*. One of these evenings I'll take you to the theater or the opera house. You can wear your jewelry and a beautiful gown and dazzle the eyes of every man present."

"I would enjoy that." I closed my eyes and smiled, imagining an evening in Paris with Pascoe, dining in a fine restaurant, enjoying quality entertainment, and—

"And you could become acquainted with *la Florinda,*" he added. "You and she share several common interests. I have been surprised more than once by the similarities."

My dream dissolved and blew away like one of his smoke rings. I said nothing. He said nothing. Much was communicated, contested, and finally dropped.

"Why was Claude in such bad humor this evening?" he asked in a leisurely tone.

"Because I won't allow him to escort Leonie Hilliard to the demonstration tomorrow without a chaperone."

This new topic would inevitably turn into another contest of wills. If he could not persuade me to associate with Florinda Mordant, he would begin a new battle and wear me down.

"And how will you prevent our brother from doing whatever he likes?" Pascoe inquired.

I could read nothing in his face by starlight or pipe-light. "He will respect my authority, Pascoe. If the doctor allows her to attend at all, Leonie will be under my protection."

"Then you should hope Hilliard will forbid her attendance, for you will have no time to attend to such an irrelevant undertaking. You have prior commitments. You must arrive at the gardens early to help organize our *section*. The people depend on you. I depend on you."

His sarcasm and tone of command produced a private revolt. "I will attend to whatever undertakings I choose, irrelevant or otherwise. What do you mean by 'organize our *section*'? I do not recall committing myself to any such duty."

He sat upright in the chair and faced me. "Colette, you are an unofficial leader of our *section*. You should know without being told that your presence is essential at any and all events. You are my right hand."

I despised his chiding tone but could not dispute that early on in our involvement with the *sans-culottes* I had promised to take part in events. Yet no amount of guilt would induce me to submit completely to his orders. "I will arrive as early as I reasonably can and do my part."

After a moment of tense silence, he said, "Do not underestimate the responsibility of your position. We expect thousands of people, from the lowest *canaille* to shopkeepers, tradesmen, and National Guard, to take part in this uprising. We intend to force the King to revoke his vetoes of recent legislation."

"I am aware," I said stiffly. "Do not lecture me, Pascoe."

"You are responsible for keeping our people informed moment by moment. Knowledge ensures order and safety."

I thought of the plan he had outlined at the meeting, thousands of citizens armed with everything from pikes to pitchforks marching first to the Hôtel de Ville, then to the Assembly, and finally to the Palais des Tuileries to confront the King himself. I remembered Doctor Hilliard's worried expression and felt a fist squeeze my gut. The doctor was not the People's enemy, but would rampaging *sans-culottes* make any attempt to distinguish friend from foe?

"You do not anticipate actual physical violence against officials and deputies, I trust?" I asked. "I don't want to lead women and children into a dangerous situation."

"I cannot predict, but we do not expect it."

I breathed easier. If there was no danger to the deputies, I intended to stay far from the Assembly. "Do our people have a designated area in the garden? A place to gather if we are separated? Monsieur Fillion spoke of leading chants and dancing the ça ira." I could take Claude and Leonie there and avoid any connection with political unpleasantness.

"Ha ha!" It was not a genuine laugh. "Colette, you do recall we are no longer planting a Tree of Liberty, don't you? Tomorrow will be an

uprising, not a celebration. We will dominate and overcome any resistance, but in order to do this, every citizen must offer *all* to the cause. You may be called to stand before the National Assembly and speak for the cause of equality and freedom."

My face went hot at the very idea. "I will attend, and I will watch over my people as I am able, but I will not speak in the Assembly."

We stared at each other in the dark, neither yielding, neither prevailing. "If you let us down, then perhaps *la Florinda* will stand at my side and speak for the women of Paris," he said quietly.

My voice was even quieter. "If she is willing, I wish her well."

I could not sleep.

After tossing for hours in my bed, I crept downstairs and picked up some mending to occupy my hands. This division between my favorite brother and me seemed to eat at the foundation of my life. What was I without him? Less than nothing.

Yet when I considered apologizing to Pascoe and informing the doctor I could not, after all, chaperone his daughter due to prior commitments, something inside me turned to stone.

If I submitted, Pascoe would make me give a speech. I could parrot speeches I had heard from him or other leaders, and once in a while I added an original thought or opinion; but knowing that Doctor Hilliard listened from somewhere on the Assembly floor would certainly freeze my brain and seize up my vocal chords.

I woke up on the chaise longue with a crick in my neck. The first thing to meet my eyes was a nearly life-sized Apollo, only one of the many Greek-style marble statues left in Maison Beau Temps by a former owner. Pale blue-and-white-striped wall coverings and ornately embroidered cushions on spindly-legged furnishings were attractive enough, but I frankly hated the half-clothed nymphs, satyrs, and demigods populating the salon and entry hall. Stark-naked Apollo was the largest in the collection. Wherever I sat in the room, its blank stare seemed to follow me.

Unfortunately, the thing was far too heavy to safely remove from its niche, so Étienne, partly in jest, had clad it in a loincloth. Claude's recent addition of a tall hat tipped rakishly over one eye and a walking stick under its outstretched hand gave the thing a startlingly lifelike aspect.

"*Bonjour,* Apollo," I said under my breath.

It was early, but I desperately wanted the comfort of my kitchen. I dressed, gathered items I might need for the day, and set out. Dawn came early in June, so the sun was well up before I entered my kitchen garden, picked a basket of strawberries, and—feeling better already—descended the covered back steps and entered the house.

And found the doctor there before me, grinding coffee in his shirtsleeves. He looked as startled as I was, and his coat was nowhere to be seen. "*Ah! Bonjour,* Doctor Hilliard," I said with false brightness and set the strawberries on the table. He returned the greeting and resumed turning the crank. The noise of grinding filled an awkward silence.

I went about my usual morning tasks, noting how he had built up the fire and started water heating. He did these tasks every day, but I had never before arrived early enough to interrupt him. I didn't mind his coatless state, but he might find it embarrassing. I could only hope he wouldn't quit brewing coffee after this.

But following his first, almost guilty reaction, he seemed to relax and accept my presence. I mixed batter for crêpes and tried to keep out of his way. I never prepared breakfast for him, since he always left the house before I arrived. Would he expect a meal today? The crêpes and warmed-over fruit compote might be sufficient; I had planned to offer this to Leonie and take any leftovers along with us to eat during the day.

With the efficiency of nervous energy, I chopped vegetables and made soup using beans I had left to soak overnight; it would simmer all day while we were away. I set the dining room table, cooked the crêpes in a skillet lightly greased with drippings, and sliced onions to fry with bacon. Eventually the silence became comfortable.

Doctor Hilliard strained the coffee into the pot and poured two cups of the brew. "Are you still certain you wish to accompany Leonie and Claude today?" he asked.

"*Oui,* monsieur. I am willing." I met his gaze squarely before carrying the bowl of compote and the platter of bacon and onions up to the dining room.

"Then I shall grant my permission." He stood at the top of the stairs, his hands braced on the doorposts. "The atmosphere in the Assembly, in the entire city, has taken a troubling turn in recent days, urged on by certain radicals and by power-hungry journalists. Be watchful, madame. I trust your discretion."

I nearly laughed aloud. "I have never been known for my discretion, monsieur," I said truthfully. "Quite the reverse, *en fait.*" I approached the doorway, and he stepped aside to let me pass.

"Nevertheless." His expression was enigmatic.

Footsteps warned us seconds before Leonie entered the dining room. "Breakfast smells good. Is there coffee?" She brushed past her father, down the stairs, and into the kitchen without a word or glance. I followed in time to see her claim the full cup.

She sat at my work table and sipped the steaming brew. "How soon do we leave?"

I met Leonie's gaze then deliberately looked to her father in the doorway. Once her gaze followed mine, I returned to my work.

Doctor Hilliard said, "You may accompany Madame DeMer and her brothers today, with the stipulation that you follow her instruction. If she gives an order, it will be obeyed promptly and without question. Is this understood?"

While sliding the last crêpe onto the serving platter, I inwardly cringed. His tone reminded me of Pascoe at his most overbearing.

"It is understood, monsieur." Leonie sipped her coffee. "Claude tells me France's war with Prussia and Austria goes badly because the Legislative Assembly is nearly useless at making decisions."

The doctor's nostrils flared, yet his voice remained calm. "France has, for many generations, depended on foreign mercenary troops to fight her battles. The officers are, by and large, faithful to the King and mistrustful of our Republic. These must be replaced with men loyal to the Republic who also have the necessary experience for training our raw recruits into an effective army; however, such men are not readily at hand. Young Girardeau is correct in one respect: The Assembly has divided into bitterly squabbling factions who see each other as the primary enemy and cannot begin to solve the crucial issues at hand."

Leonie said nothing, merely took another sip of coffee and turned an expressionless face away from her father.

I picked up the crêpes and a small crock of honey. "Your breakfast is ready."

Once they were seated in the dining room, I retreated into the kitchen and poured myself a fresh cup of coffee. With the connecting doors closed, I enjoyed breakfast in private, if not in peace.

The doctor's brief explanation of the military's trouble made sense, and the problem had no quick solution. Today's protest against the Court would not provide France with a better-trained army to fight Prussia and Austria. But then, Pascoe hoped to persuade the King to cooperate with the Assembly, to revoke his vetoes; surely this aim was worthwhile. Doctor Hilliard might even thank us for our intervention in days to come.

Or we might make matters worse.

Claude arrived just after Leonie and I finished straightening the kitchen. "Is the doctor gone?" he asked.

"*Oui.*"

He visibly relaxed. "Did he give permission?"

"He did. Leonie is upstairs getting ready." I looked Claude up and down, noting the cockade pinned to his tall hat. "You're looking rather fine today."

He grinned and squared his shoulders. "May I carry one of your pistols? Where do you keep them? I couldn't find them in your room."

"You may not." I picked up my parasol and slipped on my sabots. "And you have no business searching my room. Did you speak with Pascoe this morning?"

"I did." Claude's superior expression put me on guard. "We're to meet at headquarters and march east to join the other *sections*, but I think we're already late. Pascoe wants you to give a speech in the Assembly today, so I'll have to watch over Leonie alone at least part of the day."

I laughed. "This will not happen. Take note: I'll make your life miserable if you misbehave today, Claude Girardeau."

His grin sharpened, and a knot of apprehension formed in my stomach. Any authority I held over this brother was based on respect. If he stopped respecting me, I would have no control whatsoever.

Leonie swept down the stairs, looking like a tall schoolgirl in her simple frock. "Is Étienne coming?" she inquired as Claude bowed over her hand.

"*Non*. He said he would spend the day organizing the forge." Disdain weighted Claude's voice. "He cares nothing for our cause. I think, sometimes, he would cheer for the King if given the chance!"

"Don't say such things," I snapped. Once again our eyes clashed before he looked away.

Leonie and I tied on our straw bonnets, and I advised her to bring a parasol as well. "It will be even hotter in the streets with all those people."

Claude led us toward our *section* headquarters, but a familiar couple met us before we reached the gate. Monsieur Gallatin, a former sailor with a weather-beaten face and a roving eye, said, "They've gone ahead already," sprinkling every phrase with obscenities. "We're too late."

"We'll have to meet them partway," added Madame Gallatin.

I tugged on Claude and Leonie, motioning to let the couple go ahead of us. Most of the people in our *section* were pleasant enough folk; the Gallatins were notable exceptions. Monsieur was perpetually drunk, kept a female slave from Martinique in their home, and never spoke a civil word to anyone. Madame had an equally poisonous tongue and spitefully abused the slave girl. I would just as soon not join our *section* people if it meant keeping company with the Gallatins all day.

At my urging we took a different route from theirs, crossed the river at Pont de Louis XVI, and walked east on Rue St. Honoré until it became Rue St. Antoine. The streets seemed strangely hushed, as if all of Paris had joined the march, though I knew this could not be so.

As we neared the Hôtel de Ville, Leonie said, *"Bah!* I think I have a blister forming on my heel."

"This is a poor beginning," I commented. "We will be walking nearly all day."

"I hear them coming!" Claude announced. And a moment later the leaders appeared in the street before us, approaching rapidly. The sight of that seething mass of humanity armed with pikes, muskets, scythes, and any other sharp object that might be used as a weapon struck me with dread, and I dragged Leonie into a side street. Claude protested then thought better of it and followed us. We three waited there, watching, until the first crush passed.

"Did you see Pascoe?" Claude asked.

"Non. Did you?"

"I thought I glimpsed him, but I'm not sure." He gave me a closer look. *"Quel est le problème?* You look upset."

Leonie turned to look at me.

I tried to shrug off the question. "Why should I be upset about a mob of armed citizens rushing through a city? This is Revolution!"

Claude detected the note of irony that *would* sneak beneath my guard. "You've seen events like this before, haven't you? I mean, you've been here a long time."

"*Bien sûr.*" Actually, as far as I knew, the greatest excitement since my arrival in Paris was the royal family's failed attempt to escape over the border to Austria. I had managed to avoid witnessing any unpleasantness. "How will we ever locate people from our *section* in this crush?"

"Eh, we'll find them," Claude said with confidence, and once the marching throng thinned slightly, he dragged us into the flow of traffic.

Leonie made no complaint as we half-walked, half-jogged along the street, but her pale face and dilated eyes worried me. "Leonie, are you well?"

"My feet hurt, and it is terribly hot and crowded. Where are we going now?"

"To the National Assembly, I assume."

Her eyes went wide. "I overheard Claude say you will be giving a speech. Does my father know?" She sounded both defiant and anxious.

"I am not giving a speech; that was Pascoe's idea of humor. Claude," I addressed my brother, "I'm taking Leonie home. This is no place for her."

Leonie looked relieved and moved to follow me. But Claude gripped her wrist and swung her away from me. "Stop interfering, Colette! We are not children, and you are not our mother. Go home if you wish, but let Leonie and me enjoy the day!"

I saw Leonie's startled expression and knew my face must match hers . . . although anger quickly rose to replace surprise. "Claude! You accepted my rules! You promised."

"You have no authority over me!" And he rushed Leonie sideways through the throng. I caught a brief glimpse of her imploring face before she was lost to view.

CHAPTER 8

C LAUDE! CLAUDE, YOU COME back here!" I shouted and swore, struggling to swim across the stream of humanity. My brother's cockaded hat bobbed through the crowds, and had I been taller I might have been able to follow him. As it was, I fought my way to a street lamp, held my sabots and stockings in one hand, and climbed the post, gripping with my bare toes until I could see above the crowds.

It was an interesting viewpoint, looking down on a sea of hats. Among the women's bonnets and the ubiquitous red caps of the *sans-culottes*, I could see the distinctive bearskins of National Guard grenadiers, and a few *casques* and cockaded bicornes of other military uniforms. And everywhere, absolutely everywhere I looked, men and women brandished weaponry including not only pikes but also farm implements, a boar spear, and even some horrible spiked clubs.

Far ahead I thought I glimpsed Leonie's green parasol. Taking note of landmarks, I set the place in my head, scrambled down, and leaned against the post while donning my stockings and shoes. I received a few rude comments but paid no heed. Modesty was not a common virtue among the *canaille* of Paris streaming past me. Many of the other women hiked their skirts up past their knees and did not even own a pair of shoes.

I hopped down, raised my parasol, and pressed on in search of my chosen landmark: a café with a black cat painted on its sign. But when I reached it I was no better off, for Claude and Leonie were long gone. Had she struggled and protested, he could not have disappeared so completely. Yet I was certain she had wanted to go home when I made the suggestion. The look in her eyes had been relief, not irritation; I had seen enough of irritation in those eyes to know the difference.

There really was nothing else to do but flow along with the teeming horde. Some groups of people detoured into the palace courtyards and set up minor protests of their own, but I followed the general flow past the Palais du Louvre and the Palais des Tuileries to Place de Louis XV, then through the main gates into the Jardin des Tuileries. Seeing the crowds on the path leading to the Assembly and hearing the cacophony of chanting and shouting from that quarter, I knew our leaders must have forced their way inside. The deputies could not possibly resist such overwhelming numbers. Even now, Pascoe might be making his speech.

I stared at the roofline of the building. Would Leonie dare defy her father openly? Would Claude have the nerve to parade her right there under her father's nose? I could hardly imagine such audacity from those two . . . but then I had not expected Claude's outright defiance. If I was to slip inside, what then? Drag Claude and Leonie out by their ears? Hardly. Stand before Doctor Hilliard and proclaim my innocence? Why should he believe me? There was no predicting what Pascoe might demand if he discovered me in the hall, and I was in no mood to fight him.

I turned to scan the huge garden. I would walk its perimeter in search of the runaway pair. If they could not be found, I might sneak into the hall and . . . No, there was no purpose in entering the hall except perhaps to assure myself of the doctor's safety.

First things first. I set out along a garden path, searching in every direction for Leonie's parasol or Claude's hat. My search was unsuccessful, and by the time I returned to my starting point, my feet were hot and sore. Not only had I not found the runaways, I had glimpsed not one familiar face anywhere.

The crowd now seemed to be flowing into the building. Succumbing to the inevitable, I joined the queue and, by way of being small, managed to work my way toward the front until I entered the National Assembly. Just inside the door, I stepped aside to take stock of my surroundings. Other marchers swore at me and pushed on.

Built originally as the Royal Riding Academy, the hall was an enormous open chamber, the largest I had ever seen. Rows of benches surrounded the open floor, and galleries above allowed visitors to observe governmental proceedings.

Currently, flag-waving people filled the galleries, and the floor of the Assembly was massed with dancing, singing women. The protesters slowly flowed through the hall and out the far door, waving their banners and shouting slogans. The deputies sat still on their benches surrounding the floor, observing the parade.

I stood on tiptoe and scanned the benches but despaired of finding Doctor Hilliard amid the hundreds of deputies. Suddenly someone caught hold of my arm, and I turned to meet Saint-Jude Fillion's bright smile.

"You are here!" he shouted amid the cacophony. "Pascoe thought you failed us. He has already gone ahead to the Tuileries with the leaders. Come out on the floor and dance with me."

"*Mais non!*" I pulled from his grasp and shouted back. "I am looking for Claude. Have you seen him? I was chaperoning him and Doctor Hilliard's daughter, but I lost them in the crowds."

He bent down to speak directly into my ear. "I haven't seen Claude, but Doctor Hilliard is seated just over there." He gestured vaguely. "Everybody knows him. Pascoe used to work for him."

"*Oui,* and I still do work for him." I ducked away and rubbed my ear to remove his hot breath. Again on tiptoe, I searched the rows of deputies, my gaze snagged by each gray wig. "Where did you say Doctor Hilliard is?"

Saint-Jude pointed openly to our right. "There, about four rows from the front. He is looking right at us."

He was. I met the doctor's gaze, and my heart sank to my toes. "May I go over there and talk to him?"

"You can go wherever you want. You can say whatever you want. Ask him for a raise. Tell him what you really think of him. He can't do anything to you. We own this place today." Saint-Jude laughed, as did several people around us. Everyone in the vicinity could hear his booming voice. "They are all afraid for their lives, as they should be."

"Go on!" a strange woman urged from behind us. "Go sit in his lap and curse him to his face. That's what they all deserve, these fat fools."

Since the doctor had seen me, I could not simply rejoin the parade. I walked out among the dancers, dodging and weaving between them, and approached the end of Doctor Hilliard's bench. Once there, I had to step over several pairs of feet then wedge myself into an almost nonexistent space between him and the next deputy, whose belly occupied the space of two men. It was awkward.

I looked almost straight up at Doctor Hilliard. He looked down at me. His face was beaded with sweat, and his eyes wore a guarded look.

There was no need to shout at this range, but I made certain to speak clearly. "I lost your daughter, monsieur," I said bluntly. "Claude ran off with her in the crowd. I don't think she wanted to go; he dragged her away. I have searched everywhere else, and I thought they might be here. I never thought he would defy me this way. I don't know what to do."

Midway through my speech his brows went up and the guarded look disappeared.

The man on my other side growled something about a bold strumpet.

Doctor Hilliard spoke over my head. "This is my housekeeper, a respectable woman." The other man mumbled something that might have been a retraction but probably wasn't, and the doctor again met my gaze.

"Might your other brother help you to search? Étienne?"

I considered the possibility. "Étienne could handle Claude, *bien sûr.* I can run over to the forge and bring him back with me."

Before I realized what he was about, the doctor pulled out a purse, pressed a coin into my hand, and wrapped my fingers around it. "Take a carriage to the forge. You needn't worry overmuch: Claude will allow no harm to befall Leonie. Girardeaux are bold and protective."

His tone gave the words double meaning. "Will you be safe?" I asked. It was true, I did want to protect him too, but what could I do?

"For the present I seem to be safe enough. Do not wander the city alone, *s'il vous plaît.*"

"*Oui,* monsieur. I will bring Étienne, and we will find Leonie. I left soup cooking at home, and there is bread left from yesterday." Stated with a direct gaze, it was the closest I could come to an order: *Come home safely!*

"I shall be grateful of it, madame."

With a firm nod, I extracted myself from the bench, lost my balance and nearly sat on the fat man's knee, recovered, made my way back through the dancers, and rejoined the flowing stream of protesters.

Saint-Jude caught up with me just outside the far door. "What was that all about?" he asked. No longer inside the hall, we could converse at a tolerable volume.

"I told the doctor I lost his daughter, and he advised me to bring Étienne to help me search. *Merci,* monsieur."

But he followed me along the path. "This lost daughter is the girl you brought to the forge yesterday?"

"*Oui.* Claude ran off with her."

Saint-Jude laughed. "Let the young lovers come home when they're ready. You looked so worried, I thought she must be kidnapped by some wicked *comte*. Why bring Étienne into this? She isn't his girl."

"Neither is she Claude's girl. She is the doctor's daughter, and she is my responsibility."

He looked into my face and shook his head. "Always so serious. A pretty woman who carries the world on her shoulders. It's just not right! What you need is to have a young man run off with you. That would set you to rights. Or at least you could dance with me."

I smiled a little. "Not today, monsieur. I must make haste."

Étienne was at the forge, just as Claude said. He looked up as I rushed in, and concern creased his brow. "Sit down here," he said in his deep, calm voice. "Catch your breath, and then tell me what is wrong." He even brought me a cup of very bitter coffee, which took the edge off my burning thirst.

I poured out the story, and he listened intently, asking few questions. His steady gaze somehow bolstered my spirit. "Will you help me search for them, Étienne? The doctor told me not to worry, but I know Leonie must be frightened and exhausted in all that heat and the crush of strange people."

"*Oui,* I will come. Wait a moment while I finish up here."

My carriage had not waited, so we walked the long way back to the Jardin des Tuileries and plunged into the sea of humanity, which Étienne breasted with ease. The solid bulk of him at my side was reassuring. I do not know how long we roamed about the gardens, threaded the throng still swarming around the Assembly, infiltrated another shouting mob in the courtyard of the Palais des Tuileries, and walked along surrounding streets and byways, looking, always looking for Leonie and Claude. From an enterprising vendor, Étienne purchased watered ale for both of us, a drink I particularly dislike, and I emptied my dipper without pausing for breath. The air was stifling, and my feet were so hot, I thought my sabots might ignite like kindling.

Étienne seemed tireless. I saw him cross himself several times, and his lips were often moving. I thought God probably wouldn't recognize my voice anymore, it had been so long; so instead I clutched the Mary medal on its string around my neck and invoked the aid of the Virgin and every saint I could recall.

The afternoon passed, and shadows grew long. I worried about my bean soup burning and stinking up the house. I also worried about my garden wilting in this heat, since I had not taken time to water it that morning. I tend to focus on trivialities during a crisis, hoping to keep my mind off the real concerns.

It didn't work this time.

Étienne and I were circling the gardens yet again when he suddenly waved his arms over his head and bellowed, "Leonie! Claude!"

"You see them?" I asked, craning my neck to follow his gaze. Strangers blocked my view, many of them staring at Étienne in surprise.

I heard "Étienne?"and recognized Leonie's voice.

"Dieu merci!" I gasped in genuine gratitude.

Moments later, Leonie gripped my arm, her eyes burning with intensity. "Colette, we must find him. What if they kill him? Whatever would I do?"

"Find whom?"

"My father."

Did she truly care only for her own convenience and safety, or did I detect a note of genuine concern? "Your father is safe. I talked to him a few hours ago. He advised me to—"

"He went into the palace as part of some kind of delegation, Claude said," she interrupted me. "I saw him go. People shouted about killing him as well as the King."

I swallowed hard. "It is only talk. The *sans-culottes* would not kill an elected deputy any more than they would dare kill the King. Your father is highly respected. It will be all right."

She believed me. Relief filled her eyes, and she gave a short nod. Her lips moved, but I could not hear her above the ringing cries of "Long live the Nation!" and "Death to the tyrant!" surrounding us. And there was Saint-Jude Fillion, in his red cap, white shirt, and striped trousers, leading the chant while brandishing a pike in one big hand.

Then I realized we had discovered our *section* people, or they discovered us. Familiar faces surrounded me, including mothers and children who sang and danced the ça ira in wild abandon, beckoning to the men to join in. Saint-Jude answered the call of a plump, pretty young woman named Juneau, laughing when she slapped his backside, and then, in his turn, swinging her off the ground. To Saint-Jude, this was one enormous party.

Just then, little Martin Danican bowed before Leonie and offered his hand. A grin lit up his face. Leonie made a curtsy and laid her hand in the child's grubby grasp. He showed her the steps, and she copied them awkwardly.

I watched, both in bemused disbelief that she would dance with the child and in dismay that she would dance while her father's life was possibly in danger. Surely my assurances of his safety had not been so convincing. I, for one, was unconvinced.

Hearing angry male voices, I turned to see Claude talking and gesticulating at Étienne, whose expression was thunderous. As I approached my brothers, Saint-Jude and the two other smiths from the forge joined us, laughing and pleased with themselves. "Étienne," the smith named Hérault said, grinning in satisfaction, "you came after all!"

"What a day this has been—beyond all expectation," said Phillipe, the other smith. "We're inside the palace, and word is we've gained audience with the fat old tyrant himself. Legendre the butcher is presenting our petition even now!"

"They heard the Voice of the People today, those deputies in the Assembly," Hérault added proudly. "And now the King is hearing our demands. Pascoe and Arnaud are there in the thick of it."

"Pascoe is?" I said. My brother and Doctor Hilliard might even now face each other in opposition, Pascoe with a virtual army at his back. Why must the revolutionaries be at odds with each other? Both sides wanted the Republic to prevail!

I eyed the façade of the Tuileries, thinking hard. Étienne could escort Leonie back to the doctor's house. If I could just convince Claude or Saint-Jude or one of the other smiths to take me inside the Tuileries . . .

Étienne touched my arm and shook his head. *"Non.* Don't even think of it." I frowned and prepared to argue, but he said, "You are Leonie's chaperone." And he was right.

"Some of us prefer open-air celebrations to stuffy, crowded royal chambers." Saint-Jude caught my hand. "Come and dance with me now, Colette! This has been a great day in the history of France, and we were all part of it. Come and celebrate!"

I glanced at Leonie, who was still whirling about with Martin. But my feet were sore and my nerves were on edge. "I can't, monsieur. My heart is not in it. I think I have had enough of demonstrations for this lifetime."

His face fell. But then it brightened, reminding me how young he was. "I will let you go if you promise to join me for a picnic on Bastille Day. I'll hire a carriage and have a luncheon packed by the best café in the *faubourg,* and we'll find places right up front to watch the celebration. I would be the happiest man in Paris if you'll agree!" His big eyes pleaded his case.

It was the best invitation I had received in a very long time. "I shall consider it," I conceded. "But I cannot give an answer today."

Even this response seemed to give him a thrill. His eyes lighted up, and he gave a whoop.

All this energy was exhausting. I turned to Étienne. "Will you escort Leonie and me back to Saint Germain?"

He nodded just as Leonie hurried up to join us. "What is happening?" she asked.

"We are going home."

CHAPTER 9

O N THE STREETS NEAR Doctor Hilliard's house, life continued as normal. Most Parisians had no interest in the events
transpiring at the Tuileries that day, being too busy with the
daily struggle of keeping body and soul together. The change in
atmosphere was surreal.

At the front door of her father's house, Leonie looked at Étienne and
extended her hand. *"Merci,* Étienne. I regret causing you such trouble and
wasting your day." Her voice was humble and soft.

Standing two steps below her, Étienne briefly took her hand and
bowed over it. "Time spent in your company is never a waste."

My brows shot up at this remarkably chivalrous reply from my
introverted brother.

Then he turned to me. "Will you stay?"

I nodded. "Don't worry, I'll hire a chair. My feet won't carry me
another step."

He touched my shoulder before hurrying down the steps and

striding away.

Leonie followed me inside, and we both removed our bonnets and hung up our parasols on the tree in the entry hall before heading to the kitchen. I checked the soup, which had not burned, then built up the fire.

"You rest for a bit while I water the garden," I ordered, and escaped to my other place of refuge. Drawing water from the barrels seemed like no work at all, and I watched it soak into the thirsty soil around my flowers and vegetables. Despite the shade cast by the trees, the evening was warm; yet its contrast with the glaring heat and confusion of the day was balm to my spirit. I drew one more bucket of water, brought it inside, and set a pot to boil. The kitchen was growing dark, so I lighted a candle lamp.

I found Leonie in the salon, sprawled on the canapé like a child, her shoes and stockings in a pile on the hideous rug, her bare feet extended in full view. Open sores covered both heels and the top of her right foot.

"Oh, *ma chère*," I sighed in sympathy. My feet probably looked much the same. I lighted a few more lamps and sconces, for the house felt gloomy. Upon returning to the salon I heard a sniffle and saw wet tracks on Leonie's face. "Do your feet hurt so much?" I asked.

She shook her head, and more tears spilled over. She mopped at them with a handkerchief, and I even heard a sob or two. I was pleased to see evidence of emotion in the girl, but I could only guess at the reason for her tears. "It was a long day filled with uncertainty," I said. "I still cannot believe Claude would be so irresponsible."

I perched on the pinkish velvet chair just as Leonie made a noise remarkably like a horse's snort and muttered something I didn't quite hear and probably was happier not hearing. Then she said, "My head aches."

"It was very hot today. Are you thirsty? Would you like a glass of wine?"

She shook her head. "I should probably go upstairs and lie down. I seem to be nothing more than a nuisance to everyone today." She tucked in her feet and prepared to rise.

"It was a wild day, but you weren't the cause of the trouble. Claude was."

She hesitated then settled back on the canapé. "He did his best to show me a good time. He wanted to march through the National Assembly, but I refused to go inside. We spent most of the day at the Place du Carrousel." After a pause she added, "I heard you entered the Assembly. Everyone was talking and laughing about it."

"Laughing?" This puzzled me. *"Pourquoi?"*

"Because a little woman like you had the effrontery to march right in among the deputies and take a seat, and they were too frightened to prevent it." Her tone held curiosity and a hint of disdain, whether for me or for the deputies, I couldn't guess. "Whatever did you say to my father?"

She obviously still suspected me of having designs on Doctor Hilliard. I answered in the most matter-of-fact tone I could muster. "I told him that I lost you. I entered the hall because I thought Claude might have taken you there." I shrugged slightly. "Once your father saw me, I had to explain."

"Pourquoi?"

"If I hadn't told him, he would have wondered why I was there and where you were. It was he who suggested I ask Étienne to help me search."

She dropped her gaze to her hands knotting the handkerchief.

"It was a good suggestion," I said. "I was glad of Étienne's company, though he hardly speaks a word. And, naturally, he was the one who spotted you, being tall enough to see over the crowds without needing to climb a lamppost."

Leonie's face crumpled, and she began dabbing at her eyes again. This odd reaction set off a new train of thought. I remembered Leonie playing only with my youngest brothers, but she and Étienne could have become friends after I moved away. How such a friendship might have come about I could not imagine, for two more taciturn people did not exist. During our walk home I had chatted freely; Leonie and Étienne between them said scarcely a word. Yet their manner of parting had been . . . unexpected.

Leonie lifted her head, her expression suddenly flat. "I think my father is home."

I hurried to the entry hall, where I found the doctor already inside and leaning his back against the closed door. At sight of me, he drew a deep breath and straightened.

"We found your daughter, monsieur," I said, ready to take his hat and walking stick. "She is safe and well."

"Tiens! Of course, you did." In the flickering light of a wall sconce, the poor man seemed to have aged ten years. The lines framing his mouth had deepened, and his eyes looked too large for his face. He gave his head a little shake as if to clear it then snatched off his hat so hastily that his wig nearly came with it. I gently took the hat and stick from his hands and hung them on the hall tree. "Where is she?" he asked.

"Leonie is in the salon, monsieur." I motioned to the adjoining room.

He glanced in that direction but did not move. When he reached up to rub his forehead, I saw his hand tremble. He tried to straighten his wig and made it worse. "I think I need a drink."

"Wine?" I suggested.

"Brandy."

I offered to pour, and he accepted. But I did not immediately walk away. "Monsieur," I said quietly, "what happened at the Tuileries?"

His gaze flickered briefly over my face before he shook his head. "Later."

"There is soup and bread prepared if you are hungry."

"Oui, I remember." I thought his expression lightened. "Might we all eat together in the kitchen tonight?"

I hesitated. It must be well after ten o'clock, far past my usual hours.

Yet I said, *"Mais bien sûr,* monsieur." The story unfolding in this household fascinated me, and I could not refuse this second opportunity to eat with the Hilliards, to observe their interaction and develop my theories. But there was more going on than I yet understood.

I hurried first to the liquor cabinet in the dining room and poured a small glass of brandy from a cut-crystal decanter. From there I heard the doctor greet Leonie in the salon and noticed she sounded at least somewhat pleased to see him.

When I returned to the salon, he stood near the window, looking down on the street as Leonie related her adventures of the day. I offered him the drink on a small tray. He tossed it back, returned the glass to the tray, and murmured, *"Merci."*

And in the brief moment our eyes met, my gut clenched. Something was very wrong.

While I ladled soup into bowls and arranged the simple meal on my worktable, I concealed any outward sign of awareness. The doctor brought down a decanter of wine and three glasses. Leonie entered the kitchen soon afterward. We spoke of commonplace matters, sat down, and began to eat.

Each time the doctor spoke to me or looked in my direction I sensed uncertainty, fear, even anger. I could not blame him. If the *sans-culottes* talked and laughed about my visit to the Assembly that afternoon, what must his peers have thought and said?

How could I assure him of my loyalty when I was uncertain of it myself? What was the doctor to me besides an employer and an old family friend? Such tenuous connection could not begin to match the ties of blood and love I shared with Pascoe.

The silence was too thick. I took a quick breath and broached the awkward topic. "Did anything of importance happen at the Assembly today? I did not and do not understand why the *sans-culottes* disturbed you. I observed only a foolish display serving no useful purpose."

His gaze met mine and held it. *"Au contraire,* the display more than adequately served its purpose."

I sat there in my private crucible, enduring that mistrustful stare.

"What purpose?" Leonie asked when I remained silent.

"Intimidation."

It was no more than the truth, and I knew myself for a blind fool. Recalling the almost rigid posture of the deputies, I knew that every last one had feared for his life. I now remembered Saint-Jude Fillion saying something to that effect, but I had been too focused on finding Leonie and explaining myself to the doctor to fully comprehend the situation.

Or perhaps my conflicting loyalties had prevented honest evaluation. As if a veil lifted from my eyes, I now remembered events in the National Assembly Hall in a harsh, ugly, threatening light.

"Claude wanted to join the parade, but I refused," Leonie said. "What exactly happened?"

Doctor Hilliard shifted his attention to Leonie, and in a calm tone he described for her, with additional chilling details, the events I had witnessed that day.

"I saw you enter the Palais des Tuileries," Leonie said. "And I heard people shouting death threats." She actually sounded like a concerned daughter instead of a dispassionate stranger. Would he respond?

But Doctor Hilliard merely poured himself another glass of wine. How many had he already drained? And when he addressed his daughter, I saw and heard only anger. "Do you realize what would have happened had they assassinated the King today? Do you realize how the world would react if France were to commit regicide? Fools, and the opportunists who use them, imagine violence will force progress." He swore and slammed his open hand on the table, making both Leonie and me jump. "It can bring only anarchy and will turn world opinion against our Republic."

His voice rose in volume. "I am neither a close-minded nor a dictatorial man. As a Republican I that acknowledge women should be allowed to use their minds and make decisions. I respect independent thinking and admire courage. Fool that I am, I actually encouraged you young women to attend the demonstration today, hoping you would recognize the difference between civilized political discourse and anarchy. Did you see it? Did either of you gain any insight into the futility of civic turmoil?"

Leonie suddenly rose and rushed from the room. This took me quite by surprise, for my entire focus had been on the doctor's words. Had she been taken ill? I saw no reason for this sudden exit.

I glanced at her father. He had risen and now flattened his palms on the table, still staring at the doorway through which she had disappeared.

My mind spun out possible explanations for her behavior, but none of them were logical. "Do you want me to follow her?" I asked.

He turned to me, looking utterly confused. "Was I so offensive?"

"I am not offended, but I cannot tell what your daughter felt or heard. I could ask."

"Will she talk to you?"

"J'en doute," I answered honestly. "She met me only two days ago."

He blinked and absently rubbed the strip of stubbled scalp exposed by his crooked wig. Then he looked at me, and there was neither anger nor suspicion in his eyes. "If you will try to talk to her, I'd be grateful."

So, shortly afterward I knocked at Leonie's door and pushed it open. She sat at her toilette table, regarding her reflection in the polished brass mirror. Turning, she gave me a baleful stare. "What do you want?"

"You left suddenly. I was concerned about you, and so is the doctor."

She turned back to the mirror. "Go away."

Instead I approached and inspected my own reflection. It looked rather ghastly by the light of her one lamp. "Why did you run away? Your father was talking about women and politics. Did this bother you?"

She laughed without mirth. "What else would he rant about? What else does he care about?" Then she scowled at me. "Why would you care what I think?"

"You fear your father. *Pourquoi?*" It was a guess, but she didn't need to know this.

She closed her eyes and shuddered. "He is always angry, always shouting, and never satisfied. If ever he notices me, it is to find fault."

"I have never heard him speak to or of you with disrespect," I observed.

Her eyes opened wide, focused on me, and then narrowed in disgust. "In public he is civilized and suave, but privately he cuts and destroys with his words."

"Recently?" I asked. "*C'est-à-dire,* has he done so since you arrived in Paris?"

"As if a few minutes of polite behavior can convince me he has changed." She gave a mirthless laugh. "He claims he is not dictatorial, yet he despised my mother because she would not recant her faith. He is a monster and a liar, and I hate him."

"I thought I hated my mother because she disapproved of my choices," I said. "But I know now she was angry because she hated to see me make foolish decisions ending in heartache."

Leonie turned away and fell silent. Although my efforts to draw her out had already succeeded beyond expectation, I was disappointed.

But then she said, "Choosing to believe in God is not a foolish choice."

"Perhaps not, but your father believed it was, and this belief influenced him," I observed, thinking aloud. "I am not his daughter, but I think he is trying to be a better father than the one you remember."

Suddenly she turned in her chair and fixed her wintry eyes on me. "Did he send you up here as his spy?"

"*Non.* I offered to look in on you."

"And now you will tell him why I left. And then, for a time, he will be quiet and polite. But eventually the monster will emerge again, and he will shout and rave and blame. If you truly want to help, go and tell him to send me to England, to my grandfather."

When I stood irresolute, she snapped, *"Partez!* Get out of my room."

Descending the servants' stair, I first considered the irony of her attitude. Who was she to call her father dictatorial? And then I considered her request. Send her to her grandfather? Why would she prefer him to her father? Something did not make sense here.

Back in the kitchen, I found the doctor seated at my worktable, looking down the barrel of a pistol. I drew a sharp breath before realizing he had taken the weapon apart and was in the process of cleaning it. A second dueling pistol and a tiny gun lay on the table. I sometimes carried a similar "muff" pistol in my reticule.

He laid down a rag, took a drink from his wineglass, and raised a brow at me. "I am not planning to kill myself, madame," he said.

Feeling too foolish to respond, I began collecting the dirty dishes from the table.

"Only a fool would go unarmed in the streets of Paris at this time," he added. "Today, I was that fool."

I knew his walking stick concealed a sword, but a sword-stick would be useless against an enemy wielding a pike or musket.

"Did Leonie speak to you?" he asked.

"She did. Do you wish to hear her reasons for leaving the kitchen so abruptly?"

His brows drew together. "I am not altogether certain I do. But go ahead and tell me."

I folded my hands at my waist and fixed my gaze on the china dresser. "Leonie says you care only for politics, you tear her apart with angry words, and you say you are not a dictator yet tried to force her mother to recant her faith. She also says that once I give you this report, you will be kind for a few days, but the monster inside will again emerge."

I paused for a moment to think. *"Heu. . . Ah, oui!* And she believes you sent me upstairs as a spy and advised that if I truly wish to help I will tell you to send her to live with her grandfather in England."

I dared a look at him. He rubbed a piece of the pistol with the rag, but his eyes were unfocused.

"Monsieur," I said. "I have observed your desire to establish a good relationship with your daughter, and I pointed this out to her. I believe she will change her opinion if you continue to treat her with respect and kindness. And I would suggest avoiding political discussion in her presence."

He gave me a look. "It is hardly a topic to pursue in your presence either, I daresay."

I dropped my gaze. "Less than an hour ago you regarded me as an enemy," I said. "I cannot say I blame you, for my appearance at the Assembly today must have appeared suspect. Leonie tells me the *sans-culottes* were laughing about it. I did not pause to think how my behavior might appear to others."

A sharp knock at the front door brought the doctor to his feet. He caught up the pistol lying on the table and ordered, "Stay here."

CHAPTER 10

I NEARLY CHOKED ON PANIC as Doctor Hilliard ran up the dining room stairs. The remaining guns were unloaded, and one lay in pieces, so I snatched up the poker from the fireplace and put my worktable between me and the door.

But as soon as I heard male voices conversing, I put back the poker and ran upstairs. Étienne stood in the salon, his red brows bunched. "It is very late," he said.

My heart suddenly felt too large for my chest, and I gave my brother a warm hug. "Monsieur," I addressed the doctor, "I promise to clean the kitchen in the morning."

"It is of no consequence." His features drooped with exhaustion. "I apologize again for delaying your sister," he said to Étienne. "I paid no heed to the time."

Étienne only dipped his head, but his demeanor was respectful. My things were right there in the front hall, so I quickly collected them. *"Bonne nuit,* monsieur," I said as we stepped into the night.

"Why were you working so late?" Étienne asked once we were out of earshot.

"I'm not sure where the time went," I admitted. "The doctor asked if I would stay for dinner, which we ate in the kitchen, which is unusual . . . but then, today was unusual from beginning to end. You see, the relationship between Doctor Hilliard and Leonie is strained." And I described the situation as fairly as I could manage, placing blame on neither side. "I believe the presence of an outsider enables them to avoid confrontation."

"Or resolution," Étienne added.

"True. Did you know him well when she was still at home? Was he truly frightening?" I asked. "Obviously I know him only as a kind and undemanding employer, although this evening I witnessed his anger and suspicion. And fear," I added.

"I seldom encountered the doctor. I knew Madame Hilliard well."

"Vraiment? How did you become acquainted with her?"

"She would call me into her sitting room to talk."

This sounded strange to me. "To talk? What did you and the daughter of a marquis have to talk about?"

"She loaned me books from her library and discussed them with me afterward."

"What type of books?"

"Philosophy, theology, and history."

I tried to picture the elegant lady conversing with a hulking, self-conscious boy. "What was Madame Hilliard like?"

"She was intelligent and opinionated."

Like her daughter, I thought. "And kind to a village boy," I said.

"Oui." Étienne didn't seem to mind my prying for information. His deep voice sounded as good natured as ever.

"You say she called you into her sitting room, but why were you in the house?"

"In bad weather, Leonie and I explored the garret and attics."

So my guess was correct: They had been childhood friends. "What did you do in good weather?"

"We made up stories and acted them out in the orchard."

I smiled to myself. Digging information out of my brother was a chore worth the trouble, for some of Leonie's behavior now began to make sense. I might still be mistaken, but it seemed likely Étienne, not Claude, was the object of her interest. Gauging Étienne's interest in Leonie would not be as easy, however.

The street lamps burned like small islands of light, their glow making strange shadows on the buildings we passed. There was little traffic at this hour, only a few other rather nervous pedestrians and an occasional carriage. A few dogs barked in the night, and the noise echoed eerily. No breeze made its way down among the crowded buildings to relieve the lingering heat and stench of the streets.

We turned into the drive leading to Maison Beau Temps and saw a carriage just disgorging its passengers. Three men, two assisting the third up the front steps. "That is Pascoe," I said, breaking into a quick trot. "With a stranger and Claude helping him." Sudden fear clutched my heart. Was he injured? Ill?

"Must be his new valet," Étienne said, easily keeping pace with me.

"Pascoe hired a valet?"

"*Oui.*"

But Pascoe had always hated even the idea of a personal manservant invading his privacy. My mind could make no sense of this information and tried to reject it even while pondering what might have motivated Pascoe to change his set policy.

Just as the carriage rolled away, I rushed through the front door with Étienne at my heels. The three men, midway up the staircase, turned to stare, and Pascoe brightened and waved a languid hand. "The family arrives!"

It was immediately obvious he was very drunk. Claude and the stranger urged him upward, and he gave in, swearing roundly. None of the servants were around at this hour, so I hung up my own hat and parasol. "This has been a very long day already," I said, debating with myself whether or not to check on Pascoe.

Étienne regarded me from beneath his brows. "Better let him sleep it off."

"You are right. I need sleep as well. Tomorrow night I must organize a dinner party and dance. Most of the preparations are complete, but Madame LaRue is very little help. I'm talking too much, aren't I?"

Étienne's smile warmed his eyes. *"Bonne nuit,* Colette. Get some sleep."

Pascoe was asleep when I left for work in the morning, but to my surprise he was still at the house when I returned. "I am invited to the party tonight, *chérie,*" he said, "and thought I might escort you, if you are willing."

"I must go early to set up."

He nodded. "I'll help you."

"What about *la Florinda*?" I asked.

He blinked in apparent surprise and then smiled widely. *"Ah. Oui.* She is visiting friends in the country over the weekend and set out this morning."

"Then I shall have you to myself?"

His eyes twinkled. "Entirely."

The evening had an unpropitious beginning. We arrived only to discover that Madame LaRue had done almost nothing to prepare. Pascoe threw himself into the work, and his charm worked its usual wonders when it came to convincing madame we could not comfortably seat fifty people in her small dining room.

By the time her guests arrived, we had arranged and decorated tables in a hall along the back of the house. Silver and china sparkled in candlelight, and torches surrounded a dance floor on the second terrace in the garden. The string trio played softly while guests dined, and the meal catered by a local restaurant was exceptional.

"But the night air!" Madame protested to me. *"Enfin,* my guests will be scandalized, and what if we all take ill?"

"On such a sultry night, we would open every door and window to let in air anyway," Pascoe pointed out. "This way the dance floor will catch any cooling breeze, and your guests will be delighted."

"How marvelous!" Madame gazed at him with such wonder that I nearly gagged, but I could not deny his powers of persuasion saved the evening.

But then he had to spoil things.

"You look very pretty tonight, Colette," Pascoe told me between dances. "Several gentlemen have mentioned the fact to me. Why do you not accept dance invitations?"

"I am working." I was often grateful for the ready excuse.

"Not all men are like your captain, you know."

For a moment I thought my heart stopped. How dared he? Through stiff lips I said, *"Excusez-moi, s'il te plaît,"* and moved on to check the punch bowl.

But he followed. *"Chérie,* I don't mean to offend; I simply want you to let the past go."

"I am not offended," I lied, then beckoned to a page, saying, "Tell them we need more punch. It is already mixed." The boy ran down to the kitchen. When I turned back, Pascoe had disappeared.

Trust him to lob a cannonball into my emotions at such a time! I closed my eyes, deliberately slowed my breathing, and pushed painful memories out of my head.

But they would return.

The guests arranged themselves into groups of similar age and interest: Politically ambitious men discussed the ramifications of events at the Tuileries, young women flirted with the more socially-inclined male guests, and the older women clustered to discuss everyone's business. Pascoe passed from one group to the next, electrifying the political discussion with firsthand stories of events within the Tuileries, thrilling young women with his flirtations, and giving the gossips compliments that brought roses into many a faded cheek. He was on his best behavior, flashing his smile, murmuring insincere pleasantries, dancing with grace and precision. He drank very little and caused no scandal, to my relief.

Madame LaRue raved to her friends about my organizational services, and before the evening ended I had added a number of them to my list of patrons. Altogether the event was a resounding success.

Late in the evening when the last dance was announced, Pascoe half-dragged me to join the end of a processional. If Madame LaRue noticed me among the dancers, she made no complaint; an abundance of wine and a successful party had soothed her overwrought nerves. My brother was, as always, a delightful dance partner, and I found myself relaxing and smiling.

When the dance ended and we cleared the floor, Pascoe suddenly laughed aloud, bent, and scooped a lace petticoat from the paving stones. "Someone must be feeling a breeze right now. Did you lose these feathers, *ma petite poulette*?"

"I wish I owned anything so fine." I choked back a giggle. Whoever lost the garment must be near dying for dread of having her identity disclosed.

"Then I claim it." And he made as if to pull it over his head.

"Stop, you idiot!" I hauled his arms down, and the two of us dissolved into silent laughter, clutching each other to keep upright. By some great luck, we were in a shadowy area where a torch had extinguished, and the other guests were moving indoors and occupied with farewells and thanks to their hostess. Once we recovered our decorum, Pascoe twirled me one last time.

"Oh Pascoe, you have made this evening a treat instead of a chore." I gazed at his grinning face with adoration.

He promptly kissed my cheek. "You should tell every hostess to add my name to her list."

"I believe I shall!"

It was two o'clock in the morning before we climbed into the hired carriage. "I have not enjoyed myself so much in many months," I sighed as I leaned back on my seat. "Will you truly attend some of the upcoming events I arrange? There are dances, concerts, and even a masquerade ball scheduled this summer. My calendar is filling rapidly."

He linked his hands behind his head. "I will attend if I have the time."

"You are dear," I said in satisfaction.

"*Mais oui.* Was this ever in question?"

"You are seldom around to remind me of it. We have not talked about important things in weeks," I said. "I did not know you hired a valet. Where do you stay when you are away over so many nights? We seldom see you anymore."

"I have another place, a small place." Suddenly his tone was sober. "Quent, my valet, has experience with . . . my condition. He is proving invaluable."

Everything inside me went cold and tense. "You are still having spells?"

"*Oui.*"

"You hadn't spoken of it in some time, so I thought perhaps it ended." I so desperately wanted it to end, or to never have begun at all.

"I don't believe it will ever end, but Quent helps me manage it. He is teaching me to recognize warning signals, usually in the form of contracting muscles. I cannot express the relief it is to know he will remove me instantly from a situation if necessary."

"If the man is that useful, I'm glad you hired him. I saw him bring you home last night," I said. "He and Claude helped you out of the carriage and up the stairs."

"You were there? I don't remember. Did you hear what happened?"

"Non, what happened? Did you have a seizure?"

He brushed aside my concern. "I mean what happened inside the Palais des Tuileries. The King refused to withdraw his veto of the Assembly's decrees, though he did drink a toast to the nation of France. The boys gave him one of our red caps, so he could look like one of the *sans-culottes*. It did not fit on his enormous head."

Beneath Pascoe's mocking tone I heard something more. "You are displeased?"

"Most certainly I am displeased! We failed to convince him to withdraw his veto, and even the leaders of our group were surprised and impressed by the fool's dignity and courage under duress. Did you not hear the talk tonight? *Ridicule!*"

I wished he had not brought up politics, for his good mood vanished.

"I cannot believe such talk will endure long," I said.

"Hmph. I hear you did enter the National Assembly after all, and you made Doctor Hilliard look the fool."

My face felt warm. "What exactly did you hear?"

He sounded tentative. "I heard from several sources about your adventures. Did you really sit in Doctor Hilliard's lap before the scandalized eyes of the entire Legislature?"

I very nearly blurted out a denial but realized in time that he must be baiting me. "How better might I further the glory of the Republic?"

He chuckled. "That's my Colette! I wish I had seen the doctor's face." He sounded overly pleased. "What did he say? I assume you are no longer his housekeeper. If you are, the man has no self-respect remaining to him."

This had gone too far; for some reason he overlooked my sarcasm. "Pascoe, I did not sit in the doctor's lap; I sat on the bench between him and another man. I imagine the story grew as it was told, as stories generally do."

After a silence, he asked, "Why did you sit next to him during the demonstration?"

"I entered the hall in search of Leonie and Claude. When the doctor saw me, I felt obliged to tell him I failed as chaperone to his daughter. That is all."

"Did you find them?"

"Oui, with Étienne's help."

"And you still work for him. He still trusts you?" Pascoe's tone expressed disgust.

"I don't know if he trusts me, but he values my cooking, if nothing else."

Pascoe swore roundly as the carriage entered the short drive before our house. He assisted me as I climbed down, he paid the driver, and we entered the hall. Someone had left a candle lamp burning; only a short stub remained.

"Morning will arrive all too soon," I said. "I hope I shall see you tomorrow?"

"Peut-être." In the upstairs hall he returned my kiss but looked sulky. "You are terribly obstinate."

"Just like you, *mon cher."* And I entered my room.

CHAPTER 11

THEY SAY LASTING memories are connected to strong emotion. I believe this is true, for of the many people I visited in the poorest areas of *faubourg* Saint-Germain, those remaining vivid in my memory are connected with joy, anger, or sorrow, and sometimes all three at once.

Not long after Pascoe and I first arrived in Paris and before we joined the *sans-culottes* movement, I discovered that the dregs of Paris led a nearly animal existence, subsisting on almost nothing and living in squalor. I started taking food and clothing to the poorest families in our *section,* but only when Doctor Hilliard discovered my endeavor was I able to make a real difference. He and a few other deputies living in the *faubourg* began donating goods, entrusting me with their dispersal since I was known and trusted by the people.

I had asked for volunteers to serve as go-betweens, and three women volunteered. Goods were delivered to one of their homes every other week, and I supervised distribution. Leonie accompanied me that fateful summer on most of these visits to the *section*. Her frosty attitude had soon thawed; other than her father, I was the only person she saw on a regular basis. I rather suspect she made peace with me out of desperation.

The volunteer on Leonie's first foray into the *section* was one Minette LaVie, our laundress, a widow with four children. We arrived at her house early that last Friday in June to meet the delivery wagons and direct the unloading of sacks of beans, flour, coffee, and even sugar and salt. Sometimes thread, needles, tools, and cheap fabric came to us, and I was careful to dole these out only to people in genuine need, having discovered early on that opportunists would claim to be in need then sell the goods elsewhere.

Minette greeted us with her usual good cheer. The woman humbled me, for although she and her children worked like slaves and Minette herself had hardly a tooth left in her head, she was unfailingly positive and smiling, as was her little brood. "Mademoiselle Leonie, it is an honor to have you in my home, as well as Madame DeMer, who is an angel from heaven."

"I am honored to be here," Leonie replied, and handed out fruit from our garden to the children, who clustered around her. The little girls examined the buttons and lace on her gown with their chapped fingers.

Minette nearly gushed with appreciation: "Jesus and Mary, *merci!* How blessed we are this day! So blessed, so very grateful."

I hardly knew how to respond. But Leonie surprised me by answering with the warmest smile I had yet beheld on her face. "Yet it is more blessed to give than to receive," she said. She seemed perfectly at ease with the family, and they with her. If anything, I was the outsider.

As the *section* people began to arrive, we all worked together for a time, loading goods into hand carts, the boys sometimes delivering for those too weak to collect for themselves. Later in the morning, when we had time to breathe between visitors, Leonie took Elise, Minette's youngest and a hollow-eyed slip of a child, on her knee and sang hymns.

Her voice was fine and the children were clearly enchanted. Elise and her sister, Jeanette, regarded Leonie as if she were the Blessed Virgin herself. Even the boys gazed at her with admiration.

The last to collect supplies was a dark-skinned girl. *"Bonjour,* Tressy," I greeted her, trying to make eye contact. I quickly analyzed her condition: She was perhaps six months along now, maybe more. She was thin; but her build was naturally wiry, and she seemed healthy.

"Bonjour, Madame," she said, her voice quiet yet melodic in its cadence. When she glanced up at me, I noticed a distinct swelling of her left eye, and bile suddenly filled my mouth. The pregnant girl, little more than a child herself, was slave to the Gallatins, who treated her worse than a dog and seldom let her leave their house.

"Why are you collecting the goods today? Is Madame Gallatin ill?" I asked.

Her wary expression reminded me she might be punished for dawdling, so I began to measure beans into a sack. "You can speak freely to me, Tressy," I said softly. "You know I am your friend."

Her dark eyes expressed uncertainty of this, but she did speak. "Madame has taken to her bed."

"Is she ill?" I didn't care for the woman, but she was one of my volunteers.

Tressy shook her head as she took the sack from me and arranged it in her hand cart. "The master was arrested the other night and is in prison," she said.

I dropped my voice to a whisper. "Arrested on what charge?"

She whispered back, "He knifed a man, they say."

"Killed him?"

"I don't know."

This news came as no great surprise. Monsieur Gallatin was active among the *sans-culottes,* yet he would be regretted by no one. The ex-sailor's reputation was vile even among his peers. I knew, as everyone must that the slave-girl's baby was his.

"Are you managing?" I asked.

"Well enough," she said. "It is easier now."

She needed to say no more.

Despite his talk, Pascoe did not attend another of my social events. I had hoped rather than expected he would. Political strategizing occupied his time; I knew he met often with *section* leaders from all parts of Paris. Together they worked to unify their representatives in the Legislature.

I also suspected that yet another young woman occupied his time. *La Florinda* must not mind sharing his attentions, for although I saw him in her company at *section* meetings, he flirted as freely as ever with pretty young girls from all levels of society.

One evening in early July, I arrived home to find him lying on his back in the salon, writhing about with one hand over his eye, howling and moaning. Panicked, I rushed to his side and skidded to my knees. "Pascoe, *mon cher!* Are you ill?" I had never before witnessed one of his seizures. What should I do?

"He poked me in the eye!" he cried, then looked up at me with two bright eyes and a mischievous grin. "Look at him, so pompous and shameless, pointing that accusing finger."

"What? Who?" I sat back on my heels and felt the terror leave my body in a rush. "Whatever are you talking about?"

"Apollo, *bien sûr*. Who else would do such a thing?" Gazing up at the statue behind me, he propped himself on his elbows and raised one knee, looking gracefully casual and decidedly pleased with himself. "Have you ever noticed his resemblance to Doctor Hilliard? It's the nose, I believe, and that expression of incredulous revulsion toward all those beneath him."

I looked over my shoulder at the statue on its plinth, my anger rising. "It was all a jest? You terrified me, Pascoe!"

He laughed. "I would dress him in a waistcoat if he would oblige me by lifting his arm. But the shameless fellow is determined to flaunt his physique, undoubtedly for your benefit, *ma poulette*."

I scrambled ungracefully to my feet. With another glance at the statue, which now sported a lace jabot, I growled, "You are too absurd."

"And you are too cross." He leaped to his feet in one agile motion and bestowed a kiss on my forehead. "I am off now, *chérie*. Try to miss me a little."

Since Pascoe spent little time at our house and Claude avoided my presence, I saw Étienne more than either of them. His company was relaxing, for he let me chatter at will about whatever concern was on my mind and rarely offered a counter opinion or, for that matter, any opinion at all. Yet I knew he was listening, thinking, and not judging me. I'm not sure how I knew this, but I did.

I discovered that his interest in my monologues intensified when I spoke of Leonie, just as she always paid close heed when I mentioned Étienne. This evidence of mutual interest both pleased and distressed me, for to my knowledge their paths never crossed. How were they to know if a childhood friendship might develop into more if they never saw one another or had a chance to interact?

With such interesting puzzles to occupy my mind and so many problems to fix, I lost interest in political matters. I was aware, on the verges of my mind, that the confrontation with the King inside the Tuileries had given our cause a severe setback. Word of his royal courage and dignity spread, turning the mood of Paris in his favor. The majority of the public believed the *sans-culottes* had overstepped their bounds. Even Lafayette, the former marquis and current leader of the Republic, publically condemned the demonstration.

Despite my political ennui, I dutifully attended *section* meetings. I particularly remember the meeting a day or two after Pascoe's stunt with the statue. Even with every window ajar, the ballroom of the *section* headquarters was stifling. I sat with Elise, Minette's youngest, asleep in my lap and furtively watched the child's two brothers throwing dice with little Martin Danican.

Pascoe's was the most exciting speech of the night, a scathing reprimand of those who valued their personal comfort and misguided loyalties above the cause of equality and freedom for all. He was articulate and fervid, using his voice to stir up the crowd one moment, nearly bringing them to tears the next.

"I wonder, sometimes, if he means half of what he says." The words spoken quietly next to my ear made me start in surprise. I pulled away and turned to see Saint-Jude Fillion giving me a significant look.

"Don't sneak up on me," I hissed.

He shrugged and smiled as if in apology. I never quite knew what to make of Fillion. Observation told me he was popular with the women of our *section*, no great surprise; and he was much like Pascoe, having no intention of settling down with any of them. Yet he seemed to have a particular interest in me beyond flirtation.

Yes, he did flirt, and I knew that many of his flattering words and expressions were well practiced. But I also saw vulnerability in his face at times, an uncertainty followed by determination which I found rather appealing. Most men would have given up after my first few apathetic refusals. But Fillion never failed to seek me out, and his face brightened whenever our eyes met.

After the meeting ended and Minette collected her children with many devout thanks, Fillion stayed around. "That woman has enough religion for ten people," he commented.

"She is kind, honest, and hard-working," I shot back, although he merely voiced my own thoughts. "What did you say about Pascoe not meaning what he says?"

He bunched up his forehead and pursed his mouth, then said, "People listen to his every word as if it fell from Mount Olympus. I just wonder if anyone ever checks what he says against what he does."

I stared at him, angry yet unable to think of a rebuttal. "What are you implying?"

He raised his hands to ward off attack. "Don't blast me with lightning. I like Pascoe; we work together for the cause. *Ma foi,* I'm jealous of his style, his way with words."

I knew he was carefully not saying everything he was thinking.

His eyes studied my reaction with interest. "You think he walks on water, don't you? Even you, his sister, see him as a god. How does he do it? I don't understand."

"I do not see him as a god. He is my brother; I see his flaws clearly, yet I also admire his vision. He believes in our cause to his core. This is why he is a great leader."

Fillion heaved a quick sigh. "Always quick to forgive any fault for the sake of the cause. You are too kind and forgiving for your own good, *belle dame.* Have you thought any further about Bastille Day? Our picnic?"

"Actually, I have been too preoccupied to give it a moment's thought," I admitted. "What was your plan again?"

He brightened slightly. "I want to spend the day with you at the celebration. I will bring wine and food, and we can sit in our carriage and eat during the ceremonies. Or, if you like, we can walk over to join the crowds and cheer for our troops and for the Republic."

Despite his enthusiasm, the prospect held little appeal. "I shall think on it, monsieur" was my best response. *"Merci."*

Recognizing a dismissal, he bowed politely and moved on. I felt decidedly unsettled in my mind. Fillion's vague intimations about Pascoe would not leave my thoughts.

Across the room near the open doors, red hair glowed like the flame on a tall candle; I recognized Claude, who was talking with a pair of National Guards. Panic erased all common sense: I rushed across the room to accost the three.

"Excusez-moi," I addressed the startled guards. "Claude is too young to think of enlisting, so kindly refrain from encouraging him." And I caught my young brother by the sleeve and tried to draw him away.

He responded with a barrage of profanity that would have turned our mother's hair instantly gray, easily wrested his arm from my grasp, and caught me by the shoulders. "Don't ever interfere in my life again!" he communicated amid a storm of ugly names and accusations. I believe he barely kept himself from doing me bodily harm. But the verbal lashing was enough.

Pascoe laughed at me during our walk home. "You were forewarned weeks ago," he said. "If the boy wants to enlist, he will enlist. It is his choice, his life."

At some time during the past few weeks a sense of dread had begun to form deep inside me, growing like a tumor or a parasite. It made my stomach hurt and disturbed my sleep, and I hadn't the slightest idea how to rid myself of it other than continuing to warn and redirect my loved ones. But what good did such warnings do if they refused to listen?

It was Sunday morning, for I remember hearing church bells; I had just left the house on my way to the doctor's when a voice hailed me at the crossing. Wondering if I was hearing things, I looked around and saw Quent approaching on the cross street. "Madame DeMer," he repeated. "I hoped to intercept you. Your brother Pascoe suffered a mild injury this morning. Do not worry; he will quickly recover."

"Injury? What kind of injury?"

The man appeared hesitant. "He was slightly pinked in the arm during a duel."

My jaw dropped; my mind stopped. Once I regained control of both, I said, "A duel."

"*Oui,* madame. It is not serious."

"What became of his opponent?"

Again the man's gaze shifted away from me, and again I knew he was reluctant to answer. "He is dead."

For a long moment I could not speak. After attempting, and failing, to swallow, I said, "Pascoe killed a man in a duel. Why?"

"I am not at liberty to say, madame."

Heat rose in me like a pot about to boil over. "Where is he? I want to see him," I said, preparing to follow.

"I am sorry, but monsieur has forbidden me to reveal the location of his lodgings." The man did not look sorry. He looked impervious.

Words hissed from my lips like scalding steam: "I don't care what he has forbidden; take me to him at once."

Quent's face was deeply carved with lines. He was probably no older than fifty, yet his eyes held deep wisdom. "I cannot, madame. When monsieur wishes to invite you to his lodgings, he will do so."

I met his stare and actually found myself backing down. "Tell him he must allow me to come and help care for him," I said rather weakly.

The man bowed and turned away. Although I could have followed, something told me it would do no good. Not many people could make me yield. In some unknown way, Quent claimed my respect.

The same could not be said for my brother.

CHAPTER 12

PASCOE SHOWED UP at Maison Beau Temps Wednesday evening, looking as hale and impudent as ever I had seen him. After showing me the bandage on his forearm, he adjusted the folds of his jabot at the gilt-framed mirror over a side table in the salon. The face of a very ugly marble satyr reflected beside his, as though looking over his shoulder.

"I instructed Quent to inform you if ever I fell ill, but this little stab hardly counted," he said irritably. "Oh, and you are not to ask him where I hide out. If I want you to know, I will take you there."

Then his reflected eyes caught my gaze. I crossed my arms and stared right back. "I will ask anything I wish to ask," I said. "Was this duel about a woman?"

He looked mildly amused. "You may ask anything you wish, and I shall refuse to answer anything I wish."

"I can easily find out, you know."

He turned and gave me a mock bow. "Then do so. But never let yourself imagine you can amend me, *ma sœur*."

The unfairness of this implied charge brought so many protests welling up that I nearly choked. Yet what was the use? He would never listen.

Being at odds with Pascoe felt like a division of my own spirit; the only remedy was surrender, which I could not do. Why did I suffer while he seemed unaffected? In past situations I had allowed him to persuade me I was in the wrong, but of late I found this solution insupportable.

A change of subject might help. "What do you know about your valet? Where is he from and why did you hire him?"

"He is from the north, near the coast. I hired him because he is respectful and competent, and, as I've told you before, because he understands my condition. His father suffered seizures similar to mine." He crossed his arms as if mirroring my position but immediately uncrossed them, no doubt sharply recalling his injury. "Thus far his service has been satisfactory. He proved an able second the other day, though nearly as censorious as you are."

I could think of no reply. If a man like Quent was unable to convince Pascoe of the evils of dueling, nothing I said could make a difference. The silence stretched between us.

He heaved a little sigh then looked me up and down. "You have lost weight, and you look pale. Working too hard? Sleeping too little? Are you in love? Worried?" He sat gracefully on a chaise longue and patted the seat beside him. "Come, *ma cocotte*, and tell me what weighs on your heart."

His switch to a loving tone disarmed me, as it always did. I took the seat beside him and folded my hands in my lap like a child. "I suppose I have been working too hard. Far more people showed up for last night's concert than my hostess anticipated, and . . ." I happened to meet his gaze and found it slightly glazed. "Oh, the details won't interest you. But everything did turn out rather well."

"What do you do with all this additional income?" he inquired. "I can see you have not updated your wardrobe in some time."

"I rarely find time for fittings," I said, quelling irritation. "But when I had my fitting for my costume for the *bal masque* next month, I did order three new everyday gowns."

"A costume? But you never dance." He fixed his eyes on my fichu, and a tiny crease formed between his brows.

I glanced down, saw nothing amiss, adjusted the cloth anyway, and looked up in time to glimpse amusement in his eyes. What a time to play a boyish trick! "Nevertheless, I shall wear a costume," I said between tight lips.

"Am I invited?" He crossed his legs and extended one arm along the back of the chaise longue.

"We have not yet completed a guest list, but I'm sure you will be on it. Will you come?"

He briefly studied his fingernails. "If my schedule allows. Which brings me to the object of my visit today: an invitation of my own. I wish to request your company on Bastille Day. I plan to order a basket lunch and wine from René's café, rent an elegant carriage, and treat my companions to a memorable celebration."

My expression, which had brightened at first, fell at his last words. "Oh. Who else would be with us?"

"*La Florinda*. Now listen; you will enjoy her company, Colette. She is a good friend: intelligent, witty, insightful, and good natured. She knows nearly everyone who is anyone in this city."

I attempted to smile, although my face felt stiff. "Actually, I do have a prior invitation."

His brows lifted. "You do? Please tell me you don't intend to spend the holiday serving the Hilliards."

"I have not yet decided whether or not to accept the invitation from a young man."

He smirked and reached up to trace a finger across my forehead. "Beware your face does not settle into those lines. Is that a white hair I see?"

I smacked his hand away. "Will you please be serious?"

"I could not be more so. Invite him to join us. The carriage can hold four."

"I'll consider the option." So I said, but it was a lie.

"I am delighted to hear you are once again entertaining a man. It has been over a year." He shook his head. "Youth passes so quickly; why waste your beauty in lamenting one man when there are so many who would delight in your company?"

Inwardly I flinched, and my smile probably appeared fixed. He would persist in bringing up one of my life's greatest errors. "I no longer lament the captain; he deceived me."

"But what harm did it do? You were happy while it lasted."

"One week of false happiness based on lies." I pushed my fist into my chest. "The harm is here, and I did it to myself."

Pascoe snorted. "It is not as if he defiled an innocent maid. Jean-Antoine did that long ago; you married him and lived to regret it. Did you learn nothing by this mistake? Rejoice in your freedom! Be grateful du Coture did not marry you. *Bah!* In five years, he will be fat and old."

I studied my brother's guileless expression. Was he truly oblivious to my shame? Or did he, as he sometimes claimed, know me better than I knew myself? "I am grateful not to be married to such a man; as I said, I do not regret him."

It was true. I thought of Captain Charles-Louis du Coture with an emotion closer to revulsion than regret. The man had convinced me of his undying love, promised to marry me, and persuaded me to abandon my good sense for a few days of mad passion. Only later, after he moved on, did I learn he had a wife and two children who lived at his family estate in Burgundy, in the house he had described to me in detail as my future home.

I could forgive my adolescent self for succumbing to the wiles of Jean-Antoine DeMer; I was an ignorant child then. But to allow myself at twenty-six to blindly trust the promises of a golden-haired god in uniform, a man I now clearly recognized as a seducer on a par with my own brother—such stupidity was unpardonable. Yet the harder I tried to pretend this lapse of sanity never occurred, the more my conscience waved it before me like a white flag of defeat.

Every time I tended Adrienne, I wondered what would have become of me had I conceived a child with that deceitful man. I loathed myself for escaping her fate. I loathed my credulous folly, the quickness with which I had abandoned reason for a mere illusion of love.

"Marriage is a trap." Pascoe brushed the institution aside with a graceful wave of one hand. "With your assets—your energy, intelligence, and looks—you could easily become 'la Colette,' the toast of Paris. Let me manage your career, and you will soon be wealthy far beyond your pitiful earnings as a social organizer or housekeeper."

I laughed aloud to conceal the stab of pain. *"Mais non.* I have no wish to become a commodity. I have observed the life of a slave and have no desire to share it."

His good humor vanished. "You think I would make you a slave? Colette! I have only ever wanted your happiness."

"So you say, yet you constantly strive to end my current happiness."

Our gazes clashed and held. He understood my meaning exactly. "Colette, after working with Doctor Hilliard for a good portion of my life, I know how he manipulates people to serve his ends. You think he is a good man, but if once you caught a glimpse of what goes on behind the mask he wears, you would never again enter his house. I cannot allow you to let him direct your future."

"Because only you are allowed to do that."

As soon as the words left my lips, I regretted them.

He stared at me in shock, the first genuine emotion his face had expressed that day. Then anger flared, and he swore bitterly. "You think he is good; you are deceived. The man was my idol; I patterned my life after his. In Biron he is held up as a model of virtue only because he made a practice never to dally with any woman inside our district. His religious wife knew of his philandering and prayed for him to her dying day. Do you know that the atheist we once feared now secretly goes to confession? He is the worst of hypocrites, Colette!"

For a moment we sat and stared at each other, shaken and breathing hard. Then he sprang to his feet and left the house, slamming the front door so hard, the windows rattled and even Apollo shuddered on his pedestal.

When I arrived at Doctor Hilliard's house early in the morning, smoke rose from the kitchen chimney. I stopped on the garden path, my feet nearly engulfed in prickly squash leaves, glanced about, and noticed the water barrels were nearly empty. The boys I paid to keep them filled had apparently forgotten their task. So I picked up a pair of buckets and let myself out by the gate at the bottom of the garden, trying to inhale as little as possible. Everyone in the row of houses emptied their chamber pots into large containers adjacent to the iron fence, which sanitation workers emptied once a week. This kept the stink away from the houses but made the alley almost impassable during the heat of day.

It was a warm, gray morning. A gray sky looked down on gray stone, and even my apron appeared gray in the somber shadows of the alley. When I emerged into the street, splashes of color—the patriotic red and blue on enlistment posters—seemed only to emphasize the overall impression of a grimly colorless world.

The women already queuing at the fountain glanced over as I approached, their faces gaunt and gray. Silvery water poured from an exposed pipe emerging from the stone blocks of a curved wall of gray stone and pooled in a small basin. From a shelf above, a stone cherub with badly chipped toes looked down on all comers. I had always thought his expression more impish than angelic. He looked the sort who would make faces as soon as my back was turned.

I waited my turn to hold my buckets beneath the exposed pipe. The other women spoke of their children or of the impossible price of sugar—ordinary enough topics, yet I noticed a tension in their faces. Few of these women were known to me; none attended *section* meetings or participated in protests. Yet the decisions made in the Legislature affected their lives in ways they could not understand.

Pascoe spoke eloquently of the plight of such ragged, barefoot women as these, whose men labored long hours to feed their children and keep a roof over their heads. Would the efforts of the *sans-culottes* improve life for the ordinary people of Paris? Would these women see their children achieve a higher standard of life than they now knew?

I began to wonder.

My buckets filled, I returned to the house and entered the back gate. As I climbed the slight slope of uncut grass toward my kitchen garden, I caught the scent of ripening peaches and heard birds warbling in the tall trees. My steps slowed, and I breathed in the sweetness of my flowers. With a heavy bucket in each hand, I stopped there and regarded the back of the ugly house.

Had I really needed to fetch water? Probably not. Martin and the other boys were likely to come later that morning, when their mothers visited the fountain. I was simply delaying the inevitable. If not this morning, then the next morning, or perhaps some evening, I would encounter Doctor Hilliard again and wonder what secrets lay behind his eyes. Pascoe's parting revelation had kept me awake long into the night.

If his accusations were true . . . But how could I know? My brother was not the most truthful of men. At least that trait was not directly the doctor's fault, for Pascoe had always been a skillful liar. However, Doctor Hilliard had decidedly influenced Pascoe's political, philosophical, and social views as well as teaching him to shoot, ride, and fence.

Had Pascoe also learned his philandering ways from his mentor?

Leonie's stray comments about her father's past seemed to verify my brother's claims. And yet my personal experience with the man contradicted their characterizations at every point; not once had I so much as caught him looking at me in an inappropriate manner. Admiring, yes; a woman knows when a man finds her attractive; but never leering or suggestive.

I emptied my buckets into the water barrel, flexed my aching hands, and descended the mossy stone steps to my kitchen. A pot of hot coffee waited for me on a hook above the hearth. I poured myself a cup and sat at my worktable.

The doctor brewed coffee every morning. Only the most urgent of circumstances prevented him from building up the banked fire, drawing water from the barrels outside to fill the kettle, and bringing it to a boil over the fire while grinding the coffee beans. And then by some secret alchemy he brewed it to perfection, strained out any grounds or impurities, and filled the coffee pot.

He went to all this trouble, and some days I was not altogether certain he even took time to drink a cup himself. I could think of no reason why he would do it other than the satisfaction of knowing I enjoyed the product of his labor.

Was Doctor Hilliard truly the respectable man I admired, or was this all a skillful deception, part of some unknown nefarious plan, as Pascoe implied?

I weeded my garden until Leonie appeared at the door with a cup of coffee in her hands. She yawned and blinked. "Today is hot already," she commented. "May we visit Adrienne? I haven't seen her in a while."

"Neither have I." In fact, I felt guilty for neglecting my little friend.

So we packed baskets with produce, and Leonie added several tiny garments she had stitched for the baby.

"I want to stop at the butcher's on the way," I said.

And we set out. The streets were as busy as ever, and I noticed new posters on the store fronts and walls. "So many notices," I commented.

Leonie frowned. "Always urging men to enlist. Is the war with Austria really going so badly for us?"

"I don't know," I admitted. "We seem to have no shortage of guards here in the city."

"Is Claude still planning to enlist?" she asked.

My heart turned to stone. "He had better not even think of it," I said shortly.

She wisely dropped the subject.

Adrienne was overjoyed to see us. I set Leonie to work chopping vegetables while I checked the baby's size and observed Adrienne's condition. "Are you sleeping well?"

"Not so well at night, but I often lie down during the day. The pain in my hip is better if I move about, so I try to walk some. Minette LaVie comes by every morning now, and we talk about God. And one evening Arnaud walked me over to a garden, and I sat on a bench until I could walk home. It was so good to get out of the house."

I listened to the clamor from the forge and felt a surge of sympathy. This dark little house would seem to close in around one after awhile, and the noise must wear on her nerves. "Do you mind that Leonie came with me?" I asked softly.

"I am glad she came today," she whispered, and I noticed a new peace in her expression. "I expect she needs friends too."

Adrienne sat at the table to watch while Leonie and I prepared a ragout. Once again the girls talked about the past, and again I heard about their rag dolls and the kittens they dressed up as babies. Adrienne kept her hands over her belly, and a few times I noticed ripples of movement.

She looked up, our eyes met, and we shared a smile.

Arnaud met us outside the door as we were leaving. "Colette, I know someone with a milk goat for sale. Do you think the milk would do her good?" His eyes were dark with anxiety. Arnaud always seemed anxious these days

"Anything she enjoys eating is good for her. You are very thoughtful, Arnaud," I said. "Today Adrienne seems more peaceful."

He nodded. "She is happy when Minette comes too. Today is one of her good days."

So, I realized sadly, this change was unlikely to last. "May we visit my brothers while we are here?"

He could not meet my eyes. "*Non.* We are far behind in our orders. I am sorry."

"You needn't apologize," I assured him.

But we had scarcely left the yard when Saint-Jude Fillion jogged up beside us, sooty and grinning. He barely acknowledged Leonie before asking me, "You are coming with me Saturday, madame?"

Despite several days' growth of beard, he seemed little older than Claude. His eyes sparkled with anticipation, and even after a morning of hard labor, he could hardly stand still. I could not imagine spending a whole day in his exclusive company. It was wearing even to contemplate.

"I am sorry, monsieur, but I think not."

His face fell and his entire being seemed to deflate. "But you must come. You promised!"

"I did no such thing," I said. "I told you I would consider it."

"But I have so looked forward to the day!"

"I have work to do."

"But it is a national holiday!" he cried. "You can't work on a holiday."

I turned to Leonie, who observed us with evident amusement. "Leonie, tell him I must work that day. You cannot do without me, can you?"

"Mais non!" she said soberly. "We should be lost without Madame. What would we eat? However could we dress ourselves?"

Saint-Jude gave me a look of stark disgust. "You help them get dressed?"

I restrained a laugh. "I do not. She speaks . . . metaphorically."

He looked puzzled but let the word pass. *"S'il te plaît,* Colette?"

His familiar use of my given name annoyed me. "You should return to work before Monsieur Lamorges loses patience with you."

"I'm in no danger of dismissal. There is no one to replace me." He was still talking when I caught Leonie's sleeve and we walked away. "I'll see you tomorrow night!" he called after me. Once we were out of hearing, Leonie giggled.

"I hope you're proud of yourself," I said. "'However could we dress ourselves?' Indeed!"

CHAPTER 13

WHEN I SPOKE OF THE people of our *section* whom I remember most clearly, did I happen to mention that memories of Minette LaVie make me smile? Despite her habit of constantly giving thanks to Jesus and the saints, her cheery attitude, industrious habits, and, most of all, her kindness restored my faith in humanity time and again.

If Minette makes me smile, Madame Gallatin is the volunteer whose memory brings a grimace. The first time we met at her house I quickly realized madame volunteered only because she intended to appropriate the best goods for herself. When I refused to allow her pilfering, she threatened to stop making her home available; only when I advised her that several other women would gladly take her place did such threats cease. From then on, all work involved with distribution fell upon Tressy.

I suppose it was fitting that our distribution on Friday, July 13, would be at the Gallatin residence, or rather in front of the building in which they rented rooms. Leonie and I arrived early to set up a trestle table on the weedy walkway, and Tressy was on hand to help unload and sort the food when it arrived. Away from Madame Gallatin's critical eye, Tressy relaxed slightly, and the work highlighted her organizational skills. She actually smiled when I introduced her to Leonie. "I am pleased to meet you, mademoiselle," she said in her lilting accent.

I recognized signs of outrage in Leonie's face and posture and laid my finger over my lips. "We will speak of it later," I told her. Her expression was mutinous, but she nodded.

People began showing up before we were ready, among them Minette LaVie, who, typically, began to help us and assigned her sons to make deliveries. "We have only a few laundry deliveries to make today anyway" was her reasoning.

Talk circulated regarding the *section* meeting that night. I heard a few women describe their Bastille Day plans with anticipation and pleasure. Perhaps this celebration of freedom would remind people of all that had already been accomplished and relieve the tension and fear plaguing the city?

I wondered if it was too late to change my mind and accept Saint-Jude Fillion's invitation. A picnic in the company of friends would be a welcome change to my normal routine. Perhaps I needed a day free from responsibility. Fillion's evident admiration was flattering, yet I was in no danger of losing my heart to him. What harm could possibly result from a day in his company?

Midway through the morning, Madame Danican arrived with her children. Martin made a bee-line for Leonie and hovered as if her presence were nectar to his soul. I never saw a more besotted child.

"Come here, Martin," I ordered, and also beckoned to his brother Jeremy. The boys regarded me with their rather froggy eyes, a legacy from their father, and I thought how tall Jeremy had grown that year. "My water barrels are only half full, and the water in them is brackish. Will you please use it to water my garden then refill the barrels from the fountain?

Ask as many others to help as you like; just don't trample my flowers or vegetables."

They quickly agreed, we settled on a fair price, and I paid them in advance. This evidence of trust pleased them mightily. *"Merci,* Madame DeMer," they said in chorus. Martin threw his arms around me and then, without a word, ran to the corner and disappeared. Minutes later he returned with a lily purchased at the flower stall around the corner. This he presented to Leonie like a gift of homage to his goddess.

I smiled and shook my head, watching her pleased reaction. Leonie seemed more appealing to me now that her personality frequently emerged from behind its wall of reserve. Yet I failed to see what inspired such devotion from the child. In my opinion Leonie lacked either particular beauty or charm.

Her reactions to Tressy also added interest to the morning's activity.

The first time I encountered Tressy, her dark skin had startled and almost horrified me. I assumed, as did everyone else, that she would be mentally inferior; and although I spoke kindly to the slave as I would to a dog, I interacted with her too little to learn otherwise.

Watching Leonie now was like observing myself not too many months before; she regarded Tressy with a certain curiosity mixed with distaste and carefully avoided addressing her. For the first time I wondered how Tressy felt about living among so many pale creatures. What was it like to be so obviously different from every other human being in sight?

For she was fully human, I now knew, endowed with every emotion and capacity allotted to people with paler skin; actually, more than many. Yet among us she claimed less respect and fewer rights than the youngest child, and her value equated to that of a beast of burden. Why did the Rights of Man not apply equally to her?

I decided to broach the topic with Pascoe. Or even, if opportunity arose, with Doctor Hilliard, for he had been involved in drafting the

Constitution.

The morning passed quickly with so many hands at work. It was not yet noon when Leonie and I passed the block of houses at the end of the close and returned to the main boulevard. I could tell she was thinking hard, but not until after we visited the market and headed home did she inquire, "That slave, Tressy—how old is she?"

"I believe she is fifteen, although I cannot be sure. Monsieur Gallatin purchased her as a young child and brought her back to France, supposedly as a gift for his wife." I concealed my opinion for the moment.

"A gift for his wife?" Leonie gasped. "The creature is obviously with child. How can the poor woman bear to have her under her roof?"

I reminded myself that Leonie did not know Madame Gallatin, who had scarcely shown her face all morning and then only to demand the best cut of meat available.

"Leonie, the girl is a slave. Monsieur Gallatin legally owns her. Do you understand what this means?"

Leonie looked mortified. "I do, but still . . ."

"Tressy has no say about anything. Madame intends to sell the baby, and she frequently says if her husband dies in prison she will sell Tressy. The girl's future is bleak from any angle I can imagine."

"But how much does she even understand?" Leonie asked. "Surely she would not care so very much who owns her as long as she is fed and clothed and treated well."

"She understands and cares as much as you or I would."

Leonie looked shocked. "Surely not!"

"Tressy is a sweet-natured girl with a quick mind. She deserves so much better than this."

"You want to help her, *est-ce que?*" Leonie sounded both surprised and condescending; I chose to overlook this.

"I do, but I cannot yet think how to do it. Even if I could save enough money to purchase her, then what would I do? She is completely vulnerable, and I can offer her little protection."

We arrived at the house and parted ways. Leonie went upstairs, and I mixed a batch of dough for baguettes and started dinner preparations. But she had obviously been pondering the subject of Tressy, for after a few hours she entered the kitchen, brewed tea, and sat down at my worktable. Her forehead was creased in thought.

"Perhaps if someone took Tressy back to . . . wherever she is from, then she could live a normal life?" she suggested as if our conversation had never paused.

The same idea had once occurred to me. "Even on Martinique she would have little chance at a normal life, for she has no family to welcome her. Tressy does not remember her mother at all. She remembers only that she was stolen from a good home and sold to Monsieur Gallatin."

Leonie shook her head, clearly distressed. "What will become of her baby if madame sells it?"

"I don't know, but if we keep thinking and planning, we'll find a way to rescue them both."

She met my gaze squarely then nodded. In one afternoon she had switched from critic to conspirator. "I will that pray God provides such a way."

That evening Doctor Hilliard arrived home early and entered the dining room while I was setting the table. "The flower arrangements are very fine today," he said.

"Merci," I said. Some of the flowers had wilted during the hot day, so I had replaced them with fresh blooms only minutes earlier.

This was it, my first encounter with the doctor since Pascoe's revelations. I glanced at him furtively but noticed no marked change in my feelings toward him. He was just a tall, lean, high-strung man.

His manner struck me as unusual, however. Sweat dripped down his temples from under the wig, and deep lines framed his mouth. His shoulders lacked their usual military posture, and his gaze remained fixed upon the flowers.

Before I could speak, he said, "Since tomorrow is a holiday, I do not expect you to work. You may pursue your own plans." He gripped the back of a chair with both hands.

"This is kind of you, monsieur."

But he was not finished. I saw him draw several deep breaths before he continued. "Madame DeMer, you have been in my employ for many months now, and I have known you since your childhood. I hoped you would trust me enough to tell me of important changes in your life."

Then his formal tone changed to a note of personal distress. "Particularly following events of last year, after which I hired you back with no questions. I have even trusted you as companion to my daughter, for I hoped and believed the pain you suffered then would prevent another such impulsive decision." Pauses to swallow revealed his embarrassment.

Never before had he alluded to the episode with Captain du Coture, and I knew he hated to mention it now. He must know of something horrible I had recently done, yet my conscience brought nothing forward to convict me.

"I appreciate your faith in me, and your forgiveness, more than I can express." I managed to speak evenly. "I shall endeavor never to betray your trust."

He finally turned to look at me, and his eyes were very dark. "Madame, I must be forthright. While walking home today, I was approached by a young man who claimed to be—" he looked away—"to be your lover."

"Oh!" I exclaimed heatedly. "Monsieur, it is a lie. I have no lover."

His eyes returned to my face, narrowed and intent. "He demanded I release you from your housekeeping duties tomorrow so you might spend the holiday with him. I saw you with this man that day at the National

Assembly."

My legs were shaking. I had to release the tension somehow or I would have plopped right down on the floor. I paced across the room, gesturing with both arms. "I could have guessed it would be he, but I can assure you I scarcely know the man. If you doubt me, consult Leonie. She heard me turn down his invitation. What an arrogant, interfering fool!"

An awkward pause followed. Then the doctor spoke quietly: *"Oui,* I humbly apologize for bringing up events of the past. I never intended to . . . It is not as though my own past is pristine."

I stopped short. "Doctor Hilliard," I managed to say in a tone of abject horror, "I did not mean you! I meant—" The ridiculousness of it struck me, and I laughed aloud. "Monsieur, I am outspoken to a fault, but not even I would call you a fool to your face!"

My family blushes easily due to our fair complexions, yet Doctor Hilliard achieved a deeper hue at that moment than Étienne or Claude after laboring hours in the forge. I can't be certain, but my face was possibly just as red.

Needing to fill the silence, I shook my head. "I am horrified, monsieur, that an acquaintance of mine would presume to accost you on the street."

"Non." He held up a hand to stop me. Twice he opened his mouth as if to speak, but finally he said, *"Bonsoir,* madame," bowed, and left the room. It suddenly struck me as odd that he would bow to me, his housekeeper. Pascoe certainly never bowed to our household servants. Doctor Hilliard was a true Republican to treat a servant as his equal. My brother could learn a thing or two from the "manipulator."

At the meeting that night I sat with the other women of my *section,* helping them to jiggle fussy babies and hush noisy toddlers. No additional arrangements for the morrow's celebration were discussed; but I heard all manner of calls for bloodshed and violence upon various malefactors, particularly M. de Lafayette, the former marquis and hero of the Republic who now seemed to be universally disliked, and the usual threats and death-wishes upon the royal family and all formerly-titled nobles, including those currently serving in the elected Assembly.

It was Pascoe who brought order, reminding everyone to attend the Bastille Day celebration and cheer for the Jacobin leaders, who were united in spirit with *fédérés* from all over the nation and with the *sans-culottes*. He reminded the people, in his erudite yet straightforward way, of past wrongs, current progress, and future goals for the downtrodden proletariat of France. My brilliant brother was roundly cheered, and I fleetingly thought he might consider running for office in the Assembly in the next election. While he would be unlikely to replace Doctor Hilliard in representing our home district, his rising popularity in our Paris *section* was indisputable.

When the meeting finally dispersed I looked for Claude, who often walked home with me, but he was nowhere in sight. I was obliged to approach Pascoe, who was talking with a man I didn't know.

At his side stood *la Florinda* herself. I thought she looked rather bored, but her face brightened at my approach. "*Bonsoir*, Madame DeMer," she said politely. "Are you to join us tomorrow?"

Her genial yet respectful manner took me by surprise, and I said only, "*Bonsoir*, madame." Or was she a mademoiselle? How did one properly address a courtesan? Or did propriety even matter? Her expression of amused comprehension flustered me still further.

Just then Pascoe, having answered the stranger's question, turned to join our conversation. "Ah, Colette." He looked me up and down. "You look tired. Better ask Claude to take you home so you'll be ready for our outing tomorrow."

Then another man, a joiner, I guessed by his attire, stepped between me and Florinda to claim Pascoe's attention and relieved me of the obligation to make conversation with her. I watched my brother's face as he listened and talked, noting its pallor, the lines of strain around his mouth. Was he fully recovered from the injury suffered in the duel? Had he suffered from any fits recently?

Did Quent attend our *section* meetings, remaining somewhere in the background to keep an eye on Pascoe? I wondered—and feared—how this crowd would react if my brother suddenly suffered one of his attacks. This strange malady had overtaken him only recently, soon after our move to Paris. I had witnessed only a mild trance-like state once, from which he quickly recovered. But according to him, not all of his attacks were so mild, and he did not want me or anyone else to witness one. If people were to discover his condition, he might be incarcerated as a lunatic.

"Here you are, Colette. I've been looking everywhere for you."

Still dazed by my worried thoughts, I looked blankly into Saint-Jude's warm gaze.

He caught my hands in his and linked our fingers. "I talked to your employer today, and he promised to give you the day off work. I've hired a chaise for the day, so I'll stop by for you at nine o'clock."

His clear, carrying voice attracted an audience. I silently reclaimed my hands and led the way to a side chamber offering a modicum of privacy. There I turned to confront him head-on. "You had no right to approach Doctor Hilliard. What did you say to him?"

"I couldn't think of any other way to get you out of working on Bastille Day. He seemed surprised, but he didn't argue the point." Saint-Jude shrugged and grinned. "He's a true bourgeois in that old wig of his, looking down his long nose at a true man of the Republic. We'll show those Girondins where the real power lies. "

I wanted to take Saint-Jude by his shoulders and shake him, but this would have been about as effective as shaking one of the stone lions seated on the pillars outside, and in all probability he would have found it romantically encouraging.

"Did you tell him we were lovers?"

He took a step back, perhaps beginning to apprehend my feelings. *"Oui,* I did. Why not? The old bird looked as if he might pull his sword on me, so I reminded him that he is your employer, not your father. You are an adult woman, free to choose your own life and love."

"Exactly so!" I exclaimed. "I am delighted to hear that you share my view of the matter. Since I am free to choose my own life and love, I will bid you a good night and wish you all manner of joy in your future. I would advise you not to bring your chaise to Maison Beau Temps in the morning, for I possess a fowling piece that belonged to my late husband, and I know how to load, prime, and fire it."

CHAPTER 14

BEFORE FILLION COULD react to my threat beyond a stunned expression, I spun on my heel and headed for the door.

Just outside I would have collided with a man's chest had he not caught my shoulders. "Colette, where are you going?" It was Claude.

"Home."

He grinned, his eyes alight. "I'll escort you." He called to someone behind me, "I'll catch up with you later, Philippe. I'm walking my sister home."

From somewhere in the midst of my consuming fury, a reasonable part of my mind noted that Claude had not been talking with guards, which was some consolation. I heard laughter from within the hall, and someone calling Fillion's name. Recalling that arrogant grin of his, I boiled over again. Did I possess no discernment of character whatsoever when it came to good-looking males?

Pink streaked the western sky; the trees in the park surrounding our headquarters looked black in silhouette against it. When we reached the streets, traffic was sparse and our sabots clopped on the pavement. "*Merci,* Claude. I would have marched home alone, I was so angry."

"And heaven help anyone who dared accost you. I think nearly everyone in the *section* heard you threaten Fillion with the fowling piece." He laughed. "He'll be a laughingstock for days!"

"*Bon.* He humiliated me."

"How?"

"Never mind how," I snapped. "He overstepped his bounds."

We walked nearly a block in silence before Claude observed, "No one's ever known him to pursue one woman for this long."

"Until today I considered him a polite young friend."

"Fillion?" Claude's laugh held an unpleasant edge. "He really wanted to impress you, I guess. Why don't you like him? He's a good fellow."

"He told someone whose good opinion I value that he and I were lovers," I snapped. "I am not a loose woman, Claude."

"Oh, he told Leonie, right? That must rankle. But didn't you have an affair with a married officer last year?" he asked. "Étienne won't talk about it, but Pascoe told me all."

The casual manner in which he referenced my past history nearly earned him a clout on the ear. But I gripped my self-control with both hands and held on tight. "That was a mistake," I said, trying to keep my tone light. "I did not know I was being an adulteress."

"Would it have made a difference if you'd known?"

"*Oui,* believe it or not. It would have made a difference."

Not even my young brother considered me a moral woman; probably because I wasn't one. But in my deepest heart I wanted to be good and respectable. I wanted to feel . . . No, not just feel . . . I wanted to *be* worthy of respect.

At the house, Claude followed me inside. A candle lamp burned welcomingly on the hall table; Étienne had left it for me. "I apologize if I hurt you," Claude said hesitantly.

I stood on the bottom step and reached up to touch his smooth cheek. "I forgive you. In this new world with no rules, I suppose it sounded reasonable that your big sister would be a harlot."

He looked deeply uncomfortable, shifting his weight and twisting his cap between his hands. "Would you want to be married and have babies like Manon, Mimi, and Lorraine? I thought you escaped to Paris because you hated that ordinary life."

I quirked a brow. "My only marital prospect in Biron was a bald widower who wanted a wife to watch his eight children so he could spend his evenings in the tavern. Whatever was I thinking to refuse such an attractive offer?"

He gave me a crooked smile. "Monsieur Sorel. But have you found anything better here in Paris? Pascoe says you could never be happy tied down to one man."

Pascoe talked that way about me to our little brother? I closed my eyes, set the anger aside, then gazed up at Claude and said earnestly, "Claude, I would very much like to marry and have a family. But I do not wish to repeat the mistakes of my first marriage. I would rather remain alone than marry a man who cannot offer me the two things I desire most."

I could tell he was losing interest in the conversation, but he asked, "What two things?"

"Respect and kindness."

I saw when the words' import reached his brain. "Respect. You want respect? *Pourquoi?*"

"Why does anyone want respect?"

Claude regarded me with curiosity. "I never thought of a woman wanting respect," he admitted.

"We do." I pulled him down to kiss his cheek then headed upstairs. *"Bonsoir, mon chouchou."*

"Bonsoir, Colette."

After lying awake much of the night, I awoke with a feverish headache. I actually welcomed the good excuse to stay home. A terrible depression had settled over my spirit, akin to the low spirits I had experienced in my darkest times. My natural optimism had always before insisted better times would come. Now I was not so sure. Did anything truly good even exist?

I sent a maid down to tell my brothers I was ill. Predictably, a few moments later Pascoe breezed into my room. "Get up, Colette. How can you even think of staying home on Bastille Day? Come. Rise and dress yourself."

"*Non.* I am ill."

"*Absurdité.*" He dragged open the window curtains then took a clear look at my face. "*Ouille!* You look terrible."

"*Merci.*" I turned my face away from the brightness. "Now go away."

He stood there, hands on his slim hips. "I know you're not spending the day with Fillion; the whole world knows you threatened him with a gun." A pause. "Do you really own a fowling piece?"

"You may not have it."

"Selfish." He huffed then grinned. "Fillion has more muscle than brain, but I thought you would like him. *Enfin,* he's the type you generally admire."

"Perhaps my tastes have matured. He, on the other hand, has not." Pascoe's brash humor grated on my raw nerves. "Now will you please let me rest?"

"You are not only ill; you are angry."

I gave him a cold stare. "This is true; I am angry. I don't want you telling people about my mistakes. If I want them to know, I'll tell them myself."

His eyes widened in a look of deep concern. Suddenly solicitous, he touched my forehead with the back of his hand. "Too much night air," he said. "Or perhaps it is this heat wave. I suffer from it myself. We fair redheads thrive in a cool climate, as did our Nordic ancestors."

I shoved his hand away. "You told Claude about Charles-Louis du Coture."

"Only because he asked."

"How would he know to ask?"

Pascoe gestured helplessly. "He asked why you, a handsome young woman, live with your brothers."

"So you told him how I made a fool of myself. In future, kindly direct him to ask me anything he wants to know." I scowled. "I hate the very idea of any of my brothers treating a woman the way that dog treated me."

He was silent, his gaze fixed on the floor. Then he gave me a direct look. "The servants all have the day off, so you will be alone here unless Étienne or Claude stays home. I will leave some of our picnic food and a bottle of wine for you."

"*Merci.*"

He piled the food on my bedside table, far more than I could have eaten even when well; and he brought me a pitcher of fresh water. Pausing again at my bedside, he reached out to smooth hair from my face, frowning. "I don't like seeing you ill, Colette." He shook his head, and a red-gold wave fell over his forehead. "And I don't understand why you take these things so seriously."

"Headaches?" I asked, deliberately dim.

"Affairs. Intrigues. *Amour.* Why can you not simply enjoy life?" His tone was light, but his eyes challenged me.

I stared right back. "In that duel you fought, did you kill her husband? Father? Brother?"

He froze, his eyes wide. Then, with a sharp oath, he left the room. I heard him whistle as he descended the stairs, a sure sign of anger.

I lay there feeling guilty. I was guilty, for I intended to hurt him. It had been a duel of words, and mine drew blood. But to what purpose? Sharp words could not repair the breach between us; they only drove him farther from me.

I fell into a troubled sleep and woke hours later, damp with sweat. My headache had faded into a dull heaviness, and I no longer shivered in the heat. Rising, I dressed in fresh undergarments, took a long drink of the water Pascoe had brought, then used the rest of it to bathe my face. I donned my lightest gown, hoping to avoid overheating myself again.

Someone was thumping around downstairs. I hurried down and found Claude stamping into his riding boots. "Oh, you're out of bed!" he said in some surprise. "I came home to change clothes; someone spilled a bowl of beans down the front of me."

"Did you see the King?"

"He is fat and ugly. I couldn't see the Queen clearly, but she is thin enough. They all looked unhappy."

I had never seen the royal family in person. To me they always seemed like characters from legend or myth, despised for the tyranny they represented. Yet today Claude's offhand manner bothered me. "Wouldn't you be unhappy if you were surrounded, as they are, by thousands of people who hate you?" I said shortly.

He shrugged. "People hate them for good reason." He rose and smoothed his riding breeches. "Are you coming? I could rent a second horse for you. I don't want to miss the exhibition. Étienne is holding a place for me."

I had heard there was to be a great parade, including radical *fédérés* gathered from all over France. The king would be required to swear an oath of loyalty to the nation and then set fire to a symbolic Tree of Feudalism decorated with emblems of royalty, nobility, and the papacy.

None of it interested me. I looked at my handsome little brother, so vital and enthusiastic, and I knew he would soon enlist. War would take him from me, perhaps for always. I could not keep him safe. I could not keep anyone safe.

"You go on. I want to rest today."

He gave me a closer look. "Don't get really ill, Colette. We all depend on you." He actually gave me a quick peck on the cheek before riding off on a thin-looking gray.

The balcony was in full sun, and the statues in the salon were undesirable company, so I sat before the open window in my bedchamber, hoping to catch a stray breeze. At times I thought I heard the distant roar of crowds and the roll of drums, but this might have been imagination. Hungry, I nibbled at the food Pascoe left, drank a glass of wine, and found myself refreshed. The cheese was particularly fine, but I thought my baguettes superior in texture to the baker's. The spears of pickled cucumber were excellent, and I analyzed the blend of spices even as my mind pondered deeper topics.

Where would it all end? The movement toward a free republic had achieved success beyond our dreams, yet the people of France seemed further than ever from peace and true freedom. Was nothing in life worth striving toward?

Should I focus my energies on achieving a crisp pickled cucumber or a crusty loaf of bread and forget anything outside my immediate sphere of influence? But not even my kitchen or my garden was truly mine. When Doctor Hilliard left Paris, someone else would move in and take over my little realm of happiness.

Finally, as if compelled, I donned my sabots and bonnet, stepped outside, and walked down the short drive. I saw few people on the boulevard, and every shop along my route was either empty of customers or closed. Yet when I reached the little chapel its doors were open, and the air inside the stone building was refreshingly cool.

I found the confessional, hardly daring to hope a priest would be there. But a gentle voice addressed me: "My child, is your heart burdened?"

"Père, my heart is so burdened I can hardly stand upright," I said, and a lump nearly closed my throat. "I cannot escape the weight of it."

"Tell me," he said.

So I unburdened myself, not only of sins committed, but also of desires and longings unmet. "I long to love and be loved, yet I always choose men who despise and reject me. I long to have children of my own, but my baby daughter died. I want to help people, to make a difference, so I joined forces with those who shared my dream. But our months and years of work bring no perceptible change. The people in our *section* are as destitute as ever, and their hope fades."

After rambling on for some time in this vein, I paused and heaved a sigh. "Père, I long to know my purpose. Why am I here? Why did God allow me to be born?"

Silence followed. I wondered for a sinking moment if I had bored the priest to sleep.

But then he spoke, and his voice held such loving sympathy: "My child, you have voiced the great question of humanity."

"Is there an answer?"

"Christ Himself gave the answer to your question. Your purpose is to love the Lord God with all your heart, soul, mind, and strength, and to love your neighbor as you love yourself."

This was my answer? It sounded vague and impersonal. "But how can I love God when I do not know Him? I have trouble enough loving people I do know."

"If you seek after God with all your heart, you will find Him, for He will reveal Himself to you and teach you to love Him, and to love others." The voice held quiet confidence, as if the speaker smiled as he spoke.

"But I don't know how to seek God," I said.

He answered me using words I recognized from my catechism or from Scripture readings long ago, yet he applied them to my life here in Paris almost as if he knew me. Then he said, "When you find God, my child," he said, "you will find your purpose and your joy. Seek Him, and then return to tell me how He leads you."

"What if I return and another priest is here?"

"Only I will be here. But even if I am taken away, never fear, for until that distant day when the Kingdom is fully come and all things are made new, God will supply your needs as He has promised."

I walked home deep in thought, puzzled yet somehow encouraged.

The house felt empty, and time dragged. Seated alone on the terrace, I thought over my conversation with the priest then tried to stop thinking but failed. Deep thinking was never a habit of mine, yet once I started, it was impossible to stop. I felt as if something picked through every wall I tried to build and broke down every door I tried to shut and bar.

I whispered, "I believe you exist, God. I have to believe." Somehow I knew I did not speak into a void. "But . . . are you good?"

This question lingered in my thoughts as I passed the little chapel the next morning, heard singing, and realized early Mass was in session. Almost without thinking I slipped inside while a small gray-haired priest was praying. I recognized that comforting voice. Attendance was sparse, but several other people knelt in the pews before me, heads bowed. Light streaming through the rose window over the altar touched one of those heads, turning it to red flame. I stepped into the farthest-back unoccupied pew. The prayer bench creaked when I knelt on it, and a few heads turned.

The gray stone walls, the candles on the altar, the eucharist, the beautiful carvings and windows: although distinct to this particular chapel, they felt familiar, comfortable. Something was different, however. For the first time I sensed . . . a Presence. Once again my mind tentatively reached out. Not a word did I speak, yet the contact was real.

After the service I tried to escape notice, but in a congregation so small anyone new was obvious. Just as I opened the door, I heard my name spoken firmly. I stepped outside but held the door open. Étienne exited after me, followed closely by Leonie and Doctor Hilliard.

Étienne's eyes, silvery in the early morning light, studied my face. "I must hurry off to work, but I wanted to greet you first, Colette." He spoke quickly. "I'm glad you came."

I nodded. "I am, too. Do you come every Sunday?"

"Every day, if possible. Did you enjoy Père Benedict's homily?" His gaze flitted toward the Hilliards.

"Is that his name? *Oui,* I did. Must you work today? I'll try to bring you something good to eat." And I gave him a hug before he strode away. I hadn't hugged Étienne this much in years.

When I turned, Doctor Hilliard nodded in greeting. Leonie's gaze followed Étienne.

"May we escort you, madame?" the doctor asked.

"Mais bien sûr." I bobbed a curtsy. "Do you attend Mass every week?" I asked, falling in step beside Leonie. We walked three abreast, taking up the entire walkway, which did not matter since few other people were about on a Sunday morning. Although the government did not recognize a holy day of rest, most Parisians still observed it if at all possible.

"Of course we do," Leonie said with an edge of surprise and censure.

"I began attending only recently," her father added. I guessed that Leonie's arrival had prompted his attendance.

"Today is my first time in many years," I admitted.

Although Leonie said no more, her disapproval was evident. As we turned the corner and approached the house, the doctor spoke again. "You are feeling better today, madame?"

"I am. I believe I had too much sun while distributing food Friday."

"I suffered no dire effect," Leonie said. "But you missed nothing by staying home from the celebration; it was dull."

"So Claude informed me. I heard the King refused to burn the Tree of Tyranny. I can hardly say I was surprised." I paused then asked, "How did you know I was ill?"

Leonie answered. "In the midst of interminable monotony I looked up, and there were Étienne and Claude on horseback. We inquired about you, and they told us you were ill. Papa offered to stop by your house last night, but Claude said it was only headache and he needn't bother."

"He was right. By afternoon my fever broke and I felt better."

The doctor followed us up the front steps and opened the door, standing back to allow us to enter first. Halfway inside, Leonie suddenly turned to her father. "I want to start attending weekday Mass."

"If you rise early enough, I will escort you when my schedule allows," he said, and I caught his gaze. He understood her motivation as well as I did and seemed to find it amusing rather than annoying.

Would he actually consider a match between his daughter, granddaughter of a marquis, and Étienne Girardeau, son of a village blacksmith? If so, the man was a truer Republican than I dared imagine.

An idea took root in my thoughts and rapidly grew into a thriving plot.

CHAPTER 15

I T WAS TIME, I BELIEVED, to take matters in hand; Étienne and Leonie needed an Event to push them together. For the next several days I plotted, tweaked, and organized my Grand Scheme until it was ready to introduce to its main players.

Nearly every morning now I walked with Étienne to Mass, and Leonie sacrificed her morning sleep for the sake of meeting him there, accompanied by her dutiful father. I felt certain God would overlook her blatant hypocrisy; and I believe even Père Benedict recognized and approved the romance blooming amid the holy sacraments.

Thus encouraged and emboldened, I met Doctor Hilliard one evening as he entered the front door. He let me take his hat, gloves, and stick without question, although I think he smiled indulgently, knowing a request must follow such rare attentions.

"May I speak with you privately about an important matter, monsieur?"

"*Mais bien sûr*, madame." He gave me his full attention, all trace of humor gone. "Shall we discuss it in the salon? The kitchen?"

"The kitchen, I think. Leonie is upstairs at the moment."

He motioned for me to lead the way as if I were his equal. In the kitchen I approached my worktable, turned, and bolstered my courage by resting my hands behind me on its scarred surface. Without preamble I launched into my subject. "Monsieur, I'm certain you and mademoiselle have received an invitation to Madame Lovett's grand *bal masque*."

He nodded. "I believe we did."

Sudden curiosity distracted me. "Have you met Madame Lovett?"

"I have not had the pleasure, *non*."

"She is many years younger than Monsieur Lovett and very handsome." Monsieur Lovett, a wealthy Girondist Assembly member from Limoges, occasionally joined other conservative deputies at planning meetings in the doctor's library.

"Is she?" His gaze wandered toward the fireplace, where his dinner kept warm over the banked fire. Savory aromas filled the room.

I suddenly noticed the lines of fatigue and discouragement on his face and realized that, no matter how kindly his tone, I was keeping him on his feet at the end of an exhausting day.

I burst into explanation. "You see, I am assisting Madame Lovett in planning the event. Despite this dreadful hot weather it should be a delightful affair, for their home is well located and quite commodious. I wish to ask, monsieur, if you would accept the invitation and escort Leonie to this ball. I know you seldom attend social functions, but this will be a wholesome event; madame invited only the most respectable of people."

A slight crease formed between his dark brows. "Do you believe this is a good time for such frivolity, with France at war and our city in near chaos?"

"Perhaps not, but I believe the distraction would be good for Leonie. She would remember this event all her life! Although the time is short for selecting a costume, I think we might easily find something to tailor to fit her."

"Do you have a costume for yourself already?"

"I do, but I am not a guest, you know. I shall be working."

Again he paused and my hopes hung suspended. Then he gave me a sidelong look. "I hope you will take time to introduce her to appropriate dance partners."

My hopes soared. *"Oui,* monsieur! Then you will come?"

His eyes actually twinkled. "I shall, although I suspect there is more behind this little plan than first meets the eye. You may instruct Leonie to send an acceptance. And you may have all bills delivered here."

"Merci beaucoup, monsieur!"

But a moment later all humor vanished from his face. "I have a message not half so pleasant."

"What is it?" I asked, instantly worried.

"Merely a caution, madame. You are undoubtedly aware of certain outbreaks of violence in the city. Recent military setbacks are causing widespread unrest."

His gaze briefly held mine. A lump formed in my chest. "I . . . I shall not risk your daughter's safety, monsieur."

"Or your own, I hope," he said.

"Do you wish her to stop assisting me at the food distributions?" I asked. "And should I stop taking her to visit her friend Adrienne?"

"I trust your discretion, madame."

My discretion again. I wasn't sure I possessed any, but I longed to be worthy of his confidence.

Once more he glanced toward the hearth. "I did not realize I was hungry until I entered this room. Not every man comes home at night to the aromas of heaven." Again his expression softened into something very like a smile, and he bowed before heading upstairs.

"*Bonjour,* Adrienne," I called brightly the next morning from the doorway of the little house behind the forge. It was stiflingly hot, and dampness from last night's rain made the air difficult to breathe, outside or inside.

Hearing Adrienne's muffled reply, I found her in bed, sweaty, rumpled, and red in the face. Her belly was now a large mound on her small frame. "Did the baby keep you awake in the night?"

"It is too hot to sleep anyway. I hate being so fat."

"*Chérie,* I wish you would gain more weight, for there is a great deal here of Baby and very little of Adrienne."

She passively let me bathe her face and limbs and check on the baby's growth. I covered her belly with a thin sheet and patted it. The baby shifted beneath my hand. I never tired of this feeling, though it emphasized my own loss, my empty arms. Serving other women as midwife was strangely cathartic, except when I lost a baby or mother. Each time tragedy happened I resolved to stop assisting at births, but I could never seem to refuse a request from a frightened young mother.

"Is Leonie here?" Adrienne asked.

"She went to care for your goat. Are you enjoying the milk?"

"*Oui.*"

Her melancholy was a puzzle to be solved. "Are you lonely?" I asked. "Does Minette still visit you?"

"She does, but I am tired of hearing about Jesus. He cannot love me anymore."

I listened to her querulous voice, put myself in her position, and made a guess: "Are you feeling guilty and rejected?"

The direct question struck home. "*Oui,*" she whispered. Tears welled up and spilled down her flushed cheeks. "Every time I see my baby, I will think of *him.* I loved him so, and I love him still."

I regretted my bluntness even while congratulating myself on digging up the truth. "But you will learn to love this baby for the person he or she is, an innocent child who is in no way responsible for the father's sins."

She shook her head. "You can't know."

"I know that a baby is a gift. I know that I loved my daughter even while I hated her father."

Adrienne regarded me with sudden interest. "Did you kill Jean-Antoine?"

"Of course not! He killed himself with drink." I rose and brushed my hands on my apron. "Stop moping over what cannot be changed and start preparing your heart for a love you can't begin to imagine. There is nothing in the world like being a mother."

"But what kind of future will he have? War and battles and revolutions. I am so tired of hearing about the Republic and warnings and threats. I wish I'd never left Biron."

I could not argue, for I felt much the same. "You can give him love. It matters more than anything else."

She scowled. "Love. With you it always comes back to love."

"I hope so. Can you think of anything better?"

Adrienne blinked. After a moment her hands lifted to cradle her belly, and she shook her head.

Rarely in those days were all three brothers and I home of an evening. But after dinner on the last Thursday of July, three of us sat in those heavy chairs on the tiny balcony adjacent to our salon; Claude lounged on the floor. Below us, the unkempt community garden looked dry and wilted. No one in our block of houses had taken responsibility to tend or water the little patch of green, so it ran wild all summer and suffered for the lack of order, like the rest of Paris.

I gave Quent his due: Pascoe's stockings and cravat were snowy, and no wrinkle marred either his modest blue coat or his waistcoat diagonally striped in patriotic red, white, and blue. But his fine features bore a sharper edge than I liked. He enjoyed his pipe while gazing off over the housetops toward the last streaks of saffron and cerise in the western sky.

Étienne and Claude wore rough brown trousers and plain shirts, and soot darkened their skin. The discontent written on Claude's boyish face saddened me. He would much rather be out tonight with friends, as he was most evenings. Étienne's rough-cut features expressed his serene enjoyment of the sunset.

Claude brought up the *section* meeting scheduled for the next evening. "I heard that a group of the *fédérés* from Marseilles is to attend."

"More than likely," Pascoe responded, "they will treat us with a spontaneous performance of their song." His voice dripped venom.

"Don't you like the song?" Claude inquired. "I keep hearing it everywhere. All the fellows are talking about it."

Pascoe gave a short laugh. "It is a rousing call to arms that has captured the imaginations of patriots all over the city. And if I never heard it again, I would die happy."

I followed this exchange with rising concern. "Why are the *fédérés* still in Paris?" I asked. "I thought they would leave after the Bastille Day events."

"They declare they will not leave until action is taken against the king." Pascoe drew on his pipe and blew a smoke ring. "They are rough and provincial men, yet they serve a purpose in rousing our people to action."

"The Assembly is indecisive and weak," Claude said. "The people of Paris must take action if anything is to happen."

"By 'take action,' I assume you mean another demonstration like that at the Tuileries," I said, trying to conceal my dread.

"The time for demonstration is past," Pascoe said. "We have allowed the Assembly months in which to act, yet it has done nothing effective. We have a Republic, and we have a King. The two cannot coexist."

I glanced across Pascoe to Étienne, who shook his head in warning. I ignored him. "But our enemies have threatened to destroy Paris if any harm comes to the King."

Pascoe turned his head and gave me a level stare. "Let them try."

Many times I had seen brave men wither beneath Pascoe's censure; rarely was I on the receiving end of it. Instead of cowing me, it aroused my temper.

"And what would then become of the women and children of this city? You leaders talk so much about the *canaille,* about the People, and yet when power comes into question, the ordinary citizens are trampled underfoot."

My beloved brother addressed me as coldly as if I were a stranger. "You speak from ignorance; yet dissension among the ignorant masses can cause havoc. Trust in your leaders, Colette, and keep your mouth shut about matters you cannot understand because you lack access to certain information. And do not berate me for calling you ignorant, for regarding certain vital matters you *are* ignorant and must remain so."

I opened my mouth, again caught Étienne's warning gaze, and closed it. For the time being.

Instead of dressing for bed, I went to Étienne's room and knocked. He opened immediately and motioned me to enter. "I thought you would come," he said quietly, and I realized he too was still fully clothed.

"Do you know something I should know?" I asked.

"At the forge we have been making countless pikes, which are being distributed not to the army but to citizens of Paris. I expect forges in every *section* are doing the same. Colette, you and Leonie must not visit the *section* anymore without armed protection."

"But I must distribute food tomorrow. The people depend on me."

"I know they do. I will ask Arnaud if I might accompany you."

"Will he allow it when you are so overworked at the forge?"

"I don't know. I hope so," Étienne said.

But when Leonie and I stopped by the forge early the next morning, Arnaud met us, his expression cloudy. "I cannot spare Étienne today, so don't bother asking," he said.

"Claude, then?"

"*Non.*"

And none of my arguments moved him, not by a hair's breadth.

So I flagged a carriage to take us back to the doctor's house. I fear I was in rather a temper, so much so that I cannot remember what I said to Leonie. I left her alone in her father's house, warned her not to venture into the streets alone, then took the carriage to Maison Beau Temps. After asking the driver to wait, I rushed upstairs to my bedchamber.

And there I dug up my buried treasure, the only possession of my late husband still in my keeping. I pried up two loose boards in one corner and pulled from its hiding place beneath the floor the old fowling piece. It took precious time to make certain it was in firing condition, but I counted the cost.

The carriage driver had been content to wait, but when I asked him to drive me into the poverty-stricken area of the *section,* he balked. Even after I offered him three times the usual fare, he promised only to leave me at a major crossroads. I would simply have to walk from there. I gave him the money in advance and climbed into the small carriage, cradling my unwieldy, loaded firearm.

Just as Étienne warned, the streets crawled with red-capped *sans-culottes* and guardsmen carrying pikes and firearms. But most of those patrolling our *section* recognized me, and I encountered nothing worse than lewd comments as I walked to the Danican home.

The supplies had already been delivered when I arrived. Madame Danican greeted me with evident relief, and we set to work, helped by her older children. Minette LaVie was again one of the first to arrive, and she and her sons joined our labors with a good will. I set the fowling piece within easy reach and warned the children away from it.

The loading and deliveries progressed smoothly with so many willing hands at work. Among the women present, there was plenty of discussion about that night's meeting. "We'll be there," said Madame Danican. "I don't understand what is taking so long. All our big, strong men cannot push one King off his throne?"

"No more kings!" a small voice piped up from somewhere in hiding.

"I hear you, Martin," I said with a smile. The boy crawled from beneath the table. A dirty red cap far too large for his head hung down to his eyes. "Where is Mademoiselle Leonie?" he demanded.

"Where is Leonie?" Minette's little girls echoed.

"She could not come with me today," I told them, mirroring their sad expressions. "But next time I hope to bring her again."

As the morning ebbed and our supplies dwindled, I began to wonder if Tressy would come. Finally she arrived with her handcart, puffing slightly, and returned my greetings with her usual polite solemnity. "I haven't time to visit today, madame," she said. "But I promise to tell the mistress about the meeting tonight."

"Is Monsieur Gallatin still in prison?" I asked.

"*Oui,* he is." The girl looked tired yet healthy. From the size of her belly, it should be many weeks before she delivered her baby.

Shortly after Tressy's departure, I walked back to the main boulevard with the huge firearm over my shoulder, receiving both frightened and amused glances from passersby. Once I reached the crossroads I could have hailed a chair or a cabriolet, but walking gave me time to process my thoughts regarding conversations and impressions of the morning.

Never before had I disliked my *section* people. Today how they annoyed me! All morning I had listened while men and women foully berated the Assembly and never once recalled that the men who donated the food they were collecting numbered among its members. Not even the children had charmed me; they all wanted Leonie anyway.

And then Minette, of all people, had capped off the dreadful morning. There I was, contentedly thinking judgmental thoughts about my ungrateful neighbors while packing and loading their food; when suddenly, with no warning or apparent provocation, Minette observed in her gentle way, "I've been thinking today how God sends rain upon the just and the unjust. I am always amazed by His kindness toward those who reject Him and run after other gods."

Nothing more did she say. I do not know whether she read my thoughts or was simply making one of her random religious remarks, but the aptness of this one quite chilled me.

I stopped at the fish market and selected an eel, the key ingredient for a favorite spicy stew. After adding it to my basket along with a bottle of cream and a packet of peppercorns, I hurried home, arms aching from carrying both the heavy basket and the gun.

And while I prepared this dinner, I directed at least one sincere thought of gratitude toward the God who provided eels, cream, and peppercorns.

CHAPTER 16

THE TIME CAME FOR the final unveiling of my Master Plan.

Many hours I labored over my presentation, for even one wrong word might spoil the entire speech and drive Étienne away. For a man of few words, he was remarkably sensitive to other people's phrasings. Mine in particular, it seemed.

I waited long, almost too long, for an evening when Pascoe and Claude were both out. At last it came, and I cornered my unsuspecting brother. With good-natured patience he let me herd him into the salon and sat on the chaise longue to listen.

Watching his face for any reaction, good or bad, I poured out my plan.

When I finished, his initial reaction was exactly what I had expected. "I will not be dressed up like a fool to attend a ball."

"But it would be the thrill of her lifetime! Leonie would never, ever forget the excitement of dancing with you at her first ball." A sudden fear struck me. "You do know how to dance, don't you?"

Our mother had adamantly insisted upon her children receiving both a good education and solid instruction in the social graces, which last had annoyed Papa, who cared nothing for dancing. But what if her fervor had cooled by the time the youngest six boys were old enough to learn?

"Never fear; I know how to dance."

If my ears didn't deceive me, he sounded grudgingly interested.

I smiled at his slip. "Think what will please *her* most, Étienne. She is so excited about this ball; she can speak of little else. You must have heard her mention it after Mass the other day."

His face revealed inner conflict, so I pressed on. "I am allowed to bring an escort, so you will have an invitation. Leonie's costume must have once belonged to a countess at the very least. Your eyes will drop from your head when you see her."

He shook his head. "You and your one little chick to tend," he said, and rose to his feet. "The mother hen needs a brood of her own, I think." With a deep sigh he stretched his arms and flexed his back. "*If* I should decide to attend this *bal masque,* what would I wear?"

I jumped up and hugged him. "Oh Étienne, you will not regret this!"

While I was absorbed in plans for a masked ball, political tensions in Paris were escalating. The *fédérés* from Marseilles and *section* leaders from all over Paris demanded the King be no longer recognized as King. A few of the *sections* declared that on 5 August, a Sunday, they would march on the Tuileries and demand the King's abdication.

The mayor of Paris, Monsieur Pétion, asked them to wait until the following Friday to give the Assembly time to depose him. The leaders agreed to wait, but on Monday a great crowd was to gather at the Champ de Mars to demand the King's abdication. Pascoe told me of this important protest and fully expected me to participate.

And I forgot. Quite possibly I "conveniently" forgot.

In the confusion of the day my absence went unnoticed, to my relief. Pascoe might have suspected the truth but was too busy to make anything of it, and Claude simply assumed I was there. At any rate, the protest went unheeded: The Assembly remained unmoved, and Louis XVI was still King of France.

Unbeknownst to me, further plans were being laid.

Madame Lovett and I were entirely immersed in our own plans for the social event of the season. Perhaps we deliberately blinded ourselves to unpleasantness; not even in retrospect can I explain such oblivion. But I am certain we were not alone in our denial of the true state of affairs, for the masked ball was well attended, and nearly everyone there seemed determined to forget anything to do with revolution or reality.

Étienne had rushed home from work in time to clean up, an ordeal in itself. Pascoe was staying at Maison Beau Temps at the time, which proved a blessing, for Quent offered to help Étienne prepare for the ball.

The valet insisted that years of accumulated soot and grime required a complete bath. He scoffed at my worries over Étienne taking ill from the water on his skin, declaring, "I grew up swimming in the ocean every day and have never been ill in my life." For a servant, Quent seemed accustomed to taking command, and I submitted, if not quietly, then at least humbly. We were all appreciative of our house's water pipes that day, for many gallons of water, several scrubbings with soap, and many rinsings ensued before Quent declared my brother clean.

I dressed in my own costume while I waited. It did not compare to Leonie's gown, the creation of a famous *coturier*, but the color flattered my complexion. My appearance did not matter, I reminded myself, for I would spend the evening in the background.

Étienne was nearly unrecognizable once clean and clad in his costume. His hair was a richer red than I had realized, and his eyes looked very blue. Now he seemed to genuinely anticipate the ball, abandoning the sarcastic complaints of recent days.

To my relief, neither Pascoe nor Claude made an appearance before we left the house. But in retrospect I realize no amount of mockery would have changed Étienne's course. Once he decided to attend the ball, it was as good as done.

We arrived early to supervise last-minute preparations, and I believe Madame Lovett was rather startled by my brother's fine appearance. He truly did credit that night to the name of Girardeau.

While the first guests arrived I arranged my servers and gave final instructions regarding the food tables. I pictured Étienne supporting the walls or mimicking a post, but I needn't have worried. When I did find a spare minute to scan the ballroom, I was delighted to see him conversing with a matron and her daughter, smiling, and to all appearances quite at ease.

His costume, in royal blue trimmed with gold, I had purchased on sight before ever mentioning the ball to him, for I knew I would never find another to fit his frame. It had required some tailoring, but no one would now guess it was not made for him. A domino covered the upper half of his face but could not disguise his identity; and, thanks to Quent, a perfect froth of lace jabot underlined his square jaw. With his commanding height, breadth of shoulder, and amazing hair (which he refused to powder,) he was easy to find in the crowd.

I could hardly wait for Leonie to see him.

My duties kept me hopping, but I was lucky enough to see Doctor Hilliard and his daughter enter the ballroom. Easily the most striking pair in the room, I thought. Leonie glowed in her silk gown of deep pink organza with an exquisitely embroidered train. The new high-waisted styles were ideally suited to her tall, slim figure. Her ornate mask covered most of her head like a bonnet, fluttering with feathers dyed to match the gown. The doctor looked equally fine in a dark gray coat, matching breeches, embroidered waistcoat, white silk stockings, and buckled shoes, with a lace jabot and sleeve ruffles for a touch of elegance. Although his domino added a slightly mysterious appearance, he was easily recognizable in his gray wig.

My gaze shifted across the room to the figure now conversing with another matron and daughter. Had Étienne seen Leonie? His careless pose suggested not.

My duties then called me away from the dance floor. The next time I found opportunity to scan the sparkling room for my people, I saw the doctor dancing with Leonie. For the time, at least, she seemed pleased with her father as well as with herself. The tentatively happy expression on his face sent a twinge through my heart. Who could know how long her approval would last?

I took a moment to visit the powder room and check my reflection in a polished mirror. Beside elegant Leonie I would appear short and ordinary, and red hair was decidedly unfashionable, yet I felt pretty enough. I had debated whether the ruffles framing my gown's neckline might be excessive on my figure, but now I thought not.

The entire event seemed to be a success. My servers nearly ran their feet off, replenishing food and drink at the tables. Wax candles twinkled from ornate chandeliers and candelabra, reflecting from every polished surface. The music was not the best, for quality musicians demanded exorbitant prices; but it was adequate for the occasion, and I heard no complaints.

The hostess approached me between songs to request a rearrangement of food platters, and I gave quick orders to two waiting lads. Despite open windows and doors, the rooms became stuffy as the evening progressed. I longed to step into the garden, which looked inviting, discreetly lighted by torches. Evening had fallen while I was working.

"*Bonsoir,* Madame DeMer." A familiar voice spoke from behind me.

"*Bonsoir,* monsieur." I turned to greet the doctor and dropped a curtsy. "Are you and Leonie enjoying your evening?"

His expression softened. "Tonight my daughter is the happiest I have ever seen her. I must thank you and your brother for this, madame. Her surprise at Étienne's presence was complete; her joy, unsurpassed." He then glanced at my head. "If you will pardon the question, what exactly is the purpose of a domino worn atop the head?"

I slipped my mask down over my face. "Better?"

His brow wrinkled above his own domino. "Actually, *non.*"

I smiled. "You are difficult to please tonight, monsieur."

"A costume quite alters the personality, I suspect. Next I shall weep like Pierrot or boast like Scaramouche."

I laughed outright. "This I should like to witness."

Creases appeared in his cheeks. He was smiling! Or at least fighting back a smile. "*Touché.*" And he touched his fist to his chest and bowed slightly, as if saluting with a sword.

But then I caught sight, beyond his shoulder, of Madame Lovett beckoning imperiously. "*Peste,*" I muttered. "If you will excuse me, monsieur . . ."

Serious once again, he bowed.

As I had feared, Madame observed me narrowly through the eyeholes of her mask. "I did not hire you to flirt with my guests. See you do not neglect your duties."

"Certainly not, madame." I said humbly, wishing I dared speak my thoughts.

Shortly afterward the doctor again appeared at my side. "Madame DeMer, may I have the honor of partnering you in the next, a minuet? I have obtained Madame Lovett's permission to borrow your time."

I could only hope my domino concealed my feelings as well as the doctor's concealed his. Madame Lovett might have given permission, but she would not be pleased.

"Do you think it wise, monsieur, to dance with your housekeeper?" I kept my tone light and amused.

He matched it: "What is the good of a Republic if I cannot?"

A sensible answer.

He offered his hand. I laid mine atop his, and he led me to the floor. We took our places, the last couple in a processional minuet. I danced the first steps by rote, and we parted for a turn out. As soon as our hands touched again, I looked up, and he smiled. "Relax, madame."

I quickly discovered he was a fine dancer. More than once I lost track of the count and started turning out at the wrong time, but he corrected me imperceptibly with a slight pressure of his hand on mine. His help kept me from looking awkward, but in reality my thoughts were everywhere except on the minuet.

I caught sight of Étienne at the far end of the room, dancing with Leonie. The two of them were tall and graceful, his blue-and-gold contrasting beautifully with her pink gown. And anyone could see the attraction between them.

Before I quite realized it, the dance ended. Doctor Hilliard bowed gracefully over my hand. "I thank you for the honor, madame."

My cheeks felt so hot, I'm sure they were flushed. "The honor is mine, monsieur," I said. "And I thank you for hiding my many errors." I unfurled my fan and put it to use.

"Not so many. But you did seem distracted. Are you afraid Madame Lovett will be displeased?"

"I know she is annoyed," I answered honestly.

He led me off the dance floor. "I am certain chaos has not ensued at the punch table because you danced one minuet."

Before he could walk away, I pressed his forearm with my fingers then quickly let go. He immediately focused his attention on me.

"Monsieur," I said, "you do not mind about . . . about Leonie and Étienne?"

A certain distance entered his expression, as if his mind fled into the past. "Étienne was a great favorite with my wife, I recall. Leonie seems to bloom in his presence. He brings out a warmth and animation I never see in her otherwise."

"You have come to know him a little while attending Mass, I think?"

He nodded. "A secondary blessing."

I somehow caught the wit behind his serious comment and felt emboldened. "I was unaware they saw each other at all until I discovered you at the church. Étienne is a man of few words."

We both looked around for the young couple and saw them together in an alcove. Étienne was talking with remarkable animation. "Or perhaps he simply saves all his words for Leonie," I amended.

"And I would add she saves the majority of hers for him. Although I hope she also speaks to you." This time I heard sadness behind his light tone.

"She talked to me a great deal while we shopped for her costume," I said. "Otherwise she talks with me only about certain topics. Mostly, I have realized rather tardily, she encourages me to talk about Étienne."

I could feel my nerves stretching tight; we had stood talking too long for propriety. Yet I made no excuse to walk away. The doctor observed Leonie's progression across the dance floor as she and Étienne took their places in yet another set. No mask could hide the girl's excitement.

"I am grateful to God for bringing you and Étienne into Leonie's life," he said in calm and measured tones. "She may soon have need of such friends during these uncertain times."

CHAPTER 17

JUST THEN SOMEONE CALLED to Doctor Hilliard, and he politely excused himself to join a group of other bewigged men. One fat man clapped him on the shoulder, and the others laughed.

Gathering my scattered senses, I returned to the refreshment tables to find the punch bowl nearly empty and my servers standing idle. I quickly set them running and poured myself a glass of wine to settle my nerves. The doctor's final words rearranged themselves in my thoughts to form various meanings. Why would Leonie need friends when she had a father to watch over her?

As the evening progressed, the party divided into smaller rooms for card play, and several couples drifted into the gardens. Many of the families headed home, leaving behind those guests less concerned with propriety and more intoxicated on the host's fine wine and brandy. Newer dances were introduced, including a *valse allemande* involving close contact between the partners. False steps and errors brought bursts of laughter from the dance floor.

I did not see Étienne and Leonie on the floor, but Doctor Hilliard stood on the sidelines in conversation with several elderly men. He had removed his domino, and his wig was crooked. If he must wear the ugly thing, I thought, he should at least take care to keep it straight.

I returned to work, humming along with the music. Since no guests were at the punch bowl and the food was cleared away, I dragged one of my servers into the allemande off in our little corner. The others applauded and begged a turn. They were all near the ages of my little brothers, and I treated them so. When one squeezed me too close, I scolded him sharply. He laughed, unrepentant, so I sent them off and returned to the ballroom door.

Étienne, Leonie, and the doctor stood together, apparently in amicable conversation. The smile on Étienne's face pleased me. He looked so very happy! And Leonie was glowing. A great lump rose in my throat, and I felt as if I might cry. But why? I never cried, and happiness was a silly cause for tears. Disgusted with myself, I tried to push aside the emotion, but it would not leave.

I could no longer maintain my forced gaiety. Ever since Doctor Hilliard's remark about uncertain times, reality intruded on every side. I overheard talk, some of it sharp and angry, containing such words as Tuileries, Assembly, Jacobins, Marseilles, and *sans-culottes*.

Talk of counter-revolution did not belong at a ball! I wanted to go kick someone in the shins as I would have as a child. Sometimes I hated being an adult. The few unexpected lovely moments were usually too jumbled and nerve-wracking to fully enjoy. They would remain only as memories of lost possibility during the long stretches of ugliness that dominated life.

Dancers were leaving the floor. Among them I noticed a masked young man, slim and graceful in a green jacket and striped trousers entirely inappropriate for the occasion, escorting a giggling Madame Lovett. Whatever was Pascoe doing here? I could only shake my head at his typically brazen disregard for propriety. Quent must have told him about the ball. Had he come in search of me?

As I started forward to greet him, he bowed before Leonie as if requesting a dance. People came between me and the interesting scene, and by the time I made my way into the open, only my two brothers were there. Étienne's face was expressionless; Pascoe grinned from ear to ear.

Leonie was nowhere in sight. The doctor, too, had vanished. I turned toward the front hall just in time to glimpse a flash of Leonie's pink train. "The Hilliards are leaving?" I asked as I approached my brothers.

"With a great suddenness," Pascoe said, catching me by the hands. "*Hélas!* I believe my arrival disturbed them. I am devastated to be late and have missed the fun." He looked me up and down. "*Chérie,* you are a goddess tonight in that blue, but the ruffles? *Non. Pitié de nous, non!* You are plump like a pouter pigeon."

He kissed me, and brandy fumes made my eyes water.

"Whatever are you doing here? Did you really just dance with Madame Lovett?" I asked.

He beamed. "I did, and she loves me. My omission from the guest list was surely an oversight. Will you dance the next with me, *ma poulette?*" He bowed and extended one graceful hand.

I cannot explain why Pascoe's silly banter soothed me. He was more than slightly intoxicated, presumptuous to the extreme, and had just insulted me in public; and yet I relaxed and followed his lead, no longer caring what anyone thought.

"Why, monsieur, I should be honored!" I said, placing my hand atop his. Then I turned to Étienne. "Will you take me home after this? My work is done."

His gaze shifted to Pascoe and back to me. "Do you need me?"

"Judging by the brandy on his breath, we will both need you."

He nodded but did not return my smile, and Pascoe led me to the floor. The *contredanse* was new to both of us, but several of the other dancers were even more inebriated than Pascoe, so our odd interpretation of the pattern mattered little. Pascoe amused me with quips and comments in between flirting outrageously with the other woman in our set; and because I was so tired and stressed, I laughed harder than his jokes deserved.

Afterward, Étienne flagged a two-wheeled calèche and helped a very unsteady Pascoe to climb inside with me. "There are no larger carriages around. Don't worry, Colette; I'll catch another for myself." He closed the door and stepped back.

The carriage had not traveled a block before Pascoe laid his head on my shoulder. "Colette, if you should ever stop loving me, my heart would break," he said clearly.

"*Mon ange,* I never shall." I patted his cheek and kissed the top of his head and wondered why my heart felt like stone in my chest.

I could not sleep. Just after dawn I rose and walked to the church. To my surprise, my priest was in the confessional as if waiting just for me. "I visited you a few weeks ago," I began to explain.

"I remember you, my child."

I could have visualized Père Benedict's face, but I preferred to focus on his voice. "I am deeply confused, Père. Since we last spoke I have tried to seek God. I attend Mass nearly every day. Sometimes I sense His presence, but otherwise I feel emptiness, or else a pressing darkness. I am terribly afraid."

"Is it truly God you seek? Or is it possibly the love of man? Are you demanding your will or seeking God's when you accept the Sacrifice of the Mass?"

I could not answer at first. Events of the past few weeks rushed through my thoughts, and I could not honestly say that an awareness or need of God had occurred to me more than once or twice. The priest's insightful questions aroused a hint of resentment. He must have guessed my identity after seeing me at Mass. But still . . .

"How . . . how do you know my heart when I scarcely know it myself?"

Had he eavesdropped on conversations in the church porch? Or had Étienne spoken out of turn?

"I do not know your heart, my child, but I have been a priest for a very long time. I also know from personal experience the longings, heartaches, and weaknesses of mankind."

"From experience? But you are a priest," I protested.

"A priest is yet a man," he said mildly, "with all of a man's temptations. Being consecrated to God does not cancel out a sinful nature. Yet throughout my years of service, I have found the Almighty's power and grace to be all the greater through my weakness."

This revelation distracted my focus, momentarily, from my own woes. I blinked, trying to understand. "So a priest can sin?"

"Can you live in this present age and not have observed the corruption in the Church? Many succumb to lusts of the flesh while wearing vestments of spiritual service. Even now, judgment falls upon the unrighteous shepherds of the helpless, wandering sheep. To suffer for righteousness is a joy and honor, but woe to those teachers who lead God's children into the pit and raise themselves upon the backs of the downtrodden."

My throat tightened at the sound of sorrow in his voice. I well knew the anger of the *sans-culottes* toward the Church, and I knew that many priests had been imprisoned since the revolution began. But Père Benedict seemed to imply that such judgment came from God, not man. So many questions and fears crowded together inside my head; I could not see a straight way in any direction.

"Père, I returned to the Church to find God," I said. "But now you tell me the Church is corrupt. So where can I turn?"

"To the Good Shepherd who laid down His life for the sheep. There are still faithful shepherds in Paris. Yet days are coming, are upon us even now, when the sheep will have few under-shepherds to tend them. When the day comes, remember: Christ Himself will carry you in his bosom, if you will seek and follow Him."

In the transept of this very chapel there was a colored window depicting a shepherd holding a sheep. I had never until this moment understood why. It was interesting, and yet I found all this picturesque speech frustrating; I needed solid direction. "But what do I *do,* Père?" I asked.

"Love God and love your neighbor, and do what you know to be right. No matter how dark and dangerous the path of righteousness appears, it will bring you safely Home in the end."

I frowned, trying to absorb his words so I could analyze them at a later time. At the moment I felt lost in a fog. "I want to trust God and follow His path, but I don't know how to find it."

"Again, look to God, act in love where no love is shown you; and even if a brother, sister, parent, or your dearest friend betrays you, even if the world crumbles about you and the sky falls on your head, you will rest safely in His arms."

Somehow, hearing my fears stated so openly produced a strange courage in my soul. I could lift my head and sally forth to face the day. *"Merci, Père.* I shall do it."

I lighted candles and prayed for loved ones while waiting for early Mass to begin. Praying for them seemed to bring them closer to me. I had never before missed my parents, but somehow knowing I could no longer reach them in a matter of days made their company more desirable. I could not hear Papa's booming laugh or see his sooty countenance, but I remembered them well, and Étienne so often reminded me of him. I missed Maman's sharp lectures and her warm hugs. No letters had yet arrived from America, although this was not unusual. Even the literate

Girardeaux were poor correspondents.

It was easier to pray for distant family members than for more immediate concerns. When I thought of my brothers, the Hilliards, Adrienne, and even Tressy, I could find no words. I clutched my newly-purchased Saint-Sébastien medal, hoping a saint would pay heed to my prayers. Then my eyes lifted toward the stained-glass window of the Shepherd and the lost lamb.

Étienne entered my pew. "I thought you might be here," he said.

I glanced up at him and offered something close to a smile. He wore his usual rough attire, and in contrast his face appeared strangely clean. Something else had changed. "You look like a man who conquered the world," I observed.

His gaze dropped to the floor, but he could not hide his grin. "I feel like one."

I felt pleased for him, yet when Leonie and her father took nearby seats I wondered what coming days and weeks would bring.

Not until after Mass, when Étienne took leave of us and I fell into step beside Leonie, did I dare to glance at Doctor Hilliard. Was it my imagination, or had he aged overnight? Although his posture was as upright as ever, he seemed weighted by a great burden.

Leonie, by contrast, seemed to walk on air. Rarely before had I seen her smile reach her eyes, and the difference in her appearance was startling. I sensed that pent-up words would overflow once we were alone.

The doctor took leave of us at the front steps, his manner distant and his bow brief.

When we entered the house, Leonie ran upstairs and I headed for my kitchen, but I expected her to seek me out very soon. I built up the banked fire and hung the full pot above it on a hook to reheat the tepid coffee. The doctor must rise very early these days in order to brew coffee before Mass and still have time to drink it. Then I stepped outside to tend the garden.

It was past noon and I was kneading bread dough when Leonie finally joined me. "I thought I would lie down for only a minute or two, but I fell asleep," she confessed. "We arrived home terribly late, and then I was too excited to sleep until nearly dawn."

"I seldom sleep well after these social events," I admitted. "But I thought the ball turned out rather well. The guests seemed to enjoy the refreshments, and the dance floor was always crowded."

I knew she did not wish to discuss generalities, but I felt too contrary to make it easy for her.

"Tell me honestly, Colette: Did I look as awkward as I felt last night? I so much wanted to be dignified and graceful, yet I felt like a gawky schoolgirl, all elbows and big feet."

I hope I concealed my shock. Never before had she admitted any possible flaw in herself. "You looked like a princess from a fairytale," I answered honestly.

She looked both delighted and doubtful. "You are kind to say so, but I know I am not beautiful."

This new, honest Leonie brought out my inner mother hen. "Well, Étienne is not handsome, yet the two of you together were splendid. I heard a trio of ladies talking about you at the punch bowl. They knew you must be Doctor Hilliard's daughter, but they could not identify the man at your side. I recall hearing the words 'magnificent' and 'devoted.'"

At this, I am certain she turned slightly pink with pleasure.

I covered the dough and left it to rise. If ever there was a time to delve into the history between Leonie and my brother, it was now, while Leonie wanted nothing more than to talk about him. "When did you and Étienne become particular friends?" I asked. "I remember your playing with the little boys at our house, but not Étienne."

A reminiscent smile spread over her face. "Once when I was about eight, Adrienne and I were playing with our kittens in the orchard; you know how we dressed them up like dolls when we played house. A group of big boys walked past on the road and saw us; Étienne was with them, but he kept in the back and didn't say anything. Verel Campion snatched my tiger kitten from Adrienne and said he would hang it. He made a noose out of string, and my kitten was squawking with fright and pain."

I remembered Verel, the innkeeper's son, a powerful boy with curly white-gold hair, a few years my junior. Before I married and left town, Étienne had fought his way into Verel's gang of toughs, to our mother's distress.

"I flew at Verel," Leonie said, "and he threw me down. And then Étienne knocked him to the ground. They pounded and kicked each other until they were bleeding, and finally Verel got up and ran off, and the others followed him. But Étienne stayed. His nose was bleeding, but he got the kitten down from a tree, and that one became his special kitten when we played from then on."

"Étienne played house with you?"

My incredulous tone widened her smile. "Not exactly. He started making up adventure stories for the kittens. Adrienne didn't like playing with Étienne because he wouldn't play husband and father for the babies. So eventually it was just the two of us. We spent hours creating our stories about *du Pays de Chaton.*"

"Kitten-land! Who invented this original name?"

"Étienne did. It was a kingdom located somewhere in South America, near the Andes Mountains."

This little tale revealed much to me about Étienne. I would never have guessed that the fighter of my family possessed such a chivalrous soul. And his friendship with Leonie and, by association, with her mother must have been instrumental in his transformation from surly brawler to industrious student and conscientious worker. Étienne's brief revelations about Madame Hilliard made more sense in this context.

That evening I left the house early, after preparing a stew that Leonie could easily reheat for her father. I took a sedan chair to the forge for a quick check-in with Adrienne. She was morose but seemed to be eating well. When I asked if she wished to see Leonie again, she looked tired at the prospect and sounded distinctly unenthusiastic. Suspecting it exhausted her to keep up the façade of happiness, I dropped the subject.

By the time I entered Maison Beau Temps, I felt as if I walked in a haze of exhaustion. Having no appetite, I climbed the stairs to my bedchamber, fell across my bed, and was instantly asleep.

Which was probably a good thing, for the following days would tax my endurance beyond anything I had known before.

CHAPTER 18

THURSDAY BEGAN LIKE any other day: morning Mass, weeding in the vegetable garden and arranging cut flowers for the house, marketing for fresh meat, an afternoon of cooking, and home. I waited around until the doctor returned, since Leonie seemed lonely. Her euphoria began to wear off, for she and Étienne were back to brief glimpses of each other and hasty greetings at church. I could hardly blame her for a bout of melancholy.

And being true to my role as domineering older sister, I collared Étienne in the salon that evening. "I meant to ask you last night about helping with our distribution in the *section* tomorrow. I know Leonie wants to go along, but I don't feel confident enough about being able to protect her by myself."

His eyes widened. "You shouldn't go there by yourself either, especially not tomorrow. I don't know exactly what is going on, but everyone else, including Claude, left the forge immediately after work."

"If no one else shows up at the forge tomorrow, then you can help me," I said in satisfaction. But then my brain started to process his full meaning, and I frowned. "I wonder if this has to do with the event Monday at Champ de Mars, the one I missed. Pascoe and Claude are involved, I'm sure."

As if on cue the front door opened and Claude entered. "Claude?" I called.

"Dans un moment," he shouted back, and ran up the front stairs. We heard him tramp back down, and he dashed into the salon, bright-eyed and eager. "Be ready for the call, Colette. I can't stay; important meetings to attend."

"What are you talking about? What call?" I jumped up and ran to grab him before he could escape without explanation.

"The call to arms, *bien sûr*. Tomorrow we depose the King at last."

I shook my head in confusion. "How will we do that?"

He frowned in irritation, gazing down at me from his vastly superior height. "Where is your head, Colette? We've talked of nothing else for weeks now. We march on the Tuileries tomorrow and demand the King's abdication. The Assembly does nothing, so now the People will act."

I remembered hearing such words many times during the past month or two, but I never thought it would come to action, particularly not action involving my young brother. "Claude, you will stay out of danger, won't you?"

He gave me a disbelieving stare. "Do you think I am a coward? Everyone will be there, Colette. Our entire *section*: men, women, and all children old enough to carry a weapon. The Commune says all men who possess pikes should be enlisted as National Guard; I intend to obtain a pike tonight. We've been making hundreds of them at the forge."

"What are you thinking?" I shouted. "You are seventeen years old, Claude Girardeau! I forbid you to carry a pike."

He laughed. "You should bring along your gun. I hear you've been seen carrying it around, so don't lecture me about a pike." He twisted his arm from my grasp and opened the front door. "You'll see. Tomorrow will change the course of history, and we will be there!"

I stood in the doorway and watched him mount his hired horse and ride away. As soon as he disappeared from view, I turned on Étienne for verification. *"Est-il vrai?"*

"Eh oui." His eyes were sad. "Colette, we cannot stop Claude from fighting here in the city or from joining the army to fight in the war. These are his choices to make."

Sometime in the early hours of morning, the tocsin rang throughout the city. The nearest bells to our house were in the chapel tower. Who rang them? Père Benedict? My half-conscious mind tried and failed to picture the gray-haired priest pulling the bell ropes.

The longer I lay there, the more awake I became. I tried to pray, but the best I could do was to hold my medals and ask the Virgin and Saint Sébastien to watch over those I loved most. In that hour of darkness a deep foreboding draped over my spirit. As a good Republican and *sans-culottes*, I should be excited about the King being deposed, but I was not.

When I rose not long after sunrise, Étienne was already awake and looking as worried as I was. We attended Mass but the Hilliards did not come. Neither did Minette and her children. Only three elderly people were there besides us and Père Benedict. I believe we all felt the bond of worshiping together along with the distance of uncertainty. Only the priest seemed fully at peace with the circumstances. He spoke a special blessing on those of our flock who faced dangers unknown, and I echoed every word in my soul.

"You could come with me today," I begged Étienne afterward, while we stood before the great iron-bound oak doors on the step outside. "If you were with us, Leonie could come to the distribution. It will be at Minette's again today."

"I need to go to the forge, take care of a few things, and find out what is happening. If no one else is there, I'll come to you." He squeezed my hand.

I nodded. "Please take care of yourself, Étienne."

His only reply was a nod. I watched him walk away and suddenly felt vulnerable. Not that danger swarmed in the streets. In actual fact, there were fewer people abroad than usual. I did see a squad of red-capped *sans-culottes*, bristling with pikes and marching north toward the river, but they were on a cross street and did not notice me.

I arrived at the doctor's house without incident and entered through the kitchen door as usual. The first thing I noticed was the *couvre feu* over the hearth fire. No coffee awaited my arrival. Although I had half-expected this, the reality of it struck me with dread. I climbed the back stairs and knocked at Leonie's door. "Mademoiselle?" I inquired. "Are you awake?"

"Colette?" I heard thumping feet on floorboards, and the door flew open. *"Oh, Dieu merci!* I feared you wouldn't come."

"Where is the doctor?"

"He left in the night when the tocsin rang. He told me to wait until you came," she said. "I've been huddled alone in my room all these hours, hardly sleeping." She looked very like her father, with dark smudges beneath her eyes and her wide mouth turned down at the corners.

"I'm here now, so come on down to the kitchen. I'll make tea. We have some time before I need to leave for the food distribution at Minette's house."

"May I come with you?"

"Not unless Étienne attends us, which he might do. Everything is in upheaval today."

She snatched up a wrap and followed me down the back stairs then and there, which spoke louder than words of her loneliness and fright. Her hair bushed in wild corkscrew curls about her face, and her feet were bare. I hadn't previously realized her hair was so curly, for she never left her room with it untamed, and she certainly never appeared in her nightdress. Looking so young and vulnerable, she plucked again at my maternal heart-string.

I built up the fire while she went to the larder for the peach cake I had baked the day before. Once the fire burned hot, I drew water from a barrel outside, strained it, and set it to boil. I opened the small windows and left the back door standing open to let in fresh morning air and birdsong. And a few flies, but this was unavoidable.

Just as I sat down at the worktable across from Leonie we both heard a sharp knock at the front door. "Who could it be?" I hurried up to the salon and peeked out the window. Claude glared at me from the steps, his chest heaving. My heart nearly choked me as I rushed to open the door. "Claude, what has happened? Is Pascoe ill?"

Claude scowled. "What are you doing here? Pascoe sent me to find you, and I've led a merry chase. Everyone is expecting you, and we'll miss everything if you don't hurry." He braced his forearm on the doorpost, puffing and sweaty.

I processed the fact that Pascoe was, in fact, safe and expecting me to be somewhere. Relief and nervous tension muddled my thoughts.

"Come inside. People are staring." I caught him by the arm and dragged him through the house and down to the deserted kitchen. Leonie must have heard his voice and escaped up the service stairs. "Sit down there and have some cake. Once the water is hot, I'll brew tea. Meanwhile, you can explain what you are talking about. What is going on?"

He was happy enough to drop into the chair and plow into the cake, though he kept shuffling his feet. "You must have heard the tocsin ring, Colette. I told you last night: Our people are gathered, and everyone is asking for you."

I checked the water; it was finally hot. I poured it over the tea leaves in the pot and watched them swirl. "I don't see why my presence is necessary. I attended the march back in June, and it was a catastrophe from beginning to end."

He stopped chewing cake to stare at me, brows high. "Are you serious?" Crumbs spewed across the tabletop. "Colette, we are removing the King from the throne! This is the day when the people say 'Enough' and make the Republic of France a reality!"

His words came almost verbatim from one of Pascoe's speeches; I no longer felt their power. "I cannot leave Leonie here alone." Although I would have left her while I did the food distribution, I realized.

"Bring her along. You've brought her to the *section* before; she knows our people. She needs to see democracy in action!" He shoved the last bite into his mouth.

"The last time I exposed Leonie to democracy in action was nearly disastrous. I'm sorry."

I first knew that Leonie had entered the room through the door behind me by the change in Claude's expression. He jumped to his feet and bowed. *"Bonjour,* Leonie."

"Bonjour, Claude." She gave him a brief smile before adjusting her face into earnest lines. "Colette is right: I cannot join you without my father's permission. But I am quite able to spend the day alone in this house. If your people are depending on you, Colette, then you must be there for them. Be sure to greet Minette and her children and Martin Danican for me."

"I'm certain the little children will not attend this event," I stated, then stood there debating with myself about the right thing to do. Pascoe expected me to support him. Leonie would be in no more danger alone in the house than she was before I arrived. And I had made a commitment to the women in our *section;* they counted on me to lead. "I shall come," I said with reluctance. "But I must return in time to fix supper."

Claude shrugged. "Are you sure you won't come, Leonie?"

"I promised faithfully not to attend another political demonstration," she said. "But thank you for the invitation."

At the door, I took her hand and gave her a level look. "Make sure you bolt the doors, front and back, when we are gone. I'll come here to the back door when I return, so be looking for me. Étienne might come here if he finds no one at the forge."

Her face brightened. "I'll watch for him. And if Papa returns home before you do, I'll explain."

My decision was made. I believed it was the right thing to do. Yet a knot in my gut made me wonder: Did a right choice even exist in this situation?

"Where is your fowling piece?" Claude asked before we set out. "You should bring it."

"It is very heavy, and I would never shoot it anyway."

"Then let me carry it."

"Ha ha! *Non.*"

His face settled into angry lines, and he strode rapidly away.

I trotted after him and tugged at his coattail. "If you walk so fast, I'll not be able to keep up."

"If we don't hurry, events might begin without us."

"We could hire a carriage." I glanced around but saw none on the street.

"If you see one, let me know." His voice wielded a sarcastic edge.

"Where is everyone?"

"Most of the working people in our *section* will be at the event; I told you already."

I couldn't recall his saying such a thing but didn't care enough to point it out. "I hope it isn't as crowded as last time," I puffed. "Is there anything more I should know?"

"This will be a huge event," Claude said. "The biggest yet, I expect. The National Guard is with us; most of them, anyway. Last night their commander, who was Royalist"—he spoke the word like an epithet—"was executed and replaced."

"Executed!" My stomach dropped. "Without a trial?"

"The People found him guilty and administered the penalty. Pétion, the mayor, is being held prisoner to keep him from interfering, though he is not a half-bad fellow. The *sections* of Paris have united to disband the Commune and to form an Insurrectionary Commune of our own. It is a revolution inside the Revolution."

"Who did all this?" I asked, though I already knew.

"The People! Pascoe was there last night, and Arnaud too, I think."

A blend of horror and pique sharpened my tongue. "I cannot believe you and Pascoe kept this from me!"

"We kept nothing from you. If you don't know, it's your own fault. I thought Leonie would join us. At first she talked about showing her father he doesn't know everything, but now she won't even think of disobeying him. She's probably listened to Étienne's preaching." He sounded disgruntled and more than slightly jealous.

"Étienne doesn't preach," I said.

"He won't take part in anything, Colette. I sometimes worry he is secretly Royalist, and I know he still attends Mass."

"Attending Mass does not make one a Royalist. I attend Mass." There. I said it.

"You do?" Claude gave me a look of sheer revulsion. *"Pourquoi?"*

"Because I want to." I couldn't put my reasons into words while trotting along the city streets beside my long-legged brother, but he seemed satisfied with my answer. "And I am Republican to the core. Étienne is no more a Royalist than you are."

He shrugged. "I hope you're right."

After entering through the open gates, we found our *section* people waiting impatiently where Claude had left them in a certain corner of the Place du Carrousel. Almost immediately I heard Saint-Jude Fillion's booming laugh. Arnaud loomed among the other smiths; his expression sent a cold chill down my spine.

La Florinda was there with several other women I didn't recognize; they all carried pikes or firearms. To my surprise, she approached Saint-Jude and touched him in a most familiar manner. His response informed me that his desolation over losing me had been fleeting. I felt more annoyance than jealousy; I had always known how it would be.

Pascoe was too busy giving direction and organizing the jumble of humanity to notice this moment of casual intimacy. Or had he noticed but chose not to acknowledge it? Was jealousy the cause of his increasing stress? Had that woman broken his heart? From the beginning I had feared such an outcome. As a soldier tends to die in battle, so a heartbreaker must, in his turn, suffer heartbreak.

A wave of protective anger flooded through me, and as soon as I saw an opening I doggedly approached *la Florinda* and tugged at her sleeve. "May I speak with you privately for a moment?"

Her eyes narrowed charmingly when she smiled. "I am at your service, madame. But privacy is in short supply."

Nevertheless, I led the way to the edge of our group and spun about, fists clenched. "I am deeply worried about Pascoe."

She studied my face. "For what reason, may I ask?"

"Have you jilted him for another man?"

"Non," she answered firmly. But I saw her lips twitch. "Did he not inform you that he and I are only friends?"

I blinked twice. "I did not believe him."

She looked at the sky, obviously repressing a smile. "I cannot blame you. Lying is his mother tongue; however, in this he told you truth. Now I know he also spoke truth when he described you to me as a meddler who believes she holds the fate of the world in her hands, a naïve romantic with no conception of reality."

"He said this?"

The smile spread across her face. "How easy it is to see clearly the flaws in others while blinding ourselves to our own! I understand your concern for your brother; Pascoe is visibly cracking under some invisible stress. However, I am not the cause of it. I confess I did entertain a brief fascination, for the little man is quite beautiful; but I am not one of his young innocents to be used and tossed aside. Friendship is all we ever shared." She chuckled in a patronizing, though not unkind, manner. "In his way, *ma petite,* he is as naïve as you are: A clever child playing at being a god."

I could only stand and stare. Her eyes softening, *la Florinda* patted my arm. *"Enfant,* to survive in this world one must think only of oneself. Trying to control other people or solve their problems will cause only heartbreak and disaster for you. Enjoy pleasure while you may and don't let sorrow crease your pretty brow any earlier than it must."

As she walked away to rejoin her friends, I realized she was much older than I first thought. Heavy cosmetics and illusory glamour both melted away in strong sunlight. She was also a perceptive woman with kind eyes.

Feeling strangely numb, I gathered up my small but devoted group of patriotic women, from thin Madame Danican to stout Madame Gallatin, who came despite her husband's absence, and all sizes, shapes, and ages between. Minette was missing; I hoped she was not waiting for me to assist with the food delivery. Few people would be likely to show up.

To my dismay, many of the women brought along their children. "We left our Marie-Honore to keep the little ones," Madame Danican told me, "but I thought the older lads would want to take part. This is a historic day." The smile of anticipation lighting her gaunt face gave me an uneasy twinge.

Martin evidently numbered among her "older lads." When I caught his eye, he left his brothers to inquire why Leonie had not come. "She was obliged to stay home today," I said, smiling at his evident disappointment.

Perhaps it would not have been a mistake to bring her. This event seemed more orderly than the march back in June. However, the number of weapons present was troubling, especially in the hands of boys no older than twelve. Any misfire would have tragic consequences in such a crowd. Martin carried no weapon, but I considered him in danger of being trampled, darting underfoot as he did. Leonie might have been able to keep him in hand, yet knowing she was safe in her home gave my wavering mind at least some peace.

I wondered if Claude would manage to obtain a pike.

The number of people gathered amazed me, and more arrived every minute. I later heard that citizens from the *sections* numbered near twenty thousand strong, with several hundred *fédérés* leading the way. Somewhere in the courtyard, the Marseillais belted out their thrilling song, and many Parisians joined in with gusto.

I saw Saint-Jude Fillion pushing his way through the throng, his eyes intent on me. *"Bonjour,* Colette," he said with a bright grin. The glaring sunlight and rising heat seemed to bother him not at all.

"What do you want?"

His grin faded and I felt rude.

"I came to suggest you keep the women to the rear of the group, for safety. We don't expect trouble, but with all these weapons . . ." He shrugged.

"Merci." I softened my tone. "I'll do my best to keep everyone out of harm's way."

His eyes searched my face for a moment. Then he touched his cap and jogged away to rejoin our group's leaders.

Pascoe's slight form nearly disappeared amid those hulking smiths, yet he moved like a lord among them. I could hear him shouting orders; to all appearances, he reveled in the position of command. Perhaps I had imagined his nervous tension? His attire was pristine from tilted hat to crisp jabot to creased trousers. By contrast, the smiths wore grimy neck cloths and open shirts. Philippe, one of Arnaud's smiths, wore no hat or shirt at all, and his broad face and hairy torso were already reddened by the sun. I did not see Claude, but Quent stood quietly on the outskirts of the group, apparently unarmed.

Groups of National Guard in uniform wandered amid our ranks, greeting fellow citizens and patriots with good cheer and joining in the singing. The overall mood was watchful yet positive, with a confidence no doubt based on the power of such vast numbers of participants.

Behind us lay the ancient Palais du Louvre. The long building to our left, nearest the river, must be the Pavillon de Flore, the section connecting the two palaces. It looked different from this side. With so many other pavilions and buildings and walls surrounding me, I wondered if I would be able to find my way back to the Jardin des Tuileries without help. This courtyard was immense, yet it became more crowded by the hour, and there was little shade. I cast about for a place to station my women out of the direct sun and out of danger from the weapons flashing about on every hand.

None of my companions seemed to mind the heat or the potential for danger, and they would not allow themselves to be herded away. *"Non, non,* madame!" protested Madame Danican. "We have an excellent view from here. Why should we move back?"

View? View of what? Following her gaze, I realized that the crowd focused its attention on the main steps of the palace, where a number of guards in red-jacketed uniforms stood in military order. These were Swiss Guards, I learned by listening, hired to protect and serve the King of France. Unlike the French National Guard in their familiar blue coats, these foreigners had an ominous appearance. But some of the *fédérés* stepped forward to talk to them, apparently inviting them to join us.

Realizing to my distress that Pascoe, Quent, Arnaud, Claude, and the other smiths had disappeared, I shepherded my group of women and a few boys to stand near a low wall which probably at one time enclosed gardens. The boys and some of the women stood atop the wall for a better view. "Our leaders are over there, near the front." One of the older

Danican boys pointed.

I scrambled up beside him but couldn't see my brothers. I did see large mortars or cannons or something of the sort between us and the steps, which was alarming. Short as I was, I felt too exposed up there on the wall and scrambled down. "I think we had better stay here." The other women agreed, mainly because the wall offered a better view of proceedings.

The tone at the palace steps became more combative. Curiosity put me back on top of the wall. There was some shoving, shouting, and what sounded like a gunshot; and a red-coated guard who had come forward to talk with the *fédérés* ran back up the steps to rejoin his comrades. The guards and *fédérés* were still calling back and forth, but all of us sensed rising tension. I exchanged worried glances with Madame Danican, who suddenly climbed down from the wall and reached up to tug at Martin's trouser leg.

In a sudden hush I heard a commander of the guards cry in clarion tones: "We shall all certainly die rather than abandon our posts without orders from the King."

There was a general outcry; pikes rose and sabers flashed, and the gathering of citizens seemed to flow forward like a tide of humanity. I could not see what happened at the steps, but we suddenly heard the crackle of gunfire. Smoke from discharging guns blossomed from the palace windows. The wave of *sans-culottes* struck this wall of resistance, broke as if into foam, and then surged back toward the gates, toward our position, shouting, *"Trahison! Trahison!"*

CHAPTER 19

THE WOMEN WITH ME screamed, and several leaped from the wall and ran before the oncoming flood, deaf to my shouts. A few huddled with me in a corner of the wall. Amid the wailing and the trampling feet, I dared to climb the wall once more and look for my brothers. To my horror, the Swiss Guards had followed the retreat in orderly pursuit and reached the cannons in the courtyard. Even as I watched, the first cannon belched flame.

I jumped from the wall amid the ongoing roar of cannon fire, lost my balance, and went to my knees. But even as I surged back upright and spread my arms to gather my charges and make a run for safety, something struck me from behind and knocked me flat. My head hit the pavement and I saw stars. Yet amid the deafening din I noticed small sounds—pings and dull thuds, sharp screams and brief moans—and the crushing weight of a body on my back, its heartbeat reverberating through me, its breath loud in my ear.

"Now get up and run," a gruff voice ordered. Then the weight lifted, shoes scraped on the graveled stone, and my attacker was gone.

I don't know how long I lay there nearly insensible, but when my brain began to think and my eyes could focus, I crept on hands and knees to a body lying near. It was Madame Danican, and she was staring fixedly at the sun overhead, dead. I closed her eyes. Martin lay just beyond her, collapsed against the shattered wall, blood covered. But he was alive; his uncomprehending gaze turned to me. I touched his chest, and my hand came away red with blood. I pulled off my fichu and wrapped it around his torso, but it immediately turned as dark red as his jacket. Shaking in every limb, I gathered him into my arms. I could barely stand, and his weight made me stagger.

Around me was chaos. I aimed for the gates and focused on taking one step at a time. The cannons stopped firing. People ran past me on either side, and I vaguely realized they were now running toward the Tuileries, not away. I believe I narrowly missed being accidentally impaled on a pike, which caught the brim of my bonnet and nearly ripped it from my head.

Martin moaned, and his hand rose to grasp at my chest and neck, but then it fell limp. I looked down and saw blood oozing from his open mouth. My bodice felt hot, and I knew it was not damp with sweat.

The commotion behind me sounded like the end of the world—I tried to close my mind to it and focus on walking, but the horror seeped in. None of the faces around me were familiar. Where were my brothers? Were they still alive? I stopped, trying to gain my bearings, saw trees and green, so headed that way. After a time I emerged into the Jardin des Tuileries.

The sunlight was unbearable; the world began to spin around me. Martin was completely limp now, and my arms ached. I staggered to a tree on a patch of sun-withered grass and dropped to my knees beneath it. As carefully as my stiff arms could manage, I laid Martin on the grass.

He was dead. I think he had been dead several minutes, but my mind wouldn't accept it until I saw the dull glaze of his eyes. Still in a fog, I gently closed them, straightened his legs, and crossed his hands over his shattered chest. Then I crossed myself and silently asked God to show him mercy. Never again would Martin sneak glances at Leonie or flash me the gap-toothed grin that transformed his face from homely to charming. I could not weep, for I seemed to have no emotion.

All around me were running feet and violent death, as revolutionaries chased down fleeing guards and palace servants, but I never looked up. I don't know how long I sat there before a crowd approached, most bearing pikes topped by objects I refused to acknowledge, and shouting, "Death to Traitors!"

A woman stopped to address me. "Is that your son? Are you injured?"

I dared not shake my head lest the spinning start again. *"Non.* His mother is dead." My voice sounded abnormally high. "She was my friend. A cannon killed them." I lifted my gaze enough to meet hers. She was wiry and weathered, with gray in her brown hair.

Scowling, she consigned the Swiss Guards to perdition with a few choice words then jerked a thumb upward. "This one'll be the death of no more children and mothers at least. I took his head off after my man killed him and stuck the heart on his pike." I followed her gesture upward and could not look away.

"You needn't fear anymore, *enfant,"* she said. "They're mostly dead now, the Swiss, and the traitors inside the palace are being rounded up as well. We're chasing the vermin down one at a time, if need be. The royal fool and the whore and her bastards ran and hid in the Assembly, so we're heading there now. Where are you from?" Her tone was friendly, even cheery.

"Faubourg Saint-Germain," I said, my voice faint, my mouth scarcely able to form the words. "My brother leads our *section."* I still could not look away from her trophy.

She nodded approval but then commented, "Eh, if the sight of this one gives you a turn, best not look around. There are worse things to see." She regarded her grisly prize. "A shame, really. Just a young fellow, he was. He should have stayed in Switzerland, or else chose the right side to fight for."

She suddenly looked after her distant companions and hefted her pike again. "I'll be on my way. A good day to you, *citoyenne!*"

I stared at the blood on the ground where her pike had rested. Slowly my gaze went to my gore-covered hands. And then I was up and leaning against the tree, retching as if everything inside me must escape. When the spasms finally passed, I wiped my face with my sleeve, collapsed on the far side of the tree, and lowered my throbbing head to my knees.

I could do nothing more for Martin. If his father still lived, I would tell him what happened to his wife and son.

The *sans-culottes* were headed toward the National Assembly, just a little way ahead. If the deputies attempted to defend the royal family, would their heads end up on pikes as well? I considered heading there, but in my current condition what good could I do?

I set my heart toward home.

I have no memory of crossing the river or traveling familiar streets. Anyone I encountered probably ran screaming in another direction. I went to the back door of the doctor's house and knocked, grateful for cool shade there at the base of the steps. But Leonie did not answer. I pounded harder then tried the door. It opened.

My kitchen was tidy, and the fire was banked. A note lay on my worktable, weighted by a pewter tankard. But I could not read it. Had it been written in print I might have puzzled out a word or two, but script was scribble to me. My brain was not wired for reading.

Holding the note in one hand and clutching my medals with the other, I sat down and prayed. I cannot explain how or why I sensed God's presence so clearly during this time of horror and fear, yet it was so. I felt I might almost have reached out and grasped the Shepherd's hand or leaned against Him.

Pascoe would have attributed this to the blow to my head, but I didn't care.

I also cannot explain why I put the note back under the tankard, closed up the house, and headed directly to the chapel. I walked there without thought, without doubt.

Its weathered door creaked as I stepped into the porch. By this time, my vision was diminished to a tunnel of light straight ahead and darkness all around, so it seemed natural that afternoon light streamed through the small rose window above the altar to rest on the bent heads of two kneeling worshipers. I recognized the shaggy mop of red hair. "Étienne?" I said, and my voice filled the nave.

They both turned. "Colette! *Dieu merci!* You are safe." Leonie sprang up and ran to me but stopped short to stare in horror. "Are you . . . Is that . . . ?"

Étienne strode past her and wrapped me in his embrace. I clung to his jacket, and I shook so violently that my legs would barely support me. I heard him speaking, his deep voice a rumble in my heart, and someone else replied. And then the world faded into a muddle of voices and lights.

My next clear memory is of Étienne in a chair beside my bed, eyes closed and long legs stretched out. But as soon as my hand brushed against the bedclothes, his eyes opened. "Ah, you're finally awake." He leaned forward and gently touched my arm. "I'll tell Leonie. Would you like to bathe?"

I didn't respond. Memories came flooding back, and I wanted to block them out.

Soon Leonie entered, followed by Étienne carrying a tub. I closed my eyes and drifted off again.

Someone touched my arm. "Colette, we filled a bath for you."

"I don't want a bath."

"But you are covered in blood." It was Leonie. "I'll help you wash your hair; the maids have brought up plenty of rinse water. I promise to be very careful of the swelling on your forehead."

If a bath would help me escape the smell and sight of Martin's blood, I would risk it. *"Merci,"* I said, and let her help me upright. My head felt as if it might break in half, but at least I had full range of vision again. Leonie and the maid Hortense helped me wash. The water turned pink then reddish brown as rinse water removed the dirty suds from my hair and skin. The last rinse they poured over me was scented with rose water. Shivering, I soaked up the sweet aroma, hoping to forget the stink of death and fear.

After I dried off and dressed, the maids carried away the used bath water. Leonie combed out my hair. "Why don't you let your hair grow longer?" she asked.

"It gets too heavy," I said. My voice was dull, and I spoke without knowing what I said. But somewhere in the fog of my tired brain I knew Leonie was doing what she could, trying to distract me. "When it reaches the middle of my back, I flip it over my head and cut off a length. I don't like to bother with it."

She walked around in front of me and sat on the edge of the bed. "When I was quite young, I enjoyed watching your family file into church. I kept track of you all by the redness of your hair and would mentally rearrange your order accordingly. I longed to have fiery hair so I could be a Girardeau."

I attempted a smile. I suspect the result was ghastly. Drawing a deep breath, I tried to force my voice into light, natural tones. "I always longed for golden hair or brown. Anything but red."

"Pourquoi? It is so beautiful!" She looked shocked, almost crushed.

Beautiful on me? Or did she have some other redhead in mind? I mentally shook myself, and this time the smile on my face was more sincere. "You would not think it so beautiful were you one of so many redheaded children in a large family."

"Do you still hate your hair?"

I paused to consider. *"Non,* I don't. I wonder why?"

"Will you let it grow long?"

"Peut-être." I opened my eyes to give her a look. "I'm glad you like the red. Perhaps you will have redheaded children of your own one day soon."

A flush of pink stained her cheeks, and her gaze shifted to the floor. I saw the wall of reserve rise and wondered if she would give me one of her set-downs. Instead, the wall lowered again and she sighed. "I suppose my feelings are quite obvious."

"Sometimes obvious can be better." I might have said more but my head ached too badly. Which was probably just as well.

I didn't want to eat, but to please Étienne and Leonie I managed to swallow some bread and cheese. I felt better for it and was well enough to sit on the balcony. With my damp hair braided down my back, I watched the sky change from rose to deep blue while Étienne and Leonie talked. They asked me about events of the day, but other than saying the blood on my gown—and hands, chest, face, neck, and hair—was Martin Danican's, I could not talk about it.

Leonie cried about Martin. I couldn't cry but I loved her for it.

All afternoon and evening the servants slipped out then brought back bits of news. Then Claude burst into the house shortly after dark, assuring us first of all of Pascoe's safety. He professed exhilaration over events of the day, but I thought he might be suffering shock nearly as much as I, for his eyes, feet, and hands were constantly moving. He was sunburned and overheated and so thirsty that he emptied every glass handed to him.

He let me hug him and exclaimed over my bruised face. "You look as if someone hit you in the face with a club, Colette. Does it hurt much?"

I don't remember if I said no or told him the truth, but it didn't really matter because he wasn't capable of listening just then. He needed to talk.

The Assembly deputies, he said, had retreated into the convent adjoining their meeting hall for safekeeping overnight. On the morrow they would meet with the leaders of the new Commune and come to agreement regarding future steps for the Republic.

"The Republic is now a reality," Claude kept repeating. "You needn't worry about your father, Leonie. He is a steadfast Republican and will not hesitate to support our progress. The traitors paid with their lives today, and Paris will soon be cleansed of its hidden evil."

On and on he ranted in the same vein, and I recognized pet phrases of Pascoe's mixed with Claude's questionable use of words and phrases. Much as I loved Pascoe, I did not like hearing Claude quote him so freely. And when he spoke admiringly of *la Florinda's* skill with a musket, I had heard enough and told him to go wash.

He stared at me in surprise. *"Pourquoi?"*

"You stink of blood and death," I said. "And fear and sorrow. If this is Revolution, I hate it. Madame Danican and Martin died today because I led them to stand in front of cannons. What was I thinking?"

"Saint-Jude Fillion and several others died too."

"Monsieur Fillion is dead?" I exclaimed.

"Enfin, maybe not dead yet, but he will be."

The news hurt more than I would have expected. "What happened to him?"

He shrugged, looking uncomfortable. "It looked like he got grapeshot in his back along with a saber in his belly. But all those deaths were the fault of the Swiss Guards, Colette, and ultimately the fault of the King. The guards paid with their lives, and the King will pay with his."

I put my hands on my swollen forehead. "And you think more killing will ease the pain, will end the evil? The guards who died today were brave and loyal men who believed they were doing right in following the King's orders."

"Obviously they were wrong," Claude said stiffly.

"What memories will torment you tonight, *petit frère?*" I asked quietly.

He stared straight at me, swore viciously, and ran from the salon. His feet pounded on the stairs and a door slammed.

I met the stone gaze of Apollo, safely atop his plinth. Someone had replaced his white loincloth with a red-white-and-blue-striped one, and a *sans-culottes* red cap adorned his marble curls. His hand extended to me as if in supplication.

The guards had thought they were doing the right thing today. So had Claude. So had I. What would the priest think of my choice?

What did God think?

I spread out my hands, palms up. The blood was still there. No one but God could see it, yet it was there. Not only the blood of my friends, but also that of my enemies—of the Swiss Guard whose head topped that woman's pike, of the commander who had bravely refused to abandon his duty. And they were but two of the many who died that day. I wanted to weep for them, but I had no tears.

Leonie and Étienne were quietly talking, and I knew she must have asked him if God approved of our Revolution. As I listened to Étienne's deep, deliberative voice, I realized he was very well read. He had obviously studied the *philosophes* in great depth.

In a pause, I said, "And to think, I always considered you the brawny, mindless brother."

Étienne looked at me. "I am sorry about Fillion. He was a good fellow."

"I am sad." I could say nothing more. What could be said?

Leonie sat stiffly on her chair and shivered, certainly not from cold, for the night was sweltering. "I left a note for Papa, but he has not yet seen it."

I reached over to squeeze her hand. "Your father will be safe at the convent tonight, *ma chère*. The *fédérés* won't dare to harm the elected representatives of the people of France."

"Can we be sure of anything?" she asked and suddenly hunched over. I put my arm around her, and she leaned into my shoulder. I felt her shaking with quiet sobs.

"Étienne," I said quietly. "Why is nothing in this world ever as we think it should be?"

He regarded me soberly, his thick eyebrows twitching slightly when he blinked. "I don't know. Perhaps because we don't understand the whole of the story."

"Why is our Revolution becoming evil? Is it because our leaders have rejected God?"

"Nothing is so simply explained, Colette. Particularly not war."

I wanted answers, but no one could give me any.

CHAPTER 20

I AWOKE TO A TAPPING at my chamber door and nearly rolled off the daybed where I had spent most of the night. It was far too hot to share my bed, and Leonie both snored and kicked.

Wrapped in a dressing gown, I opened the door to see the little maid Hortense looking apologetic. "Would you like a tray brought up, madame?"

"What time is it?"

"Nearly noon, madame. Your brothers rose early and went to work, but Monsieur Étienne told us to let you sleep. Are you well today, madame?" Her gaze drifted to my forehead.

"Well enough, *merci,* Hortense." My head still throbbed. "Actually, coffee and perhaps fruit and bread would be appreciated."

"*Très bien,* madame. And may I say that we are all so very glad you are safe, and the young masters as well." Her broad, freckled face held genuine relief.

I gave her a faint smile. "As am I. Now if only Pascoe will return to us." And the doctor. But Hortense wouldn't care about him.

I dressed myself while waiting for her return with the tray. Leonie stirred and snorted but still slumbered peacefully, now sprawled across the bed. I did not envy her future husband his battles for sleeping space.

For nearly an hour I drifted about the house, wishing for something to do. This waiting around was horrible. I thought wistfully of my withering garden but knew better than to go out alone in my current condition.

I heard a horse in the drive and hurried to the front door, braced for bad news. It was Claude. "He is asking for you, Colette. You need to come."

Despite the oppressive heat, I shuddered. My lips would barely form the word: "Pascoe?"

"Pascoe is busy at meetings. You're the person he wants. If you won't come, I'll think the worse of you, that's sure. I know you don't care for him like he does for you, but you could show a little compassion."

My befuddled brain slowly grasped that he spoke of Saint-Jude Fillion. "Where is he?"

"At his place. Monsieur Lamorges brought him home. He has no family in the City besides us. *Dépêchez-vous!*"

I was already gathering my parasol and slipping into my sabots. "How are we to get there?"

"Oh." He blinked. *"Heu,* I'll go hire a cabriolet or a chair for you. Unless you want to ride double?"

"I do not."

I soon discovered that Fillion's "place" was a room shared with the two other smiths in an old building near the forge. Claude led me up the dark staircase and knocked at the door. The entire building stank of mildew and refuse, but when Hérault opened the door and beckoned us to enter, a nauseating concentration of stench nearly knocked me backward. I gasped and braced myself, trying to focus on my mission.

It is surprising how quickly a smell can lose its power to offend. I'm not sure Hérault even noticed my hesitation before I stepped into the room. His face and head were blistered with sunburn, and he limped visibly. "Are you injured too?" I asked.

"Nothing to signify," he said gruffly.

Saint-Jude lay on his pallet along the far wall. His eyes were closed, so I knelt quietly on the floor beside him. A thin coverlet spread over his shivering body, which seemed strangely small and wasted; he had always been such a solid, muscular man, more alive than most people. Without his impudent grin, his face looked very young despite a heavy growth of whiskers. "Saint-Jude?" I said softly.

His eyelids fluttered and his lips moved. I smoothed the lines forming on his forehead then found his hand and held it. "I'm here. Colette. Claude told me you wished to see me."

Slowly he dragged himself into consciousness. When his eyes focused on my face, I saw a light come into them. "You came," he rasped painfully.

"I am so sorry you were injured," I said, and my voice cracked. I turned to Hérault. "Has a doctor seen him?"

Hérault shook his head. "It's no use."

I believed him. "A priest then? Claude, go get Père Benedict at Chapelle de Saint-Germain."

My brother nodded and disappeared. I heard his feet thunder on the rickety steps.

Saint-Jude's great dark eyes studied my swollen, scraped face. Again he rallied himself to speak. "Your face . . . I'm sorry . . . I was afraid . . . the cannon."

My thoughts flew in circles before alighting on the truth. "Did you knock me down when the cannon fired?"

"*Oui.*"

"And that is how you were injured?" The words could barely emerge from my tight throat. The blood in my hair—had it been his?

"Cannon didn't stop me. I saw Pascoe—" He grimaced, squeezed his eyes shut, and took several shallow breaths.

"You saved my life, Saint-Jude." Suddenly my tears overflowed. I don't know why they came at that particular moment after all the traumatic events of the past day, but the relief of weeping was enormous. I sobbed over Saint-Jude Fillion, the rejected suitor who had saved my pathetic life.

He seemed gratified by my sorrow; a little smile curled his lips. "I was saving up . . . ask you to marry me . . . Stupid, I know."

Which only made me feel worse, for I would have refused him and couldn't say otherwise.

"You'll be pretty again," he said and tried to laugh. But the effort made him cough, and the cough made him cry out and writhe in pain.

And I wept harder than ever.

Claude finally returned with Père Benedict, but Saint-Jude did not want me to leave him. "I'll stay close," I promised, and kissed his cheek. Surprise brightened his gray face.

Claude, Hérault, and I waited across the room while the priest gave Saint-Jude his last rites. "Good idea, bringing the priest," Hérault said to Claude. "He can't last much longer. I don't know how he is alive at all. If you could see . . ." He glanced at me and let the sentence trail off. "So he ran in front of the cannon to push you out of the way?" he asked.

I nodded, still sniffling. "The people around me were killed. I would have been killed if I'd been standing."

Hérault considered this. "Fillion's got some grapeshot in his back, but that wouldn't have killed him. So don't start thinking he died in your place. He was running around afterward, took a ball in his shoulder, and then got a saber through his gut. I saw it." His face wore an expression of concentration, as if he considered whether or not to say more.

"He's got courage," Claude said, gazing at his dying friend with awe.

We could hear Père Benedict speaking softly and Saint-Jude struggling to answer. I crossed myself and begged God's mercy on the poor brave boy.

Père Benedict turned and beckoned to me. I hurried to kneel beside him, took Saint-Jude's cold hand in mine, and pressed it to my cheek. His glassy eyes slowly focused on me. "Colette."

"Saint-Jude," I said. "Thank you for saving my life. Thank you for caring so much. I'm not worthy, but I promise to honor your gift always." I kissed his big, dirty, blood-stained hand, and then I kissed his lips.

He smiled and closed his eyes. His breathing was raspy and labored.

I looked at the priest. "He will not wake again, I think," said Père Benedict. "Until he awakens in God's presence." He gently laid one hand on Saint-Jude's forehead in blessing, then rose with a great crackling of joints. At this, he met my gaze with a small, self-deprecating smile. "I told him to look for me at heaven's gate. I'll join him there before long."

For the first time in my life I sensed how very near to me eternity was. From one breath to the next, one heartbeat, one thought, one step. Saint-Jude would very soon take that step.

"You are certain he will enter God's presence?" I asked.

"More to the point, the young man appeared certain. He accepted God's mercy with a grateful heart." The priest's faded eyes studied my face. "He risked his life to save yours?" he asked.

"He did. *Père*, I made a poor choice. I—"

"Did you? Then you must trust God with the results. Also, you must trust that He spared your life for good purpose." He turned to Hérault. "When he passes, contact me, and I shall request a place for your friend in the cemetery at Église Saint-Jacques-du-Haut-Pas."

And he took his leave. I felt corrected and blessed and very confused.

Once the door closed behind him, Hérault and Claude looked to me as if for direction. "Père Benedict does not believe he will awaken again." My head throbbed, and my knees felt rubbery. "I need to check on

Adrienne while I am here."

"You won't stay until . . . ?" Hérault asked hopefully.

"I cannot." I pressed my fingers into my eyes and felt the puffy flesh of my grazed right cheek. "I must go home." Then I lifted my head. "But I must first check on Adrienne."

"I must return to work," Claude said. "Can you get yourself a ride home?"

I said I could, so he returned to the forge while I knocked and entered the little house, calling, "Adrienne?"

She set aside her broom and hurried to greet me. "You came to see me! Arnaud thought you would not." Then she got a good look at my face and cried, "What happened to you? *Pauvre chérie!* You look terrible! Come and sit down. I'll make tea."

So I told her the story while she bustled about and tried to pamper me with tea and honey cakes. "Arnaud told me Pascoe was worried because you disappeared, but then Saint-Jude told them he saw you leave the courtyard with a wounded child in your arms," she said.

"So Pascoe is safe?" I asked just to make certain.

"Mais oui. Arnaud thought he was wounded, for he could not find him after the battle and someone said they saw him carried away. But then Pascoe stopped by early this morning to speak with Arnaud and seemed surprised by the rumors."

I blinked rapidly in a wave of relief. Why had Claude said nothing of this? Most likely to avoid distressing me.

Adrienne spoke with more animation than I had seen in her for many weeks. "I knew Saint-Jude was badly hurt, but to think that he saved your life! Everyone in the *section* knew how he admired you. Minette and I often talked about you two. But then nothing came of it, and we could not imagine why." She gave me a look that demanded answers as she set two cups on the table and sat down across from me.

"He seemed like one of my little brothers to me," I said, knowing it sounded lame. Her expression verified this, so I tried again. "His interest was flattering, but he was presumptuous and interfering. I saw no point in encouraging a man I would never wish to marry. And at the time I did not know he had marriage in mind."

She sipped her tea and gazed across the room. "Always so practical. Have you no passion in your soul?"

"My small taste of passion left only bitterness behind."

"I would rather know passionate romance and live with the loss of it than never experience love at all."

I noticed that one hand caressed her belly, and my heart gave a twinge. She seemed devoted even yet to her baby's father, which saddened me, for the man was obviously unworthy of such loyalty. My one attempt at romance had been entirely selfish. Though at the time I had thought myself in love, I now saw my motivation with greater clarity.

"One can experience love without romance," I said. She met my gaze, and I saw in her eyes when she understood my meaning.

"I am grateful for Arnaud's love," she admitted. "But he is so jealous and suspicious. Sometimes he pushes me to tell him my secret."

She did not need to explain further. Telling Arnaud the identity of her baby's father would cause more harm than good. He was a man likely to think his duty lay in avenging his wronged wife.

When I said nothing, Adrienne pressed both hands into her sides and winced slightly. "Do you think the baby might come early?"

I rose and knelt to check her puffy feet and ankles. "When your feet swell up like this, you need to prop them up." I pulled my chair closer and helped her lift her feet to its seat.

"They look like old-woman feet," she complained. "And my skin is all stretched and ugly."

"Never fear; you'll soon be slim again."

When I gently palpated her sides, the baby kicked and moved away. The active life beneath my hands gave me joy, almost as if the infant were mine. Memories of my own pregnancy were both bitter and dear, and I thought Adrienne's words about lost love were greater in meaning than she knew. I loved my lost baby girl more as time passed and her true value became ever clearer to me. I would not give up my memories of her no matter how much they hurt.

I thought of Saint-Jude, so soon to leave this life, and wondered if his mother still lived. Would her son's death break her heart? Would she hold a faded memento to her bosom and picture his face, from birth to adulthood, and weep for a remembered love?

What joys and sorrows would Adrienne's child bring to this young mother?

As never before I treasured the precious, fleeting thing that was life, a gift so often stolen, wasted, or thoughtlessly thrown away.

"Dear baby," I said to Adrienne's belly. "Stay safely inside your maman until you are ready to live in this big, frightening world."

"Don't tell him that! I'm ready for him to come out," she said, teasing yet partly serious.

I sat back on my heels and looked at the little mother, hardly more than a child herself. "Are you nineteen yet, Adrienne?"

"In December I will be," she said proudly, deepening my impression of her youth, for only the young and the very old take pride in an added year. Neither she nor Leonie was young enough to be my daughter, yet the responsibility I felt toward them both fostered a motherly affection in my heart.

I rose and dropped a kiss on Adrienne's sweaty forehead. "Keep drinking plenty of milk, *ma chère*, and don't forget to prop up your feet."

Arnaud saw me leave the house. "Wait, Colette." I paused as he approached. "How is she?" he asked.

"Other than swollen feet, she seems well enough. *Pourquoi?* Is anything wrong?"

When he scowled, his swarthy face seemed to darken. "Only that she was crying again this morning. Something is hurting her, but she is afraid to tell me." His great fists clenched, and muscles tightened in his thick neck and jaw.

Intimidated, I took a step back. "Women are often emotional during pregnancy," I said. "If you wish to ask another midwife's opinion of her condition, I will not be offended."

He slumped, all the fight gone from him. *"Non,* that is not what I want." He rubbed a sooty hand over his face and left streaks in the sweat. "I want her to be well and happy." He gave me a slanting look. "You saw Fillion?"

"I did. He is man of great courage."

Arnaud sniffed and wiped his nose on his sleeve. "He did good work in the forge when he paid attention. He loved you, Colette. But you didn't love him. At least I have Adrienne for my wife, even if she never loves me."

It was a good thing Claude and Étienne emerged from the forge just then, finished with their labors for the day, for I do not think my heart could have taken any more pain just then. It began to feel numb. Claude needed to return his horse to the livery stable, but Étienne took one look at me and said he would hire a carriage.

I remember nothing else until I walked into our house, and into Pascoe's embrace. While the younger brothers went upstairs, I put the good side of my face against Pascoe's strong shoulder and wanted to rest there forever.

But he held me away, raised a brow, and said, "You resemble a gargoyle, *chérie.* I have never before seen an eye so red or a forehead so purple. Whatever you have done to your face, I disapprove."

I tried to laugh, but it sounded more like a sob. "I am relieved to see you alive and whole!"

"What else would I be?"

I looked into my brother's eyes but saw only my own questions reflected. How could he be uncertain of my love? He was the one who demanded and was never satisfied.

"Saint-Jude Fillion is dying," I said. "He saved my life yesterday."

"So I heard. I owe him a debt I can never repay. His loss is a sad blow; he was a fierce fighter and a faithful ally. And you have lost your faithful swain."

I sighed, turned, and led him by the hand into our salon. "To me, he was a friend and nothing more. I am tired of feeling I must apologize for failing to return his regard."

"Then I shall not mention him again."

I pulled Pascoe down beside me on the chaise longue. "I am tired nearly to death, and I need a shoulder to lean on."

He obligingly put his arm around me and provided the shoulder. "Does your face hurt?"

"What do you think?" I mumbled.

He chuckled softly and rested his cheek on my hair. "Your hair smells sweet."

And then I was asleep.

Although my opinion of her culinary skills was not the highest, I did feel sympathy for our cook, who never knew from one day to the next how many people she would be expected to feed. On that night, everyone was home, including Pascoe's valet, plus Leonie.

The cook herself entered the salon to announce to our gathering that dinner would be delayed, for she was obliged to add a few dishes to the menu to accommodate our numbers.

As soon as she departed, Pascoe, standing before the cold hearth, made a rude remark. I saw Leonie's eyes widen and wanted to smack him. "You hired the woman," I reminded him.

"Quite true. Our cook is a rare gem." He smiled at Leonie, a most charming smile. "Don't mind my language, mademoiselle. Everyone knows that I am a reprobate."

Leonie had no idea how to respond, so I said, "And if they do not know, you are certain to boast of your degeneracy while being introduced."

He glared. "Shrew."

"Wolf," I snapped.

His lip curled in a sneer. "Toad."

I smiled a superior smile. "I like toads. You are a slug."

At that, he laughed. "Bane of your garden."

Poor Leonie observed this exchange with dismayed incomprehension. Recalling that she had no brothers, no siblings at all, I felt a pang of pity. Silently I wished Étienne luck in developing her somewhat atrophied sense of humor.

The evening was bright and hot, as the day had been. There wasn't room for everyone to sit on the small balcony, so we scattered about the salon, hoping for a breeze from the open doors. Leonie shared a chaise longue with me, and Étienne sat near enough to her for the two of them to talk quietly without everyone else overhearing. Claude appeared to have dozed off in the other chaise longue.

Pascoe poured himself a glass of wine from the decanter on the side table and reclined gracefully in an armchair near the hearth. The gilded clock on the mantel above his head ticked away the time. "You will all be pleased to learn that France's King is no more." His voice carried throughout the room and seemed to echo off the high ceiling.

Leonie clapped her hand over her mouth. Étienne and Claude both sat upright. "What? Is he dead?" I blurted out the question everyone must have been thinking.

Smiling with gratification over our reactions, Pascoe took a sip of wine. "Today our hard-working and patriotic Assembly members voted to overturn all of the King's vetoes and suspend him from all of his functions. Until further notice, the man now known as Louis Capet and his relations will dwell under guard at the Temple. Other measures were taken today to improve government function, but none of you will care to hear those details."

I disliked the thread of irony in his voice. What could he find amusing about these events? Pascoe in this mood was a stranger to me, a person I neither understood nor liked. Nearly every word he spoke made me cringe inwardly, imagining its effect on Leonie.

"I'm sure we are all relieved to know that power has been transferred without further bloodshed," I said, doing my best to keep my voice level, "but yesterday was a tragedy. A disaster! Had I known there would be fighting, I would have taken our women and children out of that court-yard."

Pascoe held his wineglass up and swirled its contents, admiring the way the burgundy clung to the glass. After taking an appreciative sip, he said, "That would have been a mistake, for the women were among our fiercest fighters." He gave me a brief but pointed look. "Your lack of patriotic spirit is disappointing, Colette. Claude acquitted himself well; I saw him dispatch two guards, and I'm sure he was hard at work when my attention was elsewhere."

Sudden wrath filled me. "If your idea of patriotic spirit means using my enemy's head as a trophy, then I want none of it! Our people behaved like savages, like ravening beasts!"

Claude stared down at his feet. "This is war," he muttered. "Women don't understand war."

"The women of Paris do," Pascoe corrected him. "Colette was un-prepared for battle, but she will do better next time. Once their fighting blood is aroused, women are the most terrifying warriors of all."

Thinking of the warrior woman I had encountered in the Tuileries garden, I fell silent.

"Monsieur Pascoe," Leonie said abruptly. "Can you tell me when my father is likely to return home? Are the deputies still at the Assembly

Hall?"

"I really couldn't—" He broke off, for at that moment the door opened and a maid ushered Doctor Hilliard into the salon.

CHAPTER 21

LEONIE AND I BOTH turned at once to see the doctor standing behind the chaise longue. She sprang up with a cry and rushed to embrace him. I followed more sedately, feeling as if my chest might burst. The doctor looked at me over Leonie's shoulder; his eyes widened then narrowed at sight of my face, and a line appeared between his brows.

All the while, Pascoe was loudly vowing further revenge for the patriots who perished at the hands of the Swiss Guard, traitors that dared to fire upon the people of France. He was aware of the doctor's entrance, yet he offered no acknowledgement.

When he paused for breath, Étienne said, "I mourn the loss of our citizens, yet I also sorrow over the violent deaths of the Swiss Guards and the palace servants who served faithfully, hopelessly, to the end. They, too, deserved better at the hands of their people."

Sensing impending disaster, I faced my brothers just as Pascoe lashed back: "How dare you voice sympathy for the enemy's mercenaries and lackeys? All these months I have tolerated your lack of enthusiasm for the Republic, but if you do not develop some true patriotism, or at least learn to keep your mouth shut, I cannot promise to protect you from coming storms of change."

"He is right, Étienne," Claude said, sounding both belligerent and worried. "You must have heard the ugly talk around the forge. Our smiths like and respect you, but other *sans-culottes* question me about you. People are starting to say that anyone who isn't with us must be against us."

"They are wrong," Étienne said. "But I will watch my tongue more closely in future."

A soft answer turns away wrath. Père Benedict had given a homily on that scriptural saying just the week before. Was Étienne remembering as well?

Étienne rose and came to greet the doctor. "Monsieur, I am relieved to see you safe and well," he said in his quiet way.

"I cannot thank you and Madame DeMer enough for taking my daughter into your home while I was detained," the doctor said.

"I'll go upstairs and gather my things," Leonie said. "I'll be only a moment, Papa."

Étienne, the doctor, and I followed her to the entry hall and waited while she ran upstairs. "Will you and Leonie dine with us tonight, monsieur?" I asked. "I fear she will be hungry, and there is little food in your kitchen. I hope you will water the garden, for it must be withered by now. I have worried about it all day."

He bowed slightly. "Then I shall take care to attend its needs."

I felt silly, although there was no hint of ridicule in his voice.

He continued: "I thank you for your concern as well as for the invitation to dine, madame, but we must decline. I'm sure we can manage until tomorrow morning. That is . . ." Again he scanned my swollen eye, always the doctor. "May I examine your injury?"

I glanced at Étienne then nodded.

Doctor Hilliard's touch was gentle, his expression impassive as he pulled my eyelids wide. I had to tip my head way back, and Étienne, at the doctor's instruction, held a lamp to shine directly into my eyes. When the doctor asked about my eyesight, I told him of the tunnel vision and floating spots.

"Did you ever lose consciousness?" he asked.

"*Oui,* briefly."

He gave me a direct look. "What happened?"

I told my tale, from the palace courtyard to the chapel, giving only basic facts. My voice felt thick and heavy, and I could not look at him while I spoke.

"Have you lost consciousness since?"

"She walked here from the church," Étienne said, "but she seemed dazed and could not talk."

"*Oui,* everything was muddled," I added, "all flashing lights and throbbing pain and voices talking, with brief glimpses of my surroundings."

With his long fingers the doctor carefully probed the swelling of my forehead and cheekbone. "Tell me if anything particularly hurts," he said, so I did, watching his face the whole time.

"Badly swollen and bruised, but there are no broken bones. I will prescribe mild powders for the pain, and you must avoid exertion for a time. The scrape on your cheek here was also from impact on the courtyard stones?" he asked, indicating the tender area without touching it.

I nodded. "It is very sore."

"There appears to be gravel embedded in the abrasion." His gaze briefly met mine. "I will clean it for you in the morning, if you wish. My implements are at the house, and the lighting should be good."

"Will you have time, monsieur?"

"*Mais bien sûr!*" He looked affronted at the question.

"You must realize that I failed in my duty," I persisted. "Étienne, not I, was faithful in protecting Leonie from possible harm."

The doctor turned to Étienne. "Again, I am indebted to you, Monsieur Girardeau." But his inscrutable gaze returned to me while Leonie clattered down the stairs with a small bundle in her arms, and he said, "Until morning, madame."

Dinner that evening was a tense affair, and I did a lot of rearranging the food on my plate. Claude was sullen and kept glaring at Étienne. Pascoe seemed to find satisfaction in making grim predictions about the days to come. "You must understand," he said, aiming a pointed glance at me, "that recent measures taken are only the first steps. Not only do France's neighboring countries threaten us with destruction, but we also suffer further threats from within. The prisons of Paris are currently packed to overflowing with dangerous criminals and traitors, every one of which places our citizens in peril."

"How can they place citizens in peril while they are locked away?" I asked.

He chewed and swallowed, frowning. "If a few organized traitors were to break into those prisons and release the inmates, the resulting carnage would be unprecedented," he said. "Defenseless women and children slaughtered in their homes."

Étienne and I exchanged glances but refrained from further comment. I didn't want to think about Pascoe's warnings. I didn't want to think about anything. As soon as I could gracefully excuse myself, I pleaded a headache, which was certainly true enough, and retreated upstairs.

A terrible weight inside my chest prevented me from sleeping, and I tossed for hours, remembering snippets of conversation, remembering voices and facial expressions.

No amount of regret could change what I had done. Nothing could bring back Saint-Jude, Madame Danican, or Martin. Nevertheless, I determined that as soon as life settled back into its usual routine, I would talk with the women of our *section* about returning civility, honor, and decency to our revolution. For the good of our children, our future, we must not allow the evils of fear and retribution to overcome France.

The streets were quiet as Étienne and I left the house the next morning; peaceful, as if nothing ever ailed this city or ever would. Birds chirped, dogs barked, and a blue sky arched above the elegant buildings surrounding us. Perhaps all would turn out well, I thought. Sometimes people shock themselves with extreme behavior and learn their own weakness. Good always wins over evil in the end. People don't want to live in a world of death and revenge.

Do they?

I noticed that attendance at Sunday Mass had dropped. On that August morning, fewer than twenty people dotted the chapel's benches. Among them were Minette LaVie and her children; Doctor Hilliard and Leonie sat near us. I caught Leonie glancing at my brother several times during the service. Her father seemed focused on the sermon and the prayers.

The priest's gentle voice brought Saint-Jude Fillion to mind; I wondered if he had survived the night. From there my thoughts drifted to my attempts to do right, which had ended so badly. Père Benedict said I now must trust the results of my choices in God's hands. What did that mean?

Pascoe was right, I thought: Religion was all foolishness, or at best a pathetic attempt to make human life mean something when in truth we are no better than animals. A mature adult needed no imaginary friend produced by a blow to the head.

Yet I knew that I had not imagined God's presence. Reason could not erase Him from my consciousness.

After the service ended and Étienne headed toward the forge, I felt a strong premonition of impermanence. This pattern of walking home from Mass with the Hilliards would soon end. My main source of happiness, the thing to which I clung despite Pascoe's disapproval, was a transient chapter in my life.

"We watered your garden last night," Doctor Hilliard said. "It was rather wilted, I fear, and some of the marrows rotted on the vine."

"There are also peaches rotting on the ground beneath the trees," Leonie added. "And plenty of weeds to pull."

"I'm sure we can soon set things to rights," I said. "Thank you for remembering."

"Appetite is a strong incentive. I do like to eat well," the doctor said.

I chuckled, and Leonie gave me a startled look. Did she not understand her father's dry humor? Perhaps her essentially hostile view of her father prevented her from recognizing his good qualities.

At the house I made directly for my kitchen, where the aroma of coffee greeted me. It was still hot, so I poured a cup and set it on the table. A moment later Doctor Hilliard entered, carrying a leather case.

I faced him, gripping the edge of the table with both hands. "Monsieur, I told you last night that I was at the Palais des Tuileries when it was attacked." My voice cracked. "I should have stayed here with Leonie."

His gaze was steady and somehow bracing. "I understand that you carried out what you believed to be your duty."

"But you are angry." How I knew this, I cannot say.

"You placed yourself in the way of cannon fire." His voice held an ironic edge.

In that moment I clearly saw the madness of leading unarmed women and children to stand amid a revolutionary mob as it threatened a dedicated military unit. Yet I looked the doctor in the eye and flashed back with: "I warned you not to trust in my discretion."

After only a breath he retorted sharply, "Then more the fool, I; for I shall do so again."

My mind darted from thought to thought. Whatever did he mean? Not until I saw his lips twitch did the tightness in my stomach relax. At least I could understand that his anger would not end our friendship.

We heard approaching footsteps.

"If I may clean that abrasion now, madame?" He approached the table.

"Shall I sit down?"

"*S'il vous plaît.*" He opened the case and withdrew a few shiny implements. I tried not to look.

Leonie entered, glanced back and forth between us, then poured herself some coffee. She sat opposite me and frowned. "Are you feeling well, Colette? Your face is flushed."

I tried to smile. "I have felt better."

"I shouldn't think it will hurt so very much," she said.

"Will you open the door, Leonie?" the doctor requested. "For additional light."

While she complied, I picked up my coffee and took a few sips. The doctor approached and drew a chair up beside my bench. "This might sting, but it will be easier if you relax your face." I did my best. He used a small, sharp instrument to pick tiny stones from the inflamed flesh over my cheekbone. I closed my eyes and focused on the sound of his steady breathing.

"*Fini,*" he said at last. "Now some witch hazel to aid healing."

"Do you miss having a medical practice?" I asked as he gently dabbed the ointment on my raw skin.

"At times. I do frequently treat my colleagues, and they repay me with legal aid or whatever may be their specialty." Two horizontal lines marked his forehead, a sign of concentration. His wig was crooked again, showing the dark stubble of hair beneath. It suddenly irritated me.

"Why do you wear a wig, monsieur?" I asked. "They are long out of style, you know."

Leonie spluttered and started coughing.

The doctor blinked. *"Eh bien, alors!"* He glanced toward Leonie, then at the floor. "My wife always liked a wig. I suppose it became a habit." He tugged it forward to cover his hairline just as the hall clock chimed.

"I must be off." He scrambled to his feet. "Keep that abrasion clean, madame, and please be more careful in future."

He picked up his bag and slipped out the door before I could say more than a hasty *"Merci."*

Leonie met my gaze and smirked. "I've told him the same thing about the wig, but he never listens. Perhaps with our combined dis-approval, he might reconsider."

"What is your burden today, *ma fille?"* the priest asked before I was settled in the confessional booth.

After several days of thinking about the Tuileries disaster, Pascoe's explanations, and Père Benedict's comments at Saint-Jude's bedside, I was more confused and angry than ever. Pascoe had subjected me to the writings of myriad philosophers during our youth, but much of that knowledge had faded from disuse, and the little I did remember offered only a sense of purposeless emptiness.

That morning I had stood in a cluttered cemetery with Étienne, the other smiths, and a handful of other people to watch as a pine box containing Saint-Jude Fillion's body was lowered with ropes into a grave. Père Benedict spoke a few words about Christ being "the Resurrection and the Life."

I laid a sheaf of lilies atop the grave and wondered about my friend. If Saint-Jude was now with God, where was that? Could he see me standing beside his grave? If not, would God let him know that my heart ached over his loss with more sincere affection than I felt for him during his life? How could a woman not think with a touch of romantic fondness of a man who risked his life to save hers?

Yet now I asked none of these questions of the priest. Instead I asked the greater question in the forefront of my disordered thoughts. "Where was God?" I demanded, my voice tight and low. "All those people dying in terror and agony . . . Why did He not stop it?"

"God was there, gathering His children to His heart, and weeping over those who choose hatred and vengeance over His mercy and grace."

"But if He is all-powerful, as you say, why doesn't He stop the evil?"

Père Benedict, for I knew it was he, explained to me that although God is ultimately sovereign, He endowed mankind, the being created in His image, with the freedom of choice. I listened intently, but it was too much to comprehend just then. I walked away from the church that afternoon pondering one short sentence: "True love is a choice."

I was free to choose to return God's love or not. It seemed simple, and yet that choice was the most important of my life. Every other choice in my life reflected either forward or back to it.

I might have chosen to love Saint-Jude Fillion, and I now knew that he had hoped to marry me. How I regretted humiliating him with my silly threats! For he chose to love me and to risk his life in saving mine. And somehow God had used Saint-Jude's courageous choice to further His own plan to spare my life, or so Père Benedict claimed.

My head whirled from trying to understand so many vast concepts. After wandering several minutes without conscious thought, I found myself standing before the doctor's house. Leonie would not expect me to come; it was my day off. But surely no one would object if I worked in my flower garden for an hour or two.

Or I could make a choice to spend my day off with someone who needed me more than I needed my flowers. Better still, I could share the flowers with someone alive who could enjoy them.

So I carried another sheaf of lilies and a basket of fruit to Adrienne and spent the afternoon making her feel loved. This is one choice I look back on with no regrets.

CHAPTER 22

THE FOLLOWING afternoon brought more unwelcome change.

Tensions in Paris had risen even higher since the royal family's arrest and incarceration in the Temple. France's military suffered multiple losses against the superior forces of Austria and Prussia, causing distrust of the military leadership and a rising fear of invasion by these countries that had vowed vengeance if we dared depose our King. Now the government sent out a call for all able-bodied single men to defend the Republic against our enemies.

With this knowledge in my head, I should have been better prepared when Claude showed up at the doctor's house the Wednesday following the Tuileries disaster. He entered at the garden gate and surprised Leonie and me digging up potatoes for dinner.

"Toiling away like good little slaves, I see."

I sat upright and held my dirty hands away from my skirt. *"Alors, bonjour* to you! Are you off work early, or have I lost track—"

My question broke off at sight of his blue coat with scarlet collar and cuffs, white waistcoat, trousers, and gaiters—the uniform of the National Guard. A tri-cornered chapeau topped his neatly queued hair, and a proud grin nearly split his freckled face. He threw out his chest and strutted along the path. "I did it, finally enlisted. We'll be with General Lafayette's army by next week. Can you believe it?"

Both Leonie and I uttered cries of dismay. Claude threw up his hands and turned away, then faced us again, scowling. *"Ah, bah!* Can't you give a man some appreciation?"

"Claude, I wish you would return home to Biron while you still can!" Leonie said.

He laughed mirthlessly. "And be shot for desertion? I think not."

She wilted.

I could only press both hands over my breaking heart, heedless of the dirt. When I closed my eyes I could vividly recall rocking this baby brother to sleep; he had always liked to hear me sing, a rare distinction.

"Awww, Colette!" Claude stepped over a row of peppers, extended a hand, and pulled me up and into his arms. He was so tall and strong and alive! "I know you love me, *ma sœur,*" he said, returning my tight embrace. "I'll come home a hero." When I looked up, he tried to smile, held my face between his hands and kissed me sweetly, then stepped back and drew a deep breath. *"Au revoir,* Colette."

"Will we not see you again before you leave?" I asked in desperation.

"Non. I already collected my things from the house, and I must report within the hour. Three of us lads signed up together, so I'll have friends, never fear. I'll send word as soon as I may."

I started to pull my medals over my head. "Take these with you, Claude. I can purchase more."

He gently pushed my hands away. "Keep them. I have my own."

"You do?" I asked in surprise. "I thought you didn't believe in God."

He looked abashed. "I bought myself a Saint Sébastien medal. If there is a God, I could use His help; and Saint Sébastien is supposed to protect soldiers, you know."

I clutched my own medals in one hand. "I will pray for you every day," I promised.

His bright eyes softened again. "I know you will."

Then he sucked in a breath, and his brows rose and fell as if he gathered courage. "Leonie, will you walk with me?" he asked with a little break in his voice.

Leonie gave me a quick glance then met Claude's gaze to say hesitantly, "I will walk with you here in the flower garden for a few minutes."

Claude's fervent expression did not bode well. Surely he was not so blind as to believe Leonie would welcome a declaration of his love. If so, he probably deserved what was coming to him.

"Adieu, Claude, *mon cher."* My voice broke. I picked up my basket and hurried inside.

A short time later Leonie entered the kitchen alone, her cheeks scarlet and her breast heaving. She attempted a careless air, picked up a paring knife, and began to peel a carrot.

I took the knife from her hand and laid it down out of reach. *"Tiens.* I don't want blood in our food. What happened?" I asked.

She grimaced. "Claude asked me to kiss him goodbye and to promise to wait for him and marry him when he returns from the war."

"I see. What did you tell him?"

"I told him I care for him like a brother and can never marry him. Why would he imagine I would welcome his declaration?"

"Who knows what thoughts go through the mind of a boy? Or a man? Or anyone, for that matter?" She looked so crushed that I wrapped an arm around her shoulders and gave her a sisterly hug. I could offer no other consolation or guidance. But I could offer love.

As soon as Doctor Hilliard returned home that evening, I took a cabriolet to the forge. When the carriage turned the last corner I saw Arnaud, his shaggy head down, pacing the open space before the long building and viciously spearing the packed dirt with a pike, probably newly-crafted. He scowled at my appearance and called, "If you seek Claude, look elsewhere. If you seek Étienne, he is inside. Everyone must work harder now, for the government will not lower our quota because one smith enlisted in the army and another died."

I paid the driver and approached the forge, struggling to conceal my anger at Arnaud's unfeeling remark about Saint-Jude's death. The man had been his friend as well as a worker in his forge. I walked past him, heading toward the house.

Arnaud followed. "I have never seen Étienne so unhappy," he said. "He feels responsible, but I cannot blame him for this. Claude is no child to be controlled by a big brother."

The goat bleated at us from her enclosure. I walked over to scratch her head between her horns, and again Arnaud followed me. "How is Adrienne today?" I asked him.

"She complains of pains, and always I fear the baby is coming early," he said. "She drinks milk, but we have no more eggs, for all our chickens were stolen. I bring the goat inside at night to keep it safe."

I found it difficult to react with convincing outrage to the loss of poultry. "I know it has become difficult to find meat, but are the shortages that bad?"

"For people with no money it is that bad," he said. "Pascoe says we must take our rightful possessions back from the royals and clergy who've been stealing it from us for so many years. You must bring Étienne to our next meeting. We're going to form a Vigilance Committee to keep spies from helping our enemies. If we don't catch the traitors, we're doomed. The enemy is at our gates!"

Once again I recognized Pascoe's influence, if not his very words. Or, perhaps, words Pascoe borrowed from popular journalists.

"As far as I am aware, our foreign enemies are still fighting us on our borders," I said calmly, feeling numb inside. "We must be careful not to act in panic. How tragic if we were to kill innocent people by mistake! People are not guilty just because they are accused, and children should never suffer for the sins of their fathers."

Arnaud seemed baffled by this notion. "But no one would accuse innocent people or children!"

His simple, straightforward mind could not even imagine the devious designs of other men and women, which made him a useful ally to the Jacobin leaders. And a dangerous enemy to their enemies.

While he fed and milked the goat, I entered the house to check on Adrienne, who sat at her table with her feet propped on a bench. *"Bonjour,* Colette," she said with a wan smile. "I heard the news about Claude. Arnaud is in a rage."

I needed to think and talk about something else. Anything else. "How are you feeling?" I felt her ankles and frowned. They were quite swollen, and her face looked puffy.

"Hot and fat. How are you feeling?"

I smiled a little at her quick retort. "Hot and glum." I took her hand and noticed that her fingers were also swollen. Probably from the heat, poor thing.

"The baby is quiet while I am moving about and active when I try to rest. But I do find it amusing to see its little arms and legs moving beneath my skin. Don't tell him I told you so, but Arnaud gets frightened when he sees it move."

This time my smile stayed longer. "I suppose we cannot blame men for failing to appreciate the miracle of a child growing inside its mother. Yet they generally see nothing strange in the pregnancy and birth of a horse or cow."

Adrienne grinned. "Sometimes I talk to my baby when we are alone.

Do you think I am crazy?"

"Not at all. How do we know the baby cannot hear you?"

Before I left her that day, she took my hand and gave me a serious look. "If anything happens to me, will you take my baby to raise, Colette?"

I looked into her eyes and felt my heart rate speed up. "What about Arnaud?"

She swallowed and glanced away. "It is not his baby. He keeps asking me questions. Colette, he is so good to me, and I think he will be a kind father as well. But I don't want him to raise the baby without me."

"Then we will do everything possible to make certain you can raise this baby yourself," I said, squeezed her hand, and let go. "Would you like to have Doctor Hilliard check on you?"

She immediately shook her head, eyes wide. *"Mais non."*

Her strong reaction bothered me. "Do you dislike the doctor?"

She looked abashed. "He has frightened me since I was a little child; I think because he was so tall and stern, and my mother kept me out of his way."

This I could understand. "He is a kind man. I wish you would let me bring him to examine you."

"Arnaud would not like it," she said flatly, and I believed her.

"Very well. Keep drinking milk, *petite mère,* and I will bring more fruit for you soon."

The midwife I had trained under years ago in Caen, a scrawny crone known only as Old Elsa, always swore that goats' milk, eggs, and fresh fruit and vegetables were the best foods for an expectant mother. Her patients had seemed to deliver a high ratio of healthy offspring, so I saw no reason to depart from my training.

But diet and vigilant care could not prevent the unexplainable tragedies linked to childbirth, and Adrienne's request suddenly put me on edge.

When I stepped outside, Étienne waited near the goat pen, talking with Arnaud. My approach ended their discussion. "How is she?" Arnaud asked.

"As well as she can be in this heat. The baby could come soon, but I expect it will be another few weeks."

Arnaud sighed. "I just want her to be safe." He entered his house without another word.

Étienne and I walked home. I reached over and took his arm, and he slowed his pace to match mine. "Do you think Claude will be all right?" I asked.

"I don't know," he said heavily. "I keep thinking there must have been something I could do or say to stop him."

I gently bumped my shoulder against him. "It isn't your fault. None of this is your fault."

"Perhaps not, but I will suffer for it. The smithy is buried in orders for weapons. Don't expect to see me at home much in future." He sounded resigned.

We walked on in silence for several moments. Then Étienne looked down at me, his face strangely urgent. "Colette, I need to tell you something important."

His tone immediately set me on guard. "What is it?"

"Quent, Pascoe's valet, waylaid me outside the forge this morning to tell me that Pascoe fell into one of his trances during the attack on the Tuileries, so he threw him over his shoulder and carried him out of danger."

At first I could not speak. I pictured the courtyard on that terrible day and tried to imagine Pascoe standing immobile in the midst of chaos. Quent had carried him over his shoulder? Pascoe's slight frame was deceptive; he was solid bone and sinew. Quent must be very strong indeed.

"Where did he take him?" I asked.

"To a sheltered place, he said. Pascoe soon awakened and was startled and angry to find himself no longer in the courtyard. He rejoined the *sans-culottes* leaders after an hour or two and invented some story about where he had been. And he was involved in negotiations the following day."

"I think his spells are happening more often," I said.

Étienne looked grave. "This most recent one could have caused his death."

CHAPTER 23

EVERY EVENING AFTER work now I stopped at the church to light candles for Saint-Jude and Martin, and to pray for Claude, Pascoe, and my other dear ones. Sometimes I made it there in time for the Vespers service, but usually not. I often visited the confessional and asked questions about God. I never found the priest's answers completely satisfying, yet spiritual hunger kept drawing me back. I listened intently during Mass and began to form an impression of this Being known as God, although to me He was yet only a name, a concept, and a strange Presence.

Pascoe showed up unexpectedly at Maison Beau Temps one week after Claude's enlistment. Since Quent came with him, we knew he intended to stay a few days.

"I missed you two and decided to spend some time with family," he explained. "And I have news of Claude to share." We three siblings sat on the balcony to seek an evening breeze while Pascoe's valet tidied the salon.

"What have you heard?" I asked eagerly.

Pascoe always enjoyed imparting news. "Claude and other new recruits are headed north to join the Central Army, which, according to rumor, is even now moving toward Belgium. Lafayette's replacement, General Dumouriez, has just taken over command. Let us hope he is a better commander than that idiot noble was."

Étienne leaned forward, his elbows on his knees, his eyes intent and curious. "General Lafayette was removed from command? What will he be doing now?"

Pascoe brightened. "Ah, now there is another story." And he launched into a detailed account of General Lafayette's treason, the Assembly's intent to impeach him, and his subsequent escape into Belgium. "We Jacobins rule the Assembly these days, and the army is loyal to us. Lafayette's plots were doomed at the start," he concluded.

"But I thought Lafayette was a friend of the Republic," I said. "Wasn't he our ally and leader in the early days?"

"He was yet another who wanted to limit the power of the People. Unfortunately he has escaped our reach, but I cannot imagine the Austrians welcoming him with open arms." Pascoe chuckled quietly, and I felt chilled.

"He wanted France to establish a constitutional monarchy," Étienne explained to me, "limiting the powers of any one body of government in order to prevent a dictatorship from forming."

"He failed." Pascoe shrugged. "Such a government would be weak and ineffective."

"I thought the intent of the Revolution was to overthrow a tyrannical government." Étienne's tone was slightly sardonic. "What do we have now?"

Pascoe drew himself up straighter in his chair, and his tired eyes flashed. "We have a government doing its best to protect our people."

"By blocking city gates and arresting anyone who attempts to leave?" Étienne, in contrast to his brother, relaxed back in his seat, though I saw his fists clench.

"We detain only enemies of the Republic," Pascoe snapped.

Even I was aware that suspicion and fear gripped Paris. Anyone considered an enemy of the Republic and all former nobles were being rounded up and imprisoned, and internal passports were suspended.

"Please don't argue politics!" I begged. "Here in our home, at least, we should have trust and security. But regarding Claude," I said, "surely he will not be sent into battle without being thoroughly trained first."

There was a tense pause. My brothers did not look at each other; contention lay thick between them. Then Pascoe waved one hand dismissively. "Claude will learn bayonet and other basic drills when he reaches the army camp. Perhaps they are training recruits on the march. He already knows how to load and fire a musket. What more will he need?"

"He is handy with a sword," Étienne added, "so he should master a bayonet easily enough. He will learn to work together with others in his unit."

"It will be good for him," Pascoe said. "Grow him into a man." He looked away from us then, out into the withered garden below our balcony. "I'm hungry."

I rose quickly. These two argued sharply over political matters yet spoke with nonchalance of our young brother's involvement in battle. I wanted to knock their heads together.

"So sorry! I forgot to tell you that our cook quit two days ago," I said with cloying sweetness. "She finally had enough of the undependable schedules of this household and took her services elsewhere."

"Then what will we eat?" Pascoe asked. "Are you cooking here now?"

"I am not. Étienne and I dined at a café down the street last night. You can do the same." I turned to enter the house.

"Is there food in the kitchen?" Pascoe rose to follow me.

"I have no idea. You are welcome to look."

"I can do better." He brushed past me, calling for Quent.

I was too curious about his intentions to go anywhere, so I settled in one of the uncomfortable embroidered chairs in the salon, grimaced at Apollo, and picked up my basket of mending. Before long, Pascoe sauntered back into the salon, saw me, and changed course to sit in the opposite chair. "That's settled. Quent will cook for us. He has already set out to market."

I stared blankly at him, trying to form a mental picture of the burly valet with a marketing basket on his arm. "Quent cooks?"

"*Bien sûr*. Who did you think did the cooking at my other apartment?"

I spoke before I thought: "Florinda?"

He burst into laughter, and I felt my face grow warm. "I suppose she doesn't cook. At least for her there would be no duels."

His face darkened and his voice dropped. "That was an unfeeling remark."

Since I was in this far, I decided to lay my opinion out completely. "Perhaps it was. But I consider you more unfeeling for killing a man in a duel than I am for remarking upon it."

He drew and exhaled a deep breath and shifted his gaze to the open balcony doors. "The whole affair got out of hand," he said. "I didn't realize how deeply it would affect the girl, and her hot-headed brother challenged me in a public setting. I could not refuse."

"Why could you not?"

"To refuse would mean social disgrace and the end of all political aspiration." Pascoe looked more disturbed than I expected. "I chose swords over pistols because they are less often fatal; but the young fool knew just enough swordplay to be dangerous, and his intent was to kill me. I tried to inflict a minor wound but failed. He died within the hour."

He sat there blinking rapidly then rubbed the bridge of his nose with a finger and thumb, sliding them up to cover his closed eyes. "Think of me what you will, but I tell you I have hardly slept since that day. It is one thing to kill an enemy in battle. It is another thing altogether to kill a stripling lad who intended to avenge the sister I disgraced."

Sadly, my first reaction to this confession was a cynical suspicion that it was an act for my benefit. When did I start doubting Pascoe's every word? Probably around the time I realized he lied to me as glibly as he lied to the rest of the world. Exactly when this realization dawned I could not say, but it was now a reality in my consciousness.

Each morning, Étienne and I attended Mass, and on most days the Hilliards joined us and a few other worshipers. Père Benedict had recently started reading passages of Scripture and delivering his sermons in French rather than Latin, which I appreciated. I understood quite a lot of Latin, but hearing the words in French made God seem to me more accessible. None among the congregation complained, although I saw a few raised eyebrows among the faithful.

On the last Thursday morning, Père Benedict read words that remain in my mind to this day: "In the world you shall have tribulation: but be of good cheer; I have overcome the world."

I did not understand this, so after the service ended, as the others moved toward the narthex, I approached Père Benedict. "Père, please tell me how Christ has overcome the world."

When he smiled his entire face seemed to glow. "Through Christ's death He overcame sin, and by His resurrection He overcame Death. Therefore, even though we die, yet shall we live."

Friday morning when we arrived, the church was empty.

Étienne and I stepped inside and waited with a few others. "The door was ajar," said an old man with a completely bald head. Every face wore an expression of dread. We met each other's eyes, searching for reassurance but finding none.

The Hilliards were last to arrive. Leonie smiled at Étienne, but I saw the smile fade as she noticed the dark emptiness of the nave. Doctor Hilliard addressed some of the other men, and their faces were bleak. "No one was in the building," the same man told him. "The sexton is gone too. Père Benedict spent most of his time here in the chapel."

"I will ask questions today and find him," the doctor promised.

We walked to the house in near silence. To my surprise the doctor followed Leonie and me inside. Leonie ran upstairs, but her father followed me downstairs into the kitchen.

"Madame, if your brothers do not object, I would be grateful if you will take Leonie to your house each afternoon before nightfall if I am not yet home. I will collect her when I am able. If I am detained late, I hope she may stay overnight at your house; I shall, of course, pay for her board and lodging. I would have greater peace of mind knowing that you and Leonie were in the protection of your brother Étienne rather than imagining you women alone in this house at night."

With Père Benedict missing, I knew Doctor Hilliard did not exaggerate the danger. "I shall be pleased to take Leonie home with me if necessary, monsieur, and I know Étienne would protect us with his life." I made no mention of Pascoe and Quent.

After a pause he asked, "Would you consider returning to Biron to escape this turmoil? You still have family there. I believe I could obtain official travel papers for you."

Perhaps I should have been grateful, but his offer annoyed me. Turning away, I opened the back door and let a breeze brush my hot face. "I cannot leave Paris. I must be here when Claude returns home from the war. Surely it will end soon."

"I pray the war ends soon but I do not believe it will," he said quietly. "Leonie told me about Claude."

His sympathetic tone prompted further confession. "Our parents trusted my brothers and me to watch over him, but now he has gone out of our reach." My voice quivered and cracked ridiculously. I could not control it. I could not control anything.

"And you feel that you have failed your family."

"I should have found a way to stop him," I snapped.

After another pause he said, "If a way existed, you would have found it."

"Claude wouldn't listen to me anymore, or to Étienne. And Pascoe thinks the army will be good for him." Again I choked up on the last words.

"Perhaps it will."

I shot him a quick glare over my shoulder. Plenty of words came into my head, but I didn't trust my voice to deliver them properly.

He sighed. "We only imagine we control other people. Ultimately their choices are their own."

"Not children," I said. "We protect children."

"Granted. But Claude is no longer a child. There comes a time when true love and respect allows others their right to choose."

Love is a choice. I suddenly hated the very concept of free will. It allowed destructive choices. What had God been thinking?

After another tense silence Doctor Hilliard said, "I must go, madame, but I wish you to know that I shall pray for God's protection on your brothers and on all those dear to you."

A tear spilled down my cheek. I don't think he saw it. *"Merci."*

He paused another moment then headed to the door. *"Bonjour,* Madame DeMer."

"Bonjour, Doctor Hilliard."

CHAPTER 24

A FEW DAYS LATER IT happened: The doctor did not come home. I waited until afternoon faded into evening. Still he did not come.

"He told me to go home with you if he did not return before dark," Leonie said. "I think we should go. He will be angry if he comes and finds us still here at this hour."

She had been hinting strongly at this for some time, but I resisted. Surely he would step through the door at any time. As the minutes ticked by, the tightness in my stomach intensified. "Very well, gather your things and I shall flag down a carriage for us."

When we arrived at Beau Temps, Étienne greeted us at the door with evident relief. "I was about to go in search of you," he said, gazing steadily into Leonie's eyes. "Pascoe has not yet come home either."

I brightened. "Perhaps they were both delayed at the Assembly. I believe Pascoe was there again today."

Leaving those two visiting in the salon, I headed to the kitchen to help Quent prepare food for an extra person, but he shrugged off the imposition. "There should be plenty for all."

The arrangements at our house were most unconventional, for although Quent was a servant and maintained a respectful demeanor at all times, he was no lower in social rank than Étienne, a blacksmith, and I, a housekeeper. He and I enjoyed discussing food, and he had recently shared with me a new marinade which I intended to try as soon as I could obtain a decent beefsteak.

There were three of us at dinner. Leonie and Étienne talked quietly. I have no idea what they said or what I ate, for my mind was running through possibilities. Had the Assembly remained in session to untangle some knotty political issue? Perhaps the doctor was called to a meeting with his fellow deputies from Normandy. He might have gone out for dinner with colleagues. With slightly frantic determination I came up with dozens of innocuous reasons why he might be late.

Then the door swung open and Doctor Hilliard entered the dining room, followed by Quent. We three stared at him in surprise. His hat and wig were gone, his clothing was disheveled and torn, and his expression was grim. "Pardon my late arrival." His polite words lacked inflection. "I thank you for welcoming my daughter into your home and feeding her. We must be going."

"Doctor," I said. "Will you join us for dinner? I was unable to—"

He interrupted without even a glance or nod of acknowledgement. "*Merci, mais non.* Leonie?"

She had risen at his entrance to stare, open-mouthed. "Papa," she said just above a whisper. "Are you injured?"

"It is a scratch," he said. "I shall clean and wrap it at home. Hurry and gather your belongings."

This was when I noticed what she had already seen: a dark stain around one of the rents in his coat sleeve. I suddenly felt light in the head.

Without another word Leonie rose and hurried from the room.

Étienne and I followed the doctor to the entry hall. He walked stiffly, and his short hair looked much as Claude's had once, long ago, after a cow licked his head: clumps of it plastered in all directions.

"What happened?" I asked.

He finally met my gaze, and for an instant I glimpsed recognition. "Ask Quent," he said. Then he blinked and his eyes were again a dark void.

Leonie trotted down the stairs. "I am ready." But her worried gaze clung to Étienne's until the doctor ushered her outside and the door closed behind them.

I wasted no time, and Étienne followed my rush downstairs to find Quent. "What happened to Doctor Hilliard?" I asked. "He said to ask you."

Quent set aside the pan he'd been scraping and folded his thick arms. "He received a death threat today so took an alternate route home and lay in wait. Four *sans-culottes* armed with pikes attempted to kill him."

"What happened to them?" Étienne asked.

My heart was pounding so hard I couldn't speak.

"Two died, two escaped—one wounded. The doctor carried his sword-stick and three pistols, which they obviously did not expect."

I pulled out a chair and sat down, waiting for my racing heart to slow its pace. "Why would they try to kill him?"

"To silence him, I would guess," Quent said. "He is an eloquent speaker who advocates moderation and compromise in government. He is highly favored among the moderate provincial deputies. Those currently in the majority fear his influence."

I felt as if the earth shifted beneath me. Never before had I realized how heavily my security depended on Doctor Hilliard. What would I do if anything happened to him?

My event-organizing business had died out since the Tuileries attack. It would likely revive once this current crisis of fear ended, but when would that be? Pascoe would again tell me it was time to look for another employment position. But where?

As if my thoughts conjured him, Pascoe stepped into the kitchen. "Here you are. The house was strangely empty. Is there anything left to eat?"

While Quent prepared a plate for him, I rose and embraced my brother. He smelled of tobacco smoke and brandy. "Where have you been?"

"Working like a slave. It was a busy day on the Assembly floor. Much to debate, much opposition to overcome." He stretched his arms and rolled his head from one side to the other. Then he flopped into a chair and squinted up at me while circling his ankles, one after the other. "Why are you two in the kitchen? I ran into a cringing little housemaid upstairs who told me I could find you here."

"We've been talking with Quent," I answered.

"About the fine art of cleaning a scullery, no doubt." He shifted his gaze to Étienne. "Are you contemplating a domestic career now? Quent can teach you how to sponge and press a coat to perfection."

It was Étienne who told him about Doctor Hilliard's brush with death. Pascoe went still and cold as the tale unfolded. Not even I, who knew him so well, could read his face. But when Quent set a plate of food before him, Pascoe swore under his breath. It certainly was not the cold beef-and-onion pie arousing his wrath.

I glanced at Étienne, whose face revealed the same uncertainty I felt. "Did you know—" I began, then tried to swallow with a dry mouth. "Did you already know about this attack?"

Pascoe gave me a sour look. "Do you imagine I orchestrated it?"

I regretted opening my mouth, but it was too late to stop now. "I don't know what to think anymore."

"Then think whatever makes you happy."

Bright morning sunshine seemed incongruous as I took leave of Étienne at the foot of our drive in the morning. I walked alone past the closed church. Someone had barred its weather-worn doors, probably to prevent vandalism. The bells no longer rang, although someone must be sweeping the front steps. I paused a moment to pray for Père Benedict and others, whose names I didn't know, who might have been taken away with him.

When I entered the basement kitchen through the sunken door—which, as usual, I left open to allow fresh morning air and light into the room—Doctor Hilliard stood beside my worktable, pouring coffee. He looked so different! His hair was dark, nearly an inch long, and looked as curly as Leonie's. He had evidently bathed since last night, for it was shiny rather than clumped.

He glanced up then poured a second cup, using a towel to protect his hands from the pot's handle. *"Bonjour,* Madame DeMer."

"Bonjour, Doctor Hilliard. What became of your wig?" I asked while untying my bonnet strings.

He hung the pot back on its hook then ran one hand over his head, looking self-conscious. "I had intended to discard it soon, as you suggested; now I have no option, for it was lost last night, along with my best hat, in the scuffle."

My momentary amusement vanished. Since witnessing violent death, I could no longer think or speak of it lightly. "You had blood on your sleeve," I said.

His glance flickered toward me and away. "A pike scratched my arm."

"You killed two of your attackers?"

His voice lowered. "Madame, I do not take pleasure from loss of life. I killed to preserve my own life; perhaps this was the wrong choice."

"Those men attempted to murder you! Theirs was the evil choice, not yours." My vehemence surprised both of us. Embarrassed, I turned to hang up my bonnet and reticule. "Have you discovered yet where Père Benedict has gone?" I asked.

"He was arrested for treason against the Republic and incarcerated at l'Abbaye prison," he said.

I spun back to face him, gasping in such outrage that I could not articulate a coherent sentence. "Treason? Père Benedict? Impossible!"

"I agree, madame. Yet they claim he refused to take the oath of loyalty to the Republic."

I wanted to throw something, kick something. Instead I stood there and sputtered, "But why would he refuse?"

"Some priests see no conflict of interest in taking the oath; others consider it heretical. And they have a point, for certain among our government leaders intend to abolish Christianity in France. Their first step is to take control of the Church by separating it from the Vatican. It may comfort you to know that I am working for Père Benedict's release. I have visited him twice, and he claims to be content with his treatment." The doctor's tone was dubious. "But then, he would be content anywhere."

"*Oui,* it is true," I said, my anger draining away. "Père Benedict foresaw his arrest. He warned me of it weeks ago and advised me to trust in God whatever happens."

"And so we must do." The doctor handed me a cup of coffee, beckoned for me to be seated, and then sat across the table from me like an old friend. At first I felt nerveless, empty. But a peaceful silence grew as we each sampled our coffee. The chirping of birds in the garden filtered into my awareness, and soft light shimmered through the open door. Conflicting emotions filled my heart until I could scarcely breathe: a sudden supreme happiness and the aching premonition that it could not last.

He cleared his throat and said with evident reluctance, "I would request you to no longer walk the streets alone; there is much evil about."

"Obviously you should not walk the streets alone either. Must you attend the Assembly today?"

"Of all times, this might be the most crucial," he said heavily. "Terrible things are being planned. I have no power to avert them, but someone must try to speak sense into the whirlwind of hysteria. Also I must report the attempt on my life in case other lives are similarly endangered."

"I will take Leonie home with me again this evening, monsieur."

"I trust you to protect her. I hope you are armed."

"Today I brought my muff pistol in my reticule."

"Do you know how to fire it?"

"I do, and I would shoot to protect Leonie . . . although I am not a very good shot. At least its recoil does not knock me over like the fowling piece does."

One side of his mouth lifted in a crooked smile. *"Bonne fille.* And I, in turn, shall attempt to alter my predictable habits."

"You still have your weapons?"

He opened his coat to reveal twin dueling pistols strapped to his sides so that they could be quickly drawn. I had never before seen such a device for carrying firearms.

Then he pushed back his chair, rose, drew out his coin purse, and stacked coins on the table. "One more thing before I go: Food distribution days are impracticable at present, for the merchants fear to enter the *section;* one can hardly blame them. Until the city recovers its equilibrium, I should be grateful if you will purchase necessities for those in greatest need, and you may also freely share as much of our garden produce as you deem necessary."

"Oui, monsieur. *Merci."* I studied his face, noting the deep lines around his mouth and what I could only call sadness in his eyes. "May God bless and protect you."

The sadness fled for a moment. "And you, madame."

After he left, Leonie wandered downstairs, her face creased from sleep and her hair in a messy braid down her back. "Are we to visit Adrienne today?" she asked, her face weary and drawn but her eyes earnest.

"*Non*. I cannot take you there until the city calms down. We might work in the garden or straighten cupboards as we planned to do last week."

She looked less than thrilled. "I would prefer the garden. I am sick of being inside this dreadful house."

So we spent the morning hours pulling weeds, lugging water buckets, and harvesting ripe produce. "Your father seems sad," I mentioned while pouring water around a newly-weeded bed of melons.

"Probably because of the letter he received from his father," she said.

I thought back to the tale Pascoe told. Many of its details I already knew to be false. Had he also misled me about the doctor's parentage? "Did he know his father well?" I asked.

"Not at all, *en fait*. Not until after Papa's mother died did his father take active part in his life. My grandfather's legal wife was barren, which possibly explains her lack of objection to her husband's funding my father's education and training. He also purchased the estate in Biron for Papa."

"Is his wife still living?"

"*Non*, she passed away years ago. Papa always refused to visit his father, but now I think he regrets his coldness and wishes he could travel up to Dunkerque. You see, his father is ill and not expected to live out the year."

"He should go. Don't you think so? Wouldn't you like to meet your grandfather?"

"I do think so, and I would go; but it would be difficult now, with internal passports suspended and battles being fought not so very far from my grandfather's estate. Papa says he might be able to call in some favors, but he isn't sure he should."

CHAPTER 25

THE DOCTOR ARRIVED home early the following evening, relieving me of duty. As soon as I got home I asked Pascoe if he would escort me to the forge before nightfall. "We have spent so little time together recently," I added as possible incentive.

He reclined upon a chaise longue in the salon, looking almost as boneless as a cat. At my request he looked up from his newspaper with a considering frown, then folded the paper and nodded. "*En fait*, I do need to consult with Lamorges before our meeting tomorrow night. If you can promise to take no longer than an hour to complete your business, I'll accompany you."

Pascoe flagged down a carriage, and we made good time through light traffic. He asked the driver to return in one hour, paid him generously, and turned to join me. "Ah, the infamous forge," he said, looking underwhelmed.

I handed him the basket of produce to carry. "You have been here before, I know."

"*Hélas,* it is true." He regarded the straw-strewn courtyard and the goat pen with a disdainful air as he followed me to the little house. I heard him mutter something under his breath but caught only the last two words, "ended up."

Arnaud came at my knock and seemed both startled and relieved. "We began to think you had stopped coming altogether." He gave Pascoe a curious and not entirely welcoming look.

"It isn't safe to travel the streets alone," I explained as he stepped back and allowed us to enter, "and I cannot bring Mademoiselle Hilliard with me anymore." The interior of the house was shadowed, and at first I could see nothing but a rush lamp on a table.

Pascoe added, "When Colette asked me to escort her, I remembered a matter of importance you and I must discuss."

Arnaud still seemed sullen, but he nodded.

As my eyes adjusted to the dim lighting, I saw Adrienne sitting upright in the bed across the room with the coverlet clutched to her chin and her eyes wide. "If you men will go outside, *s'il vous plaît,*" I said firmly. "Pascoe, you can leave the basket here. Be careful of the jar of butter."

They obeyed without question. I was uncertain whether Pascoe even saw Adrienne in her dark corner. For her sake I hoped not. She looked rather dreadful, with her face puffy and her hair like a rat's nest.

"*Bonsoir, ma chère.* I am so sorry to disturb you at this hour," I said, unpacking the basket, "but I can no longer visit you alone. The streets are dangerous. My employer was attacked while walking home at twilight."

"I was afraid you wouldn't come back." She sounded like a lonely child.

"I will always come back; I can never forget you, *petite.*"

The dull, tired look in her eyes concerned me, and her face, hands, and feet were swollen. "Are you still drinking your milk?"

"I am. I can stomach little else."

"I brought fruit. Would you like some grapes? They are the first of the season and very fine."

"Later, *peut-être,*" she said listlessly. "Arnaud is so busy I hardly see him anymore, and I know he is worried. He works terribly hard but gets little pay for all the weapons he makes. Minette comes to visit me, and . . ."

She continued talking, but my mind wandered while I checked the baby's size and responsiveness. I could not help thinking of my last few visits in this house. A full month had not passed since Saint-Jude's death or Claude's enlistment, yet it seemed longer. I felt as if this summer had lasted a lifetime. Or as if I had become a different person during the past three months.

"Baby seems healthy and active," I said as soon as she paused for breath. "Are you having contractions?" The baby had turned in the womb and now lay in the breech position. There was still time and room for it to turn again, but I felt some concern.

"Not often. I feel enormous and ugly." Yet her hands cradled the baby lovingly.

"Would you like me to brush your hair?" I offered.

"That would be lovely." I saw her wipe tears from her eyes, poor little thing.

So I wrapped her in a dressing gown, sat behind her on the edge of the bed, and combed tangles out of her hair while explaining what she would experience when labor began in earnest.

"You will come right away when Arnaud calls for you?" she asked again.

"I will come," I reassured her. "You are dear to me, Adrienne."

Once her hair was neatly braided she seemed to feel better, but her fear remained. She clutched my wrist and blurted, "My mother's second baby died during delivery. Maman nearly died too, and she swore she would never have another. That's why my father left us."

Anger and fear flashed through me. Why had she never told me this story before? "You are not your mother, *chérie*, and I see no reason why you should not give birth to a healthy baby." My voice was calm though I was not.

Pascoe opened the door a crack. "Are you finished yet?" he asked.

"We are. You may enter."

The men appeared, Arnaud carrying a second lamp. The two were a study in contrast: Pascoe trim, bright, and elegant; Arnaud massive, sullen, and sooty.

"It is good to see you looking well, Madame Lamorges," Pascoe greeted Adrienne politely. "Are you ready, Colette? It will be dark soon."

I gave Adrienne a quick hug and reminded Arnaud to send for me immediately if Adrienne's water broke. He still looked surly, but the brief glance he gave me revealed a haunted expression that touched my heart. "Make sure she drinks lots of milk," I repeated. "And see if you can't tempt her with the grapes and plums."

He nodded. Not a word passed between him and Pascoe. *"Bonsoir,"* I said as we stepped outside, but nobody answered.

The sky was a rich blue dotted with stars and fading to pale silver in the west. Dogs barked and howled somewhere nearby, their voices echoing among the buildings like the cries of lost souls. Several bats skimmed the air just above our heads; one particularly bold swoop made Pascoe cringe and swear.

It should have been a lovely summer evening. Should have been but wasn't. Something was wrong. Anger seethed from Pascoe in caustic waves.

Our carriage driver had parked in front of the forge to wait for us. Pascoe handed me into the carriage and sat in the backwards-facing seat. The wheels rattled on the uneven pavement so loudly that I raised my voice to be heard. "I am glad I visited Adrienne tonight. She should deliver her baby soon now." When I received no response, I asked, "So what did you and Arnaud need to discuss tonight?"

"Nothing to concern you," he said. "Can you believe the idiot thinks I am responsible for Fillion's death?"

"Why would he think so?" I asked in blank surprise.

"He says Fillion was injured while fighting off a Swiss Guard who would have killed me while I stood frozen with fear." Pascoe snorted. "Fear! Colette, I fought like a mad dog the entire time and never knew a moment's fright."

"Perhaps you were frozen by . . . your condition," I dared to suggest.

As I might have expected, he burst into a swearing fury and even called me several most unflattering names. "Pascoe," I said several times, attempting to break into his tirade. At last he slowed down and I was able to speak. "Pascoe, you know it is true. Quent told us he carried you out of the courtyard while the battle raged. You undoubtedly owe your life to him, and possibly to Saint-Jude Fillion as well. If Arnaud is correct, then Saint-Jude rescued both of us that day."

"Don't canonize him now he's dead." My brother's eyes gleamed as if with pale fire. I could see little else of him in the shadowy interior of the carriage. "He was no saint."

"Pascoe, he risked his life for me."

He laughed abruptly. "And I am forever grateful to him, but the fact remains he was an idiot. All muscle and no brain."

The carriage drew up before Maison Beau Temps, and Pascoe climbed out first. I hopped down without waiting for a step then watched as Pascoe paid the driver. One thing about my brother: He was not tightfisted. The driver grinned while thanking him and sprang to his seat with energy.

Étienne had retired early, Quent informed us while taking Pascoe's hat and gloves. Somehow the valet had become our all-around servant, leaving only the most mundane tasks for the two maids. His presence was a blessing in every sense; best of all, he was a calming influence on Pascoe.

I followed my brother into the salon. Pascoe returned to his seat and unfolded the paper. I picked up my mending basket, which I had sadly neglected of late. I knew it would not be long before Pascoe's wrath again required an outlet.

"So," Pascoe said, "is Fillion now the tragic lost romance of your life?"

The newspaper hid his face from view. His pose, effortlessly casual earlier in the day, was now a sham.

My thread tangled. I spent precious minutes picking at the knot with my needle, to no avail.

"I hope you know better than to believe me a romantic fool," I responded calmly. "I still mourn his needless death and wish I were kinder in my rejections, but I could never have accepted his marriage proposal had he lived."

"Marriage proposal?" Pascoe's eyes appeared over the top of the paper.

"On his deathbed he declared his intent to marry me. I am wise enough to know he may have formed the intention then and there; nonetheless, I will treasure the thought." I kept my tone light, hoping to lighten his mood.

He shifted in his seat and lowered the paper another inch. "So you value his memory more because he wanted to marry you?"

"I said no such thing." I laid down my sewing. "Pascoe, I invited you to come with me this evening because I have missed you."

He dropped his arms, crumpling the paper in his lap. "And here I am."

"Angry and looking for a fight," I said. "I am ready and willing to listen if you need to talk about anything. Have you suffered other attacks recently? Are you feeling ill?"

He swore and threw the paper on the floor. "Stop feigning ignorance, Colette. Discussing my 'condition' changes nothing. I begin to think talking with you is entirely ineffective, for I see no perceptible change in your attitudes or behavior. You are a woman of intelligence despite your inability to read. You are handsome, articulate, and talented. Yet instead of stepping forward into a leadership role, you have pulled away from the counter-revolution effort and spend more time with the daughter of a political enemy."

His pedantic tone never failed to irritate. "I have no further interest in encouraging women and children to stand before cannon fire," I said. "And Leonie Hilliard might soon become our sister-in-law. I believe her childhood friendship with Étienne has blossomed into love."

Again Pascoe spewed profanities. "And you would encourage our brother to marry that skinny, arrogant granddaughter of an émigré? If she imagines herself in love with him, it will not last. In no time at all she will recognize the disparity of family and despise a simple blacksmith. Look at her mother's romance with the bastard son of a country *comte*; the ink had not dried on the marriage certificate before those two were discontent."

"They were very young and ignorant about the opposition they would face," I said. "In contrast, Leonie's father approves of Étienne."

Pascoe's eyes narrowed. "So the noble Republican would allow his daughter—the daughter who despises him, mind you—to wed our brother. How very grateful we should be! Always with you the conversation comes around to Doctor Hilliard, the saint, the paragon of all virtue."

I gave him a steady look. "You, not I, brought up first Leonie and then her father. You are the one who constantly reverts to the same conversational theme. Why? Why does my employment in Doctor Hilliard's household gall you so? Is there something you haven't told me? Did he ever abuse you or force you to commit a crime?"

Pascoe shook his head and smiled a humorless smile. *"Non.* He was the mentor I always wanted, for he valued my gifts as Papa could not. I wished to be just like him."

I snipped the hopelessly tangled threads and pulled out the stitching

I had done, leaving the hole in Étienne's stocking larger than before.

"What happened? When did you begin to hate him?"

"He talked too much." He linked his hands behind his head, inhaled deeply, and said, "Not long before we came to Paris, I began to see the man in a different light."

My success at drawing Pascoe into honest conversation excited me. Another question or two might reveal the reason for his change of heart.

But then I pushed too far. "You have told me of the doctor's philandering while his wife lived and of his hypocrisy in attending church. I see a man who has turned to God for forgiveness and for help in changing his ways."

My brother nearly choked. "You, my formerly lucid sister, now speak of a god as if such myths had any basis in reality? Matters are worse than I thought." He rose and scooped up the wrinkled newspaper, folded it neatly, and tucked it beneath his arm. "I require fresh air and rational company for a change."

"You are going out tonight?" I set my work aside and rose as well. What had I been I thinking, to mention God at such a time?

"Mais non! I am leaving. You will see me again once I have purged all this sanctified air from my system." He approached to kiss me, then held my face between his hands and looked into my eyes. "Never fear: I care too much to abandon you, *ma poulette.* I promise to keep trying, to do everything in my power to help you."

"Help me? Pascoe, I don't need your help. I simply want your respect."

He patted my cheek fondly and strode away. I heard him calling for Quent upstairs, and within half an hour they left the house.

As the door closed behind my brother and his valet, I wondered how we would manage without Quent.

I recall few details of the following day. Leonie and I worked many hours in the garden, harvesting onions and garlic and braiding them in strings to hang up in the kitchen; then we prepared a vegetable stew I hoped would please the doctor. I dared not take Leonie with me to market or go alone after my promise to the doctor. If he wanted fresh meat in his meals, he would need to purchase it himself.

Doctor Hilliard returned home earlier than usual that evening, so again there was no need for Leonie to come with me to Maison Beau Temps. After a brief observation, I decided the doctor was on edge and trying to conceal it. He spared me scarcely a word and did not meet my gaze. But at least he was safe.

While I donned my hat after saying my goodbyes to Leonie, he stepped outside to hail a chair for me. At that moment a carriage pulled up before the door and Pascoe emerged. His very appearance at this house was enough to inspire panic. Was he ill or about to have an attack? Had he come to confront the doctor directly about some past wrong? I hurried to intercept him. "Pascoe, whatever is wrong?"

Without a glance at the doctor, he took my hands. "Colette, you must come. It is Étienne; he has been taken to prison, accused of treason!"

CHAPTER 26

BUT WHO WOULD ACCUSE Étienne of treason?" I objected in immediate denial. "He is no traitor."

"Where is he being held?" Doctor Hilliard asked.

Pascoe's burning blue gaze held mine. "I am told they took him to l'Abbaye. Now stop arguing and get in. I'll take you there."

I turned and met the doctor's grim gaze. "Leonie," I said.

"I will tell her," he said. But his gaze fixed almost fiercely upon Pascoe. "The prison is no place for your sister."

"I'll be the judge of that," Pascoe said shortly. He helped me into the calèche, gave direction to the driver, and we were off.

"Will they allow visitors?" I asked. My words sounded strangely distant in my own ears, as though spoken by someone else, not me. I drew a deep breath but could not calm the racing of my heart. "Can we bring him food? Maybe the doctor can get him released."

"I am more likely to be of help in this regard than Doctor Hilliard," Pascoe said.

When the carriage let us out on the grounds of the Abbaye of Saint-Germain, where the prison was located, I stared up at the tall building, wondering if Étienne might be at one of its windows. "I don't understand why he would be imprisoned," I said again. "He has never involved himself in political matters at all. Surely the authorities will listen to reason, Pascoe. Don't the *sans-culottes* practically run the government these days? And you are known and respected everywhere."

He also stared up at those looming windows, his expression hard. "I warned him many times to keep silent, to avoid any connection with the Church. But he would keep attending Mass, and he refused to join our *section* meetings. *Le fou.*"

"Attending Mass does not indicate lack of support for the Republic," I insisted. My hands balled up knots of my skirt, as though clutching a lifeline. "Étienne spends most of his time making weapons for our military; how can this be viewed as traitorous activity?"

Pascoe slowly turned his head to give me a reproving stare. "The Church's leaders have conspired with the King to overturn the Republic, and they even yet refuse to acknowledge or accept their loss of power. Colette, of late you have gone passive, and I blame our zealot brother for this. Once you were a woman who made things happen; now you blind yourself to reality and allow people to use you."

I set my jaw. "Will you ask if we might visit Étienne, or shall I?" I asked.

His face settled into hard lines. "I'll ask."

And he left me standing in the courtyard. Passersby avoided my gaze. Night would not fall for several hours, yet somehow I felt shadows oppress me like a physical weight.

"*Mon Dieu,* please watch over your servant Étienne," I whispered, crossing myself. I hoped He would keep me in mind as well but didn't dare ask.

Pascoe was right. I had been reacting to life instead of taking it by the horns. Then and there, in the courtyard of l'Abbaye prison, I resolved to gather my remaining courage and do whatever I could to make things happen.

A large presence loomed beside me, and I nearly died of fright before looking up at Quent's impassive countenance. "Monsieur Pascoe has entered the prison?" he asked.

"*Oui,*" I answered breathlessly, taking a small step aside. "How did you know to come here?"

His gaze scanned my face then returned to the prison's bleak façade. "Doctor Hilliard sent me."

At the time my mind failed to seek a connection. It seemed sensible that the doctor would send Pascoe's faithful servant to assist us. "Pascoe entered some time ago. Do you think he is all right?" I asked.

"I would imagine so," Quent said, his voice not unkind. "His enemies are unlikely to number among the prison guards. Madame, my intent is to escort you home. Your presence has attracted unwelcome attention, and you do not want to enter the prison, I assure you."

I shivered. Without looking around, I knew he spoke the truth about the attention I had drawn. *"Très bien."*

"Come." And he led me to a waiting carriage. Instead of riding inside with me, he climbed on the back like a footman or guard. Within minutes we arrived at Maison Beau Temps.

Quent walked me to the door and spoke quietly. "Your two maids are still here, and I believe they can be trusted. I shall attempt to convince Monsieur Pascoe to return here tonight, but if I cannot, I would advise you to take your maids and stay at Doctor Hilliard's house." He must have read objection in my face, for he added, "Otherwise, keep your firearms loaded and ready. You would be wise to prepare for the worst."

I followed Quent's advice, setting one loaded pistol on the table beside my bed, hiding another in a drawer near the back stairs, and concealing my fowling piece behind the hat stand in the entry hall. Anna-Marie and Hortense expressed outrage over Monsieur Étienne's arrest but seemed otherwise unaware of any threat to our safety. I prepared a dull yet filling meal of scones with honey and sliced fresh fruit. Hortense wrinkled her nose, but both girls ate without comment.

Pascoe did not return. I wondered if he had attended the *section* meeting planned for that evening. Perhaps it was cancelled.

Regardless of Pascoe's movements and Quent's warnings, I made plans of my own. Early the next morning I put a muff pistol in my reticule, flagged a chair, and gave directions to the forge. If I waited for a man to escort me, I would never go anywhere. Besides, at this hour I felt safe enough.

While being carried through the quiet streets I considered the situation, fighting back waves of dread. As France's armies crumbled on our borders and our enemies threatened to invade Paris and punish all those opposed to the King, the *sans-culottes* and Jacobins inside the city were whipping its citizens into a frenzy of fear. I had recently overheard others seriously repeat the rumor Pascoe first mentioned to me about enemies intending to release Paris's murderous prisoners upon the unsuspecting population.

If the populace became convinced this was truly an impending danger . . . But I could not allow myself to follow this line of thought. There simply was no time to waste in obtaining Étienne's release. His complete lack of involvement in political matters might work in his favor, but during these insane times, who could be sure? I could leave nothing to chance. Now was the time to call up certain favors.

Arnaud met me at the door of the house, and his expression chilled me to the bone. I concealed my reaction behind a sober yet friendly greeting. *"Bonjour,* Arnaud. I brought scones for Adrienne. Since the baby could arrive at any time, I thought I should check on her more often." I stepped forward, and he made way for me to enter.

Adrienne lay in the bed with her face to the wall. When I touched her shoulder, she awakened with a jolt and rolled to her back. Blinking, she recognized me, and I saw myriad expressions flash through her eyes. "Colette," she said, her voice rough with sleep.

"I brought you scones and fruit, *petite*. I'm sorry to wake you."

"I wasn't quite asleep," she said. "The baby seldom lets me sleep." She smiled at me, but it seemed to require effort.

"You rest, and I'll fix your meal." I kept a friendly tone, but I knew without doubt that something was wrong here.

Arnaud had left the house, possibly to escape me. I slipped outside and found him mucking out the goat pen. The look on his face as I approached was anything but encouraging; but when it came to family, I had courage to spare.

"Arnaud, my brother was arrested here yesterday, yet you glare at me as if I were an enemy. *Pourquoi?*"

Arnaud stepped out of the pen to face me, folded thick arms over his barrel chest, and jutted his jaw. His was a truly intimidating presence. In his deep, gruff voice, he said, "I accused Étienne and had him thrown into prison, where he belongs."

I'm sure my heart lurched halfway up my throat, and a raging fire roared suddenly, fiercely in my head. A younger version of myself might have flown at Arnaud without another word, ready to scratch his offensive, menacing face to ribbons. As it was, I scarcely batted an eye. In a voice deadly with calm, I said only, *"Pourquoi?* Tell me why?"

"Because he is guilty."

"Guilty of what crime?"

"Trahison."

The first word from my mouth was quite unladylike, yet it perfectly described this accusation. "What treason did he ever do? He spends his days in your forge, building weapons for France's armies. He spends his nights at home, watching over me. He loves a sweet young woman and dreams of marrying her and having a family—"

Arnaud exploded, spewing profanity like a cannon spews grapeshot. Amid the almost incoherent noise, I heard an accusation I knew to be false.

I gave up waiting for his diatribe to end and broke in with one of my own. "I don't know who has been lying to you about Étienne, but you"—I reached out then and grabbed his shirt in my fist, startling him, not with the strength of my arm but with the force of my fury. I tugged until the fabric strained, forcing him to look me in the eye. "You, of all people, should know he is the last man on earth who would ever harm a woman or a child. I am well aware that some men are hypocrites who pretend to serve God while living evil lives in secret, but Étienne is not such a man. Arnaud, he is only twenty-one, and I would swear on my life he is as pure in heart and body as any virgin who ever prayed before the altar of Our Lady!"

Arnaud fell silent, his expression reminding me of a wounded bear. "But . . . but why would Adrienne lie to me?"

His words felt like a knife in my gut. Breathing hard, I forced my hand to relax, to let go of his shirt. I took a step back, unwilling to break gaze with him. But he turned from me, his shoulders sagging. So I whirled around and returned to the house.

I stood a moment in the doorway, uncertain what I would do, what I *could* do. Instinct moved me as much as rational thought. I brewed herbal tea and prepared food for Adrienne. All the while my thoughts were far away from domestic chores, racing in frantic circles.

When I approached the bed I saw Adrienne watching me, her face white and cold. I placed the tray on a low table beside the bed, within her easy reach, and then stepped back.

"Did you tell Arnaud that Étienne is your baby's f ather?" I asked quietly.

"I did," she said. Her voice was low yet defiant.

"Do you realize he could be killed for this?"

I saw her lips tremble before she cried, "He deserves to die for what he has done. He is lucky Arnaud did not tear him limb from limb!"

"Adrienne, how could you tell such a lie about a man who has ever been a true friend to you and to Arnaud? How could you do this to me?"

Her face contorted with rage and fear. "You get out of this house!" she shrieked. "Get out and never come back!"

CHAPTER 27

I COULD NOT BRING MYSELF to tell Leonie about Adrienne's lie. My own mind could hardly accept it. Why would she do such a thing? What had Étienne—gentle, unobtrusive Étienne, of all people!—ever done to her? Jealousy of Leonie's happiness might provide a motive, but Adrienne was unaware, so far as I knew, of the progress of their little romance. Leonie had not visited her in many weeks, and Étienne certainly would never have confided in Arnaud or the other two remaining smiths.

Leonie surprised me with a quiet courage that did her credit. I saw her begin to crumble more than once when some trivial thing reminded her of the horrifying truth, yet each time she closed her eyes, straightened her shoulders, and rallied. I knew prayer provided this strength, for I sought the same refuge.

We spoke of ordinary matters, and for some reason she seemed to find comfort in speaking of her mother. I let her talk and filed away details in my mind for later contemplation.

As the afternoon hours ticked past, I wondered if the doctor would expect me to take Leonie home with me now Étienne was no longer there. Such a move seemed pointless, yet I could not leave her alone in the house after nightfall.

The doctor relieved me of this choice by returning earlier than usual. At his request, Leonie and I entered the salon and sat on the canapé side by side. He took the red chair, and his posture alone revealed much. After a short silence he sighed and looked up. "I visited Étienne this morning. He is in a room on the fourth level in the back. There are eight other men in the chamber, including Père Benedict."

We exclaimed in unison.

"Étienne told me the priest was the best possible cellmate; his faith and good humor never waver." He continued, "I brought Étienne a loaf of bread and a block of cheese, for they are given little to eat."

"Knowing Étienne, he will share it," I said.

He nodded acknowledgement and looked me in the eye. "Your brother asked me to tell you to pray and to trust in God's love and goodness no matter what comes. And Leonie—" He met her gaze and paused to regain control of his voice. "Étienne asked me to tell you he loves you more than life itself. He begged me to find a way to return you both to Biron." His voice recovered its steadiness at the end. "I told him I fully intend to send you to safety."

Leonie lowered her face into her hands. I put my arm around her shoulders and let her lean on me to weep. A fierce protectiveness filled my heart, the same feeling I recognized in the doctor's face as he looked upon us.

When I indicated my desire to head home, he accompanied me to the front door. "Madame, I advise you to be very careful what you say to anyone; and above all, I beg of you, do not go to the prison again."

I looked him in the eye. A mystery nagging at the back of my brain suddenly asserted itself, and I asked, "How do you know Quent?"

He paused before saying, "Quent is my cousin. He is a man of integrity. You may safely trust in him."

"You sent him to watch over Pascoe?"

"I did. He reports back to me regarding your brother's health; he is not a political spy."

"*En fait,* such a suspicion never once entered my mind. Tell me, *s'il vous plaît:* Is Pascoe's condition worsening?"

I read my answer in his eyes before he spoke. "In recent weeks his attacks have occurred with increasing frequency and intensity. Quent has removed him from a few situations without arousing public suspicion, but at times Pascoe almost seems eager to invite disaster upon himself."

I could easily imagine this. "He has always tested his limits to the extreme," I said quietly. Turning away, I drew an unsteady breath. All three of my brothers were now in imminent danger, and I was helpless to intervene. "I will not tell Pascoe about Quent, monsieur; and I promise not to go to the prison."

"*Merci.* I have hinted to you before; now I must speak plainly. I have called in favors from influential friends to obtain travel papers for you, Leonie, and Étienne. Once he is released, I intend to send you all to safety—you will learn details when it becomes necessary."

"What good are such papers with Étienne in prison?"

His face clouded. "No matter what comes, you must leave Paris."

"What about you?"

His gaze shifted. "I must complete my work here before I think of leaving. First we must focus on Étienne's release. Then we'll take the next step." He stepped outside to summon a chair for me.

I kept further objections to myself. If he thought I would leave him to face danger while I saved my own skin, he would soon learn better.

The next morning, the last day of August, soon after the doctor left the house, Leonie and I were startled by a knock at the kitchen door. I opened it and stood staring dumbly at our visitor.

Just as she had that fateful day last winter, Adrienne waited there at the base of the garden steps, her face dirty and tear-streaked, her eyes red-rimmed. This time, however, her belly was enormously distended. "I came to confess," she said, looking beyond me at Leonie.

"Come in, *ma chère*. You must sit down and put your feet up." I stepped back to allow her entry, leaving the door open. Leonie poured a cup of coffee and gave her a pastry.

Adrienne drank thirstily while Leonie and I exchanged glances. Then she coughed, held her side, and winced. "Did you tell her?" she asked me. "Did you tell Leonie what I did?"

"I have told no one." I had not allowed myself even to think about it, because my thoughts tended to run toward hair-tearing and eye-gouging when I did.

Adrienne took a deep breath then let her words pour out. "Étienne has loved Leonie since we were children. When she went away to school, I tried to get him to notice me. All the girls did." She shrugged. "He was a Girardeau, and they're the best husbands around. But Étienne never gave me a look. He was always true to you, Leonie, and I think every girl in town hated you for it. Not really, but . . . *oui*, really.

"Last winter, when I got pregnant . . ." She blinked hard and struggled to control her voice. "I came here to Colette because I didn't know where else to go. She happened to take me with her to the forge where I met Arnaud, who was an old friend, but that is another story. I told him I was pregnant, but he didn't care; he married me."

"This is all well and good, but why did you suddenly tell him the baby's father was Étienne?" I broke in.

Leonie gave a sharp cry.

Adrienne fixed her gaze on mine. "The baby's father told me I must tell Arnaud that Étienne Girardeau was the father. He said if I didn't, he would kill me, and Arnaud, too."

She shot a glance at Leonie then up at a string of garlic hanging from a support beam. "He would do it. If he ever finds out I told you, he will kill me!"

"Then why are you telling us?"

Again she met my gaze, her eyes wide and slightly defiant. "Arnaud asked me this morning if I lied about Étienne being the baby's father, and . . . and I couldn't lie to him again. I'm afraid he might try to break into the prison; he feels so guilty about accusing Étienne." Her gaze returned to the garlic. "You've got to do something, Colette!"

At least this last part of her revised story was credible. "Did you tell him about the baby's father threatening you?"

"I did, and he is furious that I won't tell who it was." She stared boldly at me. "But if I told him, Arnaud would end up dead!"

I gave her a level look, and this time she shifted her gaze to Leonie, then to the floor. Leonie's expression revealed fury and disgust. A reflection of my own sentiments.

Yet for the first time that day I felt hope. My original plan might work after all, and with the added incentive of guilt, Arnaud was more likely than ever to cooperate.

"Come along, Leonie," I said. "This is an emergency. We will all three take a carriage to the forge and, Adrienne, I shall tell your husband something useful he might do. God willing, the doctor will be able to have Étienne released and none of this will be necessary. But in case the situation worsens, I have a plan."

I cannot honestly say I felt a great deal of concern at the time for Adrienne, who was seriously fatigued from walking to the doctor's house. As a midwife, as a friend, I should have paid more attention, but personal resentment blinded me.

Within the hour our plans were laid. Not only Arnaud, but Philippe and Hérault also, eagerly volunteered their time and energies toward saving Étienne's life. It warmed my heart to witness their determination to rescue a young man who had never joined in their political or social activities yet won their respect with his good humor and quiet dependability.

Now we could only wait.

CHAPTER 28

THIS TIME WHEN THE tocsin rang early Sunday morning, I felt the heaviness of dread press me into my bed. Exactly what form it would take I could not know, but retribution would soon fall upon all prisoners considered dangerous.

Someone knocked at my chamber door. "Madame, what do the bells mean this time?" a small voice inquired.

I dragged myself out of bed and opened the door to see the maids' frightened faces in the light of Hortense's candle. "It means something bad will happen again. We need to pack up clothing for a few days and go to Doctor Hilliard's house."

"Pourquoi?" Hortense asked.

"Quent told me to," I said.

It was reason enough. Apparently Quent had earned their unquestioning loyalty during his few days in the house. The doctor might not appreciate a sudden influx of domestic help, but he had no choice in the matter. I could not leave these two frightened young girls alone in this house during crisis.

Soon we all three tramped along the city streets amid frightened yet orderly crowds. Word of enemy invasion, of prisoners rioting, of plague, of any number of other disasters reached our ears along the way. As we passed the chapel's blocked doors I suddenly wished we might enter, kneel in the quiet, and pray—but there could be no sanctuary in a church.

I could only hope Arnaud, Philippe, and Hérault would keep their word. And I could pray for the eternal souls of those doomed to perish in this latest move of the *sans-culottes*.

Why did I ever encourage this anarchy? How can I ever repay the damage I've caused?

Doctor Hilliard must have seen us coming from a window, for he met us at the front door and shepherded us into the house. "Prepare rooms for the servants and for yourself," he ordered me. "I must find out what is happening. Do not open the door to anyone, and I beg of you, madame, do not go outside again."

"May we gather some food from the garden?" Leonie asked.

"And we'll need to carry water," I added.

He looked disturbed. "Do it quickly and latch the doors once you are inside."

I left Hortense cleaning and arranging the servants' quarters adjoining the kitchen, instructed Leonie to collect fruit and vegetables, and took Anna-Marie to the fountain to draw water.

Anna-Marie followed me like a cringing shadow. "You needn't be frightened, child," I told her with a smile. "Two servants carrying water are unlikely targets for an angry mob." She tried to smile to humor me, but her round eyes held stark fear.

Few other women queued at the fountain. No one knew what was going on; all of us were frightened. Yet we politely waited in turn and hurried home as soon as our buckets were full.

Leonie bolted the kitchen door once I followed Anna-Marie inside.

I baked bread and pies throughout the morning and into the afternoon, and set the maids to work dusting and polishing throughout the house. All of us stripped down to the fewest layers of clothing possible. Even so, the oven's heat was nearly unbearable, and once I sneaked outside to splash my face and arms with water.

Leonie helped me a little in the kitchen, drifted off to supervise the maids, and then took up her sewing. I understood her restlessness but wished she would settle on something instead of wandering like a lost soul. She quoted Scripture about God's faithfulness, which I found encouraging or annoying by turns; and she sang hymns in Latin. Although a part of me would have liked to find fault with her singing, her rich soprano voice was lovely, even soothing.

Hearing a sharp knock at the front door, I charged upstairs, pausing only for a precautionary glance through the salon window before I let Doctor Hilliard inside. He entered and told me to double-bolt the door again. I took his hat and watched him peel off his gloves. His eyes were fixed and unfocused. Despite the sweat running down my face, I went cold inside.

Leonie joined us. "What has happened?" she asked, her voice taut with anxiety.

"Come into the salon, both of you." We followed him and sat down, Leonie on the canapé, the doctor and I on the ugly chairs. He bent his head and rubbed his eyes with both hands. I thought his lips were trembling, but when he straightened they were tightly closed.

"Today, a short distance from here, carriages transporting priests to l'Abbaye prison were openly attacked on the city streets. An organized mob followed the carriages and finished the job when they reached the prison grounds. Every last priest was slaughtered, and more prisoners were brought from inside the prison and killed. Now the killing has spread to other prisons throughout the city."

He spoke coldly, as if relating historical facts rather than the day's events. Yet his shattered expression told me he had witnessed things he would never tell.

"Étienne?" Leonie whispered.

"I do not know. I could learn nothing of him."

I lowered my forehead to my knees as despair swept through me. First Claude, now Étienne. Would I lose Pascoe next? Were all those I loved most to be stripped from me?

We ate together in the kitchen that night, though none of us had much appetite. I ate without tasting and stopped when my plate was empty, and I suspect Leonie did much the same. The maids cleaned up the kitchen without being told; I think they needed something to do. The rest of us drifted into the salon and took our places.

But in the place of my usual seat, the green chair, stood a fat wingback chair with brown leather upholstery. "I brought it in from my office," the doctor explained. "I never used it there."

"Never" was not entirely accurate, but since none of his colleagues had visited him in months, I didn't quibble.

"You should have told me about the green chair's broken seat," he added in a reproving tone. "I would have switched with you."

"Why not switch with me now?" I asked. But he would not hear of taking the comfortable leather chair for himself. Leonie watched me settle into it, and there was a cool glint in her eyes. For the most part she viewed my presence as non-threatening, but she still seemed to resent any particular notice her father might offer me.

Doctor Hilliard closed the front curtains tightly and moved the faded red chair to a spot from which he could see the front door, placing himself between possible intruders and us. Two dueling pistols were holstered under his coat, a third lay beside him on a table, and his sword stick, my fowling piece, and a musket leaned against the wall within reach, along with ramrods, powder horns, and ammunition pouches. Leonie and I each kept one of my muff pistols at hand.

One candle lamp burned on a side table, its small flame insufficient to light the salon. A sconce in the entry hall still burned, but the candle was low. I tucked my feet beneath me in the chair and rested my head back on its wing. But this position put that appalling still-life directly in my view. As luck would have it, the candle lamp highlighted the lifeless pheasant with its head dangling off the painted table. Just looking at it made my neck ache.

I rose, tried to pick up the massive chair, realized I couldn't lift it, and let it fall with a thump. By this time both Hilliards had leapt up to assist in whatever I thought I was doing. I communicated my desire to move the chair across the room. Leonie's expression clearly revealed her opinion of my dearth of sanity, but the doctor placed the chair where the red one had been and arranged it so I would be able to see both of them in their seats. I think he guessed about the painting, but he said nothing.

The street outside buzzed with traffic; occasionally we heard what sounded like shots and the distant roar of many voices. After an extended silence I noticed Leonie quietly crying, and my heart went out to her. I tried to think of something encouraging to say, but it had all been said at some point during that interminable day. Repetition made even truths seem trite.

"Tell me, Leonie," the doctor said, "What is your happiest memory connected with Étienne?"

So our evening passed with trivial conversation. Leonie spoke unwillingly, though once or twice I saw her lose herself in a fond childhood memory. I silently thanked the doctor for his kindness to his daughter. After all he witnessed that day, I doubt he felt much inclined to listen to Leonie's hesitant, meandering memories. But listen he did, and when her words wandered too near the present and the sorrow so heavily surrounding us, his gentle questions guided her back to the past.

I accepted this kindness as partially for my benefit as well, though I do not know if he intended it so. For I, too, needed a distraction. I, too, wanted to hear good words, to indulge in cheerful reminiscences. When Leonie, stumbling a little over her words, spoke of *du Pays de Chaton*, I was even tempted to laugh. Guilt stifled the urge. What kind of heartless beast would laugh while a beloved brother's life either hung in the balance or had already been violently taken?

Strange, how we could sit around the room and discuss insignificant things at such a time!

At long last, Leonie curled up on the canapé to rest, tucking her legs beneath her skirts and her hands beneath her head. I leaned back in my chair, my eyes fixed upon the flame of a flickering candle, watching it writhe in a breath of air then stand still and straight once more. What a fragile little thing it was—one small candle against all the darkness of night. And yet it burned so bright, its tiny glow encouraging the soul with the promise of a sun to rise soon . . . soon . . . .

CHAPTER 29

IT SEEMED AS IF ONLY moments passed before I was rubbing my burning eyes and twisting my neck to fight a terrible cramp. I sat up in the chair. Someone had draped a shawl over me.

Although the candle was extinguished, I could see Leonie sleeping on the canapé. Pale light squeezed in around the window curtains. The doctor was asleep in his chair, his mouth open, his long legs at spider-like angles. Both he and Leonie snored softly.

The sound that awakened me came again, a soft tapping at the front door. I laid aside the shawl, rose from the creaking leather chair, and lifted the curtain to peer out.

Pascoe, standing at the door, turned and met my gaze through the window. Hurriedly I slipped on the sabots I had left near the door and stepped outside, shivering.

My brother's usually neat attire was rumpled, his boots were filthy, and the hems of his trousers were stained several inches deep with what looked horribly like blood. His jabot hung loose at the neck of his shirt.

But it was his face that struck dread into my soul.

"Is it . . . Étienne?" I croaked.

He shook his head. "I tried to find him . . ." His voice trailed off.

Relief that was not relief left me feeling faint. "At the prison?"

"At l'Abbaye." He stared at me, but I knew he did not see me. His eyes seemed to gaze into a private hell.

And then he slowly lowered his gaze to his right hand, which opened and closed repeatedly.

"Pascoe, you are unwell," I said with certainty. "You need to come inside and sit down before you fall down. Where is Quent?"

"He is somewhere near. Colette, I feel—" First his voice broke off. Then his eyes rolled up in his head, and his head began to jerk. He lurched forward, collapsed, and rolled to his side, in immediate danger of tumbling down the front steps.

"Pascoe!" I cried, catching him by the coat tail.

Suddenly Quent and the doctor were there, the one running up the steps to capture Pascoe's flailing feet, the other appearing from behind me to grasp his stiff shoulders. They carried him into the house and laid him on the entryway floor. I followed, closed the door, and pressed my back against it.

As helpless as if I dwelt in a nightmare, I watched my brother's body arch and convulse, listened to his guttural groans. This was far worse than anything I envisioned. I clasped one hand over my mouth to hold any sobs inside.

Doctor Hilliard and Quent hovered over Pascoe but did not touch him.

"Do something!" I begged. "Help him!"

"There is nothing to do but wait for it to pass," Quent said firmly.

Pascoe at last lay still, his eyes half open. Quent turned him to his side. Blood oozed from my brother's mouth. Had he not been breathing heavily, I might have thought him dead.

Doctor Hilliard wiped the blood from Pascoe's face and checked his pulse, then looked up at me. "He will soon return to his senses."

"He has done this before?" I asked. "He isn't dying?"

Quent's gaze turned to me. "He is not dying. You have never before witnessed his attacks?"

I shook my head, and I am certain the horror I felt was written on my face. My legs were shaking, and my hands were tight fists.

"It is shocking to see the first time." He sounded sympathetic. "But he is strong and recovers quickly."

"What causes it?" I asked, almost fearing his answer.

"Doctor Hilliard believes it is caused by some malfunction in the brain."

I looked to the doctor, whose attention was still focused on Pascoe. "It is only a theory," he said. "Science has not yet discovered the cause." He looked up at me. "But I can tell you with confidence that your brother is neither demon-possessed nor insane."

My breath came short and fast. I did not want to know, yet I needed to know: "Might it kill him one of these times?"

"My father suffered from such seizures yet lived nearly seventy years," Quent said. "But my son died before he turned two." His eyes were sad.

"I am sorry," I said. "My daughter died in infancy as well." And I remembered the doctor's son who died at birth.

Quent nodded. "One does not forget such a loss. My son would be twenty-seven had he lived."

"Pascoe will be twenty-seven in January."

Quent's dark eyes studied my face. "He is jealous of your love."

Feeling my face grow warm, I shook my head in frustration. "He has no need to be. No one can replace him in my heart."

"One love does not supplant another."

"*Exactement.*"

Doctor Hilliard said abruptly, "Jean-Baptiste, help me move him to the canapé."

I looked into the salon and realized that Leonie was gone. Had she witnessed Pascoe's attack? He would hate that. Oh, how he would hate it!

Once they had shifted Pascoe's limp form, I helped arrange his limbs into a more comfortable position. "Will he be all right?" I asked, still needing reassurance.

"*Oui,* madame." Again, Quent answered. "Physically, he will be himself by tomorrow. But the horrors he has seen are not so quickly shrugged off."

"You were there too," I observed. "At the prison."

Quent said nothing, but his expression darkened in such a way that my hope for Étienne nearly extinguished. I knelt beside Pascoe and smoothed the bright hair from his waxen forehead. Lines appeared beneath my fingers, and his eyes fluttered open. He grunted and blinked at me, recognition dawning.

Then he glanced around, and more wrinkles appeared, this time between his brows. As he became aware of his location, his expression darkened and he growled like a large dog.

I turned around, but Doctor Hilliard was nowhere in sight. Pascoe's body tensed, and his hands flailed for something to grasp. One gripped the carved back of the canapé, the other clamped upon my shoulder. With another grunt, he sat up, shoving me back on my heels. The first words out of his mouth were curses.

Quent capably removed me from my brother's painful grasp and helped him to stand. "Out of here," Pascoe growled. "Now."

"*Oui,* monsieur." Taking Pascoe by the arm, Quent gave me an apologetic yet comforting glance. I knew I could safely trust this man to care for my brother like his own son. Yet I could not escape the sense that even Pascoe was lost to me now.

The rest of Monday passed much like the day before, although Leonie's spirits were lower, as were mine. Pascoe's name was never mentioned.

Doctor Hilliard attended the Assembly but could offer us no encouragement upon his return. I knew very well that no legislative body on earth possessed the power to stop the flood of murderous, mindless fear engulfing the city of Paris.

We three spent a second night in the salon, unwilling yet to be alone in the dark. I wrapped myself in the shawl and prayed using the beads of my rosary. Although it seemed impossible that Étienne could be alive, I was not yet ready to accept his death. My prayers were more like arguments, as if I could convince God to intervene on behalf of one quiet, red-haired blacksmith. Hearing Leonie sniffle, I dashed a tear from my own face and ran through the beads once more.

When I first woke up, I didn't realize I had slept. Leonie still lay curled up on the canapé and the doctor sprawled in his chair, rubbing his eyes with one hand as if he, too, had just been awakened. The lamp on the side table burned low.

Then we heard it again: a pounding fist at the front door.

The doctor bolted upright and snatched up a pistol. "Stay here," he warned. Leonie sat up and blinked at me from the canapé, her hair rumpled about her face. I glanced at the mantel clock. It was three o'clock Tuesday morning, the fourth day of September. We heard the bolts snap back, the front door creak open, and the doctor's sharp exclamation: "Étienne!"

CHAPTER 30

LEONIE WAS IN THE entry in a moment.

I rushed after her. It didn't seem possible, yet I saw Leonie wrapped in the embrace of a blood-covered man with a mop of tangled hair that reflected a dirty red in the lamplight. "Oh, Étienne! Étienne!" Leonie was sobbing, and I heard my brother's hoarse exclamations in response.

The sleepy-eyed maids emerged from the kitchen amid the excitement and joy. The doctor ordered Hortense to draw and heat a large quantity of water, for Étienne insisted he was too filthy to sit on the furniture until he bathed and changed into clothes not infested with vermin.

The doctor pried him from Leonie's arms long enough to bathe, and when he reappeared he looked much more like himself. The doctor's shirt and waistcoat were a snug fit across the chest, but at least the sleeves and trouser legs were long enough. Étienne's old clothes were thrown into the back of the garden to be burned.

Dawn was breaking before my brother was fed, the tired little housemaids returned to their beds, and we four gathered in the salon, too excited even to think of sleep. Étienne and Leonie seemed intent upon occupying the same space on the canapé simultaneously. The joy in their faces as they looked at each other was so beautiful, I could hardly bear to witness it in more than quick glances.

Étienne told his story that morning, adding details in following days as they occurred to him. It was a difficult tale, and for a man of few words like my brother, more difficult still. I will relate it here as close to his own words as I can recall, omitting interruptions and questions.

He began:

"You can imagine my surprise when the National Guard arrived to escort me to prison. I had noticed a change in atmosphere at the forge and wondered if trouble might be brewing, but an accusation of treason never occurred to me.

"L'Abbaye prison itself was like a glimpse of hell, as the doctor can attest. At first I panicked and raged at the injustice, reminding God of His promises and nearly ordering Him to free me. But then one of my cell mates approached me with a welcoming smile; as you know, it was Père Benedict.

"Imagine! I was imprisoned with the very priest who had mentored, counseled, and encouraged me in the faith during the past two years of turmoil and uncertainty. He said the Lord long ago revealed to him that he would die a martyr's death, and he was ready and willing. His desire was to serve his fellow prisoners and share God's grace with them to his last breath. The other prisoners in our cell were businessmen and priests, none of them enemies of the Republic.

"Sunday afternoon, as I know it was now, we all heard screams and shouts from outside but could not tell what was happening, for our window did not overlook the courtyard. Sometime later we were told by a guard about the ongoing slaughter of priests. All through the night we heard doors slam open and prisoners shouting protests as they were dragged downstairs. Each time we anticipated we would be next. Père Benedict and I prayed together throughout the night, and the next day a priest came to our cell and gave us last rites. He looked as horror-stricken as we did, and who can say whether he survived that day?

"A guard bringing us food and water kindly advised us how best to position ourselves, when the time came, in order to have the quickest possible death. We did see a few executions from our window; when prisoners attempted escape they were hacked to pieces by the surrounding crowds.

"I must tell you I experienced a strange sense of peace while awaiting my certain death. I prayed for comfort and healing for you who would mourn my death, and for your continued safety. Rather than waste time on dread or recrimination, I also talked and prayed with my fellow prisoners until, at last, our group was called down to stand trial late Monday evening.

"The trials were a mockery. The verdict was always guilty, no matter the charge, no matter the testimony. One after another, I watched my companions brutally killed. Some screamed and fought, but most met their deaths bravely. Père Benedict was among the latter, and I saw glory in his face at the end.

"When my name was called, I stepped forward to stand before the small tribunal of filthy, blood-soaked men. I answered their questions honestly. I proclaimed myself innocent of treason and described my job of making swords and arms for the French military.

"Imagine my surprise when one of the executioners, a huge man so covered in blood and gore as to be unrecognizable, stepped forward and spoke in my defense. It was Arnaud Lamorges, who retracted his accusation, saying he had mistaken me for another man. Next, Philippe joined him, and then Hérault. All three who, only moments before, were hacking the other prisoners to death, testified that I had always labored long and hard on behalf of the Republic and never once spoke in favor of the former King or any of France's enemies.

"The crowd roared approval at this, and suddenly I was a hero! After the tribunal declared me innocent of all charges, Arnaud and Philippe hoisted me to their shoulders and carried me out through the cheering crowd. Women threw their handkerchiefs to me, and one ran forward and pulled off my shoe. The faces around us glowed orange in the firelight, and eyes and teeth glittered as they cheered . . . I shudder to think of it.

"Arnaud and Philippe carried me all the way out of the crowds before they set me down on a street corner. After Philippe ran back, Arnaud told me to hurry home and to keep my head low. I went first to the other house and found it empty, so I came here."

After completing this narrative, Étienne ended with a weary shake of his head, saying, "Now it all seems like an evil dream, yet I know it is true."

He answered a few questions for us then lay down on his side with his head on Leonie's lap, his feet on the floor, and his legs angled in all directions. Despite the impossibility of his position, he fell soundly asleep. Leonie gazed down at his face, her expression blissful, and smoothed the hair from his forehead.

"Would either of you ladies like a cup of coffee?" the doctor asked.

Leonie declined. "I shall sit here and rest while Étienne sleeps." She would be asleep herself within minutes.

"*Merci, s'il vous plaît*" was my reply. I followed the doctor downstairs into the kitchen and sat in my usual place to watch while he ground the coffee beans, boiled water, and worked his magic with the brew.

Then he set my coffee before me and seated himself, wrapping his long fingers around his cup and regarding it pensively. I took a sip, burned my lip, and set my cup down. Silence reigned, a silence filled with portent I felt unwilling to break. Any comment I might make on the miracle of Étienne's return would seem superfluous.

Recalling my angry, doubt-filled prayers, I could only marvel.

When my cup was nearly empty the doctor finally spoke. "Time is short." His gaze held resolve. "I believe it is imperative Étienne be removed from Paris as soon as the barriers are raised. Whoever wants him dead will not be pleased to discover he has been released."

"Leonie told you Adrienne's story?" I asked.

"She did."

"I think she was lying or telling a partial truth, but I have no proof. Étienne will not leave Leonie, you know," I said.

"I fully intend to send them to safety together. I have obtained papers for you as well and would be relieved if you would accompany them."

"If they marry first, they will have no need of a chaperone."

He frowned, holding my gaze. "Even now you will not leave?"

"Do you intend to leave Paris as well?" I asked.

"Not immediately." He looked down at his empty cup, rubbing its rim with his thumb. "I cannot compel you to leave, Madame DeMer, but I earnestly entreat you to consider the possibility. Civilization within this city is breaking down; I fear for its future in the short term. If you go, you can just as easily return someday."

He met my gaze, and my defenses weakened. "Whether I go or not, we need a priest to marry them first, and we need a strategy. His friends might be willing to help again."

"Again?" His dark eyes studied my face. "Did you arrange for Étienne's friends to be at l'Abbaye?"

How did he guess? "I did not know they would be executioners at the prison; I merely asked Arnaud to try to protect Étienne, and all three offered to help."

"You, madame, are a powerful ally."

Satisfaction undoubtedly showed on my face. "Be grateful I am on your side, monsieur."

"Most assuredly I am." He pushed back his chair, and rose. "I must at least show my face at the Assembly and perhaps pick up useful news." At the door he turned back. "Please take no risks today. I'm too old for this sort of thing."

Leonie and Étienne were still sleeping when I took the maid Hortense with me to market. But vendors were few, and selection was poor in quality as well as quantity. Eventually, after walking a long way, we found a fish seller's stall at the riverside. While I haggled over the price, Hortense let out a hoarse scream. I followed her fixed stare and saw a naked, mutilated body float past in the Seine.

"*Beurk!* It's one of those prisoners," the fish seller said, wrinkling her nose. "Blood runs in the streets, they say. Bodies pile up faster than carters can haul them away. But we're safer now, *est-ce que?*"

Hortense looked greener around the gills than did the carp in our baskets when we headed back home. I'm sure I looked no better. My heart was like a stone in my breast. I felt it beating a heavy *thump, thump.* But at least it still beat.

Étienne was standing in the kitchen when we entered. He turned his head to acknowledge me but remained solemn. I told Hortense to leave her basket on the worktable and go upstairs to straighten the bedchambers. Then, despite my fishy hands, I walked into my brother's embrace, and we stood there drawing comfort and strength from each other.

"Merci, Colette," he said. "Arnaud told me what you did, asking them to be there."

"I didn't know they would be executioners." I shuddered, thinking of Père Benedict. But, no. I couldn't allow myself to think of him. Not yet. I gently pulled out of Étienne's grasp, forcing my thoughts to focus on here and now, nothing more. "You must be hungry, and I know Leonie will be starving when she awakens. We could hardly eat while you were imprisoned, and I'm sure you ate very little."

He didn't argue.

I prepared crêpes and fruit for a light brunch and mixed bread dough to rise. Anna-Marie cleaned the fish while Hortense did the basic housecleaning. "Madame," Anna-Marie said quietly. "I heard mention of needing a priest for a wedding. My brother is a priest at Église Saint-Jacques-du-Haut-Pas. He will come here if I ask him."

"Are you certain he will come?"

"He swore loyalty to the Republic, so he is safe," she said. "I have told him of Monsieur Étienne's kindness, and yours. He will do this for you."

So one difficulty could be overcome. More challenging would be my interview with the prospective groom. But I had talked him into wearing a costume to a masquerade ball; a wedding should be easy in comparison.

As it turned out, no convincing was necessary: Étienne and Leonie had already decided to marry and were grateful for my offer to provide a priest. I made arrangements with Anna-Marie to accompany me to the church. The doctor would no doubt have considered this outing dangerous, but I counted the cost and took the risk.

When Doctor Hilliard arrived home that evening, he found a very nervous young priest seated on the edge of the wingback chair in the salon. I introduced them: "Doctor Hilliard, this is Père Jerome. Père Jerome, this is the bride's father."

I give the doctor full credit; he greeted the priest politely then asked to be excused for a moment. I was not terribly surprised to have my elbow taken in a firm grasp or to be hustled unobtrusively into the library. "What is this about?" His voice was dangerously quiet.

I slightly raised my brows and spoke. "Étienne and Leonie wish to marry."

"Does it follow that they must have this wish fulfilled tonight?"

I ticked off reasons on my fingers. "They will be staying together in this house for several days, and neither you nor I can always be near to chaperon. Very soon they will be traveling extensively together. Do you honestly think it proper for them to postpone their vows?"

After a brief yet eloquent pause he said, *"Non,* but I shall add a stipulation. If I agree to this wedding, will you agree to accompany them to England?"

It was the first time he had openly stated their destination. My eyes widened, and I repeated the word silently, "England?"

"I have been in contact with Leonie's grandfather. He is making the necessary arrangements for a rendezvous late next week."

I swallowed hard. Almost I asked what he would do if I refused, but instead I nodded.

The wedding was a quiet, sober affair. The doctor loaned Étienne a suit, and from the depths of a trunk he produced a shawl of Brussels lace. Leonie wore this family heirloom over her pink masquerade gown.

My little brother and his bride, both drawn and pale from stress and fatigue, exchanged vows there in the salon. But through the exhaustion and the ever-present fear, their love for each other shone in their eyes, lending them a special radiance.

There were smiles and congratulations. Above all, there was love centered on the young couple. They represented all any of us could hope for—a promise of life in the midst of death.

The doctor pressed me to stay another night at the house, since violence continued throughout the city, not limiting itself to the execution of prisoners. So I slept in my small chamber next to the kitchen, discovering too late that the bed was musty. The two maids in the next room talked in hushed, frightened voices long after I wanted to be asleep, but eventually I was allowed to think and, truth be told, shed a few tears in peace.

CHAPTER 31

I T WAS STRANGE TO awaken in the doctor's house, not in a chair in the salon, but in the servants' quarters. I rose and dressed myself then slipped through the kitchen and out into my garden to enjoy the freshness of dawn. I disturbed a toad on the path between marrows and melons, but nothing else stirred on the ground at this hour. After gathering ripe fruit and vegetables enough to fill four baskets, I paused to stretch my back and studied the house, feeling rather melancholy. A very ordinary building it was in a forgotten corner of the *faubourg*. Yet I had spent some of the happiest hours of my life here.

Later in the morning I set out to visit my particular friends in the *section*, taking along Hortense, who yawned openly at every stop. Knowing I would soon be leaving altered my viewpoint. Nothing was the same. My friends, who always looked weary, now seemed to carry the added burden of impending doom. They thanked me for the fresh produce with wan smiles and an air of hopelessness.

Despite my dislike of Madame Gallatin, I made a stop at her door. To my surprise, Madame herself opened at my knock. "Eh, bring it into the kitchen. Tressy can put it away when she comes down."

Something in her tone alerted me. "Is Tressy ill?"

"She is well enough. Her infant died in the night, and she's taking it hard."

"Infant? She gave birth? I didn't know." Sorrow and guilt filled my throat.

"It came last week. It never thrived. Better off this way." The woman's flat tone infuriated me, but I did my best to remain pleasant and asked if I might see Tressy. She motioned me on, so I climbed to a closet of a room in the garret with Hortense at my heels.

To my further surprise and increasing anger, I discovered that no one had told Tressy what to do with the tiny body.

"I named him Fabien," she said heavily, holding the still little form tenderly in her arms. "He never cried much."

"Hortense, go downstairs and send a lad for the undertaker." I pressed a coin in her hand. "Tell him it is an infant."

While we waited, I washed the body and dressed him in one of the gowns I had brought to his mother weeks before. The undertaker, a small man with a lined face and a bald head, surprised me with his respectful manner and quiet consideration. He had actually nailed together a small box before he arrived. Tressy and I lined it with an old shawl, laid the baby inside, and took a moment to admire his delicate features and soft, curly hair. Tressy wept on my shoulder while Monsieur Lazarus nailed down the lid.

Grateful for his rare kindness, I paid the man extra. After regarding the coins in his hand, he gave me a diffident glance and said, "If you'd like to ride along to the burial grounds . . ."

We three girls sat in the back of the hearse beside the little coffin. The guards at the city gate knew Monsieur Lazarus and let us through, which was a blessing. Little Fabien Gallatin was buried with other outcasts and foreigners at the far end of a weedy graveyard dotted with ancient trees. "He'll have shade in the afternoons," Tressy remarked as the gravedigger stood in the deepening hole, tossing loose earth into a pile.

He dug until he reached another small box, then made room and gently laid Fabien's coffin atop it. "It was another child," the gravedigger said. "A little Turk, as I recall."

"They can rise together at the resurrection," Monsieur Lazarus said. The unexpected compassion of these two men nearly brought me to tears.

At Tressy's request, I spoke a few words over her baby's grave. It seemed appropriate to relate the story of the little children coming to Jesus and his rebuke to his disciples to "Let the little children come to me, for the Kingdom of Heaven is made up of such as these." Perhaps I embroidered the tale a bit, but I think Père Benedict would have approved.

I wrapped my arms around Tressy's bowed shoulders. "The saints have welcomed little Fabien into heaven. Christ Himself holds him on His knee even now, making him smile and laugh as he never could here on earth."

"Jesus would hold *my* baby on His knee?" she asked, her dark eyes filled with unshed tears.

"Certainly he would. Remember? He said the Kingdom of Heaven is filled with innocent babies from everywhere in the world. All the little ones who never knew happiness here, they are happier than we can imagine there with Him." And as I spoke the words, I believed they were true. Even Hortense stared at me in undisguised awe.

We rode into the city on the undertaker's cart and walked back from his shop. On the way, Tressy told me that Madame Gallatin looked every day for news of her husband's fate. I considered his survival most unlikely.

Tressy's situation weighed on my heart. She was one step away from a life of total degradation, at the mercy of a woman who hated her and considered her a burden. Just paying for her baby's burial had emptied my purse; I could never afford to purchase Tressy. So I prayed for the bereft young mother. Surely the Jesus who loved children would not despise this helpless girl, hardly more than a child herself. Surely Mary, the Holy Mother, would look with mercy upon the plight of another humble young mother.

After such an emotionally draining morning, I almost dreaded seeing Adrienne. Despite her repentance and Étienne's rescue, our interactions would be strained. When we arrived at the forge, Hortense was pleased to wait outside in a patch of shade. I believe she feared encountering another death in my company. The forge itself was silent; I assumed the smiths were all still at the prison.

To my surprise, Arnaud responded to my hail and brought me inside. Adrienne was asleep, so we spoke in undertones.

"I served out that night at the prison and part of the next day," he said, "but once Étienne was safe I lost interest." A troubled look flickered across his face. "Not many of those prisoners looked like a threat to public safety, no more than Étienne is." Then his eyes widened warily. "Not that I'm speaking out against things, you understand."

As I unloaded grapes, plums, vegetables, and Tressy's unused baby garments and blankets from my basket, I thought of Père Benedict with a sharp pang. I knew he would not have wanted me to harbor anger, but I could not look at Arnaud without wondering if his hands had slain the gentle priest.

I replied with forced composure: "I do understand, Arnaud, and you needn't fear me. Friends don't betray friends. You rescued Étienne, and I am forever in your debt."

He shrugged his great shoulders as if they bore a heavy load. "I was wrong to accuse a good man. Adrienne says the baby's real father is dangerous, a powerful man who would have us all killed if she were to tell his name. If he finds out Étienne is alive . . ."

I snatched at the opportunity. "Étienne needs to leave Paris. He and

Leonie were married last night," I said. "They both need to leave Paris."

He nodded. "If they don't, Étienne's enemy will try to kill him some other way. And he might come after Adrienne, too." To him, the story made perfect sense. "What about you, Colette?"

"Étienne and Leonie want me to come with them," I admitted. "Étienne thinks I might be in danger too." Which was true, although not from the enemy Arnaud suspected. We all had our doubts about this "powerful man" of Adrienne's invention.

"But what about Adrienne's baby?" he asked. It was strange to see such desperation on his tough face. "If you go away, who will help her?"

"Colette?" Adrienne called, her voice tremulous.

I hurried to her bedside, grateful to avoid Arnaud's question. *"Bonjour, ma petite.* How are you feeling?"

She mumbled something and avoided meeting my gaze until I caught hold of her pale face and looked directly into her eyes. "Adrienne, you are my friend. I forgive you for endangering my brother's life. You are forgiven. Pray to the Virgin to intercede for you before the throne of God. He will forgive you too."

I do not know how sincerely I meant the words. But I knew I must say them. Perhaps, if spoken, they would become truth in my heart.

"What about Leonie?" Adrienne mumbled.

I could speak for neither Leonie nor my brother. So I said only, "I know you don't hate Étienne and weren't plotting to have him killed. In time, they will know it too."

She closed her eyes and remained passive while I checked on her baby. I was not happy with its position. I pushed and prodded, trying to discern knees from elbows. "The little one is getting crowded in there." I pressed a bulge in her belly, and the baby moved away in response. "Adrienne, I know you don't like him, but please let me bring Doctor Hilliard to see you."

"Why?" she inquired sharply.

I did my best to explain without alarming her. "I think the baby might be turned the wrong way. I have never encountered this situation before, and the doctor would more likely know what to do."

"I have heard of babies coming feet-first before." Her tone revealed uncertainty, but she set her jaw. "Doctor Hilliard doesn't like me; he won't care about my baby."

"Why do you think that?" I asked in blank surprise.

"He shouted at me once." She resembled nothing so much as a sullen child. "I knocked a crystal brandy decanter on the floor."

"I don't remember that."

She shrugged. "You weren't there. I was only thirteen. It was the only time I ever drank his liquor, I swear."

My brows rose high. "You were drinking it?"

"The decanter wouldn't have smashed if he hadn't frightened me." She paused. "It made an awful stain."

I struggled to keep frustration out of my voice. "Adrienne, if he disliked you, he would not have brought you along to Paris with the rest of us."

"*Non,*" she repeated firmly.

"Then may I at least ask his advice?"

I'm afraid I sounded angry, for she adamantly shook her head. But then her face drooped. "I only want you, Colette." Her voice and eyes were so imploring, my heart went out to her—she was so young and miserable and frightened. For the moment I truly did forget my anger at her. I kissed her forehead and left her to rest.

Arnaud followed me outside. "What do you think?"

"I wish she would let me consult Doctor Hilliard. See if you can't convince her, Arnaud."

He looked nearly as despondent as his wife. "She never listens to me. What will we do if you leave the city?"

"If I must leave before the baby comes, I will make Doctor Hilliard promise to care for her. Perhaps this will be best anyway. You know where Adrienne keeps the rags and blankets and necessities I've been bringing to her all these months, and I'm sure the doctor will show you how to care for the baby's needs."

Arnaud looked no happier, but he nodded. "I don't fancy having a Girondin in my house, but I will do it if you say so. Anyway, I promise to help you all to leave Paris safely. It is the least I can do."

Hortense and I took a carriage back to Doctor Hilliard's house. I smiled when she told me about the goat biting a hole in her basket, but my thoughts were elsewhere. Tressy. Adrienne. Pascoe. How could I leave them behind and run off to a strange country? What would become of Hortense and Anna-Marie? My garden would go to ruin . . .

The following days passed in a whirl of preparation and dread of the unknown. Anna-Marie left us to keep house for her brother, and Hortense found a new position in the household of a prominent Girondin deputy. I was sorry to see them go, but we could speak more freely of our plans when only family was present. When the prison massacres finally ended that Friday and the city gates opened once more to limited traffic, we were able to settle on Monday as the day of departure.

Sunday evening, Étienne, Leonie, Doctor Hilliard and I sat in the salon, discussing routes to the coast and how far a pair of mules could be expected to travel each day. At least, those three discussed travel plans; I was waiting for the right opening to make my announcement.

"I do not think I can leave Paris tomorrow."

"Why not?" Doctor Hilliard spoke sharply.

"Nonsense," said Leonie.

Étienne frowned.

Defensive and outnumbered, I shook my head. "Pascoe is unwell.

Adrienne has not yet delivered her baby. Tressy needs my help. So many people need my help. And what would I do in England? I don't understand more than a few words of English."

"If you don't come along with us, I won't leave Paris," Étienne said. "I don't trust Pascoe to protect you, and Claude is gone."

Leonie gave him a startled look but remained quiet.

"You need protection yourself, Étienne," I pointed out. "You are the one in danger, not I."

"If such danger even exists," he returned sharply.

"Pascoe is in good hands, and I have promised to assist your friend with her delivery," the doctor said in a level tone that failed to conceal his anger. "Who is this other person? If I can assist them, I will."

"Tressy is a slave girl owned by Madame Gallatin. Other than purchasing her, I don't know how you could help," I snapped in response.

"You promised to come, Colette," Leonie said, obviously distressed. "We need you."

I could not imagine how I would be needed, unless as a cook or housekeeper. She and Étienne had each other and would be quite content. But there was no point in arguing, for she was right: I was bound by my own word.

CHAPTER 32

W E RUSHED ABOUT THE the dark house, making last-minute preparations. Arnaud delivered the cart and the mules, which he had stabled at the forge, before dawn. Our journey lay to the northwest, yet Arnaud instructed us to take a west gate from the city. The guards there were his friends and would give us no trouble.

There had been a chilly distance between the doctor and me since that conversation the night before. I racked my brain for a way to make amends but could think of nothing beyond my reluctant capitulation. What more did he want from me? I could not feign delight or gratitude about this situation, although I knew he risked much for my sake.

Doctor Hilliard and Étienne loaded baggage and bundles. I brought along very little; Leonie's trunks occupied most of the cart bed. When she returned to the house for something forgotten, I approached the doctor.

"Have you made arrangements yet to visit your dying father?"

"I have not as yet." He sounded guarded.

"You need to do so. You will always regret it if you neglect this chance to reconcile with him." I stared up at him.

His eyes traveled over my face.

Then Leonie slipped between us. "You will try to come to England soon, won't you, Papa?"

"I shall endeavor to do so, but the future is not mine to control." His voice was husky.

"I will pray," she said. "You must pray too."

"I am trying," he replied. "I am learning."

She gave him a light kiss in parting, and I hurt for him. Even her request for him to join them sounded distant, as if she spoke only as required.

I made a quick decision, stepped forward, stood on tiptoe, and pulled his head down until I could kiss his cheek. *"Au revoir, mon cher docteur."*

Then Étienne helped me into the cart bed, where I sat on a trunk, and the doctor helped Leonie up to her seat. She held on to her father's hand while Étienne climbed to the driver's seat beside her and released the brake. "Thank you again for everything, monsieur," he said to his father-in-law, his voice also gruff.

"You have the papers?" Doctor Hilliard asked once more.

Étienne patted his waistcoat. "They are safe, monsieur. *Adieu.*" He clucked to the mules, and the cart lurched away.

Seated in the back, I was able to see the doctor without turning around. Leonie waved to him, and he waved back; then she faced forward.

He was still watching us. I lifted a hand. In response Doctor Hilliard lifted his, and then he deliberately placed his hand over his heart. I hurriedly pressed my hand over my own pounding heart and watched until the curving road hid him from view. I did not regret my audacity. Perhaps now he had some idea how much his kindness to me was valued. I smiled and wiped tears from my face while rattling along the city streets.

Traffic entering the city gate was particularly heavy with farmers bringing crops and animals to sell at market, since for most of the past week they had been denied entry. Our cart was one of a few waiting at the gate to leave the city.

"Colette!" I thought I heard my name. "Colette!"

"Is someone calling you?" Leonie asked, turning on her seat.

I stood up in the cart bed and stared along the street behind us. A figure appeared, large and dark. Hatless and coatless, he approached at a shambling run. "Colette, wait!"

It was Arnaud Lamorges. The answer to my prayers.

"Adrienne, she is in labor and the baby won't come," he gasped. *"S'il vous plaît!* You must come! You promised to be there for her. You promised!"

No longer in doubt, I turned to Étienne. "I cannot go with you. I have a promise to keep."

He looked me in the eye, and for a moment I feared he would argue. Then he nodded. Quickly he withdrew the packet of papers, selected mine, and handed them to me. "Keep it safe."

I tucked them into my reticule. The wagon in front of us was moving on; there was no time for prolonged farewells. I kissed my brother and my sister-in-law. "Take care of each other. *Adieu.*"

Arnaud took my bag and helped me down, and the cart rolled forward. "Take care of Papa," I heard a thin voice say.

I turned back. "I will."

The gate guards took the papers from Étienne without delay. After what seemed an age but was probably moments, they returned them and beckoned him through. One of the guards waved a greeting to Arnaud, who returned it.

After all the worry and flurry, it was that easy. God willing, the rest of their journey would be equally uneventful.

I flagged a carriage, and we were quickly on our way to the forge. "Why did you not call for Doctor Hilliard?" I asked. "He promised to come."

"Adrienne wanted you, and I thought I might catch you before you reached the gate," he said. "When I got home from delivering the cart, she screamed at me to go back and get you. She said she'd been in labor for hours. But how was I to know? She didn't tell me." Leaning forward on the seat, for the top of the carriage was too low for him to sit upright, he rubbed his huge hands together.

"We will be there soon," I said in a soothing tone. When we approached the forge, I gave him the money to pay the driver; and as soon as the carriage stopped, I was out the door and running to the house. I could hear her keening cry before I opened the door.

I dropped my things and ran to the bed. Only one rush lamp lighted the house, revealing Adrienne on the bed, shining with sweat and deathly pale. "Colette!" she cried. "Help me. Oh, please help me!"

I took a moment to look into her eyes and grip her hand before I checked the baby's progress. She was mostly dilated, but something was seriously wrong. "When did your hard labor begin?" I asked.

"Just before Arnaud left this morning."

A few hours of hard labor. And she already looked nearly limp. I turned to Arnaud, who stood at the bedside. "Get Doctor Hilliard. Now. If you hurry, he will not yet have left for the Assembly."

Arnaud's face looked stricken. "She is bad?"

"I don't know," I said. "I just don't know."

But I did know.

While he was away I heated water and bathed Adrienne's face and body, removing layers of dirt and a few parasites. Although she was sweating profusely, the warm cloths I laid over her belly seemed to soothe her. I brewed tea and gave her sips of it between contractions.

And I changed the bed linens, slipping the sweaty, smelly sheet from beneath her and replacing it with a clean one. I also covered her naked form with a second sheet for modesty. Even these changes seemed comforting, and she was visibly calmer despite her pain. "Colette!" she called when I was out of her sight for a moment. "I must tell you something before Arnaud returns."

"What is that, *petite?*" I hurried back with a fresh cup of tea. I was no herb woman, but I did know the soothing power of chamomile.

"The baby's father—" Her face crumpled, and she sobbed too hard to speak. Another contraction came, and she screamed in pain and frustration.

"Pascoe," she wailed as soon as she was able. "It is Pascoe. And he doesn't know it!"

As if turned to stone, I could only stare as she poured out her jumbled tale in a raspy whisper. "He doesn't know about the baby. I never told him I was pregnant. He didn't threaten me or Étienne; I made that up so Arnaud would stop pushing me to tell him who it was. I thought Arnaud suspected Pascoe after that night you brought him here, so I told him it was Étienne because he likes Étienne and I didn't think he would hurt him like he would hurt Pascoe. And"—she finally stopped to draw breath—"I want you to know so you will take the baby and raise her to be your daughter if I die. But on your brother's life, don't tell Arnaud! I know he would kill Pascoe, and I could never bear that . . . ." And she began sobbing again.

I could think of nothing to say, and even had I thought of something there would have been no time to say it, for just then the door opened and Doctor Hilliard entered, carrying his medical bag and a lantern. "Leave the door ajar," he ordered. Arnaud, visibly cowed, followed him inside and hovered near the open door.

I had never before realized quite how thoroughly the doctor's presence filled a room. He surveyed the place in a glance and advised Arnaud to remove the goat, which was placidly chewing its cud in one corner, and to leave both doors and all windows open for better air circulation and for light. "I will also require a large quantity of boiled water."

As Arnaud hurried to comply with these demands, the doctor removed his outer garments, laid them and the big dueling pistols neatly on a bench, and rolled up his shirtsleeves. At last he turned his gaze on me, and I saw a confusing mix of emotions in his eyes—the foremost being anger—before he blinked and again focused on duty. "Tell me everything."

I related details of Adrienne's pregnancy and labor, answering his questions as best I could. He washed his hands with soap before examining her; I took note of this for future reference. And he greeted her politely, mentioning her mother. Adrienne stared up at him with a sort of spellbound awe and could scarcely answer his questions.

Stepping back after examining her, he wiped his hands on one of the clean rags I provided for his use and beckoned me aside. "You are correct: The presentation is breech and the infant is large. Madame Lamorges will need to push very hard when the time comes, and even then I do not know if the birth will be possible. I could attempt to remove the infant surgically . . . ." He shook his head. "Madame's chances of survival are slim."

"I think she can deliver the baby," I said. "She loves it very much."

His gaze softened briefly. "And you love her very much. I shall do my best to save them both." He glanced back at Adrienne, who was beginning to tense up with another contraction. "You bathed her?"

"I did." The poor girl was still pale, but she looked less ghastly without the grimy streaks on her face and the ring of crusted dirt around her neck.

"*Bonne fille.* If you can encourage her to breathe deeply during her contractions, it will help both her and the baby. Will her husband wish to be involved?"

"I don't know. What can he do?" I had never considered allowing a man in the birthing room.

"He might hold and support her while she pushes. I will ask him while you help her."

And we each moved to our stations. Adrienne did her best to follow my instructions, concentrating with all her might on breathing deeply through the labor pains. Arnaud came to sit behind her, and she leaned against his broad chest, draped in the clean sheets, which were no longer quite so clean.

When her water broke, Doctor Hilliard told her to push with the next contraction. She pushed with all her small being, squeezing my hands until my fingers turned purple. How she labored to deliver that baby, screaming and groaning and wailing in agony and frustration!

I could not see what the doctor was doing, but the sounds I heard indicated his efforts to help ease the baby into the world. Several times he wiped his face on his shoulder to remove sweat. Always he talked to Adrienne, telling her of the baby's progress, encouraging her in soothing tones that contrasted with his anxious face.

Adrienne's tortured screams wrenched my heart; I knew this was not ordinary labor pain. Arnaud wept as he talked to her. "You can do it, Adrienne," he said with every push.

At last I heard a gush, and I saw intense concentration on the doctor's face. With the blood-smeared baby cradled in his hands, he sat back on his heels and placed his mouth over the infant's face. A girl, I saw. Several times he sucked liquid from her nose and mouth then spat on the floor. Next he held the baby up by her tiny feet and firmly struck her back. And then I heard the cry, a bubbling, angry wail that signified life. He handed her to me and turned quickly back to the mother.

I wrapped the baby—my niece!—in a new blanket and rubbed her vigorously all over, stimulating new cries and cleaning off the blood and mucus. I clamped off the umbilical cord with two clothespins and cut it with a sharp knife. The baby looked perfect to me despite her bowed legs and puffy features. Already she seemed alert and aware and furious.

"May I hold her?" Adrienne asked, her voice scarcely above a whisper. Quickly I laid the bundled baby in her arms, watching in approval as the infant latched on to nurse as if she had always known how. Arnaud looked pale and frightened, gazing at his wife with something approaching worship.

But Adrienne was still in terrible pain. She had delivered the afterbirth, but there was far too much blood. Along with pride and joy in her face as she fed her baby, there was something else, something I did not want to see.

When the doctor first handed the baby to me I had read triumph and joy in his eyes, the joy of a life saved. Now I turned to him again, and this time I read a message that turned my heart to lead.

What was happening? What could be done? My thoughts raced madly as I worked. The doctor washed his hands and arms in a bucket, but his sleeves were still blood soaked. I did everything possible to make Adrienne comfortable, then bundled the soiled linens for Minette and her boys to collect on laundry day and stepped outside to dump the bowls and buckets of dirty water.

Doctor Hilliard followed me outside and closed the door. I turned to meet his gaze, noting the dark circles beneath his eyes. His white shirtfront was spattered with blood. "For a time," he said slowly, "I believed we would lose them both. The baby's survival . . ." He shook his head. "I dared not even hope. Even so, these next hours are crucial."

"What is wrong with Adrienne?"

"I believe she is bleeding internally. I have seen it before after breech births. Unless by some miracle the bleeding stops, she will die."

CHAPTER 33

ADRIENNE KNEW. No one needed to tell her. When the doctor and I returned to the room, she gave me a direct look. "You will raise her for me, Colette? My little Elodie Faye."

I nodded, my face working as I fought back tears.

Arnaud gave a wrenching sob and swore. *"Non! Non,* Adrienne. God cannot take you!"

"He does not take me, Arnaud. I need only take a step to be with Him." Adrienne's voice had an ethereal quality so very different from its usual tone.

Doctor Hilliard took her wrist to find her pulse. "Are you in pain, madame?" he asked.

She scrunched her face. "Not anymore. My body feels heavy and my head feels light. But there is nothing else. Even my arms feel heavy." She looked at me. "Colette, my baby will need a nursemaid."

The answer was already there, waiting for me. "Tressy. We need Tressy," I said to myself, and turned sharply to the doctor. "May I speak to you again in private?"

He rose and followed me outside, where I whirled to face him, standing close and keeping my voice low. "The slave girl I told you about. She lost her baby a few days ago. She would still have milk for . . . for Elodie."

"Will her master allow her to nurse this baby?" He crossed his arms as if to put distance between us.

"Her master was in prison, quite possibly killed in the massacre. The man's wife is a hard, cruel woman who would never allow Tressy out of her control, but I think she might sell her."

A strange look crossed the doctor's tired face. "So now I am to purchase a slave?"

"It is the only way, monsieur." I touched his arm.

He looked down at my hand then met my gaze again. "I will purchase her for you, Colette. Tell me what to say and where to go, and it will happen."

We left the baby sleeping in her cradle and Adrienne sleeping in Arnaud's arms. The doctor smelled slightly of blood, but his outer garments concealed it from view. Anyone passing us would undoubtedly have thought the stink came from me, for my travel gown bore several stains. He was obliged to visit a bank and then, since no driver or carriers would go there, we walked to Madame Gallatin's house.

"If she sees that you are eager she will ask a higher price," I told him on the way. "And you must not mention my name. If she connects me with you in any way, she might refuse to let her go at all, for I know she wishes Tressy ill."

When we reached the house and I explained my plan to wait for him outside, I had to show him the muff pistol in my reticule before he would leave me there. At last he entered the building and knocked at Madame's door. I resisted the urge to peer around the corner, but I could hear at least some of the conversation.

"*Bonjour,* madame," the doctor said in his splendid voice. "I require a wet nurse for an orphaned infant and heard through rumor of a slave in your possession who might serve the purpose."

"I . . . Ah . . . *Oui,*" Madame stammered. I smiled in grim satisfaction. Let her just try to dominate Doctor Hilliard.

His tone hinted at boredom and distinct impatience. "Might I see the slave, madame." It was not a question.

"*Mais bien sûr,* monsieur." Her obsequious voice nearly squeaked. "Step into the parlor, *s'il vous plaît?*"

A pause. I could easily picture his expression as he surveyed her filthy apartment and would hardly have blamed him for refusing. But he stepped inside, no doubt obliged to duck through the low doorway, and I missed the rest of the transaction.

A short time later the door opened again, and I heard madame advising the doctor to keep an eye on Tressy, for she was a sneaking liar and thief. By her tone I could tell she was not entirely satisfied with the outcome of her haggling.

"Come along, and never fear. There is someone waiting here who knows you," I heard the doctor say in a far different tone from that he had used toward Madame Gallatin.

When Tressy stepped outside and saw me, her expression transformed from sullen fear to surprise, and then to overwhelming relief. "Madame DeMer!" She rushed toward me, and I put my arm around her shoulders.

"You!" Madame Gallatin stepped outside and pointed at me, clutching her thin wrapper around her shoulders. Her glare turned to the doctor. "You tricked me!"

His voice and manner turned frightfully cold. "In what respect were you deceived, madame? I purchased the slave on behalf of Madame DeMer at a fair market price. You counted and accepted the money, which is there in your hand; and you signed the bill of sale, which transfers ownership of the property in question to Madame Colette DeMer. Had you bothered to read it, you would know this." He bowed with devastating hauteur. *"Bonjour."*

As he turned his back on her to join us, I heard several cheers and saw familiar faces in windows and doorways. "Good luck to you, Tressy *fille,"* one woman called.

"Our Lady's blessing upon you, Madame DeMer," another cried from her window as we progressed along the street. "And upon your fine gentleman friend."

When we reached the forge, Doctor Hilliard stopped us in the yard. "I must attend the Assembly for at least an hour or two." He shook his head slightly. "The entire world is in chaos, it seems. I believe you can handle what needs to be done here for the present. I will return this evening to check on Madame Lamorges. Is there anything you would like me to bring to you?"

"Perhaps some meat or fish? And some vegetables from our garden."

He touched his hat and returned to the street, where he quickly flagged a cabriolet. I watched the small carriage until it disappeared.

Then I looked into Tressy's eyes. "He is a kind man," she said quietly.

I gave her hand a squeeze. "Come inside and meet Elodie Faye."

Adrienne was asleep, and a harassed-looking Arnaud patted the fussing baby still in the cradle. "She smells very bad," he explained with some distaste. "I didn't know what to do."

"Never mind, Arnaud. We found her a wet nurse. Has Adrienne been awake?"

"A little. But she won't drink any milk." He wandered outside and vanished into the forge. Perhaps working would help him face his impending loss. I prayed that it would.

I exchanged the baby's dirty *couche* for a dry one, wiped her clean, bundled her into yet another clean blanket, and handed her to Tressy. Without a word the girl moved to a stool in a corner and put the baby to her breast. Peace returned to the household.

When I checked on Adrienne, she hardly seemed to breathe. Her face looked grayish, and her eyes were sunken.

Only that morning I had intended to leave Paris! How could one day contain so many life-changing events? Adrienne's labor and delivery had comprised no more than a few hours. And Tressy's purchase, perhaps two hours more. So much emotional strain, so much change in such a brief amount of time!

Tressy had charge of the baby, so I cared for the goat, mixed bread dough, cleaned house, and watched over Adrienne as she faded from this life. My thoughts scattered like mice before a cat, darting from one topic to another.

Pascoe. My beloved brother had won Adrienne's heart, used her, and discarded her like all the others. No wonder she had avoided *section* meetings or events. Her pregnancy was both her reason and her excuse for staying away. And then I, in all ignorance, had brought him here, into her home. To torment the poor girl and rub her face in the fact that he cared not a whit. Not even enough to realize that her baby might be his!

And Étienne had very nearly died for his brother's sin.

Anger boiled through me as I worked. Had Pascoe stood before me, I would have blistered his ears with accusations and truths. In my imagination he listened and repented, eyes downcast, lips drooping. But then I paused to recollect reality. Pascoe would simply have pointed out my own sins, which were many. Judging him accomplished exactly nothing. He simply judged me right back.

Now that I thought about it, Pascoe had come to the forge once or twice on his own, and Adrienne's mood swings reflected her strong reaction to him. Small wonder that even Arnaud, hardly the most perceptive of men, became suspicious.

Tressy reluctantly brought the baby to me, and I discovered that she didn't know how to care for a child beyond nursing it. I realized as well that my angry face and mutterings frightened her.

"Come, Tressy, and I will show you where to find *couches* and fresh blankets for Elodie. You are feeding her very well. Look how round and full her belly is!"

My encouraging tone removed some of the apprehension from Tressy's eyes, and she followed my directions, burping the baby with gentle hands and changing her *couche*. Elodie was alert for a newborn, her skinny arms and legs flailing the air, her squinty eyes apparently studying her surroundings. The memories she evoked in me of another tiny girl with a fluff of glorious hair were exquisite pain.

Just as I settled Tressy at the table with some goat milk and bread, I heard Adrienne call weakly for me. She was up on one elbow, looking around with a lost expression. *"Mon bébé?"*

"She is here in her cradle, sleeping and content. Would you like to hold her?"

Adrienne slowly lay back, and I tucked the baby against her so she could admire the sweet little face. *"Elle est si belle.* Like him." She looked up at me. "Like you."

"Do you want tea? Or I can make gruel."

Her gaze fell back to the baby's face. "Tea, *peut-être.*"

But when I brought it to her, she could manage only a few sips then closed her eyes to rest. "Colette," she said a few minutes later.

"I am here."

Her eyes fluttered open again. "I'm not afraid anymore," she said.

I thought she must be losing her senses. "Just rest, *chérie.*" I smoothed her forehead. "Don't try to talk."

When the doctor returned with an eel, a basket of assorted vegetables, and several blankets, I cooked up a stew to serve with the bread. It warmed my heart to see Tressy enjoy my cooking; she had a big appetite.

Doctor Hilliard accepted a bowl of eel stew. To Tressy's consternation, he sat across the table from her. "The baby is thriving," he said to both of us. "I could not be more pleased with her condition. Tressy, I am most grateful to you for agreeing to feed her." He gave her a polite nod.

Tressy dropped her shocked gaze to the tabletop and sat immobile. Hoping to soothe her sensibilities, I sat beside her at the table. "And Adrienne?"

Sorrow darkened his expression. "She might last until morning. I gave her a tincture to dull the pain. She says she is numb, but I see it in her eyes."

After a protracted pause during which I regained control of my voice, I said, "Tressy and I must stay here overnight, *bien sûr.*"

"*Oui,*" the doctor agreed. "I have asked Monsieur Lamorges to make straw pallets for you, and I shall sleep in the loft."

"You? Why will you stay here?" I asked rather bluntly.

Just then Arnaud entered with an armful of straw and proceeded to make beds for Tressy and me. I still gave the doctor an interrogative stare, but he ignored me, finished his stew, then helped Arnaud bring in bedding materials. I gave up and sat with Adrienne.

"Colette," she whispered with a slight smile. "He prayed with me."

"Who did?"

"*Docteur.*" The word emerged on a breath, and again she drifted away. I shed a few tears as I hovered over her, stroking her hair and forehead. Her skin was cool and clammy, and her breathing was shallow.

Arnaud brought the goat inside for the night; and although Doctor Hilliard grimaced, he held his peace. The animal settled down quickly, munching straw and chewing her cud. The smell inside the house was no worse with the goat than without her.

Despite his long legs, the doctor scaled the loft ladder with the agility of a monkey. I doubt he slept any better than the rest of us did. Adrienne wanted the baby with her, so whenever Elodie fussed I would take her from Adrienne's side and carry her to Tressy. Once she was fed and changed, I returned her to her mother.

I heard Adrienne and Arnaud talking quietly in the night; to my wonder, Adrienne actually had her voice back. I honestly tried not to listen, but I overheard something about Christ and the Blessed Virgin. I could only hope her words would give Arnaud peace in his sorrow.

Daylight gleamed through cracks in the window shutters the last time I returned Elodie to her mother's bed. This time Arnaud was holding his wife in his arms, so I laid the baby in the cradle and returned to my pallet for another brief snatch of sleep.

The next time I opened my eyes I saw Doctor Hilliard seated at the table, decidedly rumpled and unshaven. He caught my eye then looked toward the dark corner where the bed stood. I pushed myself up on one elbow and twisted around to follow his gaze.

Arnaud sat up in bed, holding Adrienne's limp body in his arms and gazing blankly into a distance far beyond the narrow confines of the little stone house he had shared with her for a few tumultuous months. I immediately knew she was gone.

Poor Arnaud. Once we persuaded him to relinquish Adrienne's body, he wandered out to the forge and worked himself to exhaustion. When I brought food and coffee at noon, he stared blankly at me as if he had quite forgotten my presence. The other smiths expressed their concern, but I could offer them no answer other than the standard platitude: "Time will ease the pain of his loss."

I hated saying it. Well-meaning people had said it to me when my baby died, and I had hated hearing it then.

However, although the pain never left me, time truly had smoothed its jagged edge. My heart no longer felt lacerated when I remembered that sweet bundle in my arms, the tiny toes and fingers, the pink lips and wondering eyes. And now when I pictured the smile that lighted up her entire being, I could even smile in response. Perhaps I had not been the best mother in the world, but not for lack of love or effort. As the years passed I felt more sympathetic toward the ignorant young mother I had been; perhaps knowing Adrienne had aided my healing.

Yet now I chastised myself for neglecting Adrienne during the long, hot summer when she so needed a friend. Leonie Hilliard had commanded my time and thoughts, and to myself I could not deny the main reason for this preoccupation, a reason other than Leonie herself. Had I erred in bringing her to visit Adrienne? I could not fool myself into thinking either girl had particularly enjoyed the visits. But perhaps Leonie had benefitted from seeing through adult eyes what her life as the wife of a blacksmith was likely to be. She could never claim ignorance of the hardships to come.

My friendship with Adrienne, like all relationships, had been a mixture of loving and selfish deeds and motivations. However, even while weeping over her death I squirmed under the shameful awareness that my sorrow, though sincere, was nonetheless diluted by secret joy; for her timely labor had prevented my leaving Paris.

Although I remained at Adrienne's house all that next day, I was neither useful nor productive. Minette LaVie showed up as soon as news of the tragedy reached her; and she made herself indispensible, praying all the while to Jesus and Mary and the entire canon of saints. She sent the soiled linens home with her boys to be laundered, helped me wash and dress Adrienne's body, then sent me to lie down and rest while she prepared a meal and carried it out to the forge for the smiths.

Between her testimony and Doctor Hilliard's influence, permission was granted for Adrienne to be buried at Église Saint-Jacques-du-Haut-

Pas even though she had neither attended Mass nor taken last rites. Doctor Hilliard made arrangements with Monsieur Lazarus, the undertaker, for a burial service the following day, and Minette's oldest boy notified all the nearest neighbors. The coffin delivered that afternoon was a plain wooden box, but once we laid her in it, Adrienne looked peaceful despite her pallid hue.

Several neighbors brought gifts of food for Arnaud, which we stored where he would find it; a few brought flowers, which I arranged around Adrienne's body; and many generous hands helped straighten and clean the entire house. Everyone admired the baby and expressed sorrow over Adrienne, and everyone except Minette looked through Tressy as if she did not exist.

Minette's generosity, gratitude, and goodness heaped coals of fire on my hypocritical head until I could bear it no more. "Minette, you must be the kindest person on earth!" I said during a brief space between visitors. "You were ever a faithful friend to Adrienne, and even now that she is dead you serve her without a thought for your own convenience or benefit. No matter how I try and pray to be genuinely loving and good, it seems there is always some selfish motive mixed in."

Minette's eyes widened and her gaze shifted away. "Don't make me a saint, madame. I'm no better than the next woman."

To my surprise, many of the neighbors returned that evening, bringing food until the table was laden and the atmosphere seemed more festive than mournful. "How long will they stay?" I asked Minette.

"Most will remain to share the meal, and a few of us will stay the night," she answered. "Monsieur Lamorges should not be alone with his grief. Do you intend to stay?"

It had never once occurred to me that Tressy and I could not stay alone in the house with Adrienne's body and her widower. Neither could we expect to sleep at Doctor Hilliard's house; yet I could not imagine returning to Maison Beau Temps at this hour. "We will stay." I had no idea where everyone would sleep in the tiny house, but it didn't seem to matter.

To escape the clamor inside, I set out to milk the goat and clean its pen. Just as I finished the job, I heard footsteps approaching and looked up to see Doctor Hilliard. *"Bonsoir,* madame," he greeted me and took the full milk pail from my hands. "The house appears to be filled with people." His expression was inquisitive and slightly concerned.

"With neighbors who brought an abundance of food to share," I said, giving the goat a parting pat before I closed her pen. "Madame LaVie is keeping order, and she and her children intend to stay the night. Monsieur Lamorges is still in the forge, working late. I suspect he dreads the crowds, but I cannot tell them to leave."

He fell in step beside me. "I will not intrude on the gathering. How are the baby and Tressy faring?"

"Very well, monsieur. But what will you eat?"

He looked amused. "Never fear; I can fend for myself at need."

"May Tressy and the baby stay at your house during the burial service tomorrow?" I asked. "I feel uncomfortable leaving them at Maison Beau Temps until I speak with Pascoe."

"Mais bien sûr. I wish you will make any arrangements you please, in future." His expression was uncertain.

I stopped a short distance from the house. *"Ma foi,* I have found scarcely a moment to ponder future plans."

He suddenly looked ill at ease, glancing about as if we might be overheard. "Madame, I beg of you to make no definite plans until I have opportunity to speak with you in private," he said in an undertone.

Anxiety gripped me. "Has some new tragedy occurred in the city?"

"Non, only more of the same fear and unrest. I'll not attend the burial service lest my presence be unwelcome. You should have plenty of protection in such a crowd."

"I imagine so." I reached for the pail of milk, and he gave a little start that told me he had forgotten all about it.

"Tiens. If you have no other needs . . ." he said, but remained standing there staring down at me, his eyes wide and dark in the evening shadows. "I suppose you must stay here tonight. You have your pistol with you?"

"It is inside the house in my reticule, but I will keep it with me tonight and tomorrow." I gave him a reassuring smile and extended my free hand. *"Bonsoir,* monsieur. If I can find a duck tomorrow, I will roast it for you."

He took my dirty, goat-smelling hand in his, and for a moment I thought he might bow over it. I had never seen him more awkward in his manner. "I shall look forward to whatever culinary delight you create, madame."

"Tressy and I will arrive at the house early," I said as he released my hand. "Will you make coffee?"

A smile spread across his face and warmed his eyes. *"Mais oui!* I will make coffee."

CHAPTER 34

MORNING HAD BARELY DAWNED when Tressy and I gathered our few possessions. Baby Elodie had just eaten and now slept securely in the sling Tressy formed from my shawl and wrapped around her own body. Arnaud had spent the entire night beside Adrienne's coffin, with Minette and another woman keeping vigil with him. All three now slept hunched over in awkward positions.

One of Minette's children stirred and whimpered when we rose to leave, and the goat bleated. We both froze in place and waited for them to settle. Then we tip-toed across the creaky floorboards to the door, and I eased it open. Not until the forge was well behind us did I dare speak. "I doubt we will find a carriage at this hour."

"The streets should be safe enough," Tressy said. "Thieves are seldom early risers."

"I hope you're right." I kept my pistol within easy reach, and we walked at a quick pace until we entered the alley beside the doctor's house and passed through the garden gate. Tressy's exclamations were immensely gratifying. Beyond the dividing fence my annuals made a spectacular show of color and the lilies still bloomed profusely.

"Perhaps I shall make a wreath for Adrienne's grave," I said. "But not this morning. I need to freshen and change into a clean gown."

My two best day gowns were in the bag I carried. The rest of my wardrobe was still at Maison Beau Temps. After wearing my travel gown since Monday morning, I was desperate enough to change into just about anything.

Just then it occurred to me that Tressy owned only the garments she currently wore. My face went hot, but she was too busy admiring my garden to notice.

That thought led to another: My attempt to fix Tressy's situation had resulted in my becoming her owner. This was not a pleasant realization, and a load of responsibility suddenly slumped my shoulders. But I could do nothing about it just then. I hate recognizing a problem and being helpless to fix it. So I put it out of my thoughts.

As we entered the kitchen, the rich aroma of coffee stopped me in my tracks. Tressy gave me a quizzical look but, being Tressy, didn't comment. Nevertheless, I immediately removed the silly smile from my face, hung up my hat, and removed my shoes. "You may hang your things here with mine," I told Tressy. "The bedroom we can use is through this door."

She followed me into the room the maids had been sharing, then stood stock-still, staring around with wide eyes. Two small beds and a chest of drawers nearly filled the chamber. A window high in the far wall revealed a wrought-iron fence, passing feet, and a view of traffic. Yet when compared with that dark garret hole at Madame Gallatin's, this room must seem luxurious.

"Feel free to lie down and rest on a bed while I am away," I said gently. "Your only task is caring for Elodie."

She opened the bottom drawer of the chest and began to line it with a blanket to make a nest for the baby. "May I walk in the garden?"

"*Mais oui!* I hope you enjoy it. That garden is my greatest accomplishment," I said.

Again she gave me a look but said nothing. I explained anyway. "I am Doctor Hilliard's housekeeper. My brothers and I came to Paris with him several years ago. He was our village doctor when I was a child. Now that Leonie is married and gone, there will be less work here for me to do, but I will keep growing fresh produce for as long as the doctor employs me."

Tressy lifted the sleeping baby from her sling and laid her in the drawer. Elodie fussed for a moment then dropped back into sleep. I smiled at the sight. "Babies are not particular about where they sleep. When I return we'll need to make a trip to the forge house to collect her cradle and her clothing and take them to my house. You and she can share the room that was my brother Claude's until I make a decision about where we will live."

"You do not live here?" Tressy asked.

"*Non,* I have lived with my brothers all these years, but one is now in the army, another is married, and the third lives elsewhere." I frowned, again feeling guilty of procrastination. "I need to visit Pascoe today."

Once Elodie was settled we returned to the kitchen. While pouring two cups of coffee, I observed as Tressy looked around. Dried herbs and strings of onions and garlic hung from the low beams; worn pots and pans hung neatly on hooks in the wall. The wide hearth with its multitude of cranes, hooks, jacks, and a gridiron would seem luxurious to Tressy's eyes. "It is a fine kitchen, is it not? I do so enjoy cooking here."

She nodded. "*Oui,* madame." Her face concealed her thoughts, but I could imagine how uncertain she must feel. This new relationship between us would require some adjustment. We were both uncomfortable in it.

I offered a full cup of coffee to Tressy, who accepted it hesitantly. "Sit here at the table with me," I said. "I have missed my morning coffee, and a few minutes' rest will do us both good. Do you take sugar?"

She pulled out a bench, sat down across from me, and added a spoonful of sugar to her cup. At that moment we both heard the murmur of voices. "Is someone else in the house?" Tressy asked.

"I would imagine the doctor is still here, for it is quite early. But I cannot imagine who else . . ." Quent, perhaps? Setting down my cup, I rose and said, "You stay here, and I'll go see if anything is needed."

Curious and slightly concerned, I climbed the stairs, passed through the dining room, and entered the salon. The first thing I saw was light from the front window reflecting on the bright hair of a figure seated in the red chair, creating almost a halo effect.

"Pascoe, you are recovered!" I exclaimed happily. Then I noticed the pistol resting on his knee, its long muzzle pointed toward the wingback chair. I took a quick step forward. "Why do you have a gun out? Are you in danger?" Dozens of dire possibilities whipped through my mind.

A pair of dueling pistols lay on the table beside him, and a walking stick very like the doctor's leaned against his chair.

Very like.

Only then did it register that Doctor Hilliard sat across from Pascoe in the wingback chair, his long fingers splayed on its armrests, his posture perfectly upright.

Everything inside me went still.

"Colette." Pascoe's voice sounded peculiar. Slowly I looked back to him. His face was deathly pale. His gaze never left the doctor. "I thought you left Paris."

"Obviously I did not leave Paris." Somehow I kept my tone light. "I am standing here before you. Put that gun away, Pascoe."

"I came here to arrest Doctor Hilliard for treason."

"What treason has he committed?" I shifted slightly to my right, trying to catch Pascoe's gaze.

"Where is Étienne?"

"The doctor sent Étienne out of Paris, doing everything he could legally do to remove him from danger."

Pascoe raised one brow. "Legally? I have strong doubts that our brother and his bride—*oui*, I heard about the quick wedding—will long remain in the country." He gave a derisive sniff. "Not that it signifies; I'm relieved Étienne is safe. But you—I need you here with me."

"And here I am. So put the gun down. The doctor has committed no treason." I shifted again.

"If you try to get in my way, I will shoot him," he said. "As you say, here you are, Colette. But where is 'here'? In the doctor's house." He shook his head. *"Non,* I shall simply put an end to this farce with a bullet. Then you and I can walk away and finally be free."

My heart rammed so hard in my throat, I feared it would choke me. "Pascoe," I said, trying to maintain a calm and reasonable tone. "Why is my working as Doctor Hilliard's housekeeper such a terrible thing? Why does it so infuriate you? How can it affect you at all?"

He let out a sharp laugh, giving the pistol a jerk that caused my heart to stop. "Why not ask him?" Pascoe said. "Ask the fool how long he has been obsessed with you and see what he says. I was delighted when you quit your job last year to run off after that officer. The noble doctor was so jealous I thought he might die of it or commit murder; I was sure his grand passion was at an end. But days later, when you came crawling to his feet, instead of taking revenge he hired you back again. Imagine my disgust! The man has no pride where you are concerned."

While he ranted, I wordlessly prayed for a way to convince him to put down that gun. But Pascoe gave me no opportunity to speak. And every word he spoke pierced my heart.

"As if that were not injury enough," he continued, "he began to change his views about life, about politics, about everything of importance. He started attending Mass, told me revenge was not the answer, and asked me to reconsider leading the *sans-culottes* and, more particularly, to consider the possible danger to you arising from your involvement. At that point I broke off our association and vowed to do all in my power to remove you from his corrupting influence."

"But Pascoe!" I nearly choked on my own tongue, so urgently did I speak at his first pause. "Pascoe, he has done nothing to corrupt me! Not once has he even made an improper suggestion."

"An 'improper suggestion'? And there we arrive at the crux of the matter. I would not have minded had he made you his mistress. *En fait,* I encouraged him to do so! Why do you think I suggested he bring you along to Paris? But the old fool refused to behave like a normal man and instead simply adored you from afar. *Ridicule!* I thought; she would scorn him if she knew. Yet you refuse to behave like a sensible woman, and I even begin to think you might care for the man! This is the corruption of which I speak, and it must end now."

Pascoe finally met my gaze, and in his eyes, along with rage, fear, and hatred, I recognized the familiar determination to win, to dominate. Everything in life that mattered to me hung on my response.

"If love is corruption then I am thoroughly corrupted." I quaked in every limb, and even my voice shook. "But you are badly mistaken, Pascoe, if you believe killing the doctor would free me from loving him."

In one quick move I fell to my knees so that the pistol's muzzle nearly touched my chest, pointing directly at my heart. Pascoe could not react in time to stop me.

"If you kill him, you kill me," I said quietly, "so why not make direct work of it."

"Colette, *non!*" The doctor's voice sounded strangled.

I saw Pascoe try to swallow, and his voice, when he managed to speak, rasped in this throat. "You admit it then; you love him and no longer love me."

There I was, my life and the doctor's hanging in the balance, yet all I could see was the loneliness in those angry blue eyes, all I could hear was the emptiness in my beloved brother's voice. Tears filled my eyes and overflowed. *"Oh mon cœur,* love isn't like that! Pascoe, you are my brother always. How can any other relationship in my life change this? No matter where I go, no matter if we are parted or together, married or alone, you are in my heart."

It was a simple statement of the obvious, nothing brilliant or compelling, yet somehow it eased my brother's senseless fear. With both hands he raised the pistol until it pointed upward. I wanted to reach out to him but was uncertain I yet dared. "You are the only person I have ever really loved," he said softly. "I—I cannot lose you."

"I understand," I answered. "We loved each other to the exclusion of everyone else and felt safe. But you and I must learn to love others as well; to love without trying to change or control them. It is a terrifying risk. But it is a risk we must take."

"And your happiness is with him now," he said dully. "You will marry him; I know it."

Suddenly a deafening roar and flash startled me so badly, I nearly fell over. Amid a cloud of smoke, Pascoe stared at the pistol in his hands and dropped it to the floor with a crash. I saw his hand jerk open then shut, and his horrified eyes lifted to meet mine; his mouth opened, but he could not speak.

Quent, who I had not even realized was near, suddenly hurtled past me and caught Pascoe's body as it slumped forward.

"Non!" I cried.

Strong arms encircled me from behind, raised me to my feet, and guided me toward the canapé. I looked back, keeping watch over my brother's inert form as Quent laid him on the floor. Urged by the doctor, I sat down and watched helplessly as Pascoe's body began to convulse.

He was having a seizure.

"He is in good hands, Colette," the doctor said into my ear.

"I thought he somehow shot himself," I admitted. "Or you." I finally looked up at the doctor's face.

"By God's grace he didn't start seizing up any sooner."

The lingering fear in his expression made my breath catch. The realization that Pascoe might have shot either one of us without intending to pull the trigger frightened me even more. I put my hand on the doctor's arm, and he covered it with his.

At last Pascoe lay still. Quent rolled him to his side, washed the blood from his face, and placed a cushion beneath his head. He picked up all the weapons, returned the doctor's pistols and sword-stick to him, and placed Pascoe's discharged weapon on the table near the door.

As anxiety drained from me, I felt limp, shaky, and inclined to weep, although I allowed no further tears. When the doctor put one arm around my shoulders and gently drew me to lean against him, I did not resist.

Quent sat on the edge of the red chair, observing his charge with an experienced eye. "Since the prison massacres began, he has had attacks like this every other day."

"He used to have one every several weeks," Doctor Hilliard said.

"So far he has been able to conceal his condition." Quent laid one of his broad hands on Pascoe's forehead, and by contrast I saw more clearly than ever how pale my brother was. "Only twice before has he suffered a seizure in public: once during the attack on the Tuileries and once here. Now he can hardly recover from one attack before the next is on him."

I felt Doctor Hilliard heave a quiet sigh. "My guess would be that stress increases their severity and frequency. He looks as if he has not slept in many days."

Stress about losing me? I wondered.

"He slipped out of the apartment this morning while I slept," Quent said quietly. "I arrived too late to be of use. I failed you, cousin."

The doctor shook his head. "Do not apologize. None of this is your fault."

"He is starting to recover," Quent observed, watching my brother's face. I slipped out of the doctor's loose embrace to kneel at Pascoe's side. He moaned, blinked, and focused first on Quent and then on me. "Don't try to talk, monsieur," Quent told him. "Rest and let yourself recover."

But not until Doctor Hilliard knelt beside me did Pascoe's tense expression relax. He lay there looking crushed and limp, and more blood trickled from his mouth.

Quent wiped it away. "You bit your tongue rather badly, monsieur," he said calmly.

"Another seizure?" Pascoe spoke with great effort, his voice sounding thick and heavy.

"*Oui*, monsieur," Quent said.

Pascoe raised his hand before his face. It opened and closed slowly, but this time he controlled it. "I might have killed . . ." He lacked strength to say more.

"But instead you shot that painting." We all followed Quent's gaze to the wall above the wingback chair. A neat hole perforated the pheasant's neck.

"As if that bird wasn't dead enough already," I said. "The horrid thing." I smoothed Pascoe's hair off his face. "Pascoe, *mon cher,* I need to apologize."

He gave me a guarded look. *"Non."*

I explained anyway. "Instead of being a sister I tried to mother you, and I nagged you like the worst kind of wife. I tried to change you instead of simply loving you for who you are. Can you forgive me?"

A faint smile curled the corners of his mouth, and he managed to say, "You forgive me, I forgive you."

The sight of Pascoe lying there so peacefully almost frightened me. I wanted to hear a sarcastic remark from those relaxed lips just to ease my mind.

At my suggestion, Quent helped him rise and stagger the short distance to the canapé. Once he lay on the seat with his feet propped on a footstool, I bent over him and finger-combed his hair.

"Now you can rest. Would you like something to eat or drink?"

"Oui." He closed his eyes.

"I'll prepare a meal," Quent offered, and headed toward the kitchen.

I took a seat in the wingback chair, my fingers gripping the armrests just as the doctor's had . . . an eternity ago.

Doctor Hilliard stood gazing out the front window, his profile sharp against the light. I remembered Pascoe's wild outburst and wondered how much of it was true. The doctor often found me amusing, and sometimes I thought—or at least hoped—I saw particular warmth in his eyes when he looked at me; but in my saner moments I knew I must be imagining affection where he intended only friendly attention. What true bond could a brilliant surgeon and politician have with his housekeeper, the illiterate widow of a drunkard?

He must have sensed my gaze, for he turned and looked at me across the salon. His eyes, which I had so often thought distant and expression-less, revealed emotions I could never explain away as mere friendly attention.

If I were to claim this as the moment I fully appreciated how Doctor Hilliard had wooed me with kindness, respect, and a trust I did not de-serve, it would be a gross exaggeration; I am not that perceptive. However, I believe I can safely pinpoint it as the *dawning* of my appreciation.

Reality distracted me from thoughts of romance. Hearing the baby cry, I remembered Tressy. What must the poor girl be thinking? I started to rise, but the doctor forestalled me. "I'll check on the baby and the girl," he said. "Pascoe needs you most right now."

I reached out as he passed, and he paused to give my fingers a gentle squeeze. When he had gone, I struggled to catch my breath and laughed at my own foolishness.

"It is real love this time," my brother said clearly.

Startled, I met his penetrating gaze.

"I must say, the man waited and worked for it," he continued. "I suppose I can't fairly begrudge him the joy of winning you." His eyes glinted. "So I'll do it unfairly."

Obviously I needn't have worried about his loss of sarcasm. I tucked my joy safely away where he couldn't puncture it with nasty little gibes. "You must be feeling better."

He looked away. "Stronger, not better. And well practiced at disguising my chewed-up tongue and cheeks." With articulate clarity he told me in colorful terms exactly how he felt, then added, "I should have turned the gun on myself."

"Pascoe, never say or even think such a thing again," I snapped, my hands gripping the armrests. "Not even in jest."

"Why need it be jest? I am obviously insane. I am subject to uncontrollable fits, and I threatened to kill a man because my sister is in love with him. In what respect, may I inquire, am I beneficial to society? If word of my 'condition' got out, I would be locked up forever, Colette."

"You are not insane. The doctor believes stress is causing your attacks to intensify," I said. "I have worried for weeks now; one has only to look at you to see that you're under terrible strain. I thought it was heartbreak over Florinda at first, but she set me straight."

"I told you she was merely a friend."

I caught that wicked gleam again. Even in despair he was ornery.

"You did, but I never know when to believe you. Was it the strain of leadership? Was it this anger about me and the doctor?"

The gleam extinguished. "I did my best to wreck your romance." Out-flinging one arm, he addressed the ceiling: "God forbid that my best friend should win the love of my sister!" Then he draped the arm across his eyes and spoke in a conversational tone. "What is stressing me? Fear of myself, perhaps. Fear of what I have become. You despise me and I cannot blame you."

It took me a moment to decide he was sincere, and even then I doubted. "I do not despise—"

He forestalled me with a lifted hand, keeping the other arm over his face. "Listen! I seduced a young woman then killed her brother, a boy Claude's age. I led the ignorant, trusting people of our *section* to follow a movement that has brought Paris into anarchy and mass murder. I hated the doctor for making you happy and very nearly hated you for being happy. I called evil, good. I called good, evil."

Pascoe lifted his arm from his face to look at me. A deep and tremulous sigh filled and emptied his lungs. "When did I become a villain, Colette?"

CHAPTER 35

"B UT YOU DON'T BELIEVE in good and evil," I said, not entirely convinced of his sincerity.

Pascoe rubbed his eyes with both hands and sat up with a groan. "Ah, philosophy. One can excuse virtually any behavior by skillfully quoting the masters. And I did; oh, I did."

I came to sit beside him and reached over to massage his bowed shoulders. "Does this help?"

"A little. I feel as if a plough horse lay down and rolled over me. Maybe two plough horses." He stretched his arms and groaned softly.

"Pascoe, I need to tell you something."

"Ah, 'tis only fair that you bare your heart now, since mine is naked and shivering!" he said. "And, *bien sûr,* desperately wicked."

Hoping I didn't entirely imagine sincerity amid his absurdity, I plunged in: "A wise man told me recently that God can bring light out of darkness and goodness out of evil." I stopped, suddenly uncertain how to continue.

When the silence stretched on, Pascoe remarked, "That was the shortest sermon I've ever heard." But when he turned and looked me in the eye, he flinched. "This is about me, something else I've done."

I nodded.

The humor drained from his expression. "I suppose I deserve to hear it."

I pressed my lips together in thought and came to a decision. "You sit there and wait. I will show you something lovely and then tell you a story."

He raised one brow but lay back on the canapé and humbly agreed to wait. I hurried down to the kitchen. Doctor Hilliard laid aside a newspaper and rose politely from the table at my entrance. "Where are Tressy and the baby?" I asked.

"She carried the baby into the garden a few minutes ago," he said.

I found her chatting with Quent, who was testing melons for ripeness. The girl brightened at sight of me. "You are well, madame?" She then covered her mouth with her hand and gave me an apprehensive glance.

"I am well, and you needn't worry about speaking to me first, *ma fille*. Is Elodie asleep? I need to take her inside."

Tressy obligingly lifted Elodie from the sling and laid her in my arms. *"Merci,"* I said. "Enjoy the garden."

"She will be safe?" The question seemed to burst from her.

Remembering the gunshot, I understood her concern. "She will be safe. All is peaceful now."

When I passed back through the kitchen, the doctor was gone. My happiness dimmed slightly. I should have paused to speak to him before.

Pascoe appeared to be asleep when I entered the salon, but I spoke up anyway. "Here she is: Elodie Faye." When he sat up, I settled beside him and tugged the blanket away from the baby's face. She frowned in her sleep.

Pascoe looked at the baby and mirrored her frown. "I don't think I'm going to like this story."

"Listen anyway." Cradling the infant, I began my tale. "Last winter, Adrienne Picot came to me in desperation with the news that she was pregnant, but she withheld the father's name."

Pascoe's face went blank.

"I helped her inadvertently," I continued, "by bringing her into Arnaud's company. He had long admired her, and he offered her marriage despite her condition. Her pregnancy was difficult, so I visited her often throughout the spring and summer, helping her around the house, keeping her company. She struggled with depression and guilt, but she loved her baby and did her best to forgive its father for rejecting her."

Pascoe's expression was now a mixture of emotions, astonishment foremost among them. As I related the rest of Adrienne's tragic tale, he lowered his face into his hands. When I finished with the fact that I was even now missing her burial ceremony, he startled me by abruptly sitting upright and revealing tear-reddened eyes. "So Étienne nearly died on my account, and I killed Adrienne," he said. "Add her to the list of my victims."

"You did not kill her, Pascoe," I said shortly. "And Étienne was rescued. You treated Adrienne badly; but your baby is a gift from God, not a mistake or curse."

"It's not that simple, Colette. You can't change what I did into something God approves."

"No one can do that. But there is forgiveness."

He made no response. Then, a few moments later, he indicated the baby. "May I hold her?"

I laid his daughter in his arms. He stared at her with what I can only describe as fearful fascination. "She looks like a Girardeau baby," he said. "You will be a wonderful mother to her." He gave me a sideways glance. "I don't doubt she is mine, yet I can't quite make my mind accept it. Elodie

Faye Girardeau." He nodded. "It sounds good. But then, she will be raised as a Hilliard. Elodie Faye Hilliard sounds passable."

I suddenly felt too warm, tried to conceal my embarrassment and pleasure, and failed miserably.

But then the slightly smug smile slid from his face. "Will she have seizures?"

"*Je ne sais pas*. I suppose she might."

A deep sadness filled his eyes. "I did this to her. Do I hurt everyone connected with me?"

"Pascoe, your illness is not a sin or a curse. If she has seizures, we will help her to handle them just as you do. She is precious to me whether she has seizures or not, just as you are."

He surprised me by bending his face to his daughter's and rubbing his nose in her soft hair. "I wish I could be around to help her out."

"Why can't you be?" I asked sharply.

He shifted the baby to a more comfortable position in his arms and gave me a pensive look. "I need to rest. May I keep her with me here?"

I wanted an answer to my question, but I knew he wouldn't give one. Not yet, anyway. "Not if you plan to sleep. You might drop her or roll on her without knowing."

Reluctantly he returned her to me. "Later, Elodie Faye," he whispered into her tiny ear.

Pascoe looked and obviously felt better by evening. Quent privately told me that my brother had stopped eating during the past week; but confession was evidently good for the soul, for, without urging, Pascoe ate two hearty meals and took two long naps. I mentioned a similarity between his schedule and his daughter's, which amused him.

Whenever Pascoe was awake, he wanted to hold Elodie. As big brother to nine siblings he was expert at baby care and didn't blench at soiled *couches* or spat-up meals. His pleasure in her both pleased and worried me, but I couldn't refuse him his daughter. The sight of him reclined on the canapé with his knees up and Elodie sleeping on his thighs while he played with her tiny hands brought such a powerful blend of feelings, I could hardly bear it.

I felt unsettled all day. Perhaps my reaction to events of the morning was delayed, but it hit me hard that afternoon. I escaped to the garden and vented my anxiety by digging up and rearranging perennials, questioning the Almighty's goodness, ripping out unwanted vines, crossing myself and weeping tears of relief, shoveling rotted fruit into my rubbish pile, thanking all the saints for the Divine intervention that preserved not only my life but also the doctor's, and cutting the grass.

Late in the afternoon Quent stepped outside to request vegetables for dinner, which I was pleased to supply. "This is a very fine garden, madame," he said. "You have made this house into a home for my cousin."

"I enjoy gardening," I said, determined not to blush or otherwise betray immaturity.

A smile softened his features. "I am sure you do. While we have a moment of privacy, I would assure you that although I applied for my current position at my cousin's request, accepting wages from him as well as from your brother, I shall continue serving Monsieur Girardeau regardless of Bastien's future plans."

With this, he bowed to me and returned to the house with his basketful of produce.

"Bastien," I said. I could not imagine applying the name to Doctor Hilliard. Using his full Christian name would seem daring enough.

A short time later I heard the garden gate squeal open. Taking a deep, calming breath, I rose, pulled off my work gloves, and brushed loose hair from my face. Doctor Hilliard walked along the next row between the slightly yellowing leaves of my pumpkins and stopped across from me. "I thought I might find you here." He pulled off his own gloves and tucked them in his coat's inner pocket.

In his face I read the same blend of fear and hope that had assailed me throughout the day. The complications of our relationship would not be easily overcome.

"I'm glad you're home. I missed you." My throat felt tight. "Terribly," I added in a burst of honesty.

The hope in his eyes brightened. He reached a hand to me as if requesting a dance. "Will you walk with me in the garden, Colette?"

I laid my hand on his, and we paced along either side of the row of pumpkins as if dancing a minuet. "We need to talk," I said as we left the vegetable garden and descended the grassy slope.

"Regarding the future?"

"*Non,* regarding the past. Your past. I have heard many rumors regarding the death of your wife, and I need to know which, if any, are true," I said bluntly.

He seemed to shrink into himself. "I would wish to pretend some things never occurred, but I cannot take back either words or deeds."

We stopped beneath the trees. I gave his hand a reassuring squeeze then stepped back. "I know that feeling well," I said, studying his shadowed face. "You needn't relate your life story, monsieur. But I am told the marquis, your father-in-law, arrived at Maison Cerisier in a coach-and-six. How can it be that no one in the village saw it?"

He gave me a wry smile. "I do not know where that tale originated. He came on horseback to the house one summer afternoon; no one would have recognized him as nobility."

"And Leonie was there with her mother."

"*Non.* Leonie was away, probably playing with your brothers."

"Were there any other witnesses?" I leaned my back against the nearest tree, pressing my hands into its bark. Now that the question was asked, I did not really wish to hear him speak of his wife.

"I am aware of none but servants."

"Pascoe was not there?"

"He was not, and I have never told anyone what happened that day. When I returned home from making a professional call, a servant told me that a gentleman was in the parlor with Madame. I found Marie with her father, looking happier than I had seen her in many years." His voice trailed off, and pain flickered across his features.

"Had you truly forbidden her to correspond with her family?" I asked, fighting off mounting jealousy.

"Oui." His tone was grim. He turned and took two steps away, arms folded across his chest. Then he turned back. Twice I saw him begin to speak, pause, and try again. At last he said, "I shouted often in those days, Colette. I was . . . an angry man. But that day, for the first time ever, Marie shouted back at me." His brows raised, and he shook his head. "She told me she was leaving."

I was too surprised to react beyond a blank stare.

He paused for a long moment, staring at nothing. "I begged her to stay, promising to change, to be a faithful husband. Even now I can see her cold expression, and I that know she despised me. She eventually agreed to think and pray before making a final decision; but before the marquis could escort her upstairs, she collapsed. I tried everything I knew, but nothing could revive her." Being a doctor, he added, "I believe the shock was too much for her weakened heart to endure."

I could too easily sympathize with the wronged wife. "So you never knew what she would have decided."

Again he shook his head, tightening his folded arms like a shield over his heart. "She had every reason to doubt my word."

I kept my mouth shut. I could not say with any certainty what I would do in such a situation. How could I speak for another woman?

The doctor studied my face, his expression somber. With a little sigh, he resumed his tale: "Monseigneur asked permission to bury Marie in their family crypt, and I agreed. But when he offered to take Leonie and raise her with her cousins at his chateau, I refused. He left the following day, taking Marie's body with him. Soon afterward I sent Leonie away to school and kept her location secret, worried he would find a way to take my daughter from me. I never once considered what might be best for her."

I stared at the ground, struggling to control the emotions rushing over me, particularly the urge to say something cruel and cutting. I had known this would be a difficult conversation. I had not expected to feel jealous and insecure. I hated that he had been the husband of another woman. I hated that he had been unfaithful to her.

He spoke into the silence. "I was a bitter, self-absorbed, angry man; and that is the father Leonie remembers. When she arrived here you witnessed her opinion of me; it was well deserved."

"And she wished to live with her grandfather." At least I could speak of Leonie without distress.

"Monseigneur has proven himself a forgiving and reasonable man. I believe he will be good to her and her new husband. He would have been kind to you as well, Colette."

I folded my arms and gave him a defiant stare. "You seem to make a practice of sending people away without considering their wishes."

He spun away on his heel then rounded back on me, scowling. "I did so only to protect you, as you must know. When Lamorges told me you turned back to care for his wife, I nearly went apoplectic. I wanted to snap your head off."

"But you were also happy," I said sharply. "Don't try to deny it!"

He flung out his hands. "I do not deny it. To that point, it was the happiest moment of my life!"

Our raised voices died away, leaving behind the chirps of my evening birds and a rustle of leaves overhead.

"I couldn't leave you," I said quietly.

"I didn't dare let myself hope," he responded.

Warily we eyed each other. Exhilaration picked away at the layers of pessimism protecting my heart, but I couldn't be certain. "Hope for what, monsieur?"

"I want to marry you," he said flatly. "But my record is that of a most unworthy husband."

"As a wife, I was a nagging harpy," I admitted. "If you shout at me, I will shout louder."

His lips twitched. "I do not doubt it."

"And if you so much as look at another woman, I expect jealousy will be the death of me." I frowned. "Or of you."

He locked his hands behind his back and paced before me, up and back. His expression had brightened considerably. "I have learned self-control in the past few years, as you must know." He glanced my way. "I was afraid to speak to you."

"I was frightened of you," I said, concealing a smile.

He stopped to face me. "Love is terrifying. I never knew. I never knew how to love."

I looked up into his hopeful, fearful face, and I smiled. "But now you do."

We ate around the kitchen worktable that evening. Tressy took her plate and sat in a quiet corner despite my urging her to stay at the table. "She will be affected by our plans," I told Pascoe when he questioned my judgment. She said not a word and kept her eyes downcast throughout the meal and subsequent conversation, yet I think she appreciated my attempt to include her.

I had wondered how Pascoe would behave toward the doctor after the events of that morning. The one thing I did not expect was for him to behave as though nothing at all had happened. I know that the two of them did talk at some time during those last days together, but I was not privy to the conversation.

"Pascoe." Being the first to finish eating, I started the conversation. "Have you given thought to your future plans? Have they changed, or will you continue leading our *section?*"

Pascoe laid down his knife. "As I told you earlier, I can no longer deny the dangerous direction our Revolution is taking, a path I blindly followed until something you said knocked the scales from my eyes." He lifted his gaze to me.

"What did I say?"

"Something profound, as always." He looked away and I was left wondering. To this day I have no idea what I said that changed his mind. Typical of Pascoe.

"My future plans are uncertain," he continued. "I know only that I am disillusioned with the Revolution and the Republic. Even if I were not, my condition will soon be impossible to conceal. If stress exacerbates my seizures, I must find a less stressful way of life." He turned his gaze upon Doctor Hilliard. "What are your plans now, monsieur? Do you intend to marry my sister?"

To his credit the doctor did not bat an eye. "I love her too well to push her into any decision."

"You don't need to push me," I said promptly. "I'm already there."

The doctor took my hand and squeezed it. "Listen before you commit yourself, Colette." His tender expression removed the sting from his words, and I nodded. But I already knew that nothing he said would change my mind. He announced, "I have obtained travel papers signed by Danton, allowing me to travel to Dunkerque to visit my father, who wishes us to reconcile before his death."

Quent spoke up. "The *comte* lives quietly, but his tenants run a lucrative smuggling operation from his property. Despite his title he is well loved and respected in the region. The locals would jump at the chance to help him smuggle Bastien and his wife out of the country."

Wife! My heart picked up its beat at the word. "I still have my travel papers, but they are to Biron, not Dunkerque," I said. "And we need travel papers for Tressy and Elodie anyway." I looked to Pascoe. "Do you have any ideas? Can you help us get travel papers without arousing suspicion?"

He pushed his plate away, leaned his elbows on the table, and looked at me with a smug smile. Switching his focus to the doctor, he said, "Bastien, old boy, you have everything you need right here in this room; except minor items such as paper, ink, and quill. As you are well aware but my sister is not, my work at the Assembly consists largely of writing up legal documents for deputies and other luminous public servants. I can easily write up travel papers for everyone in this room, using yours as my template. And as for a signature . . ."

He turned his bright gaze upon me. "We have in our presence one of the most gifted forgers ever to grace the streets of Paris. May I present Madame Colette 'Ladyfingers' DeMer?"

All eyes turned to me.

"Pascoe, do be serious," I said. "I haven't attempted anything of the sort in years."

He brushed off my objection and tucked his thumbs into his waistcoat armholes. "You haven't lost the knack. Bastien, my future brother-in-law," he addressed the doctor, "may I run to your office and acquire the necessary materials for the execution of this crime?"

"*Tout à fait!*" The doctor's expression was a study. But as soon as Pascoe disappeared through the door, Doctor Hilliard turned to me, clearly amused. "Ladyfingers?"

I closed my eyes and shook my head. "Never. He invented that just now, I expect." I heaved a sigh and explained. "You know I cannot read or write. But I can copy handwriting very well, particularly upside-down."

"You are a woman of many talents," he declared, "this one being quite fortuitous." My suspicious study of his expression revealed plenty of humor but no hint of disdain.

So it happened that, while Quent cleaned the kitchen and Tressy cared for Elodie, the rest of us forged official travel papers. Pascoe recopied my papers with what would soon be my married name as well as new dates and locations matching the doctor's; and for Tressy and the baby he created new papers for a slave and for a child, with descriptions and ages. Next he wrote up papers for himself and Quent, leaving blanks for the unknown details, and asked me to sign them with Georges Jacques Danton's scrawl.

When we finished and the ink was blotted and drying, Pascoe and I wiped our ink-stained fingers and sat back with satisfaction. "Now, on to the next detail," he said. "I can obtain a decent coach and pair for you, but a driver would complicate matters."

"I will drive the carriage," the doctor said. "Or, at need, I can ride postilion. If you can obtain the carriage and horses tomorrow, I shall plan to leave Friday."

"Then there is but one remaining detail to discuss," Pascoe said. "I wish to attend my sister's wedding."

To my surprise, Minette appeared at the back door the following morning. *"Bonjour,* Madame DeMer." She handed me a great bundle of clean laundry. "For the baby, *bien sûr.* She is well?"

"Oui, she is thriving. Will you come in?"

Her face lit up. *"Merci."* She stepped into the kitchen and gazed around in awe. "Such a fine house you work in! Is Tressy here with you? Did your employer object to her and the baby being here? I heard how he bought her for you. People are saying you're his mistress, but I tell them that cannot be." She looked eager to have her opinion confirmed.

"I am not his mistress, Minette; you needn't worry. And I hope I deserve your confidence in me. Tressy and the baby are thriving, and

Doctor Hilliard has no objection to their presence. He is seldom here in the daytime anyway, as you must know. Will you have a cup of tea?"

I could only hope Pascoe and Quent would not return from their errands until after she left. They had stayed overnight in the guest bedrooms upstairs while I shared the servants' quarters with Tressy and Elodie. At sometime during the day I would need to run over to Maison Beau Temps to collect the last of my things. Pascoe had promised to settle the rent and clear out the rest of our family's possessions.

Once I explained that illness had prevented my attending Adrienne's burial service, Minette related every detail of the event, nibbling at Quent's honey-lavender pastries between sentences. Her incessant praise to Jesus, Mary, and the saints no longer annoyed me. She backed up her professed beliefs with loving action, and I respected her genuine faith.

Our tea was nearly gone and she had just finished describing the various flowers placed on Adrienne's grave when silence fell. And lingered. I waited for her to begin a new description, but she sat there looking distressed.

I cleared my throat. Had I said something shocking without realizing it? "Minette, is anything wrong?"

She heaved a sigh. "I fear you will despise me, but it cannot be kept secret; and I wish to tell you myself rather than let it come to your ears from someone else, since Adrienne was your special friend."

"What has happened?"

She gulped then blurted it out. "I married Arnaud Lamorges last evening."

I sat there staring at her. "You . . . married Arnaud." This news required time for digestion.

"I suggested it to him the other night while you were sleeping. All was upright and moral, I promise! I simply thought it the best solution to his problems and mine. My children like him, and they like the forge house and the goat. I'll keep my laundry business, and if we both work hard and save our earnings, we might be able to move up in the world."

From a purely practical point of view it made good sense. Minette would be a thrifty, hard-working, faithful wife to Arnaud. Could I fairly blame her for snatching at happiness and security for herself and her family?

But Arnaud had loved Adrienne with such tender devotion! How could he replace her with a new wife on the day of her burial? Inwardly I writhed, but to Minette I showed a smile. She had been a good friend to Adrienne—visiting her, counseling her, and nurturing a faith that sustained Adrienne to the end and gave her peace. In her every action Minette was true and good.

But I could not help wondering how long she had contemplated Arnaud as a potential husband. Although Minette could not have predicted Adrienne's death, she certainly was on the spot to pick up her leavings.

But who was I to criticize? With this thought in mind, I walked her to the garden gate and gave her a congratulatory hug that pleased her immensely. "May God richly bless and keep your new home, Madame Lamorges," I said in farewell.

"May our Lord and Savior bless and keep you, too, Madame DeMer," she responded.

When she was gone, I started pulling weeds. As if it mattered. Tomorrow, if all went as planned, I would leave Paris as Madame Hilliard, never to return. For the first time I realized the many uncertainties that lay ahead and regretted the many people I would leave behind.

I might never see Pascoe again.

CHAPTER 36

BY THE TIME MY BROTHER returned, I had worked myself into an emotional storm.

Unsuspecting, he walked through the front door and gave a loud whoop. "Praise me, one and all, for today I have accomplished wondrous things." He grinned at my appearance. "A fine pair of Austrian coach horses purchased from an impecunious patriot by means of your intended's hard-earned cash, and a dashing landau—*Ouf!*"

My fierce embrace interrupted his announcement.

"*Hé*, Colette, whatever is wrong?" With unaccustomed tenderness he patted my back and rocked me gently back and forth. "Having second thoughts, *mon chouchou?* Marriage and emigration are colossal changes, and taking both in one bite would frighten anyone."

I only wept harder, making a wet patch on his coat front that must have sorely tried his limited store of patience. He handed his hat and gloves to Quent, who had quietly entered the hall behind him, then gently led me into the salon. We sat side-by-side on the canapé, and I rested my head on his shoulder, trying to impress details of him in my memory: his long-fingered hands, the hint of pipe tobacco and cinnamon that lingered in his breath, the way he jiggled his knee to expend nervous energy.

"I never thought I would say this, Colette," he said once my sobs subsided into an occasional hiccough, "but I think you should marry Doctor Hilliard."

I sat up to give him a look, shoving tears off my face with the back of my hand. "You tried to kill him yesterday."

He shrugged and handed me a handkerchief. "So that failed. Today I say you'll never find a man who loves you more than he does. I think he would have done anything, given everything for you even with no hope of winning your love. I don't understand it, and I don't like things I can't explain; but for you I'll make an exception."

This little speech brought fresh tears; hearing him praise the doctor meant the world to me. And this solid indication of unselfish love, a love that desired my happiness before his own, told me clearly that he was changing for the better.

"I very much want to marry Doctor Hilliard, and I don't mind a bit of adventure, though I would enjoy it more if I could know that all will go well for us. It's you I regret. Pascoe, if I leave France I might never see you again! So many terrible things are happening in Paris."

The tender tone vanished. "All this weeping over a *possibility?* Don't be foolish, Colette. What was it you preached at me about God bringing good out of evil?"

I was still confused but willing to ponder his words. "I do not fully understand it, but I thank you for reminding me."

"Don't expect that to happen again." He turned from me then and brushed off his trousers. "Ah! I have something for you." And he reached into an inner coat pocket to withdraw a letter. "From our parents, who are settled in America. I have recorded all pertinent information for my use, so this is yours now."

After a quick look at our mother's familiar handwriting, I pressed the paper to my heart. *"Merci,* Pascoe."

He pushed himself upright and stood, swinging and stretching his arms. "I'm still sore and stiff from yesterday, but I will get by. I am stronger than I seem!" He smiled at me, though I thought there were tears in the corners of his lovely eyes. "I'll be fine, *ma poulette dodue.* I'll make my way in the world."

"I am not plump!" I protested.

"Which is why it is fun to tease you."

With his usual quick and certain stride he crossed the room, turned back, folded his arms, and gave me a contemplative look. "One more matter: I have deduced that my valet and your intended husband are related, which leads to the conclusion that Quent's opportune arrival in my life was no coincidence."

"But Pascoe, I truly think he is—"

One out-flung palm stopped me. "No lecture necessary." Grinning, he shoved his mop of hair back. "However it happened, I fully accept that his arrival was propitious. He has saved my life and my reputation on various occasions, and I could not ask for a truer servant. Or friend."

Although I wasn't brave enough to speak further of God, I suddenly felt peace about leaving Pascoe. His future was not my responsibility. "I will raise Elodie as my own child," I promised. "And Doctor Hilliard will be a kind father to her."

"Uncle," Pascoe corrected. "She has only one father." He gave me a hesitant yet determined look. "I don't want her to grow up without knowing about me. I intend to become a man she will be proud to call her father."

His declaration seemed impossible. And yet, perhaps it was not so far-fetched a notion after all. "I will raise her to know that she has a papa who loves her and wants to come to her if he can," I said.

And Pascoe gave me his most beautiful smile.

After we packed and all arrangements that could be made ahead had been made, Doctor Hilliard and I walked in the flower garden. "I regret taking you away from your garden," he said. "You truly have made it a small paradise."

"I shall miss it, but I can grow another garden someday. I confess now that the deep happiness I felt when I worked in your gardens or your kitchen was entirely because they were yours. I loved to feed you well and to know that you enjoyed my cooking."

His responding look snatched my breath away. "Each evening I waited for you to go home before I would enter the house, but I sensed you as soon as I walked through the door. The wonderful smells coming from the kitchen, the flower arrangements—comforts I had never before appreciated but suddenly treasured. I thought I could never have you, but I confess I often imagined stepping through that door to find you waiting for me."

"And I eagerly anticipated fresh coffee when I arrived each morning," I admitted, a little shyly, which went against the very grain of my nature. But I would be shy with him for a time now, at the beginning of our new love.

"I shall never bring you here as my bride," he said with some regret, "for we must leave tomorrow immediately after speaking our vows. Père Jerome expressed no surprise at the news that you and I intend to marry."

"He has grown accustomed to hasty weddings in the Hilliard family, I expect." I gave his arm a squeeze, and he smiled down at me. "It is unnatural for me to sit home and wait while others make arrangements. Yet I do trust you to make wise choices, and I know that I lack the necessary connections, money, and worldly knowledge to accomplish anything toward our goal, so here I sit. And prowl and fret and imagine all manner of impediments in our path to freedom."

We circled the garden once before he spoke again. "I cannot promise success, Colette. I would like to profess such power, but you would know better."

"I have no doubt of God's power to intervene on our behalf, and Père Benedict assured me that He loves us dearly. Yet God allowed him and other priests to be brutally killed," I said quietly.

"We would likely meet the same fate, *mon cœur,* if we stayed. This city is so terrified and so filled with hatred that it consumes itself in the name of protecting itself. Pascoe and Quent agree that escape is our best option. If we fail, we fail. Live or die, our souls are God's. When our time comes to die, I trust He will grant us the same courage and peace He gave Père Benedict."

The idea of his death, not mine, frightened me most. I stopped and pressed my forehead to his arm, and he drew me into his embrace. *"Je t'aime, mon cher docteur,"* I said, my voice muffled by his waistcoat.

His strong arms drew me even closer, and I wrapped mine around his waist. "God knows I don't deserve your love," he said, his deep voice sounding rather ragged.

Although the sun was setting, a flock of starlings chattered overhead in the shade trees, and a breeze rustled through the branches, holding a hint of autumn crispness. With my cheek pressed against the doctor's chest, I could hear his heartbeat beneath these louder sounds.

And then he said, "I cannot recall exactly when I began to sense God's presence, but once I did, everything changed."

Nothing more needed to be said. God was present now, and He would be present tomorrow.

Friday morning, September 14, 1792, I married Sébastien Pierre David Hilliard, my beloved husband, at Église Saint-Jacques-du-Haut-Pas. Pascoe and Quent were our only witnesses.

I wore a quiet gray gown with purple trim, and my newly-washed hair made a smooth, thick coil on the back of my head. New gold earbobs, a wedding gift from Pascoe, dangled from my ears.

The doctor also wore gray, and I thought him handsome. Happiness and a hint of awe glowed in his dark eyes whenever he looked at me. His hair had grown into curls that no amount of dampening could flatten, very like Leonie's.

Amid towering white pillars and glorious arches, beneath the kindly eye of Père Jerome, I spoke my vows with conviction, determination, and joy, feeling peaceful confidence that this marriage would succeed. The priest declared us man and wife, and then spoke a blessing over us. It was in Latin, but I understood enough to make gooseflesh rise on my arms.

When the ceremony was complete and we turned around, Pascoe wrapped me in a boisterous hug and kissed me. "First to kiss the bride," he claimed. And then he quietly added, "You are beautiful, Colette, and I know you will be well loved. For the first time in my life, I truly desire someone else's happiness above my own. Savor the miracle but don't expect it to proliferate." He winked, then turned to congratulate my husband while Quent spoke to me.

Tressy awaited us in the narthex, for the baby had been fussy all morning. Pascoe took Elodie from her and rushed outside. For a moment I feared he would run off with her, but a glance at Quent reassured me. My brother simply desired a few minutes alone with his daughter. This parting was difficult for him in more ways than one.

The morning was fine and clear, and our carriage waited, loaded with our baggage. The horses, a pair of speckled gray geldings, looked powerful and better fed than most of the animals in Paris. Tressy climbed into the carriage and began to arrange a nest of blankets for Elodie on one of the capacious seats.

Pascoe was still some distance away in the churchyard, half-seated on a tombstone with his leg dangling, talking animatedly to his little girl.

My heart gave a twinge, for she would have no memory of these moments with her father.

I looked at Quent, who met my gaze squarely. "Please take good care of him," I said.

"I'll do my best, madame, but you know he has a strong mind and will of his own." Then he shook hands with his cousin and clapped him on the shoulder. "You are one lucky man."

Doctor Hilliard agreed. He then looked toward Pascoe and said, "We must be on our way, Colette."

I could not ignore the urging in his voice.

Pascoe looked up at my approach, and his eyes were sad. "I love her, Colette. She is so much like you. I want to protect her. I want to hear her laugh and help her learn to walk." He sighed as I took her from his arms. "The penalty for my sin is harsh, yet I know it is best for her. I know you will love her, so I won't bother to ask. Everything has been said that needs saying."

"Go with God, Pascoe."

He gave me a sharp look. "Perhaps that did need saying." Then he bent to kiss Elodie once more, kissed me gently and stroked my cheek with one finger, and walked briskly away, shoulders square and head high. Quent followed him, and the two soon disappeared around a corner.

I leaned into the carriage to hand Elodie to Tressy. "Don't forget to pray," I reminded her. "Only by God's grace will we escape from Paris." She nodded. My husband placed the step inside and closed the door.

I looked up at the church tower, crossed myself, and silently requested Divine intervention on our behalf. Pascoe trusted in our forged travel papers, but I did not. Doctor Hilliard helped me up to the driver's seat then mounted beside me. At his bidding the boy holding the horses released them, and he guided the pair into light morning traffic.

"*Très chère épouse,*" Doctor Hilliard said quietly, turning to me. "Your expression alone would cause the gate guards to arrest us. Try to look like a bride on her wedding day. For my part, I am the happiest man alive."

I met his smiling gaze and felt the tension melt away. I had not ridden in the driver's seat of a carriage in many years; the view was excellent. To my surprise, the doctor hummed and sang while he drove, and the horses seemed to enjoy it. "These are very fine animals," he commented. "They will make our journey pleasant."

Our wait at the gate was surprisingly brief. When our turn came, I thought again of God's presence and managed to present a pleasant expression to the guards. The doctor handed over our papers. *"Bonjour, citoyens,"* he said with just the right amount of dignity.

The guard looked at the top paper, which was Doctor Hilliard's, straightened abruptly, and spoke with increased respect. *"Bonjour,* Monsieur Hilliard. You travel north to Dunkerque?"

"Oui."

"And the lady?"

"My wife. Our child and her nurse ride inside."

The guards quickly compared our physical descriptions and Tressy's with those on our papers, checked the carriage's boot for unauthorized passengers, and took record of our exit. Within a few minutes they returned the papers to my husband, who carefully folded them and inserted them back into a leather case.

"You are free to travel, monsieur, madame," the senior guard said with a nod to each of us. *"Bon voyage."*

Doctor Hilliard prompted the horses, and we rolled through the gate and on toward freedom. After all the drama and trauma of recent weeks, our exit seemed anticlimactic. "We did it," I said for his ears only.

"Perhaps God truly is laying a path before our feet," he replied with a touch of wonder.

We enjoyed fine early-autumn weather for our journey: hazy, sunny, and not too warm. We passed fields with stacks of drying hay and fields with grain crops ripening in shimmers of gold and green. Cattle and sheep grazed at pasture, and most of the villages we passed through seemed peaceable. There were many flags flying, and I recognized the occasional revolutionary slogans posted, but as yet there was little of the anxiety and distrust we had left in Paris.

Clopping hooves, jingling harness, squeaking leather, and rolling wheels all became background to my thoughts. How my life had changed since I entered Paris years before! Never would I have dared imagine myself married to the enigmatic Doctor Hilliard, who had fascinated me since the first time I laid eyes on him. I tucked my hand through his arm, and he smiled down at me.

"Tired?"

"Not very. Shall we stop soon?"

"*Oui.* The horses will need a rest. I do not expect pursuit, yet I prefer to put many more miles between us and Paris before we stop for the night."

As we journeyed on, I thought of Étienne and Leonie's journey as newlyweds. At that time I did not know whether they were safely in England.

Thoughts of my other brothers made me solemn. Claude was away somewhere with the army; Pascoe would soon leave Paris to find a new home. Their stories, too, were unknown.

For that matter, an exciting chapter of my own life was just beginning, my life as Madame Hilliard. New adventures lay before us in new lands with new people. Until that distant day when I would again be united with my beloved brothers, I left them in God's hands and satisfied myself with loving those near me.

It was a good beginning.

French Translation Guide

Absurdité—Ridiculous!
Ah bon?—Oh really?
Au contraire—On the contrary
belle dame—beautiful lady
Beurk!—Yuck!
Bonjour—good morning, good day
Bonne nuit—good night
Bonsoir—good evening
Cabriolet—hired carriage for one person
Ça alors!—How about that!
Ça suffit!—Enough!
Calèche—common carriage that came in several sizes and varieties but always had a folding top
Canaille—the lowest class, dirt poor
Certainement—definitely, certainly
C'est-à-dire—that is (I mean)
C'est pas vrai!—No way!
Chut!—Hush!
Citoyens—Citizens
comme d'habitude—as usual
comte—count
coturier—fashion designer, dressmaker
couche—diaper or nappy
couvre feu—curfew (literally: covers fire)
Dans un moment—In an instant
Dépêchez-vous!—Hurry!
Dieu merci!—Thank God!
Domino—mask

dodue—plump

Eh bien—oh well

Eh bien, alors—Well, then

Elle est si belle.—She is so beautiful.

en fait—in fact

Enfant—Child

Enfin—Well, I mean . . .

est-ce que ?—(turns a statement into a question)

Est-il vrai?—Is this true?

Exactement—Exactly

Excusez-moi de vous déranger—Pardon me for disturbing you.

faubourg—suburb

fédérés—the revolutionaries from outside Paris

Fini—Done

galette—cake

Garçon fou—silly or crazy boy

Hé—Hey

Hein? Hein !—Huh? or Eh !

Hélas!—Alas!

Heu—Um

Jardin—garden

J'en doute—I doubt it

Je ne sais pas—I don't know

Je t'aime—I love you

Landau—a large, four-wheeled carriage

Le fou—The fool

Ma chère, mon cher—my dear (*ma chérie, mon chéri*—my dearie or darling)

Ma cocotte—my hen (an endearment)

Ma fille—my daughter or my girl

Ma foi—frankly, indeed

Ma poulette—my pullet (an endearment)

Ma sœur—my sister

Mais non!—But no!

Mais oui!—That's right! Definitely!

Maison Beau Temps—Fine Weather House

Maison Cerisier—Cherry Tree House

Merci—thank you

Mon ange—my angel (an endearment)

Mon chouchou—my darling (literally, "my little cabbage")

mon cœur—my heart (an endearment)

Oui, bien sûr—Yes, of course

Ouille!—Ow! Ouch!

Palais—palace

Partez!—Go!

Patron—boss, employer

Pauvre chérie!—Poor darling!

Peste—literally "Plague," an exclamation

petite mère —little mother

petit frère—little brother

Peut-être—Perhaps

Pitié de nous—Mercy on us

Pont—Bridge

Pourquoi?—Why?

Quel est le problème?—What is wrong?

Ridicule—Ridiculous

Sabots—wooden clogs

Sans-culottes—literally, "without breeches." The upper- and middle-class men wore breeches; common laborers wore trousers.

S'il te plaît—Please (singular, familiar)

Tais-toi!—Shut up! Hush!

Tiens—And there you are!

Tout à fait!—Absolutely! Exactly!

Très bien—Very well

Très chère épouse—Dearest wife

Très drôle—Very funny

Voilà!—That's it!

Vraiment?—Really?

About the Author

Jill Stengl is the author of numerous romance novels including Inspirational Reader's Choice Award- and Carol Award-winning *Faithful Traitor*, and the best-selling novella, *Fresh Highland Heir*. She lives with her husband in the beautiful Northwoods of Wisconsin, where she enjoys her three cats, teaching a high school English Lit. class, playing keyboard for her church family, and sipping coffee on the deck as she brainstorms for her next novel.

Great titles from
ROOGLEWOOD PRESS

Like us on Facebook
www.RooglewoodPress.com

When a stowaway is discovered aboard the merchant ship Kulap Kanya, the entire crew is put at risk . . . for the vengeful goddess of the sea demands all stowaways be sacrificed to her greed. Can a young cabin boy find the courage to stand up to forces beyond his control?

GODDESS TITHE by Anne Elisabeth Stengl
www.AnneElisabethStengl.com

A timid stepsister.
A mistaken identity.
A disinherited princess.
A seething planet.
An enchanted circus.

Here are five enchanting retellings to bring new life to the classic Cinderella tale!

Stories by: Elisabeth Brown, Emma Clifton Rachel Heffington, Stephanie Ricker, and Clara Diane Thompson

www.ingramcontent.com/pod-product-compliance
Lightning Source LLC
Chambersburg PA
CBHW021528250626
47154CB00006BA/2016